KU-723-952

THE PILLOW FIGHT

NICHOLAS MONSARRAT

THE PILLOW FIGHT

THE BOOK CLUB
121 CHARING CROSS ROAD
LONDON W.C.2

First published in Great Britain 1965
by Cassell & Co. Ltd.
35 Red Lion Square, London W.C.1
© *1965 by Nicholas Monsarrat*

MADE AND PRINTED IN GREAT BRITAIN BY
MORRISON AND GIBB LIMITED, LONDON AND EDINBURGH

Nicholas Monsarrat's new novel, beautifully written, with a most moving tragic undercurrent, is the story of a man and woman who begin their marriage with strongly-held, utterly opposed beliefs and find that time and circumstance reverse their attitudes so completely that each finally reflects the other's earlier convictions, thus perpetuating a state of unremitting conflict.

Moving expertly from Cape Town to New York, to Barbados and back to Cape Town, Mr. Monsarrat studies the corrupting influence of wealth and fame on this ill-assorted couple—on Kate Marais, a brilliantly successful young Afrikaner devoted to the preservation of the life of luxury she had enjoyed since childhood; and on Jonathan Steele, an idealistic, impecunious young writer from England with whom Kate falls in love, and whom she marries after a stormy courtship, despite his violent and infuriating endeavours to arouse her social conscience.

Jonathan's crusade brings him literary fame and a considerable income and, in New York, he succumbs to its more obvious advantages; Kate finds herself appreciating to an ever-increasing degree, her husband's earlier idealism. Their brittle, abrasive relationship develops into internecine war, and the marriage reaches breaking-strain on Jonathan's acceptance of a lucrative contract to make a musical out of the book into which he had once poured his soul.

In the West Indies, where Jonathan sets about writing the script for his musical, Mr. Monsarrat injects the final shot of poison. But he is too skilful a story-teller for any preconceived denouement to be taken for granted, and in this book he is very much in his element. The result is a pungent, intensely-felt story of marital conflict, completely convincing and superbly told.

BOOK ONE

EX AFRICA

CHAPTER ONE

JOHANNESBURG from the air is *not* like a miniature New York, whatever the South African Tourist Corporation may claim; but its compactness and modestly tall buildings do vaguely recall a stunted Manhattan Island surrounded by sand-castles. The sand-castles, of course, are grown-up toys; they are mine-dumps, to be exact, the yellow dross of a full half-century's frenetic burrowing for gold. For the rest, it is a sprung-up, counter-jumping town, as brash, nervous and noisy as its newest millionaire.

One could never return to it without wondering who had gone broke, who had shot himself, which of one's best friends had been raped or robbed, who was sleeping with whom, and who, incredibly, was not. But it was still my town, and I loved it dearly. And to set the record straight, no one who lived there would dream of calling it Joburg.

As we dipped and circled for our landing at Jan Smuts Airport, the man in the next seat, who had been trying all the way from Cape Town to project his personality (and much else besides) in my direction, leant across and said:

'Can I help you with your seat-belt?'

He had called me 'young lady' eight times in three hours. He had small boiled eyes, bristly hair on the backs of his hands, and a snake's head belt straining across a bulging stomach. For me (and perhaps, desolately, for himself) he was a natural Doctor Fell.

'No, thank you,' I answered. 'I can manage.'

'Is anyone meeting you at Joburg?'

Reacting to 'Joburg', and also to the more rare annoyance that he did not know who I was, I answered curtly:

'Yes.'

'Your family, eh?'

'Yes, my family. One Jew, one Greek, and one Afrikaner pansy.'

'Ha! Ha!' His hand reached out to pat my knee, and changed its mind half way. (One of my dearest friends swears that she stubs out her cigarettes on such hands. Myself, I have never gone further than

9

flicking hot ash on them.) 'The young lady has a sense of humour, I can tell.'

The young lady busied herself making up her mouth, while the youngish gentleman watched her sideways. Presently, remembering the word 'Jew' in my last answer, he said: 'Well, they call it Jewburg, don't they?'

I paused—eyes to mirror, lipstick to mouth:

'Who?'

'That's what Joburg is called,' he laboured. 'Jewburg. Because of all the Jews.'

'What Jews?'

I said it like that, because yet another of my dearest friends claims that all you have to do in these circumstances is to keep on asking silly questions, until the intruder shies away from the charge of molesting female lunatics. But suddenly I thought: To hell with this clod. . . . I ran my own advertising business, with three branches and an annual turn-over of four hundred thousand pounds. I wrote a weekly column that had half the adult delinquents in South Africa permanently scared into good behaviour. I had large grey eyes, and the legs that God allowed me. I didn't have to give anyone a gentle brush-off, not at any time, and especially not when there were anti-Semitic overtones hanging in the air.

Thus, before he could answer, I jumped in, with the necessary vehemence. 'The Jews made Johannesburg!' I proclaimed loudly. 'In fact, they made most of South Africa, too! We're proud of that. My father, the Chief Rabbi—' suddenly, alarmingly, I couldn't remember whether rabbis were meant to be celibate or prolific; but I took a chance, '—was the first man to build an opera-house on the Witwatersrand!' (That sounded unlikely, and not only for the fact that it would make me approximately sixty-two instead of twenty-six; but it was a moment for plunging on. If I was going to be a Jewess, I'd be a damned good one, like Jael . . .) 'Both Caruso and Melba made their débuts there. Don't you think that's something to be proud of? If there *are* a lot of us in Johannesburg, it's a bloody sight more than dirty old fascists like you deserve! What the hell do you mean, "Jewburg"? Are you trying to insult me?'

If he hadn't been strapped in, I swear he would have jumped straight out of the window. Admittedly, I had the advantage, as girls who are prepared to scream and wave their arms always have; but still, I could not repress a warm feeling of accomplishment. . . . His mouth made a wet and foolish 'O', which God knows was all I wanted it to do: and then he hunched away from me without another word, while the heads that had swung in our direction turned regretfully back again. In silence we glided down and touched the tarmac, making the sort of landing that South African Airways pilots reserve for their nicest passengers.

I was first off the plane (a man called out: 'Miss Kate Marais, please!' and I obeyed, but hesitantly, as a shy young lady should). The wonderful Johannesburg air surrounded me with an immediate, insistent relish as I went down the steps. Johannesburg is 6,000 feet above sea level; it is hot and dry during the day, cool and dry at night; like Mexico, it is ideal for eating, drinking, love-making, working, or doing nothing in comfort and elegance.

Only occasionally—say, once every two years—does the roof fall in; then lightning strikes and burns up rows of houses, hailstones as big as the traditional pigeon's egg shatter tiles and windows, tornadoes rip through the native locations, killing and mutilating anyone who gets in the way.

But today was not one of those days, and as I crossed the airport apron, I felt that fabulous climate invading my lungs, caressing my skin, pricking my spirit. It was no wonder, I thought, that they all behaved so badly here. What else could happen, when one had this daily and nightly injection of potency?

The three figures I had been expecting to see were waving to me from behind the barrier. I waved back, and kissed my hand to my family, the one I had described to the short-winded Casanova on the plane as consisting of a Jew, a Greek, and an Afrikaner pansy. A few moments later, I was with them.

Perhaps only in Johannesburg would one be met at the airport by three men named, respectively, Joel Sachs, Eumor Eumorphopulos, and Bruno van Thaal.

Joel Sachs was all that his name implied: a young, brown-eyed, Johannesburg Jew, smart, hardworking, uniquely honest, capable. He was the Johannesburg representative of Kate Marais Advertising, and I could not have wished for a better man—nor, incidentally, for a nicer person. The Jews in Johannesburg (and I had not been far wrong when I told the man on the plane that they had built this city) fell roughly into three categories: the old-time magnates, who fifty years ago stole

11

more money before breakfast than latter-day, mundane thieves do in an entire life-time of crime, but who were now monumentally respectable; the cultural strata, who made of this city an oasis of entertainment; and the youngish, smartish operators who knew a good thing when they smelt it.

Joel Sachs, of course, was one of the last. In the cut-throat world of advertising, his knife had so far proved the sharpest, his own throat the most durable, and his sense of timing the most acute. I was very glad to have him on my side, and I hoped—or let's say I knew—that the feeling was mutual.

Eumor Eumorphopulos was really my favourite man, if a young woman of twenty-six heavily involved in business must have a favourite. He was a Greek (what else, indeed?), about fifty-five, small, compact, indestructible, wonderfully knowing. I don't know what had brought him to Johannesburg, with empty pockets, thirty years earlier, but he was certainly an asset to this city, and incidentally to me.

Eumor did a little of everything: he owned finance companies, teashops, hotels, landscaping firms, bicycle repair shops, garages, bad racehorses, good asbestos mines. Starting from nothing, he still had nothing —in the sense that if you possess or control a million pounds' worth of property, owe eight hundred and fifty thousand to your creditors, and play the stock-market, the horses and the chemmy tables with the balance, you still have nothing.

Eumor had an impeccable financial sense; I had once watched him leaf through a dozen assorted balance-sheets, of companies ranging from marginal gold mines to semi-derelict tyre-factories, and pick out the only two which, a year later, proved to be solvent. Naturally, those had been the ones that he himself had bought—and, again naturally, he had made his choice in the interval between the second and third acts of an Old Vic production of *Hamlet* at the Empire Theatre.

We had never been in business together, though four years earlier, when Kate Marais Advertising had just been incorporated, he had been generously helpful. He was always pretending to be my lover, though privately he lamented an uncertain virility with the recurrent and memorably words: 'But Kate, dar-r-r-ling, it won't t-r-r-ravel!' Little wonder that Eumor was my favourite man.

Bruno van Thaal, my 'Afrikaner pansy', certainly had no concern about his virility; he had long disdained to put it to the test. I must

12

confess to an inherent affection for homosexuals; they are amusing, well-groomed, gossipy, and above all no bother to a girl. Bruno was that somewhat rare thing, an Afrikaner of taste and sensibility; he was small, slim, good-looking, and fundamentally kind-hearted.

His family and mine had landed on these dubious shores about two hundred years earlier; the Marais descendants took to gold-mining, the van Thaals to farming and land-speculation. Now (and a student of heredity would doubtless find it intriguing) the last of the Marais was in advertising, and the last of the van Thaals did almost nothing at all, with perverse and continuous enjoyment.

There was, however, one thing which Bruno van Thaal did, and he did it for me, extremely well. My weekly gossip column, carried by the three Sunday newspapers which was all that God and the Dutch Reformed Church allowed us, needed local contributors; although I lived and worked in Cape Town, I tried to cover also the varied misconduct of Johannesburg, Durban, Bloemfontein, and Pretoria. My 'locals' (of whom Bruno was one) had to work under cover; there was really no other way in which they could attend the necessary parties, report accurately on what happened, and still be invited out in the future.

Of the four people I had working for me in the field, Bruno was certainly the most dependable, the most observant, and the most malicious. But of course, he had the best material to work on.

My column was written for my own pleasure, and for the edification of those people interested in misbehaviour—a wide readership indeed. Personally, I subscribed to the reputed motto of that merry monarch, King Edward VII: 'I don't mind what people do, as long as they don't do it in the streets and frighten the horses.' In Johannesburg, they were a trifle inclined to frighten the horses.

There was, indeed, a remarkable amount of high-pressure drinking and casual fornication in this city. It was not as intense, of course, as what went on in Kenya, where the upper crust of 'white settlers' really behaved very badly indeed, when judged by anything except farmyard standards. Someone should one day write a little piece called *A Day in the Life of a Kenya Nobleman*; the quota of drinks downed, maidens overthrown, husbands duped, lovers maimed, and bullets hitting the pillow would overload the most elaborate Bureau of Statistics.

But Johannesburg really did very well, in its own quiet way. There was little or no prostitution—the essential yardstick of a moral community; pleasure was public, violence was funny, and love, above all, was amateur.

All of which made it very easy to write a gossip column—especially with the beady blue eyes of Bruno van Thaal to help me.

Those beady blue eyes were now surveying me, with an appraisal all the more intuitive and feminine for being utterly neuter; I knew that Bruno was taking in every last detail, from gabardine suit (slightly crushed from the flight) to *maquillage* (repaired as good as new). Finally he said:

'Kate, you look wonderful!'

'A man tried to pick me up for *three* whole hours!' I said, kissing him.

'My dear, you must have fainted dead away!'

Eumor swept off his Panama hat, and declared, in his unusual Balkanised English: 'I kill him to the death! Where is he? How tall?'

'Nine feet.'

'I surrender.'

Joel Sachs said: 'Hallo, Kate! Nice to see you again.'

'How's our business?'

'Booming.'

'Darling,' said Bruno van Thaal, 'yesterday's column was really rather naughty, wasn't it?'

'I tried to temper justice with malice.' Out of sight of the others, I winked at him. It had been mostly his own material.

We moved inside the airport building, where it was cooler, and the noise of planes was deadened. A few people greeted me; one of the Customs men whom I knew smiled as he touched the peak of his cap; a mining man, a friend of my father, raised his hat with the courtesy of a much earlier age. Then the good-looking young steward who had elected to carry my stole and my cosmetic-case off the plane, and to collect the other luggage, said: 'All ready, Miss Marais.'

'You should come up more often,' said Bruno, as we moved through the dry sunshine towards the car-park. 'Johannesburg is really very *ordinary* without you.'

'Four times a year is all that the traffic will bear. . . . How about the party tonight?'

'All laid on, darling.'

'I bring a young girl, no?' asked Eumor.

'No.'

14

'The daughter of my inn-keeper?'

'No. . . . How are the horses, Eumor?'

'Not so nice as the daughter of my inn-keeper.'

'There'll be lots of girls there, Eumor,' Joel Sachs reassured him 'You'll do all right.'

'But this one is different.'

'Two heads?' I asked.

'With but a single thought,' said Bruno.

A couple of minutes later we were in Eumor's fancy-looking Cadillac, driving towards the mine-dumps and the gleaming white towers of Johannesburg.

We lunched, as usual, at the most civilised restaurant in Johannesburg, Fraternelli's; this was a four-times-a-year ritual, and the ritual allowed us to be greedy, self-indulgent, and just a little bit high at the finish. We all had *caviar au blinis*, with Akvavit as a lubricant, to start with; then Bruno and I had *truite au bleu*. Joel Sachs grappled with a steak obviously culled from the biggest ox in the Transvaal, and Eumor, grumbling all the time, went off into the kitchen with Fraternelli and came back presently with the oddest-looking Italian confection, loosely labelled *cannelloni*, that I had seen since my last visit.

Pol Roger eased it all down; Armagnac pronounced the blessing; and Fraternelli came up with a rich and rare cheese from the Bel Paese stable, by way of farewell. And lest anyone should think this a specially Lucullan lunch, by Johannesburg standards, I can assure them that it was not.

Fraternelli served us, with much theatrical sleight-of-hand and finger-snapping; though disappointed that we had not ordered anything in the *flambé* category, so that he could attract attention to his favourite customers by applying a blow-torch and singeing the chandelier, he still contrived to make a *La Scala* production of the meal. He was a unique Johannesburg institution, capable, talented, and enormously successful; in this city, whether you wanted a directors' dinner for twenty or a seduction snack for two, food meant Fraternelli, and that was all there was to it.

He was a middle-aged Italian with two crosses to bear: the English language, which gave him every conceivable kind of trouble, and women, who served him even worse. If he could have mastered the one with the doomed facility with which he succumbed to the other, he would have been a happy man indeed.

15

He always called me 'Miss Mary'—near enough to Miss Marais, and much nearer than he came to a lot of other words.

We were cheerful, rather noisy, and talkative in a slanderous sort of way. It was a well-lit, beautifully decorated room with a lot of elegant wrought iron-work framing the windows, and it was crammed with people who behaved according to their several public habits—eating stolidly, drinking deep, staring round them, table-hopping, waving, quarrelling, spilling water-jugs, falling down when they paid the bill.

People table-hopped a good deal in our direction; it is a habit I can do without, particularly when one is hungry and fond of food; and we were not very forthcoming to such visitors. But it isn't easy to be dismissive with one's mouth full.

Women tended to dress well when they went to Fraternelli's, and I noticed several people I knew who had obviously shot the works on their spring outfits. My dear silly friend Mrs. Marchant, wearing a hat that I coveted, waved to me from across the room; another grim-looking woman whose name I couldn't remember stopped as she neared our table, remarked somewhat coldly: '*So* sorry we can't come tonight,' and passed on.

'I didn't invite her,' said Bruno, with relish.

'Why not?' I asked.

'Don't you remember?—last time she got as high as a kite, and started juggling with the stuffed avocados.'

Fraternelli, who according to his custom had been listening closely, leant over and confided: 'When wine is in, brain is out.'

'Well said, Fraternelli,' I answered. 'You're getting positively colloquial.'

He beamed, and hurried away to his dictionary.

'And anyway,' said Bruno, pursuing his theme, 'she's so ugly.'

'*I* am ugly,' said Eumor, with conviction. 'This party is for beautiful people only?'

'It is for my friends,' I answered. 'It is also for my many enemies, for the business connections of Kate Marais Advertising, for people I grew up with when I was a pretty little Johannesburg girl, for old chums of my father, and for odds and sods paying a visit to darkest Africa. It is to give me pleasure, and for Bruno to enjoy himself, fiddling the invitations.'

'*Were* you a pretty little girl?' asked Joel.

16

'No, hideous. People would gaze at my brother, and say: "What a perfect angel!" and then they'd look at me, and say: "This is going to be the brainy one." Very mortifying.'

'You've come on since then, dear,' said Bruno.

'I was *always* ugly,' said Eumor.

We talked about that night's party, a yearly function for my firm, wildly expensive and great fun. Bruno and Joel Sachs did the invitations between them; I, first at long range and then a good deal closer, laid down the law about the decorations, the food, the entertainment, and the service. In a city of parties, some of them excellent, we always tried to give ours a special quality—partly for prestige reasons, partly because that is the only kind of party to give. Not for me the dusty *canapés* and tepid drinks, the crenellated fish-paste sandwiches which only a professional caterer could possibly dream up.

Generally, about three hundred people came, stayed for four hours, and then went on their way, much elevated. Already there had grown up a fissionable tradition, a tendency for our guests to split into smaller and smaller groups as the remainder of the evening progressed. Many was the continent girl, indeed, who had bestowed her all after the Kate Marais spring gallop, and many the maturer lady who had bestowed it all again.

Towards three o'clock that afternoon, Johannesburg being a very hard-working town, the restaurant began to clear. We sat back from our table, enjoying the Armagnac and an easier view of our surroundings. Joel and Bruno were arguing about the exact proportions of a dry martini, a traditional area of disagreement among Americans which was only now setting Johannesburg in an uproar. Eumor was giving me the horrid inside story of why one of his horses had failed to win, over the week-end.

A man whom I had subtly insulted in my column, twenty-four hours earlier, cut me so dead in passing, with such a defiant toss of the head, that I choked, and had to be revived. Fraternelli, now preoccupied with our catering for that evening, brought in (with suitable fanfare) a 16-lb. Cape salmon in aspic for me to look at; I complained about the colour of the lemon-peel decoration, which clashed with the creature's eyes, and he retreated again, hand to head, promising much better things in the future.

Across the wastes of the emptying room, I became aware that I was being stared at.

It was a man, of course; in spite of the aura of oddity which surrounds any woman who lives alone and likes it, I was not an *aficionada* of any other club. He was sitting across the room from us, alone at an inconspicuous table; I had an impression of slimness, leanness, black hair, careless dress, disdain, poverty, male-ness. (Several newspapers pay me substantial sums every week to recognise such things, even at thirty paces.) He was drinking his coffee, and staring, without insistence and with a certain detachment, at our table, and in particular at me.

I wondered why he was lunching at Fraternelli's, and if he were finding it worth the snob-surcharge on the bill, and if so, for what reason.

I leant across to Eumor, cutting short his sad tale of bribed jockeys, colour-blind race-stewards, and trainers sunk in debt, and asked:

"Oo dat?"

Eumor's creased olive face wrinkled even further, as if plumbing yet inkier depths of woe. He suddenly looked like the oldest Greek in the world, hearing the final results of Thermopylae.

'Kate, Kate. . . . You're not listening to me the least little bit.'

'Yes, I am, Eumor, and I think it's all perfectly terrible. But who's the shady customer with the black hair?'

'That's me, darling.'

'Eumor. . . .'

Eumor, who (when he was not pretending to be my lover) liked to do a little social pimping on the side, half-turned and glanced in the direction I indicated, though with such a hammed-up air of *insouciance* that he might as well have fired a signal-rocket. Then, to my surprise, he waved in acknowledgement, and turned back to me.

'*Stupido!* That's Jonathan Steele.'

'I'm a country girl,' I said. 'Who's Jonathan Steele?'

'English,' said Bruno over his shoulder. He always followed other people's conversations, no matter how preoccupied he seemed to be. 'Been here about three months.'

'Doing what?'

'Writing a book.'

'Oh, God. . . .'

Nowadays, everyone wrote books about my poor country, and about Africa in general; ranging from Alan Paton (wonderful) to John Gunther (worthy); from Ruark's blood-and-guts melodrama to Monsarrat's ponderous headstone over the colonial civil service. Most of the ones written by visitors were trash, ready-minced for the literary supermarket, like parti-coloured hamburger meat; seldom were they better than slick reportage.

In South Africa especially, we were by now bored to extinction with week-end 'special correspondents' who flew in, flew round, and flew out again, confident that they had exhausted the potentialities of this enormously complicated country in seventy-two hours, 2,000 miles of air travel, twenty conversations, three almost traditional love-affairs, and one under-cover session with devoted Anglican priest, heroic native leader, courageous Jewish advocate—whoever the current journalistic queen-ant might be.

Personally, I took little interest in South African politics, and still less in race relations. My family had played no small part in all these things, since 1750; and it now seemed to me high time for the Marais clan to take a rest, and concentrate on some kind of selfish personality-cult, by way of a change.

Nor was I especially enamoured of visiting Englishmen who (if they were not rumpled, know-it-all journalists) were mostly those modern versions of the *rooinek*—terrible pink-faced City types, who arrived with £500 and a third-hand introduction to Harry Oppenheimer, and expected to assume control of the gold and diamond industries by the following week-end.

True, the English had made an unmatched contribution to my country, far greater than most Afrikaners (even non-Nationalists) would admit; their missionaries were opening up the country, and their soldiers stemming the black tide sweeping down from the north, when many of my ancestors were loafing down in Cape Town, complaining about the heat or slipping off to the slave-quarters for a refresher course in sexual callisthenics. But latter-day Englishmen, with their E-string vocal chords and their intact colonial superiority, gave most of us a deepseated pain which not even a title could assuage.

I woke from my acid day-dream to hear Eumor say:

'But this one is different, Kate. He is serious. He is going to remain a year.'

'So long?'

'He has written some earlier books also.'

'All same Mickey Spillane.'

'He is paid for by his publishers.'

'Huh?'

19

Bruno—and this was exactly the sort of thing he ferreted out—explained. 'Whoever they are, they've advanced enough money for him to live here a year, and write a book about it.'

That attracted my attention; all the publishers I knew were the hardest of hard-headed people, not at all given to this kind of wagering. 'What sort of book?'

Bruno sniffed. '*With Rod and Gun in Darkest Johannesburg*,' he said spitefully. 'With full-colour illustration of the author wrestling a stock-broker in the lounge of the Carlton Hotel.'

Eumor looked mystified. 'Nonsense. It is a *roman*.'

'Again?'

'A romance. A novel.'

Sipping my brandy, I took another look at Jonathan Steele. This time our eyes met. He seemed to be smiling faintly. He must have been aware that we were talking about him.

'You want to meet him?' asked Eumor, the old-time fixer.

'Yes.'

Close to, he was disappointing, for reasons grounded in a personal foible of mine. Whatever their size or shape, there is no reason why men should not be neat, clean, well-dressed; if we pay them the compliment of taking enormous trouble over our clothes, our make-up, and our grooming, they should certainly be prepared to do the same. Rumpled suits, grubby cuffs, wrinkled ties, hair at the nape of the neck, yesterday's shave—all these are within the spectrum of curable masculine faults.

Jonathan Steele was as clean as a new nail, but he *was* untidy, dressed in a rather shabby seersucker suit which should have been sent to the cleaners once more, that very afternoon, and then thrown away. His hair was suitable to a writer, his tie something less even than that. There was a further annoyance. Just as all women who wear high heels with slacks or a bathing-dress look like whores, so all men in scuffed suède shoes carry with them a fatal air of poverty and neglect. Steele's shoes were scuffed to the inner lining.

Eumor introduced him all round. He waited until I asked him to sit down. He lit my fresh cigarette with the minimum of delay and fuss. He looked at me with a neutral air, neither as if I were the target for tonight (the majority reaction), nor as if his time for such friviolous contacts was severely limited. He seemed in fact a shabby man with brains and good manners; slightly withdrawn, somewhat proud,

20

inwardly confident, as if he alone had the secret but wasn't boasting about it. An Irish face, vaguely; pale, lean, potent. . . . In a horribly feminine way, I felt that he was working his way into my good opinion, just by sitting there. I didn't like that at all.

I asked him what he would drink and, after looking round at all our glasses, he said: 'Brandy, please,' with that slight edge to his voice which indicated that brandy would be a treat. Fraternelli took the order, and went behind a screen to execute it. (For some reason, grounded in heaven-knows-what morass of religion, teetotal fanaticism, and misplaced care, women in South Africa were not allowed to see bottles actually uncorked in public; there was thought to be something inflammatory in the gesture—though I should have thought the reverse operation was the more suggestive. No matter; the result was that there were no mixed-company bars open to our shy gaze.)

While we were waiting, I asked Jonathan Steele about his book.

'It's still in the planning stage,' he answered, with diffidence. His voice was deeper than I had expected. 'I've only been here three months. I'm still wandering around, and talking to people.'

'What sort of people?'

He looked at me. 'You probably wouldn't know them.'

I didn't like that either, though I disguised it with a mock sternness when I spoke next.

'Tell me,' I commanded, 'exactly what people you talked to yesterday!'

He answered, with ironic deliberation: 'I was in Pretoria. There was a Black Sash demonstration. I watched, and talked to some of the women.'

I made the usual face. The Black Sash was an organisation which had grown up during the last few years; its members (all women) followed Cabinet ministers around, or picketed them at their offices, or lined up outside the House of Assembly, standing completely silent and immobile, wearing a black sash to indicate that they were in mourning for our somewhat tattered Constitution.

It was a good tactic, and effective to a limited extent; the police didn't appreciate it at all, and a number of Cabinet ministers had reacted with a degree of rudeness and crudity which showed that it had got well under their skins.

Steele noticed my expression, and asked: 'Don't you believe in the idea?'

'In a way,' I answered. 'But I just don't want to be a lady in a black sash.'

'You just want to be a lady?'

Our drinks had arrived, and in the pause that followed his words we all sipped them, as if signalled to do so. Bruno was watching Jonathan Steele and myself, with malicious interest; it was the sort of thing I paid him to do, in other circumstances and with other people; now it was rather disconcerting.

'I'm a working girl,' I answered curtly. 'My family have lived a long time in this country—two hundred years, to be exact. Good or bad, we feel it belongs to us. And good or bad, we can choose whether to get involved in politics, or whether to do something else instead.'

'But I don't see,' he said, again with deceptive diffidence, 'how you can possibly live in South Africa, and *not* get involved in politics.'

'It would take too long to explain,' I answered. 'But you can.'

At that point, if I had been ten years younger and my mother still alive and present at the table, she would have raised her eyebrows gently yet decisively, and changed the subject to one of her own choosing; later, in her bedroom, she would have said to me: 'Katherine, I did *not* bring you up to be rude to your guests, however *odd* they may be. . . .' It was true that Jonathan Steele had made me angry; and the process was still continuing.

I watched him now, smiling faintly as he surveyed the four of us over the top of his brandy *ballon*, and I put into my own mental quotation-marks the things he was thinking and saying to himself, like the disgruntled, declamatory, round-the-table list one makes up in one's head at a dull dinner party.

To Eumor he was saying: '*You are the classic type of financial juggler.*'

To Joel: '*You are the wrong kind of Jew.*'

To Bruno: '*You are a pansy. I don't like them.*'

To myself: '*You are beautiful, and unimportant.*'

And to all of us: '*How can you play like children, living on top of this disgusting volcano?*'

It was therefore with the utmost surprise that I heard myself saying to Jonathan Steele:

'If you're not doing anything else this evening, come to our party.'

Apparently he was the only one who was not surprised; he answered: 'Thank you—I'd like that very much,' as if the invitation stemmed from a half-hour's easy social intercourse. Eumor was staring at me in sardonic inquiry; Bruno frowned petulantly; Joel Sachs went so far as to choke on his Armagnac. But it was Joel, the perceptive Jew, and the only person at the table with a built-in, hereditary preference for peace, who smoothed the moment out.

'That's fine, Mr. Steele!' he said. 'Marlborough Hotel, any time after six o'clock. . . . I'm sure there'll be a lot of people you know.'

'Oh yes!' said Bruno van Thaal, whose personal preference was for strife. 'We've got the Black Sash running the bar.'

'Then my constitution will be safeguarded,' said Jonathan Steele, and rose to make his farewells.

I thought that a very adequate retort, and, in the circumstances, defensively brilliant. Watching Steele leave the restaurant, I was not sorry that I had invited him.

But I was in a minority.

'Now why on earth did you do that?' asked Bruno peevishly, as soon as Steele was out of earshot. 'The Marlborough holds three hundred people in agonising discomfort, we've got three hundred and fifty coming for certain, and the people I *haven't* asked are all in screaming sulks already. And yet you go and invite that *agitator*!'

'I heard my mother whispering to me,' I answered.

'You and your mother,' said Bruno, who had been fobbed off with this excuse for eccentricity on many similar occasions. 'I wish you two would work out your timing beforehand.'

'He was not in good humour,' volunteered Eumor, belatedly conscience-stricken over his protégé. 'But it will be a great book, I swear to you. I have listened to him talk. Brilliant! *Fantastique! Fabelhaft!*'

'Nuts!' said Bruno, who was in a bad mood, and determined to stay there. 'He's not a genius—he just needs a hair-cut. I'll bet you he never even writes a book.'

'How much?' asked Eumor.

'One million pounds.'

'Five hundred thousand,' said Eumor prudently. 'Cash.'

'Done.'

'Besides,' I said, wishing for no special reason to make up some ground, 'if he's writing about South Africa he ought to meet lots of other people, besides those dreary Black Sash matrons.'

'And *communists*,' said Bruno darkly.

'And natives.'

23

'And Father Billingsgate, or whatever his name is.'

'And the African National Congress.'

'And us,' concluded Joel Sachs, on a sensible note.

'Gentlemen,' I said, rising, 'Kate Marais Advertising has to do a little work. I'll see you all in three hours' time.'

'If we can get into the hotel,' said Bruno, 'past all these *hordes* of new people.'

I walked back with Joel Sachs to our office on Commissioner Street. It was one of my favourite times of the day, in Johannesburg; the shadows were lengthening, the caverns of the streets were growing cooler, the first edition of the *Star* was just out and being bought at the street corners, where groups of people who looked as though they didn't have a cent in the world thumbed through the stock-market prices, the race-results from England, the sweepstake draws, the cars-for-sale.

These were the white men, poor and not-so-poor, but most of the other faces in the street were black, of course; we were outnumbered (for that was how an Afrikaner thought of it) nearly five to one in this city, and the main throng was native.

There were women selling lemons and pears and limes and paw-paws; women with babies strapped to their backs; women in brightly-coloured clothes, the élite from the native brothels. The men were office messengers, mine-boys trudging in convoy to the railway station, beggars squirming on the pavement, loafers, pickpockets, shabby black clergymen of the 'bush Baptist' variety, young idlers (whom we called *skellums*) on the lookout for the unlocked car, the coat or suitcase forgotten on a back seat, the handbag hanging open, the American tourists who were fair game for everyone.

From the groups playing dice at the street corners came an occasional pungent drift of *dagga* smoke, the home-grown version of *marijuana* which gave a man courage—sometimes too much courage for his own good.

On the sunny side of the street, the colours were gaudy and eye-catching; in the shade, we walked in a cool twilight, part of a restless drifting throng approaching with pleasure the idle hours of the day.

Of course, one never really *saw* faces, unless they were white; if they were anything less, they were part of the scenery, part of the huge

24

amorphous element known as 'them'. The thought recalled Jonathan Steele to me, and I decided that I had given him quite enough attention already, that afternoon.

'Bring me up to date,' I said to Joel Sachs.

Joel, who was always the quietest person at our lunches (since they spanned a number of different worlds, while he had only one), came swiftly to life.

Kate Marais Advertising was going through one of its spells of unpopularity, he told me. Turnover was up, prestige was high, bigger and bigger accounts were showing a tendency to gravitate in our direction; and since such gravitation always looked, to the loser, like bare-faced stealing, we were both of us branded as thieves, murderers, and worse, at the moment.

I was pleased. I kept Joel up in Johannesburg to conduct the biggest poaching operation he could manage; that was the essence of the advertising business, and if we didn't deliver first-class copy and service, we in our turn would be poached out of existence. I loved the whole thing, because I had built it up myself in four years, starting with a single room in Cape Town and a loan of £500 from my father; now, with the main office still in Cape Town, but with branches in Johannesburg and Durban, we were at the very top of the heap.

If I was any sort of a snob, it was an achievement snob. It gave me unique pleasure to have got so far, remembering the very early days when setting up the firm had been a driving, heartbreaking scramble for a marginal profit, in an area where, if you were a woman, the marginal profit was you. . . . It had meant very hard work, complete self-discipline, and the cultivation of a sexless, emotionless life in the face of a male world which didn't believe in such a thing for a single moment.

'Come and have lunch,' they used to say, when I was trying to negotiate an intricate contract that would leave me with something to show for it besides bruises. And later: 'Come and have dinner. Come to bed. Come.' In a way, it was no wonder that I had made good in advertising. Everyone else was thinking of something quite different.

The gossip column had been an alternative kind of achievement. K.M.A. made money in the business world, and 'Kate Marais Calling' kept *people* hopping, in a fashion vaguely related, vaguely complimentary. The column held people at arm's length, also, the way I

25

liked to have them. A man with whom I was trying to do business was going to think twice about staring at my bosom or crossed legs, or trying the frontal approach in a nightclub, if his wife were certain to read a fragrant little paragraph about it, the following Sunday morning.

Between the ages of twenty-two and twenty-six, I had wanted, progressively, a highly successful business (I ticked the items off in my mind), the odd glamour attached to being a good-looking woman in the business world, and the power (overt or under-cover) that went with being able to say in cold print what lesser operators were whispering, hinting at, or ignoring.

I had got all these things, and it hadn't taken as long as I had feared, nor as my father had forecast.

Joel was saying: 'There's a good chance that we'll get the Anglo-African account as well.'

I laughed, so that a man outside the Carlton Hotel turned and stared. 'That will make us *very* unpopular.'

Anglo-African was a big mining house—nearly the biggest. They did not take a great deal of space in any one year (they had no reason to, gold being a commodity which really did sell itself); but it was an excellent account, and they also paid a great deal at the 'consultative' level, for somewhat pedestrian copy.

Joel dodged an early drunk at the next street corner. 'And I'd like you to call on Sliemeck's for me.'

'Why especially?'

'It's a big firm, as you know. They're thinking of making a change, in our direction. But Sliemeck hasn't *quite* made up his mind.'

I laughed again. 'I'm really getting too old to sell my body for a real-estate account.'

'Just show it in profile, dear.'

I felt good that afternoon in Johannesburg, walking down Commissioner Street with Joel Sachs. Later, in the air-conditioned office, we did ninety minutes of concentrated, detailed work that made me feel better still. If there was a nicer way of being a woman, I hadn't discovered it yet, and I didn't need to.

26

CHAPTER TWO

THE Marlborough was not the best hotel south of the Sahara, but it was a good one, and, for party purposes, nearly ideal. The management were inclined to be sad that they were not supplying the food that evening, but they bowed to Fraternelli's undoubted eminence—the more so as it would save them a lot of trouble, and they would make a minor fortune anyway out of the bar, the flowers, and the hire of two rooms big enough to accommodate 350 people. Between five o'clock and six, I had all the flowers changed, from mainly pink to mainly yellow; initiated a good stiff row about the servants' uniforms, some of which were less than spotless; and drove Fraternelli quietly round the bend with a variety of complaints. But by six o'clock we were ready for the rush, and by seven o'clock the rush was on.

By and large, South African parties were all the same; you gave people lots to drink, enough to eat, and let them do whatever they wished. If they were actors, they wanted to slander or hug each other; if they were socialites, they wanted to be seen and to be photographed; if they were writers they wanted to talk about their books—past, present, and to be. Painters got drunk and argued; lesbians got drunk and cried; business men got drunk and made passes; newspapermen got drunk. By seven o'clock, all these people were doing all these things, in circumstances which Kate Marais Advertising had tried to make as nearly perfect as possible.

To begin with, I was kept busy, greeting people I hadn't seen for three months; introducing the minority of characters who didn't know each other, pointing out to the photographers the people I wanted for my column, and the old, old faces not worth the cost of a flash-bulb, even at wholesale prices; and seeing that the genuinely shy guests (of whom there were still a few left in the world) didn't get stuck in a corner by themselves, with an empty glass and a vase of flowers to stare at. Then the incoming tide slacked off, and I started to make the rounds, and thus to enjoy myself.

I talked to my Johannesburg editor, Francis Kellaway, a small, monosyllabic, foxy man who liked to think of himself as my employer, with the power of life and death, fame and ignominy, clasped within his hot little hand.

'Wonderful party, Kate,' he proclaimed, rocking slightly. 'As usual.'

'Thank you, Francis.'

'About your column.'

'M'm?'

'I'm really very satisfied.'

'Me too.'

'Except for one thing.'

'Oh, dear!'

'Tends to run a bit short. After editing. Think you ought to watch that.'

But I wasn't in the mood for Napoleonic editors, on this or any other evening. 'My dear Francis,' I said, 'if the column runs short after you've finished with your little blue pencil, that's because half the interesting people in South Africa seem to be on your shit-list.'

He blinked. 'My *what* list?'

'You heard. . . .'

'I can assure you——' he began.

'Save it, Francis,' I reassured him. 'It's your newspaper, and if you've banned for ever any mention of Jack Cotterell—' (I took just one example, though a good one; Jack had been discovered trouserless in a taxi with one of the Board of Directors' wives, and his name was never to sully their expensive newsprint again) '—then you're quite within your rights. But *I* haven't got a personal S-list, so I'll go on mentioning him whenever he does something interesting.'

'Cotterell is a thoroughly disreputable character.'

I shook my head. 'He's just a swordsman. One of many. People like to read about him. Then they don't feel such bastards themselves.'

'You're in a strange mood tonight, Kate.'

'Hostess Runs Amuck,' I said, and moved on.

I moved on to my dear silly friend Mrs. Marchant. Peggy Marchant and I had been at school together in England; she a prefect, myself definitely not. At the age of sixteen, hideous in orange taffeta, I had been a bridesmaid at her first marriage, to a rich elderly Italian who was now in prison on a baffling variety of charges. I shall always remember Peggy, a month after her wedding, swearing me to secrecy and then confiding:

28

'Darling, Mummy said that sex and the honeymoon and all that stuff would be awful, but I honestly didn't realise it would be quite as revolting as it is. It's so *sticky*!'

Well-read but still innocent, I could imagine that it might be sticky. I made comforting sounds.

'Every single night!' she went on. 'Sometimes strawberry, sometimes raspberry. Last night it was marmalade.'

Marmalade?

'Darling, I know you're not married, but you *must* know about these things. . . . He throws it at me, from right across the room, and then he *spreads* it with a butter-knife. Honestly, I don't see what a woman *gets* out of marriage. And how it makes *babies* is just a mystery to me.'

Dear Peggy. . . . She had shed her Italian eccentric and married a tall Australian, a good-looking young man definitely not in the jam business; there were three enchanting children to prove it. But Peggy still maintained the same wide-eyed, dewy innocence of ten years ago. We never talked about the Italian, but we talked about everything else under the sun; giggly, inconsequent, girls' dormitory talk that relaxed and refreshed.

'Hallo, Mrs. Marchant,' I said now.

'Hallo, Miss Marais. . . . I was just thinking. How much does a party like this cost?'

'That's an extremely rude question.'

'*Is* it? . . . How much, darling?'

'Seven hundred pounds,' I said.

'Heavens!' she exclaimed. 'That's more than I've got in the whole world.'

'But you have your three treasures.'

'Bless their little hearts. . . . I think Caroline is getting a teensy bit bow-legged. . . . Isn't that tragic?'

'Not necessarily. You can call it the Invitation Look.'

She sighed. 'Oh dear—you're so sophisticated. Did you have a nice lunch?'

'Very.'

'I hear that awful man is coming to the party.'

'Now how,' I asked, 'did you hear that?'

'Darling, it's all over town. You know he's terribly rude to everyone he meets?'

'Is he?'

'He as good as told Maxine Ware she was *wasting* her life.'

'That's not rude. Just accurate.'

'Are you in love with him?'

'Oh, yes. . . .'

'It *is* time you got married, you know.'

'As long as you do it before the change, I always say.'

There was now an agreeable monotone roar filling the room and the one beyond it as well; token, if not of a good party, then at least of a large number of people pretending it to be so. Weaving my way through the crowded room, glass in hand, I passed Bruno van Thaal and a knot of his chums; small, elegant, soft-eyed young men on the fringe of everything—art, theatre, radio, interior decoration, dress designing, and the more precious aspects of authorship.

Fringe Men, I thought, beaming at them because I liked them; a good title for a book. . . . As I passed them by, they stopped twittering like wrens and stared at me like baby weasels, appraising my clothes and my hair-do. Finding no fault, they called out 'Hallo, darling!' and 'Wonderful party!' and 'Kate, you look heavenly!' But I moved on; I would come back to their little nest later, for that preferred party session, the *post mortem*.

Joel Sachs was talking rapidly and persuasively to one of the newspaper-women, an earnest female scribe who had once delighted us all by writing, of a wedding reception: 'The bridesmaids wore bouffant skirts and little Dutch caps.' Joel winked at me; he was working, as he always was.

At Eumor's group I stopped for a moment. Even more dwarfed than usual, he was deep in conversation with some of his gambling friends, large fleshy men who grasped their tumblers of whisky as if they were Indian clubs, and constantly stared about them in search of something to bet on—the number of people in the room, drinks on a tray, flies on the wall, waiters with spectacles, women without hats, men with blue eyes.

It was a world that Eumor loved, though it had often dealt him serious blows; I already knew from other sources that the bookmakers had taken him to the cleaners, the previous week-end, and that this was one of those recurrent moments when he needed £12,000 by Wednesday, without fail. . . . He would get it, of course; he always did. But for gamblers like Eumor, Monday and Tuesday were often bad days.

'Great party, Kate,' said the largest man in the group, whom I recognised vaguely as a nightclub owner, splendidly indifferent to the law, with such diversified interests as roulette, wrestling promotion, and the illegal importation of brook trout from Lourenço Marques. 'Always the best party of the year.'

'But can I sell you any advertising?' I asked seriously.

He guffawed. 'I don't want to advertise,' he said, between wheezes. 'The police wouldn't like it at all.'

'Then you must be nice to Eumor instead.'

He laughed again. 'Nice to a *Greek*? Do you think I want to cut my own throat?'

Eumor kissed my hand, with that air of sexual promise which for him took the place of performance. 'Thank you, dar-r-r-ling. . . . I really need friends tonight.'

'Anything except money, Eumor.'

His eyes gleamed. 'For you I do it free. Later on, yes?'

'I'll leave the key under the mat.'

There was a vague disturbance behind me, and a commanding voice said: 'Here she is!' I turned, to be confronted by the gimlet eyes, lacquered smile, and loathsome personality of Mrs. Arkell.

Mrs. Arkell, for me, existed on a very odd plane indeed. I could only see her in social-page headlines; not as a woman at all, but as a *portmanteau* word, expressing entertainment, charitable blackmail, and unremitting social activity. I had only to shut my eyes, and there she was, in black and white, but endlessly so, like old-fashioned ticker-tape.

I saw her now. FLASH! *Mrs. Arkell Entertains Visiting Polo Team.* FLASH! *Johannesburg Hostess: No. 8. Mrs. Arkell.* FLASH! *Mrs. Arkell and Doggy Friend.* FLASH! *Arkell Home Thrown Open to Boy Scouts.* FLASH! *Prime Minister Takes Tea at 'Little Cherrystones'. Gracious Home of Mrs. Arkell.* FLASH! *Cripples Express Thanks.* FLASH! *Mrs. Arkell Ends South Coast Holiday.*

I was always hoping to read: FLASH! *South Coast Holiday Ends Mrs. Arkell*, but alas, it was not to be. . . . She was a Johannesburg institution, like gambling or criminal assault: traditional, regrettable, old-established; and though we had the most cordial dislike for each other, it was for some reasonunthinkable that I should not invite her to my parties, or that she should not attend——arriving rather late, leaving rather early, exhibiting throughout a rather special blend of snobbery and

31

discontent. And here she was now, all ready with the acid dropper and the bared bodkin. I braced myself.

'Darling, such crowds!' she began, on a shrill note of disapproval. 'You really do invite *everybody* to your parties, don't you?'

'No.'

'But yes!' It came like a rifle-shot. 'I've noticed! You like lots of people! So original! Makes us all look like snobs!' She half turned, towards a man at her side; then, as if the words made up for all the patent shortcomings of her surroundings, she intoned: 'Darling, I've brought Lord Muddley!'

Lord Muddley looked like an exceptionally stupid farmer; large, blond, ruddy, wearing a hound's-tooth suit that gave me a jumping abscess just to glance at. He stared down at me with pale, glazed eyes, as if I were a marginal pig at some unfashionable show; and on being introduced he said, 'Delighted,' on a note of such absolute indifference that for one wild moment I thought he might be a tremendously bad actor impersonating an English peer. (We do occasionally entertain false baronets, princes of less than noble blood, Hungarian counts whom the police later establish as absconding valets and chauffeurs; it lends to social life in South Africa a certain frontier hazard.) But after a few moments it became apparent that Lord Muddley, alas, was true.

'I'm very glad you could come along,' I said.

'I knew you wouldn't mind, darling,' said Mrs. Arkell.

Naturally I did mind, since we had had to limit the invitations very severely indeed, and no one save Mrs. Arkell would have dreamed of bringing an extra guest without at least ringing up beforehand. But there seemed no polite method of showing this.

'Of course not,' I answered insincerely. 'Never let it be said that I invited so many people that there wasn't room for one or two uninvited ones.'

If Lord Muddley had been an actor or any other kind of impersonator, he would at that point have made some remark, however brief or off-hand, excusing his presence. But his lordship continued to gaze at me, wordless, invincible, doing us all a favour by standing there in an agricultural trance, and I knew he must be genuine.

I asked: 'Are you staying in South Africa long?'

He considered this for some time, and then, as though negotiating a very special brand of patrician, high-pitched hot potato, answered:

32

'Just looking round.'

'Brilliant financial brain!' said Mrs. Arkell, *sotto voce*. 'Absolutely uncanny!'

'Just looking round,' said Lord Muddley again. 'I may even—ah—*settle* here.'

He was now staring at me as if I might faint or break down for very joy.

'Doing what?' I asked.

'Doing?' he repeated, as if this were a particularly foreign word.

'Don't be silly, darling,' said Mrs. Arkell. 'Finance, of course! I told you!'

'I am meeting Sir Albert Ireton in the morning,' said Lord Muddley. Once more I had the feeling that I ought to go to pieces completely, burst into tears, kiss his ring. 'Ireton is connected with the Anglo-African Corporation, a mining company,' he went on, after a suitable pause. 'Gold mines and—ah—things like that. . . . You know Sir Albert?'

I decided that I had had enough of this. 'He's on one or two of my father's boards,' I said. I looked at my watch. 'Actually you've missed him by about ten minutes. He doesn't really like parties.'

The predatory gleam in Lord Muddley's eye was slow in appearing, but eventually it was there, shining like an old-fashioned stable-lamp.

'I would like to meet your father,' he said.

'He's a poppet!' said Mrs. Arkell, who was my father's least favourite woman in the whole of the English-speaking world.

'He's never here at this time of the year,' I said, delighted to be speaking the truth. 'He's down at the Cape. Fishing.'

'*I* fish,' said Lord Muddley.

As a loving and loyal daughter, I knew I had to close this one off.

'Then he's going on to Durban, and then to Lourenço Marques,' I improvised swiftly. 'He'll be so sorry to have missed you. . . . Well, do enjoy yourselves. I must shake a few more hands.'

It was rude, but necessary, I assured my dear mother as I moved away.

My wanderings had now brought me up to the buffet tables, presided over by Fraternelli and four of his own waiters. They were all busy; huge and flattering inroads had been made upon the iced soup, trout in aspic, cold barons of beef, curried prawns, avocado salads, asparagus tips, and the eight different cheeses which comprised Fraternelli's meagre selection. I wanted to speak to Fraternelli; blocking my way was a large black beflowered hat, suspiciously face-shading, which could only belong to one person.

I touched that person on the shoulder, and Salome Strauss swung round slowly, manœuvring with great skill a plate piled as high as any plate could be.

'Darling!' said Salome, pecking my cheek carefully. 'I must have missed you at the door. . . . Isn't it awful?—nowadays, food is *literally* all I care about!'

There must, I thought, have been nearly fifty years during which that was definitely not true. . . . It was a frequent point of discussion, in many other large cities besides Johannesburg, as to how many lovers Salome Strauss had had; five marriages, argued the experts, all of them disrupted in various circumstances of rage, violence, and uproarious scandal, must have involved at least fifty other men—and then there were all the other customers, from kings to commoners, who had slipped onto the stage in between.

Salome was at least seventy years old now; but her wonderful faded beauty still shone out from behind the brittle pink make-up, the dyed yellow hair reinforced with God-knows-what assortment of switches and transformations, the gauzy veils, the tremendous strapped-up cornucopia of the bosom. To say that fantastic beauty and a generous heart had been her downfall would be quite wrong; those things had been the making of her, and if some people disdained or derided the finished product, I was not one of them.

To listen to Salome, on a good day, in a good mood, reminiscing about the past was an entertainment and an education unlikely to occur again in our dull century; her portrait gallery of the king, the two dukes, the millionaire Greek, the Texan who slept in his boots, the titled actor, the untitled cabinet minister, the visiting Indian cricket team, the twin head-waiters in Budapest, the precocious French student (destined for the priesthood) who turned out to be fifteen years old, the bull-fighter who shouted '*Olé!*' and twirled his cape with such agility and fire—these, for the past twenty years, had been my constant, envious inspiration, whenever I day-dreamed of love.

Salome Strauss had been one of my mother's greatest friends; they used to talk interminably on the *stoep*, while I eavesdropped without shame. To this day I could remember Salome saying: 'Darling—do

you know the most revolting thing that can happen to anybody?—
to wake up in the morning with a fearful hangover, in an empty bed,
and there on the bedside table is a cigar-butt stubbed out in a brandy-
and-soda! Can you *imagine* that?' To which my mother had replied,
correctly. 'I do not know, Salome. My husband does not smoke
upstairs.'

Now I eyed her piled plate, which did indeed reflect a changed if
still catholic appetite, and encouraged her:

'Salome, you can do any darned thing you like, at any time.'

'Thank you, darling, So reassuring. . . . Kate, that man behind you,
the big farmer's boy type.'

'Name of Muddley.'

Her brilliant violet eyes flickered. 'I thought so. I knew his father
very well.'

'For heaven's sake, Salome, don't tell me he's yours!'

She affected to shake her head. 'My terrible memory . . .'

'You would surely remember that particular product.'

Across the loaded buffet table, Fraternelli beamed at me. '*Prego!*
You want, Miss Mary?'

'I want, Fraternelli. I want a teaspoonful of everything, except the
beef, which is fattening, and the *gnocchi*, which still look horrid.'

'*Pronto!*'

A gentle yet commanding voice at my elbow said: 'Muddley's the
name.'

I turned, amused, and startled in a rather odd way.

'Mr. Steele, you've been eavesdropping.'

He shook his head. 'No. But I was watching your reaction a moment
ago. His lordship is a well-known menace. My apologies, on behalf
of the British upper classes.'

'You speak for them?'

'When people like Muddley are around, certainly.' Noticing
that I was examining him in some detail, he said: 'This is my other
suit.'

His other suit was of a light-weight flannel, neat, somewhat old-
fashioned in cut, acceptable. But I still didn't like his approach, which
was several notches in advance of our tenuous, three-hour-old relationship. It combined an assumption of familiarity with a certain prudent
self-effacement; it carried the unmistakable odour of re-insurance.
When he went on to say, in a cautious tone: 'You look even more

beautiful than at lunchtime,' I was confirmed in my view that Jonathan Steele, in this present version, just wouldn't do at all.

Without acknowledging the remark in any way, I introduced him to Salome, and turned away as if to speak to Fraternelli again.

The particular brand of romantic humility exhibited by Jonathan Steele was something which, in a man, I could never endure. If it was genuine, it was a bore; if assumed, a trap for the unwary. When a man, for example, murmured how little he deserved your favours, that was the time to watch his other hand. It might well start weaving.

Nor did I enjoy the company of poor young men, however good-looking or accomplished. They added complication to a way of life which, with great effort and concentration, I had made reasonably smooth—a feat which for the majority of women, with their silliness, their vulnerability, their emotional lunacy when confronted with decisions of the greatest importance, receded further and further out of reach.

A small part of that life was solvency, which I could have had from my father at any time, but which I had preferred to fashion for myself. I could now pay for my own drinks, meals, travel, luxuries; why on earth should I have to worry whether a casual escort could foot the bill without turning grey at the temples? Besides, they always wanted to change my personality, from an individual to a dependant, at the cost of two whiskies-and-sodas and a tomato sandwich. That would be the frosty Friday. . . .

There was another aspect of poverty which I found particularly repellent. When a poor man wanted to make love to me, it was always as if he were watching the meter in a taxi (sometimes, indeed, literally so). All the time, I could feel his mind running on shillings and pence, while the conversation was inexorably levered round to a quite different transaction. Was this promotion going to pay off?—so his prudent speculation seemed to run: could he get me into bed on one bottle of wine, or two? It would be nice to do it on one, but a chap needed to protect his investment, a chap liked to make absolutely sure.

Lovers, lovers. . . . For me, the worst venereal disease was love. There had been no one for more than two years now, and I wanted to keep it that way, as much in the interests of personal efficiency as anything else. So far I had found love disconcerting, untidy, and pro-gressively time-wasting; at the age of twenty-six, there had still only been three people altogether, ranging from the ludicrous to the shattering.

The first was in Rome, where I had been holidaying with some older people, loosely styled 'chaperones', who seemed to find something uproariously funny in the fact that at the age of nineteen I was still a virgin. To escape this stigma, and the screams and giggles that went with it, I simply sallied forth and gave my dearest jewel away to the first man I could pick up in a bar. He was a mechanic, Roman, swarthy, rather dirty. First he was disbelieving, then complacent, then violent and gross; it had been a horrible evening, from which I retreated as fast and as far as I could.

Then there had been an American, so considerate, worshipful, and awed that I soon tired of talking him into bed; and then the deep and unhappy time with Lucien, bearing all its own fatal complications—the rationed ecstasies, the lies, the quarrels, the subterfuges, the promise of a divorce next year, and the final cool walk-out which left me defenceless and astonished.

Looking back on it, it had been an effective sign-off from the lists of love, at a time when at last I had won a foothold in the work I wanted to do, and concentration was therefore essential. But for long afterwards, pain was all I awoke to, and betrayal the only taste upon the tongue.

In between times, of course, had been the ones that didn't count, the promising ones that petered out, the ones that just never got off the ground. Basically, they had all foundered on one of three things: either the man tried too hard, or he wanted to rescue me from a life-time of gross materialism, or he insisted, as of divine right, on appro-priating every available moment of my day. The overriding kiss of death was that none of these things fitted in with Kate Marais Adver-tising; and K.M.A. had clearly emerged as my true and lasting love.

Jonathan Steele was still deep in conversation with Salome Strauss, whom he obviously found an absorbing sociological study; and my mind went off at a tangent again—with a slight cautionary twinge as to why I was thinking about love at all, on a visit to Johannesburg at the height of the annual party there. The English, God bless them, never seemed to enter into Nature's grand design, as lovers; they might have conquered many worlds, but this was not one of them. I always remembered overhearing, in a London hotel lounge, two well-bred matrons discussing the newly-married daughter of one of them.

37

'They really are an ideal couple,' declared the mother. 'Enid is deliriously happy, though of course she finds the *love* side of it rather tiresome.'

'That will take care of itself,' said her companion.

'Oh, naturally. In fact, I gave her my solemn promise that in a year or so, all that nonsense will be over and done with.'

That for me seemed to sum up love in England, a particularly daunting climate which encouraged men to get out of bed and screw the universe instead.

Salome had edged towards a corner, to demolish her supper in peace and Jonathan Steele turned back to me.

'What do you do in your spare time?' he asked.

Oh dear, I thought: *that* one. . . . 'I read.'

'Novels?'

'Philosophy.'

He did not laugh or turn pale; he looked at me and said: 'I should guess Schopenhauer.'

For some reason I liked that diagnosis (which was correct) even less than if he had made the usual pretty-girl-shouldn't-bother-her-little-head rejoinder. Steele was moving in on me at a rate which, if not alarming (I was too old to be alarmed by such traditional manœuvres) bore signs of becoming a nuisance. I decided to draw the curtain on Kate Marais, once and for all.

'That's enough about my hobbies,' I told him, with finality. And then, following straight through: 'Eumor says your publishers have actually commissioned a book about South Africa.'

'That's roughly the arrangement.'

'They must like what you've written before.'

He grinned. 'There are men of faith in every profession.'

'Not so many in publishing. . . . Do you think you're getting the material you want?'

He became wary; this was *his* area of privacy. 'Gradually.'

'But you haven't started writing yet?'

'No.'

Feeling the resistance under the probe, and being a woman, I applied some small extra pressure.

'Would you call this a wasted evening?'

'Of course not. It's a particularly pleasant one.'

'But the people here? How would they fit into your book?'

38

'I'm not writing that sort of book.'

'What sort of book are you writing?'

He was becoming fidgety, turning his eyes away, sipping his drink rather fast. I was delighted.

Finally: 'A book about South Africa,' he said, somewhat grumpily. 'Eumor told you.'

'But this room is full of South Africans.'

'They're not the sort of South Africans I want to write about.'

'Then it won't be a book about South Africa.'

Apparently I had probed accurately, and just deep enough. 'It *will* be a book about South Africa,' he answered, so loudly that one or two men nearby turned to stare. 'But these people—' he gestured round him, —'they're just the thin upper crust. Superficial. They don't really count. They don't *mean* anything.'

'How do you know that?'

'I feel it.'

'Then you'd better feel again.' This was my particular hobby-horse, and I gave it a touch of the whip. 'The people in this room, and people like them in other towns, *run* this country. They run the mines, the politics, the banks, the business world, the newspapers. They count tremendously, because they're on top, and if they've clever enough, they're going to stay there, till you and I are old and grey.' I hadn't intended to link myself in that or any other way with Jonathan Steele, and I went on swiftly: 'If you leave them out of a book on South Africa, the book will be only half true.'

But he caught up the point I hadn't wanted to make. 'When you and I are old and grey,' he said, smiling more easily, 'South Africa may be a very different country.'

'But these people are here, now.'

'All right,' he said. 'They're here, *now*.' He gave the last word a slightly satirical emphasis, neatly reversing the sense of my remark. 'I'm looking for something more enduring.'

'It's right here, under your nose.'

'Let's disagree,' he said suddenly. My mother would have approved of the courteous withdrawal. 'This is much too good a party to spoil. . . . What happens afterwards?'

'We move on somewhere else.'

'We?'

'The stayers, and the people I like.'

39

'Can I be a stayer?'

'Among all these *worthless* characters?'

'I want to keep them under my nose.'

I had to agree that this was a laudable idea, and we left it like that. I hoped that he would forget, or find something better to do. Certainly I myself had lots of better things to do, than listen to half-baked criticism from this wandering, myopic scribe, peering through pre-set spectacles at something he would never comprehend.

Not on that night, nor or any night thereafter, did I know for certain whether or not Jonathan Steele was drunk. Clearly he must have had a lot to drink; but it did not show in his manner, nor in his speech, and the crude clash which took place later that evening might well have been a habit with him, or a way of attracting my attention, or simply an expression of violent disagreement with his surroundings. It certainly made its mark on a number of my friends.

By midnight, we were reduced to a party of five: Steele and myself, Bruno van Thaal, Lord Muddley (who had attached himself unshake-ably to my entourage), and Gerald Thyssen. In any list of the ten richest men in South Africa, Gerald Thyssen always figured; my father, I know, was prepared to shorten such a list to five, and still keep Gerald in. He was a youngish mining man, chairman of his own company which had extensive interests in the Free State; most of his wealth was inherited from an intensely hard-working German grandfather, but Gerald himself was sufficiently capable to have doubled that fortune, at a time when cramped investment and political unpopularity had made South Africa no paradise for money-spinners.

Intermittently, he was one of my suitors; now and again, when I was tired, or overworked, or depressed at the mink-less, chinchilla-less, diamond-less state of my wardrobe, I toyed with the idea of sinking back into the state of cushioned respectability which a community-property interest in twenty million pounds seemed likely to ensure.

But it hadn't happened yet, and Gerald Thyssen stayed as he was —one of the world's most eligible men, the target and the despair of hordes of mothers in London, Paris, New York, Italy, and South Africa, and (rare among the very rich) a thoroughly nice man who gave heartening significance to the word 'generosity'.

Midnight found us at the Cascade, a small restaurant-night-club with nothing at all to commend it except that it was in the centre of town, and could be relied on to stay open for ever, until the last drunk had broken his last leg on the last flight of steps. We were eating Polish eggs, an agreeable form of blotting paper, and drinking whisky. I danced once with Bruno, who was full of gossip and waspish comment about the party, and then, returning to the queue of three other men who probably didn't want to dance at all, I said: 'Gentlemen, my feet are killing me—I'd much rather talk,' and we settled down in the twilight of our table again.

I had Gerald Thyssen on one side, Muddley on the other. Jonathan Steele, looking rather grim and withdrawn, was at the further end of the table.

It was Lord Muddley who sparked the scene. I must admit that we had all found him rather trying; he had a fruity, ecclesiastical pontificating tone, coupled with an absolute lack of experience in any field save country-gentlemanship, which made him very hard to take. He lectured Bruno on how to make money in real estate; he instructed Jonathan Steele how to write books, and myself how to make good in advertising. It was while he was telling Gerald Thyssen how to run his gold mines that the balloon went up.

'South Africa,' proclaimed Muddley, in that high-pitched gargling voice which must have declared many a Conservative fête well and truly opened, 'should really do very well, if the cost-price structure remains constant. In your particular field, Thyssen, you have only to make sure that the wage costs of your labour force are pegged at their present level, and that the supply of labour itself——'

'What you really mean,' said Jonathan Steele, breaking in on a harsh, rather strained note, 'is that the gold mines will continue to make lots of money if they have an inexhaustible supply of slave labour, labour that isn't allowed to strike and for whom there's no alternative employment.'

There was a moment of surprised silence. Then:

'I don't mean anything of the sort,' said Lord Muddley, speaking over his shoulder in a way I would have found infuriating. 'Those of us with experience in the management field——'

'You couldn't manage an automatic sewage farm,' said Steele crudely. 'Major contributor though you are.'

It was rather too rude to be acceptably funny, but I smiled in spite of myself, and Bruno laughed out loud. Steele seemed to find this even more infuriating.

'You're all the same, you people,' he said, with extreme bitterness. 'Everything in South Africa is either a joke or a racket. You bleat about wage costs and the supply of labour, but you never think of those things in human terms at all. You don't see, behind the words, millions of wretched natives sweating their guts out, cooped up in this stinking squirrel's cage——' his voice tailed off, as if he were going to cry.

Gerald Thyssen, a gentle yet authoritative man, tried to intervene in a situation which, even for a Johannesburg night-club, was somewhat embarrassing.

'I wouldn't say things were exactly like that.'

'*You* wouldn't say,' said Jonathan Steele rudely.

Gerald smiled. 'Yes, *I* wouldn't say. We certainly couldn't run our mines properly if we kept our mine-boys—how did you put it?—cooped up in a stinking squirrel's cage. We try to do a lot better for them than that.'

Gerald Thyssen was, I knew, personally on very strong ground there. No one in the modern mining industry had done more for his mine-workers; apart from special safety-gear in the shafts themselves, his compounds, with their married quarters and recreation halls, and spotless cafeterias, were probably the finest in Africa, a show-piece which the Nationalist Government (not strikingly intent on cherishing its humblest citizens) were constantly inspecting, chivvying, complaining about, and trying subtly to sabotage.

'What do you do for them,' asked Jonathan Steele, 'that's so different from anyone else?'

'It's not so very different from anyone else,' answered Gerald, still equable, 'though we like to think that we have the best-run mines in the country. To begin with, we spent nearly a million pounds last year on housing, improved diet, hospitals, medical care, and welfare generally.'

'Princely,' said Lord Muddley. 'Positively princely.'

'Bunk!' said Jonathan Steele. 'It's just to keep your workpeople in prime condition.' And to Lord Muddley: 'You do the same for your pigs, don't you?'

'Darling,' said Bruno to me, in an undertone, 'I have a feeling that this is going to end in tears.'

'Pigs?' repeated Lord Muddley, his jaw dropping. 'What on earth do you mean, pigs? We're talking about gold-mining.'

'We're talking about the pig aspect of gold-mining,' said Steele, 'and all the other aspects of life in South Africa that make pigs out of men.'

It now occurred to me that he was drunk, although it was not apparent in his speech; and I wondered (as a girl does) what form it usually took with him—whether he remained a talking drunk, or graduated to a fighting drunk, or a crying drunk, and if he threw lamp-shades and felled waiters, or just knocked over tables and crumpled to the ground. The present situation bore many of the classic earmarks of a night-club brawl, the only difference being that nowadays this sort of thing very seldom happened to me.

It became apparent that Steele was a talker; and, truth to tell, I was never too sure about the 'drunk' part of it, since his enunciation remained embarrassingly clear.

Now: '*Pigs out of men?*' repeated Lord Muddley, who made a good, if slow, straight man. 'Upon my soul, I don't know what you're talking about!'

'I'm talking about race-relations,' said Jonathan Steele, 'and a system which keeps millions of people permanently poor, and a few thousands rich.'

'Here we go!' said Bruno. 'London School of Economics.'

'There'll always be rich and poor,' said Lord Muddley.

'Very likely,' said Steele. 'But in most parts of the modern world they won't always be the same lot of people, permanently anchored in one class or the other. Even the British Conservative party,' he said, ironically, 'endorses a system of private enterprise, by which a man can rise from the bottom to the top, if he works hard enough.'

Lord Muddley said: 'Quite,' expressing, I had no doubt, a limited allegiance to this view.

'You can't do that in South Africa,' said Jonathan Steele. 'There's a line between the negro and the white man, and the negro can't cross it. There's a wage level dividing the negro and the white man, and the negro can't rise above it. There's an educational barrier between the negro and the white man, and the negro can't climb it. You've got the poor bastards hamstrung, and you're going to keep them that way.'

'And a bloody good idea, too!' said Bruno van Thaal, who had his own notion of paradise, and was not ashamed of it.

'Of course it's a good idea, from your point of view,' said Steele, 'but I'm talking about *real* people. . . . That means that you have a

43

permanent slave economy in South Africa, something unique in the twentieth century. Do you wonder that the rest of the world thinks of you as barbarians?'

Gerald Thyssen shook his head. I think he shared my view that this could be an explosive occasion, and didn't want to touch it off; but he had his own personal convictions as well.

'I wouldn't call it a slave economy,' he said reasonably. 'We're lucky to have a large labour force, with a relatively low standard of living. All sorts of countries have that—England is one of them, the United States is another.' He raised his hand as Jonathan Steele, who had been taking a deep draught of whisky-and-soda, made as if to break in. 'Just a minute . . . I know that there are opportunities of rising from one class to another, in both those countries, and that those opportunities don't exist in South Africa, though they may do so in the future. But the net result *now*, after less than a hundred years of industrial development from very crude beginnings, is a prosperous country, based largely on gold, diamonds, and uranium, but with substantial industries as well, which supports twelve million people.'

'The net result is a criminal mess!' Jonathan Steele burst out. 'Good God, don't any of you use your eyes as you walk about? You're living on top of the worst ghetto in the world. . . . It wouldn't be so bad, in a way, if you made something worth while out of your slave-state, like Athens did, or Rome—something handsome, creative, cultured, to justify all the misery at the lower levels. But all you make is money.'

'That's bad?' asked Bruno sarcastically.

But Steele couldn't be bothered with the fleas on the body politic. 'The same goes for women,' he said, though not looking at me. 'Here they are, with unlimited servants, unlimited leisure, unlimited opportunity to make something out of their lives. What do they do with it all?—just bridge teas, gossip, triviality, love affairs, a six-hour siesta every day. They're the laziest, most expensive harlots in the world.'

'Come on, Steele,' I said suddenly, edgily. 'You haven't said a damned thing yet. . . . What else don't you like about us?'

His eyes came round to mine, very straight, very direct; I decided that he wasn't drunk at all, just explosively keyed up, bursting with things he had wanted to say for a long time, to the people he thought deserved them.

'The way you treat your natives,' he said, as if reciting from some inner rubric. 'The way you just don't *see* them, on the street or in a

44

room. . . . The way old natives can be barred from using the lifts, and have to walk up eleven flights of stairs. . . . The way servants, regardless of sex, are herded together in the sleeping quarters at the backs of houses, like a kennel full of mongrels. . . . The 'Whites Only' labels on benches, trains, lavatories, shop counters. . . . The brutality of the most degraded poor whites, tramps, the sherry-gang type, towards *any* black man, regardless of his worth. . . . The way the police treat a native when they stop him in the street, or pick him up for forgetting his pass. . . . Johannesburg, especially, is just an appalling square mile of jungle, surrounded by black civilization.'

Gerald Thyssen burst out laughing. 'Now I've heard everything.'

'You've heard it,' said Jonathan Steele, 'but you haven't listened to it.'

Lord Muddley expelled a deep breath. 'The fellow's just a communist!'

Thinking to lower the temperature: 'Are you a communist, fellow?' I asked.

'Not yet. If I stayed here I would be.'

'Then don't stay here,' said Bruno.

'I suppose you want us all to be the same,' said Muddley.

Steele looked at him, and answered: 'God forbid!'

My irritation returned. 'But if you feel like this, what are you doing here? Why aren't you out in the streets, binding up the wounds and throwing open the ghettos? I notice all these classy ideas haven't stopped you spending nearly six hours with us top-flight barbarians, accepting our hospitality on a fairly extensive scale.'

Steele smiled, not humorously. 'I've always had a weakness for the expense-account aristocracy.'

It was a very rude remark indeed, and it brought Gerald Thyssen to life.

'I think you ought to apologise for that,' he said, very much the chairman of companies with scores of men jumping whenever he told them to. 'It was unforgivably rude.'

After an uncomfortable pause: 'I'm sorry,' said Jonathan Steele. 'I didn't meant to be personal.'

'Forget it,' I told him.

'But it does seem to me true that——'

'Jesus Christ!' exploded Bruno van Thaal. 'Can't you leave it alone?'

'——that if you ignore politics and race-relations, you're just running

45

in blinkers,' Steele went on, as though Bruno had not spoken. 'It's almost as if there were parts of South Africa you were afraid to look at.'

I knew he was needling me again, but I took it up anyway. 'Such as?'

'Well, have you ever been round a native location in Johannesburg?'

'No. But I'm not afraid to.'

'Come with me tomorrow, then.'

'I have to work.'

'Ah, well. . . .'

One of these days, I thought, Jonathan Steele was going to get a knife in the back, and I envied, in advance, the man or woman who would wield it.

'Which location?' I asked.

'Teroka.'

'Don't go, Kate,' said Bruno crossly. 'It'll be *grisly*.'

'Don't you have to have a permit?'

'I'm meeting Father Shillingford. He can fix it.'

'Oh, God!' said Bruno. 'I knew it. That *monstrous* man!'

The others were watching me—Muddley somewhat mystified, Gerald Thyssen uneasy, and still prickly-tempered on my behalf.

'I've never met Father Shillingford,' I said.

'He's a very remarkable person,' answered Steele.

'What time?'

'Ten o'clock.'

'God damn it!' I said, half angry, half amused. 'It's a deal. . . . And now I want a *really* big whisky-and-soda.'

CHAPTER THREE

I was not at my sunniest next morning, and if it had not been for a cast-iron rule never to break appointments, either personal or professional, I would have left a message for Jonathan Steele, and forgotten the whole thing. Joel Sachs and I had a ton of office-work to get through; I had lots of people to see, and a good many other ways

46

of passing the time; the very last thing I wanted to do was to throw away the morning in trudging through a native location which I knew in advance would be dirty, mean, and depressing.

Moreover, looking back on it in cool sober daylight, I could appreciate the weapons by which I had been bounced into making the trip; a combination of argumentative blackmail, induced irritation, and a mood of anything-for-a-quiet-life which the unedifying scene at the Cascade had promoted. Whether intentional or not, Jonathan Steele had done an adroit job, and I had long graduated from such haphazard pressures.

Nor was I at all enamoured of the idea of meeting Father Shillingford, who had hitherto been only a name to me, as to most of my friends. He ran a mission in Teroka, one of the native locations; he was always figuring in the headlines as coming into collision with the authorities, preaching a near-the-knuckle sermon, defying the *apartheid* laws, joining protest marches, and peddling his particular brand of fraternal saccharine.

Overseas, they called him, among other things, the 'conscience of South Africa'; here he was just a pain in the neck, one of the Bleeding Hearts brigade who intermittently displayed the wounds of mankind for the edification of the readers of the London *Observer*. If there had to be people like that, I still didn't want to meet them.

The fact that Jonathan Steele, looking exceptionally shabby, called for me in a small English car, not less than ten years old, whose battered appearance made even the Carlton Hotel's luggage-boys laugh aloud, put the dunce's cap on the whole excursion.

Jonathan Steele was not at all repentant about the previous night; indeed, he only mentioned it once, and that indirectly, when he said: 'I thought Muddley excelled himself, didn't you?' There were so many answers to that one that I didn't make any of them. Instead I said:

'I have to be back by half past twelve.'

'That'll give us about an hour there,' he answered, rather off-handedly. 'Probably your saturation point.'

I forebore to say that in some ways I had reached this already.

We took the Main Reef road, through busy traffic, and then branched south, towards Teroka. Tall buildings gave way to smaller ones, and then to the open *veld*; the surfaced road trailed off into a yellow dusty track, bad alike for the hair and the nerves. Steele drove his horrid little car well, but our progress was not easy; deep ruts, corrugations, and that enveloping ochre dust all conspired with the heat to complete our discomfort.

Then, on the skyline, I saw the outlying shacks of Teroka Township.

It was what I had expected—not better, not worse; a sprawling mess of tin shanties, hessian shelters, lean-to sheds made of planks and barrel-staves. The buildings (for want of a better word) seemed to have been planted higgledy-piggledy, but there *was* a road system of sorts; a distorted lattice-work of pitted tracks, deeply scarred by wagon wheels and rivulets of drainage, and cluttered by every sort of refuse and every breed of goat, dog, and child.

It was stiflingly hot; the air smelt acridly of wood-smoke, natives and excrement; a pall of dust enclosed it all like a murky blanket. I wanted to turn back, admitting without argument that I wasn't this sort of person. But for a number of foolish reasons, compounded of pride, good manners, and simple obstinacy, it had already become too late.

As we drove towards the entrance gates, Jonathan Steele said: 'Fill your lungs. This is the authentic stink of South Africa.' My conviction that this was a special promotion, designed to shame Marie Antoinette under the cruel spotlight of reality, returned anew.

Then came two minor surprises, the two things I remembered best about that morning. At the rusty barbed-wire gate which marked the entrance to Teroka, a native policeman waved us to a standstill. He looked indulgently at the car, which might indeed have served as a Class II taxi: then he looked at us, and his bearing changed. He said to Jonathan Steele, with not too subtle insolence:

'Sir, no entrance to Europeans.'

It was easy to understand why he enjoyed saying it. Normally, no white man in South Africa could be disciplined by a native; here was one of the few special cases where the policeman's writ enabled him to step across that line, since under the new *apartheid* laws certain civic areas were barred to the 'non-designated' race, whichever that was. While appreciating the fact that this was the policeman's big moment, I still disliked the implications.

'Tell him to get out of the way,' I said, loud enough for him to hear.

The first surprise was that Jonathan Steele answered him, not in English or Afrikaans, but in a native language which I took to be Zulu. They talked rapidly for about a minute, Shillingford's name occurring here and there; and then the policeman stood aside and we went through.

'Do you really know Zulu?' I asked, impressed.

He looked puzzled. 'Zulu? He wasn't a Zulu. That was Shangaan.'

'Now how did you know *that*?'

'The earrings,' he said. 'They had the Shangaan tribal emblem.'

'You seem to be doing things very thoroughly.'

He grinned. 'I'm writing a book about South Africa.'

The second surprise was Father Shillingford himself. We found him at the door of his 'church', a wretched tin shanty with a yellow pine cross over the door. Shillingford was a small, modest, rubicund man, far from Christ-like—if Christ-like means bearded, lean, and dramatic, as the painters persuade us. He had a dusty brown cassock, and cracked boots. Only the eyes were out of the ordinary—pale, looking at you, and at the horizon behind you, in one embracing glance. I suppose they were the give-away; the rest of him couldn't have been less distinguished.

He greeted Jonathan Steele like an old friend, and myself with the reserve normal in a priest.

'It's very good of you to come,' he said. 'We don't have many visitors.'

'Miss Marais writes for the newspapers,' said Jonathan Steele, as if trying to put in a good word for me.

'Oh yes, I know,' said Father Shillingford.

I decided that they weren't going to get me down. 'This isn't my usual area of operations, Father,' I said.

He narrowed his gaze until it reached my face, and answered: 'There are many different kinds of slum.'

'But she *is* interested,' said Jonathan Steele, rather harassed.

Once again he seemed to be apologising for me—for the way I looked, my jewellery, my shoes. It was true that I seemed out of place in Teroka's grimy ugliness, and for my part I was going to take damned good care to keep things that way. . . . There was a naked boy-child sitting on the lowest of the church steps—coal-black, innocent, and very beautiful. He was a small, engaging fellow creature now, but in a few years he would be a native, probably criminal or sexually danger-ous. Father Shillingford wasn't going to change that fact, and he wasn't going to change that feeling in myself, either.

These were odd thoughts for me, Teroka thoughts, and I turned

49

away from them. I wanted nothing so much as to be back in my suite at the Carlton, preferably drinking the second of two dry martinis. But that respite was still some distance, and many ugly sights and people, away from me.

Father Shillingford led us first into his church. The sunlight fell pathetically on the worn pews, the beaten earth floor, the altar-cloth stained by rainwater at one corner.

'We are very poor, as you see,' said Father Shillingford.

He seemed to be waiting for me to say something, but I had nothing to contribute. This was a shanty-church in a native location: I had expected it to be poor and shabby. To remark on that aspect of it would be as silly as attending a strip-tease act, advertised as such, and then saying: 'But she's naked!' I had known Teroka would be naked.

'And of course people break in at night, and take things,' Father Shillingford continued. 'I used to be able to sleep here, but that's not allowed any more.'

'He bicycles here from Johannesburg every day,' said Jonathan Steele. 'Fourteen miles.'

I had known about that, too.

Our excursion now became progressively more dull, as well as hot and irritating. Outside the church, we walked slowly down one of the streets, picking our way past the children and the goats, occasionally pausing to peer inside some wretched hut or sacking shelter. We were freely stared at; some of the men looked at me in a way I considered impermissible (it would certainly have had my father reaching for his *sjambok*). But throughout our tour Father Shillingford was seldom greeted, and never with any particular enthusiasm.

When I commented on this: 'It's true,' he said, rather sadly. 'It's something which has happened the last year or so. They think all Europeans are either spies or exploiters—even me, and I've had this mission for nearly eight years.' He was staring at a fat old woman selling a horrible confection that looked like pink peanut butter, and staring beyond her, as usual, at some ultimate horizon. 'They've got to move on soon, you see. Even from this wretched place.'

'Under the Group Areas Act?'

He nodded, his cheerful red face sombre. 'That's the magic phrase the Government uses. . . . In future this is going to be a white area; all these people have got to get out, by the end of the year.' He looked round him, at the squalor and filth of Teroka. 'You wouldn't think

50

that would worry them much, would you? But this is home. It's been home for twenty years or so. They *own* these houses and these bits of land. Now they've had orders to leave and start somewhere else, further out of town.'

'But it's part of the overall plan,' I said austerely, 'to get Johannesburg properly zoned. There's going to be a white area, and a native area. That makes sense, doesn't it? You don't want them all mixed up.'

'But it's so cruel!' broke in Steele. 'My God, they already have to get up at five o'clock every morning, to queue up for those bloody buses to get to work by eight! Now they're being pushed even further away. And this place *belongs* to them! It's theirs. How would you like to be kicked out of your house or flat or whatever it is, with no compensation and no appeal?'

'I wouldn't like it at all,' I answered, 'and I'm taking very good care to see that it will never happen.'

'To you.'

'To me.'

'But that's so selfish!' said Steele, exasperated as I had intended him to be.

'I *am* selfish,' I said.

To my surprise and annoyance, Father Shillingford was smiling at me. It was not an amused smile; it even had elements of compassion and understanding, which I did not care for at all. Finally he said:

'Miss Marais likes to be her own worst advertisement.'

It occurred to me suddenly that he and I were illustrating two aspects of integrity, the sacred and the profane, and that I much preferred mine. I engaged his intrusive blue eyes for a moment before replying: 'I don't fool myself, and I try not to fool other people.'

We did not stay long after that; I endured a few more streets, a few more smells, a few more insolent or sullen stares. More strongly than ever, I felt that I knew all this without being told it; I *knew* that Johannesburg natives were poor and meanly housed, that there was violence and theft, that they did not like or trust the white man. If it was Father Shillingford's self-imposed task to try to soften this hard core of maladjustment, well and good. But when brought face to face with it, no bell tolled for me, nor would ever do so.

It was like getting involved with other people's children on an aircraft or a train. If you betrayed the smallest interest in one of these deceptive brats, you were likely to become mother for the duration.

Its sticky fingers would explore your hair, its wringing-wet pants would be pressed to your skirt; all its terrors and boredoms would be your own. There was only one tactic to be employed on such occasions; to ignore it utterly, and if necessary pull a horrible face and frighten it away for good.

When we were driving away from the smells and the corrosive dirt of Teroka, Jonathan Steele said:

'I'll bet that's one social engagement we won't be reading about in your column.'

I was now comfortably beyond such minor strifes, but I wasn't speechless on that account. 'You really *are* rude, aren't you?'

His hands on the steering-wheel of his rotten car were, for a moment, steady. He said, with what seemed to me to be extreme care and concentration:

'Kate, you are very beautiful and very accomplished. But whether you are lying flat on your back, or striding along to victory, Teroka is still there.'

CHAPTER FOUR

I forgot Teroka speedily, though the words 'very beautiful and very accomplished' stayed with me, echoing for two busy days in many different places—in Joel Sachs' office, at conferences in my suite, at parties, in the street. At the advanced age of twenty-six, I still received enough compliments to satisfy a not-too-swollen ego; it was odd that I should remember Jonathan Steele's, particularly since he had tacked on to it a sexual image—'lying flat on your back'—which normally would have annoyed me very much. I decided that I wasn't working hard enough. . . . I did not see Steele again; Eumor said that he was 'busy on his master-work', and Bruno van Thaal said: 'He can fry in hell for all I care,' which seemed to dispose of the matter to the satisfaction of all parties.

Meanwhile I was enjoying Johannesburg, which I always thought of as 'my town' because I was born there, at a time when my father was emerging as one of the bigger stars in the gold-mining firmament.

Working and playing there was always a tonic, after the more leisured pace of Cape Town. The Reef mines of the Witwatersrand were only sixty years old; the city which had grown on top of them was still a glorified mining camp, wide open, available for all comers. It wore always a flushed and hectic air, like a bride who might die tomorrow or an actor grown famous overnight.

People—young and old, thin or fat—threw their bodies on it at eight o'clock each morning, extracted every ounce of gold or profit during the next eight hours, and then rushed home in the evening to gamble it all away again. It lived perpetually on its nerves, hopes, fears, and suspicions; and since there was no limit of any sort to human greed and gullibility, the whole place was jumping, on a round-the-clock, twenty-four-hour basis.

Civic happiness was geared to the mining section of the stockmarket; not just for operators or investors, but for everybody. When the market was up, even the poor whites running the lifts were buoyant as bees; when it was down, there was not a smile to be had from a derelict taxi-driver. To hold aloof from this fever was an eccentric blasphemy; even the silliest women, restless, wayward, and palpably insincere, chattered of margins and coverage, stopes and assaye-reports, a clean-up in this and a sell-out in that. I sometimes wondered whether their terms of endearment, their loving words-on-a-pillow, were not darling West Driefontein, beautiful Blyvooruitzicht, dreamy De Beers. . . .

To match this nervous financial tic, there were some astonishing crimes and misdemeanours. 'Salted' bore-holes, peppered with alien gold, sent mining shares rocketing, only to plunge earthwards again when the perpetrators went to jail. Huge bets went awry as horses responded too readily to doping, and jumped the railings or sped backwards round the course. Only in Johannesburg would a horse, having broken its leg in a scuffle at the finishing-post, be shot dead by a spectator who ran across with his revolver from the Ten Shilling Enclosure.

Members of 'sherry gangs' kicked each other to death, and blamed it on tropical rain. 'Fishing-pole burglars' angled for loot through open bedroom windows, hauling out trousers, bedclothes, lovers. . . . A combination of altitude and aptitude gave people the world's strongest heads; there might be heavy drinking in other parts of the globe, but here it touched unique peaks of glory, and the altitude took care of the hangover.

53

Above all, it was a generous town. Involved in any kind of charity, I would rather raise ten thousand pounds in Johannesburg than ten shillings in London or Paris—particularly Paris. Partly it was due to a very strong Jewish community—acquisitive, cultured, and open-handed. A by-product of this was an anti-Semitism of an odd and disgusting kind; not the unselfish disliking the acquisitive, but the acquisitive disliking the ones who had out-manœuvred them. Johannesburg, however, had room for them all.

For two days I worked and wandered in this unique climate. We succeeded in sewing up the Anglo-African account, in the teeth of convulsive opposition from another firm; and I discussed with Joel Sachs about a dozen different lay-outs which were now due for production (the actual art-work was done in the main studio at Cape Town). Gerald Thyssen gave an exceptionally pleasant dinner party for me; we all went racing at Turffontein, where I lost at least a week's profits on one of Eumor's ungenerous crocodiles. Then it was the eve of my departure, and by way of farewell I dined with the boys and took them all to watch a wrestling match.

Like the act of love, all-in wrestling in South Africa was the same as all-in wrestling in any other part of the world; predominantly crooked, patently rehearsed, and (as far as I was concerned) hilariously amusing. We arrived at the end of one bout (the loser was just being finished off with a folding chair as we walked in) and wangled enough space at the ring-side Press table to make ourselves comfortable. Flanked by Eumor and Bruno van Thaal, I settled down happily to watch Honest John *versus* the Demon Barber (one fall, twenty-minute time limit, championship of the Lower Transvaal).

Honest John (a new arrival from Rhodesia) was one of the least honest performers I had ever seen in the ring. He was rather old, rather bald, rather cynical about the whole thing; but he was still a splendid character, versed in all the strategems which make ' show wrestling ' such a meaty conjuring trick. He gave us (and the Demon Barber—who was entirely hairless) the works; closed-fist punching, elbow smashes that missed the chin and took the larynx, eye-gouging, knees into the groin, muscle-plucking on the referee's blind side. He was up to all the tricks of defeat also; quite unsurpassed at cries of pain, the groggy-knees routine, fist-shaking at the crowd, and appeals to high heaven for justice.

Once, when he touched my shoe in landing outside the ring, he

54

whispered: 'Excuse me, lady,' and then roared at the top of his voice: 'Foul!' Thrown out of the ring a second time, he pointed at a projecting nail in the floor at least a yard from where he landed, and screamed in agony: 'Oh, my knee!' Naturally we backed him to the limit of our lungs.

And then, half-way through, suddenly I was bored; and just as suddenly I knew why.

The Demon Barber was taking time out on the ropes, simulating a profound coma; Honest John was protesting his innocence, and pretending to dispose of a knuckle-duster at the same time. Bruno was talking to the sports-writer sitting next to him. I tapped Eumor on the arm.

'Where's Steele, Eumor?'

He turned, surprised. 'Who,'

'Jonathan Steele.'

'I don't know, dar-r-r-ling. Why?'

'I'd like to see him again.'

Eumor's olive face creased into a grin. 'You have some plans?'

'No. I'd just like to see him.'

'No, you have plans,' declared Eumor determinedly. 'You wish me to procure for you. . . . It disgusts me. . . . I will do it gladly.'

'Hush,' I said.

'Trust me, Kate,' he hissed, wonderfully conspiratorial. 'I find him and bring him to your bed.'

'Just bring him here,' I said.

'You want his body. I arrange.'

'I'm sure you've done this sort of thing before,' I said, resigning myself to the trend.

'Not for some years.'

'What are you two children whispering about?' asked Bruno.

'Nothing,' answered Eumor. 'I go to the gentlemens.'

When he came back he stood at the end of the Press table, and called to me rather loudly: 'It's all fixed!' earning himself a malevolent glare both from the Demon Barber and the referee. Honest John was momentarily senseless on the other side of the ring.

Beside me again, Eumor whispered: 'He was home. Comes straight away.'

'But what did you tell him?'

'Everything!' exclaimed Eumor, with a gleaming eye. 'He feels same way about *you*.'

When a man whom you want comes into a room—even so wide a 'room' as a wrestling arena—and moves towards you, some tell-tale chemistry goes to work, quickening your heart, stabbing your womb. I knew, seconds before Bruno said distastefully: 'Darling, there's your *bloody* communist!' that Jonathan Steele had travelled swiftly, and was here.

Across the noisy, crowded, smoke-wreathed arena, I met his eyes, and smiled, and looked away again. He made his way through the rows, pulled out a chair, and sat down just behind me. In the ring, Honest John (the ordained winner) was getting in a few last licks at the Demon Barber, drawing his thumb-nail briskly across his opponent's eye-lids. I called out, as loud as I could: 'Come on, Johnny! Come on!'

Behind me, Jonathan Steele said: 'The black sheep of our family,' and I laughed with exquisite relief and pleasure.

I had already stopped thinking, or trying to work any of it out.

When Honest John's hand had been raised aloft in victory, and he had delivered the customary kicks at the prostrate form of the Demon Barber, we walked across from the arena to the night-club on Commissioner Street where I wanted to spend my last evening.

Jonathan Steele and I were companionably silent; Bruno, who seemed to have guessed what had happened and how it had been engineered, was deep in sulks. Eumor was beaming like Mephistopheles himself. We must have looked a very odd quartet.

As we turned into the door of the Springbok, and the bright lights of Commissioner Street gave place to the warm, indulgent twilight which is standard atmosphere for all good night-clubs, Bruno muttered to me:

'Darling, you *are* letting the side down!'

'Am I, Bruno?'

'The boys will *refuse* to believe it.'

'I refuse to believe it myself.'

But I did believe it. Already I thought the whole thing was wonderful.

Jonathan Steele was listening, saying nothing, quite unconcerned. Bruno glared at him.

'I hope you're not going to give us the same performance as the other night.'

'I'm not going to give any performance,' answered Steele reasonably.

'Of *any* sort,' said Bruno, looking from him to me. 'Frankly, these flowers are *not* for you to pick.'

I giggled at the ridiculous phrase, but I was cut short by Jonathan Steele saying to Bruno, with easy-going, confident disdain:

'Why don't you just go home?'

'One of my oldest friends,' I said, when Bruno had turned on his heel and swept out again.

'He'll be back,' said Jonathan Steele. 'But not tonight.'

Eumor, who had gone a few paces ahead, turned round to us, anxiously.

'I stay?' he asked.

'You stay,' I answered.

'Certainly,' said Jonathan Steele.

Neither of us specially wanted to be alone yet. That was in the entrancing future.

Eumor beamed at us. 'So you like my promotion, Kate?'

'Yes, Eumor, I like it very much.'

'You guess its title?'

'Title?'

He was nearly overcome with sudden laughter. '*Call Me Madam.*'

'Why, Eumor!' I said. 'I'm quite shocked.'

'Or *Kiss Me Kate*,' gasped Eumor, who seemed momentarily to have lost his head.

'Now *I* am shocked,' said Jonathan Steele.

His hand rested lightly on my arm, for the first time.

'Let's get a table,' I said, 'before we knock ourselves out completely.'

The Springbok was bouncing, as it usually was, seven nights a week, from dusk till dawn. The man who made it bounce, Skip Shannon, now came forward to greet us.

'Kate, my darling one! I've been looking for you these five days.'

'I've been terribly busy, Skip. But you knew I'd drop in some time, didn't you?'

'It wouldn't have been spring without you.'

Skip Shannon, whose guiding hand guaranteed the Springbok as my favourite night-joint, was a rubbery, durable Irishman who had spent his life doing all the things that Irishmen are traditionally meant to do.

He had boxed, he had played the music-halls, he had fought in odd wars, usually on the wrong side; he had acted in bad documentary films, followed the horses with even less success than Eumor, and served his time as a night-club chucker-out (broke his leg), model-agency proprietor (married the nicest one), and sacramental wine salesman (confessed all). I had absolutely no doubt that somewhere or other there was an ancient white-haired mother, down on her gnarled old knees among the pigs and the potatoes, praying the blessed saints above for her son's safe return to dear old Bally-go-phut.

But in spite of this checkered background, Skip was an infinitely honest and capable man, who gave everyone their money's worth, worked like a beaver, and knew (from hard experience) the exact height of the bounce of every phoney cheque in South Africa. Now he had graduated as owner (on someone else's money, no doubt) and operator (his own particular talent) of the Springbok, which was the night-club you went to when you felt in a mood of high exhilaration —or hoped to feel that way.

If I had known about Jonathan Steele, and the unladylike somersault which was to bring me thus suddenly to his side, I probably wouldn't have chosen the Springbok, which was for public rather than private accommodations. It wasn't bold or brassy, but it *was* popular—and popular among so large a cross-section of the city that whatever kind of person you were, some of your friends were certain to be watching you.

It was beginning to be crowded now, with the usual Johannesburg mixture, the late-night flotsam of which people like Bruno and myself had a good working knowledge, and Skip Shannon had the definitive blue-print.

There were upper-crust sight-seers, soft-goods merchants, brokers, bookmakers, and bankrupts. There were some of those foolish fellows who thought they could beat the Illegal Diamond Buying laws; there were whores, and models (whatever that meant nowadays), and way-ward financiers out on bail. There was a sprinkling of old women who should have known better, and girls shortly to learn worse. There were visiting newspapermen, as wide-eyed as children on their third birth-day; and professional escorts to middle-aged ladies—escorts who were liable to transform themselves, between sunset and sunrise, into jewel thieves, blackmailers, or conventional, free-swinging thugs.

There were people like Eumor, talking about money; like Bruno, talking about people; like Mrs. Arkell, talking about parties; like Joel

58

Sachs, talking business; like Salome Strauss, talking about past loves; and even like Lord Muddley, talking about the colonies and their eternal challenge to the wide-awake investor.

But there was no one, thank God, either there or in all the wide, world, exactly like Kate Marais and Jonathan Steele. . . . I felt that and *he* felt it, and perhaps dear Eumor, our personal procurer, felt it also, as we crossed the dance floor and settled down at our wall table, midway between the orchestra and a delightful notice which read: 'FIRE ESCAPE! NO EXIT!'

Skip Shannon, introduced to Jonathan, said: 'Mr. Steele, you've got a look of the Irish about you.'

Jonathan, bridging the important chasm between private joy and public elevation, said: 'That's very interesting. Actually, my mother's name was Cromwell.'

Eumor asked me, for the last time on that evening: 'Kate dar-r-r-ling, are you sure I am not *de trop*?'

Jonathan Steele surveyed Skip Shannon, Eumor Eumorphopulos, and all the *fritto misto* of gamblers, models, and musicians preparing to play *flamenco* guitar, and said: 'Your friends are really quite odd, aren't they?'

I said: 'I'm writing a book about South Africa,' and we both laughed, not caring any more about the details of surrender.

I don't know what happened to us on that night, but it did happen, and it happened to both of us.

We didn't do anything special; just talked and drank from eleven o'clock until six next morning; danced three or four times, and enjoyed or forgot the dreamy music. I had a Durban plane to catch at eight, and I caught it—fresh as a daisy, unharmed, yet borne now on a tide of gentle desire which was, we knew, to flood when next we met.

We didn't 'make love', even with our eyes, certainly not with our bodies; when we danced, it was unsensual, even sedate; there was no clutching, no intrusive thigh, no hand wandering upon my breast nor hardening pressure at the groin. That was going to happen, but not on this night.

Maybe that was why we kept Eumor as our chaperone. . . . Truly I couldn't have borne it if Jonathan had made any sort of sensual approach to me; whatever form it took, it would have been too early.

Perhaps he knew that, and felt the same way. Or perhaps, though ambitious, he wanted to earn my regard by his forbearance. It did not matter, either way. On that tender night, I was in the mood to forgive a hundred double-bluffs.

But he did say, towards the end, when we were still circling the floor sedately:

'Of course, dancing is for people who can't go to bed together.'

That was all he needed to say, for that occasion and for the precious future.

On that strange night, Eumor was there, and he was not there. He faded in and faded out of our consciousness, like a character in a trick production of *Blithe Spirit*. Of course he knew what was going on, and normally (if it had ever happened under his eyes) he would have bent a satirical gaze in my direction, and never stopped smiling. But tonight we were all out of character. I was a woman; Eumor was our small Greek godfather, Jonathan Steele an uncomplicated male. We had no worries, no fear of the net. We were playing every card face up.

Meanwhile, we enjoyed ourselves, at the traditional level also. Skip Shannon, generous soul, was giving employment that week to a forlorn old night-club comedian who should really, forty years earlier, have made up his mind to be something quite different—a book-keeper, or a jockey.

As a comedian, he was terrible, and he knew it, and we knew it, and everyone else knew it; only on that evening could we have found him uproariously funny, and communicated that feeling to a lot of other people in the room, so that his jokes presently began to get real laughs, and, on the creased old grease-paint mask, nervous tension gave way to pathetic surprise, and surprise in its turn to a perky self-confidence. Midway through his act, he must suddenly have decided that his ancient 'material' was pure gold after all, for he never looked back.

He did a rickety tap-dance, wildly off the beat, while we stamped out the time—any time. He did imitations of Greta Garbo, Bing Crosby, and Al Jolson; it did not matter that they were virtually indistinguishable. He did an Englishman in a Paris restaurant, with all the terrible jokes, including such hallowed plums as:

'*Garçon!*'

'It *is* on, you fool!'

And:

'*Je t'adore!*'

'Shut it yourself!'

He finished with some really bad juggling, dropped the balls, and murmured, in ambiguous reproof: 'Oh, balls!'

Roaring with laughter at this unique rubbish, we couldn't have been happier.

When it was all over, and we were comparatively quiet again, Eumor looked at us and suddenly said, out of the blue: 'Love is a jewel above rubbies.'

This was one of his better mispronouncements, and it made us both start laughing afresh.

'Are you fond of rubbies?' Jonathan asked me.

'Nothing I like better.'

We both laughed again. Later, it became our word for lovemaking.

At two a.m., my dear silly friend Mrs. Marchant waylaid me in the Ladies' Cloaks.

'Darling,' she said, 'do my eyes deceive me?'

'No.'

'What, then? All that merry laughter? And that *awful* man?'

'I just changed my mind, that's all.'

'Heavens! I know *I* do that. But I thought it was only me.'

'It's not only you.'

It was not only her. . . . Back at our table, in the warm twilight, with the band playing a gentle, sensual version of *Younger Than Spring-time*, I asked Jonathan Steele what he had been doing during the last forty-eight hours.

'Nothing much.' He was leaning back against the cushioned wall, idly watching the dancers in the gloom; he did not need to look at me, he knew what he would find there. 'I was thinking of you quite a lot. And I went down a gold mine.'

'Which one?'

'Free State Deep.' He grinned, almost shame-faced. 'Gerald Thyssen fixed it up.'

'In the circumstances, very handsome of him.'

'Undeniably. . . . But it was wonderful, Kate!' (Why was it such foolish bliss to hear my name thus pronounced?) 'It was one of his brand-new mines; in fact, they were still hacking away at the shaft. There must have been about twenty natives there, five thousand feet down, at the bottom of a crazy little pit about ten feet square. There was one bucket to take us down, one glaring floodlight, and the water sweating and cascading off the walls as the mine-boys tore away at the floor. It was as hot as hell, but they were grinning all the time, hopping about like maniacs in that tiny oven of a shaft, a mile below the surface. . . . We had the whole weight of the earth pressing down on us. . . . Their helmets were shining, their naked bodies glistening. . . .'

I looked sideways at his intent, remembering face, and said.

'I've been down a gold mine, too.'

He grinned, content to forget all that had moved him, and answered: 'Yes, I've read your column.'

We had no malice any more. Not even when he added: 'You know they're only paid twenty-two shillings a week?' and I answered: 'You can go quite a long way on twenty-two shillings a week, living in a compound with no rent to pay and no food or medical bills,'—not even then did we fear to strike any kind of abrasive spark. Indeed, it was Eumor who, surprisingly, picked that particular question up, as if with an unsuspected left hand.

'That is why we live in Africa,' he said suddenly, from his listening-post across the dark table.

'Why, Eumor?'

'Slaves. Twenty-two shillings a week.'

'They're not slaves.'

He spread his hands. 'They are comparatively slaves. We live on their backs. I make thirty thousand pounds a year, mostly because *they* are paid twenty-two shillings.'

Impressed, I said: 'Do you really, Eumor?'

Jonathan said: 'If you feel guilty about it, why do you stay?'

'I don't feel guilty. That is the terrible part. I feel I deserve it.' His olive face was somehow sombre and triumphant at the same time. 'We were very poor in Greece. My father was *petit fonctionnaire*, and I would have been the same. If I had stayed in Greece, I would be poor still. No slaves in Greece, only greedy *canaille*. . . . So I come here, use the slaves, use my brain, make money. More money that I could make anywhere else in world, except South America perhaps. Brains and slaves—that is all you need to be rich. Of course I stay in South Africa!'

Jonathan started to say something, and then stopped. It was part of our evening, part of the curious magic, that he didn't want to argue or criticise, though on any other occasion I was sure the flames of contempt would have roared and spouted.

'But you've contributed plenty to South Africa, Eumor,' I told him.

'I've contributed most to myself. I am very glad, and I do not mind to sound selfish.'

'I've never heard you say anything like that before.'

His face relaxed to a smile. 'Feeling funny tonight.'

We were all feeling funny tonight, and it didn't matter, and it didn't count against us.

'You think the same way, too, don't you?' Jonathan asked me presently.

'About what?'

'The slaves.'

'Not quite. In fact, not nearly. Of course, cheap labour is the mainspring of South Africa. But I don't think of them as slaves, I don't treat them as slaves. Naturally, I expect them to work hard, the same as I do, but I feel all the time that we owe them—oh, consideration, care, guardianship, whatever you like to call it. It's different down at the Cape, anyway. There's a different atmosphere there. You can feel it all the time at places like Maraisgezicht, especially.'

'*Where?*'

'Oh, don't be so English! Maraisgezicht. It's our family house—huge, old, beautiful, with acres of vineyards and about five hundred natives and Coloureds to work them. We're very proud of our vintages, and we always try to look after our people. That's what they are—our people.'

'Is that where you live?'

'I go there most week-ends. But basically I live in a flat in Cape Town. We have a couple of agents to run Maraisgezicht, and my father's there, now and again.'

'Doesn't he live there either?'

'Not any more. My brother was killed there.'

Jonathan said: 'There's so much I don't know about you.'

'But so much time also,' I answered.

Then we were staring at each other, gently intent, gently entranced. 'Do you ever come to Cape Town?' I asked, as naturally as I could.

'Now and then. When shall I come down next?'

A beating heart was all I was conscious of. 'In about a fortnight, if you like.' There was even a conventional reason for setting the date

63

thus: I still wasn't shocked. 'I have to go to Durban, and then clear my desk. I'd like to be free when you come.'

He nodded, and said: ' "Free" is the best word in any language.'

We had stopped being astonished, and it was thus that we made our assignation. Much later, with dawn coming up pink and pearly-grey, I walked back to my hotel down the very centre of Commissioner Street, arm-in-arm with my English lover-to-be and my small Greek uncle. I was blissfully happy, soberly drunk, treading the champagne air of enchantment, wanting to give everyone we saw at least a thousand pounds.

It was the end of our night, but the beginning of everything else in the world. As I had said to Jonathan Steele, so shyly, so boldly, we had so much time.

CHAPTER FIVE

TIME was extremely hard to manipulate during the next fortnight; try as I would, I could not make it move fast enough. I toiled as necessary, first at Durban (all heat, humidity, and sharks working, like pickpockets, the shores of the Indian Ocean), and then back at Cape Town, where the office grew quiet again, the people strolled up and down Adderley Street as if all the world were on their side, and the enormous bulk of Table Mountain loomed above us like a poised cliff.

Over the telephone to Johannesburg, I made up my tiff with Bruno van Thaal; all he said was, 'Darling, you really have a whim of *iron*!' and went on immediately to relay some truly acid copy. (Of an ageing play-boy, he commented: 'Fancy making love through a cascade of falling hair'; and, of a woman proud of her new house: 'They must have connected the plumbing wrong, because all she gets is hot flushes.' Dear Bruno. . . .)

But mostly I daydreamed, and especially so in the street, wandering often in happy vacuity, wearing that kind of idiotic grin which makes other people turn and smile. Waiting for Jonathan Steele, I seemed to have shed years of discipline, decades of growing up, and to be joyfully vulnerable again.

Stendhal, pontifical writer on love (but how was he *personally?* One sometimes wonders), once evolved a theory of 'crystallisation', which advised a period of separation for lovers between their first meeting, and the act of jumping into bed. (A courtly fellow, he phrased it somewhat more elegantly.) During this interval, he maintained, their thoughts and fancies about each other could have free play, conjuring up the ideal man and woman, fashioning out of the lover a crystallised object of intense desire. Stendhal, I found, was right. . . . It was not simply an erotic exercise, by any means; but during that fortnight apart I certainly had time to make of Jonathan an image for my delight.

We wrote each other every day; treasuring each other's handwriting (his was terrible), warming to each other's voices. On long distance, across nine hundred miles, the operator would say to me: 'Johannesburg wants you,' and I would answer: 'Cape Town wants *you*,' knowing that he could already hear.

Our letters were love letters, though not really in so many words; we were tacitly assuming that we would be lovers as soon as possible, in the sense that the actual fact was never mentioned, though it was implicit in every sentence, every inflexion. He once quoted the words of the rude French sailor to his sweetheart: '*Je t'écris avec la main droite, et je pense à toi avec la gauche.*' That was as nearly erotic as his letters ever became, though admittedly it was reasonably near.

Mostly, he wrote of his 'admiration', which was flattering, and disarming also. It recalled a moment in the night-club, when he had picked up my cigarette case and looked at its design. I had said: 'Gold is the prettiest metal, don't you think?' and he had smiled and said: 'Valuable as well,' and I said: 'That too, I suppose,' and he had smiled again and answered: 'Kate, you're *not* going to get me down!' But I knew that, in spite of himself, he liked that sort of thing, and he liked it in me; I was the kind of success which appealed to him, and when I seemed to shrug it all off, that appealed to him even more.

Waiting, I read his books. They were two: a traditional first novel about school and university, and a curious, somewhat moving story about a soldier unable to settle down to the drab routine of peace-time. Since he was only fifteen when the war ended, he could never have been a returning soldier; but somehow he had caught the discomforts, miseries, and dangers inherent in that misfitting moment of life.

Both books were well-written, slight, and promising—that grisly word. But they had attracted no attention at all; they were lightweights. As a writer, he had still to prove himself, and there was long way for him to go.

Perhaps the raw themes of Africa would develop the talent that was waiting to emerge. Equally, he might just produce the usual South African novel, about the noble savages held in bondage by oafish Dutch *boers* with ox-hide whips. I found already that I wanted very much for him to write the good book, not the bad one.

I wanted lots of other things, during that fortnight; the inside of my head must have looked like a teen-ager's stocking drawer. I wanted him to grow up. I wanted him to keep his innocence, hold his odd ideals, yet shed the rancour and the touchiness which had sparked that scalding row in the night-club with Gerald Thyssen. I wanted to help him to be a man, and a wonderful writer as well, if that were possible. I wanted him to want me. I wanted him.

Of course, down at Cape Town, dealing death and destruction at my desk in a flourishing office, or isolated in an astringent flat which had seen no lover, and scarcely any man, for years, the thing made even less sense than it had, that last night in Johannesburg; and just occasionally I caught my breath in mid-dream and, like any love-lorn lass gazing into a mirror, asked: *Can this really be you?* . . . Anyone who seriously tried to answer that one was heading straight for the couch; I didn't attempt it. Instead, treading water in this private whirlpool, I wondered, while I still had time, what was happening to me.

He was a man. I didn't especially want a man, but I wanted this one. He was an Englishman. Afrikaners don't especially like Englishmen, and I am sure it is thoroughly mutual. He was a writer, which was all right, and a socialist, which was not. He was good-looking, but so was every tenth man one met in the street, and I still had no decimal urges.

Indeed, I had almost everything else that worked against them: a self-made job, a self-made reputation, a contempt for those weaker sisters whose determined whoring made my column worth reading, and an absolute conviction that the head must rule the heart, from here to breakfast-time. Yet somehow, somewhere, Jonathan Steele had got under my skin, and the only thing I truly wanted was for him to stay there, all of him, for a long, long time.

66

I didn't even want to keep the thing a secret, which opened up further horrid vistas. All sorts of people were going to be astonished, as I was myself. There was Mrs. Patch, my secretary, tremendously feminist, slightly Lesbian, who only recognised men as the root of all evil. There was my darling father, who sometimes said: 'Time you got married,' but always added: 'He'll have to pass *me*, remember!' There was Julia, my maid for the past eight years, who had seen them come and seen them go, and was permanently fiercely, protectively jealous of the empty side of my bed.

There were people like Bruno van Thaal, who relied on me to behave quite differently, and like Joel Sachs, whose livelihood might depend on it; old friends like Peggy Marchant, who expected me to be an angel; and old enemies like Mrs. Arkell, who had known all along that I was a complete harlot.

Sometimes, I thought of it in terms of my own un-pretty columnese: '*Kate Marais, who tells us all how to behave, cosily installed with left-winger Jonathan Steele. Such beautiful music. . . . He writes as well, though not just now. . . .*' But the sub-cutaneous smear had not yet been coined which could make me feel second-rate, nor tarnish this idyll. This time, *I* was doing it, and so it was all different.

Thus, at the mirror, in the street, on my bed, all the foolish lineaments of love. . . . I got the flat ready. I bought six bottles of champagne, and some masculine-type soap that smelt of hot tar. I alerted Julia who, as expected, was shocked to the back teeth and refused to speak anything but Cape-Coloured Afrikaans for three whole days. I visited my doctor, whose eyebrows rose a full inch before he said: 'Of course. . . .'

Then suddenly it was the day, and, more suddenly, the night.

CHAPTER SIX

I MET his plane at the airport. Standing in the sunshine, looking across the sandy expanse of the Cape Flats towards the broad bulk of Table Mountain, still dominant against the blue flag of the sky even at a distance of twenty miles, I felt sure of myself, and happy, and excited. When his plane came winging in from the north-east, dropping steeply as it crossed the last outcrop of the Drakensberg Range, I stared at it—a tiny silver bird catching the sun joyfully on its wings —and thought: All that I love, all that I am going to love, is up there in blessed suspension, coming towards me, keeping our appointment. . . . But that turned out to be the last moment of certainty, of assurance, for several long hours.

He seemed taller than I remembered, and pale ('We came down too fast'), and nervous ('I always forget that I *hate* flying'). I was suddenly nervous too; the words I spoke, the answers I gave, were wayward and nonsensical. There were two or three people I knew, among the disembarking passengers; I felt that they were looking at me, and then at Jonathan Steele, as if we were a strange couple indeed, undoubtedly suspect. ('Kate Marais was at the airport,' I imagined the dark commentary, 'meeting someone we'd never set eyes on before! He looked so *odd*! Do you suppose . . .') I felt odd also, for the first time within a now shaky memory.

I drove into town abominably, earning horn-blasts from other, infuriated road-users, and a harsh glare from a motor-cycle cop on the watch for just such female mavericks as myself. It was nerves, of course; I wanted to do everything well that day—driving cars, mixing champagne cocktails, organising a meal, making love—and the omens already were quite otherwise.

It grew worse later on; in my flat which should have been a warm, exciting refuge from everything and everyone that was not us, we found ourselves talking with ludicrous constraint. It seemed that we had said all that had to be said, on that last night together in Johannesburg; the next stage could only be a headlong dive into action, and it was too early for that, too light, too soon.

Serving amid lengthening silences a dinner which as not as good as I had planned, Julia looked at me as if I were out of my wits, and at Jonathan as if he were a burglar. If this was madam's idea of love, her caustic glances said, then madam should see the head-doctor, now. Tomorrow would be too late.

Ten o'clock came, and then eleven. Julia had long since gone home, though the resentful clatter of dishes in the sink still rang in my ears. I sat feet-up on the couch, wearing a house-coat which had seemed just the thing when I bought it, two days earlier, but which now felt indecorous, even indecent. Jonathan was at the radiogram, changing the records over—we had had an hour-long session of Dixieland, which had proved about as inspiring as a programme of Sousa marches. In sudden panic, I was just about to tell him that I had changed my mind, and that he must go home, when he took charge.

He turned towards me. He was pale still, and tense, but suddenly he was a lover instead of an intruder, looking down at me with a kind of despairing tenderness, as though searching for the exact words he thought I deserved.

When they came, they were forthright, the way I was accustomed to talk myself, and had unhappily forgotten.

He said: 'I want to stay with you tonight. The way we imagined it in Johannesburg. Things haven't changed—they've only come to a crisis. But it's *our* crisis. Can I stay?'

I had to match his spirit, or be a coward forever.

I said: 'Give me twenty minutes start.'

He kissed me before I left the room, a sweet kiss, our first. It sustained me as far as my bedroom, but there I lapsed horribly again, the prey to every kind of paralysing emotion. In my bath, at my dressing-table, in bed at last, I was conscious only of foreboding, last-minute fears; fear that I was wrong to throw away the years of discipline, that I would be no good with him, that it wouldn't work, that we had staked too much on the chance of physical concord, that I would cry or suddenly run away, that as a lover he would be 'finished' within a few seconds, leaving us both marooned on a foolish limb. First-night nerves. . . . I swallowed my whisky, half-smoked three cigarettes, threw off the eiderdown and drew it back on again.

I was trembling. I knew it was absolutely hopeless. I wanted to lock the door, or faint, or die.

I need not have worried at all. Indeed, half-way through that wakeful night, I wanted to laugh for joy at my foolish fears. For he was wonderful, and *we* were wonderful. Taking charge again, first calming my thundering heart and jittery body with words and soft hands, he made love to me with enormous care, and gentleness, and potency. Failure never threatened us, every moment seemed pre-ordained by some singing pattern of success.

When I was ready, he was ready. When I grew wild, he was there to match it. Presently he was like a warrior at the gate, and, in the end, like a god.

We had been right all the time.

In our day-long, night-long, week-long dream, where we wandered over such a vast area of delight that we could never see nor feel its confines, music aided and abetted us at all hours. It happened that we shared, normally, a somewhat austere musical taste—Bach, Brahms, the later Mozart—but this was not a time for the attentive ear. Softer airs, warmer climes, were our need and our pleasure.

We fell in love, not only with each other, but with oddments of music which forever recalled that first meeting; and though they 'dated' us later, we were not then ashamed to be the step-children of such dreamy old nonsense as the tunes from *South Pacific*, and *My Fair Lady*, and even *Guys and Dolls*. Among a host of other things, some cerebral, some lustful, our love was deeply sentimental. Dance music of this sort, we found, linked many moods, many desires, all of them pricking the spirit, warming the tender flesh, or piercing the heart at will.

'What did you really think when you first met me?' I asked.

'I thought you were a very beautiful, complete bitch.'

'I am.'

'Oh, I know. But not all through. Not for ever. And not for me.'

'We're so unlike each other, really.'

'It doesn't matter. . . . What did you think of me, Kate?'

'Untidy. Mixed up.'

'I am.'

'But *good*. I'm not good.'

'Perhaps you will be.'

'Perhaps we'll both change. Wouldn't that be funny?'

'No. It would be very awkward indeed.'

'Why, Johnny?'

'If you became a good-natured columnist, and I became a self-regarding, self-centred novelist, we'd both be out of a job.'

'I have a little money.'

'Give it all to me.'

The fact that no man had made love to me for more than two years involved some physical intractibility. It did not last, but in our shared mood of candour, I had to speak of it.

70

'You made me feel almost virginal, the first few times.'

In the darkness, I felt one of his eyebrows gently raised. 'That was not apparent,' he told me.

'But it's true.'

'Then you are *my* virgin,' he said. 'Let's call it a special category.'

He was so very good for a girl's morale; not only in the obvious ways, such as being ready to make love to me whenever I gave the smallest signal, but in his admiration of attributes that I myself was somewhat shy of. For example, so far from laughing at my modest configuration —34–25–36—he seemed to adore it.

'They are perfect, Kate,' he said, at an appropriate moment, 'and they're perfectly in proportion, too. Don't believe all this American nonsense about men really liking 42-inch busts. That's just the pressure of advertising; they want to sell more elastic. When you see it in the flesh, it looks top-heavy, ungainly. All those Italian film stars look like cows walking backwards on their front legs.'

He was an only child, and an orphan since the nursery days. He had never had anyone close to him, to cherish and to be cherished by. Indeed, he was astonishingly lonely. For him, no sister had ever talked the night out; no fond mother had warmed the cocoa and held the jealous inquisition; no other woman had told him, in honest ecstasy: 'Come close to me, it is mine, it is yours, enjoy it, murder it, slake it, take it.' There was a moment when he said to me, in true wonderment: 'Kate, *you are all things.*' It was my happiest, the moment I had been born for.

Now he was overwhelmed by love. But he was the pilot still. He seemed able to channel and control my heart and body; I could caress and adore him towards our goal, but when he said: '*Now!*' it was I who obeyed, I who gasped and drowned. He had, after all, never stopped being a man, and with me, near me, on me, in me, he proved it in steady mastery, beyond any doubt in the world.

There was one special afternoon, in the warm sunshine, on the screened balcony, when I wore (or rather, discarded) a white robe which was a favourite of mine. We made love then with such shared tenderness, such unique eloquence, that I remembered it always. We slept for

71

three hours afterwards, and woke to hear each other murmur: 'I adore you.'

'Oh Steele,' I said, in the middle of the night. 'Steele, Steele.'
 'The name in bed is Jonathan.'
 'But the feel is Steele.' I looked past his bare shoulder at the luminous clock. 'I can't still be drunk, at five?'
 'No. Steele it is, Steele forever.'
 'How many babies was that?'
 'About eleven million, they say.'
 'Darling, so lavish.'
 'The last of the big spenders.'

What a good word, suddenly, was 'man'.

CHAPTER SEVEN

I NEVER went near my office, during that whole week. Ordinarily I would have been shocked at such indiscipline—indeed, it would have been inconceivable; but now, wandering as if drugged and dreaming, in a private world, hand-in-hand with Jonathan Steele, I found it impossible to care. When I woke up, that would be time enough to feel ashamed. . . . Mrs. Patch, my secretary, rang up two or three times, more to check on my sanity than to relay any vital problems. She could not have been reassured by any of my answers.

Mostly we did nothing, and yet, as with a Chinese box-within-a-box, we did everything at the same time. We slept, made love, ate and drank, listened to our sentimental music, became aware of successive dawns piercing the curtains, watched Cape Town harbour far below beyond our private drawbridge, heard by day the street-sellers' cries and the strange 'fish-horns' that announced the morning's catch, and by night the dogs and the drunks and the church bells counting our loving hours.

We talked and listened to each other with longing attention. We laughed, and stared at each other in enraptured silence. We kissed in tenderness, and then in wild excitement. We learned all of each other's bodies, and much of each other's hearts and minds.

We only went out three times in seven days, and that grudgingly. We drove along the coast to Hout Bay, a fishing village haunted by artistic human flotsam reputed to be homosexuals, lesbians, half-and-halfers; our own preoccupation was with lobsters. Once, on Julia's night out, we dined at Cape Town's most monolithic hotel, where the resident clientele was very old indeed, and (it was rumoured) the waiters conducted a running sweepstake on who among the customers would die next, and watched their own candidates greedily for signs of dragging feet, failing appetite, a bad colour at nightfall. . . . And once we went racing, and made a little money, and had a little quarrel.

On the race-course, I had the feeling that everyone was staring at us, and I had never felt more glad of it. I borrowed some money from one bookmaker, got a side-of-the-mouth tip from another, and, thus armed, took a third one for a ride with a walk-away winner at eight-to-one. I talked to an old flame of mine, who, searching my face, said: 'My God, you never looked like this for me!' and perhaps some of my intense happiness overflowed into my manner, because Jonathan, watching us with shadowed eyes from the Pay Out queue, grew quite livid with anger and would scarcely utter a word when he returned. We made it up *ad interim* in the Stewards' private bar, when he said:

'Jealousy will be very dull later on. But now it's desperately important, an essential part of loving each other. I want you to keep *all* of your-self for me. . . . Can we go home now?'

We went home, practically running the last few yards, and falling into each other's arms behind the slammed front door of my flat. And then, with no hurry at all, it was Sunday morning, and we drove out, as promised, to Maraisgezicht, my home.

I had hoped all along that he would love the place, since Maraisgezicht to me was irresistible; it was my one piece of family snobbery that everyone should instantly feel the same way about it. Jonathan did. . . . Maraisgezicht means, in the old Dutch tongue now bastardised into Afrikaans, 'Marais View'; and Marais' view was obviously that he should live in the utmost elegance and comfort, and his children's children after him. To this end he had bought, two hundred years earlier, a whole slope of a mountain in the Constantia district, spent a fortune on building and landscaping, and produced one of the world's most beautiful houses.

Andries Marais had settled at the Cape in 1750, when people came to stay and built to last; much of the stone of the house, every stick of timber, and all the furniture had been brought from Holland or the Dutch East Indies, and there assembled on a pattern in which good taste, home-sickness, and a frank burgher-like self-esteem all played a part.

There were not now remaining more than half a dozen such great houses, in the classical Cape-Dutch mode; for us, their builders—Van Riebeeck, Van der Stel, Serrurier, Cloete—were part of the fabric of South Africa, and their very names were like jewels—Vergelogen, Stellenberg, Steenberg, Groot Constantia, Morgenster, Alphen. But no jewel shone brighter than Maraisgezicht, on that or any other morning.

We approached it slowly by a mile-long oak avenue, past the low-lying vineyards, with the sun through the interlaced branches dappling our pathway; and I heard Jonathan catch his breath as the house came into view, unfolding in a fantastic backdrop of gleaming white walls, great curving gables, massive window shutters of polished teak, and a flagged courtyard with the twin white-washed columns of a slave bell at its further margin. When the perspective was completed, all was noble and peaceful, as far as the eye could reach.

'But it's wonderful, Kate,' said Jonathan, rather breathless, as we came to a stop. 'And the view. . . .' His eyes turned from the house to the Constantia valley below us, twenty hazy miles of trees, vineyards, and sunny pastures. 'I can't understand why you don't live here for ever.'

'Nor can I, sometimes.'

Simeon, the major-domo, came down the wide steps to greet us, splendid in his white frock coat, scarlet tasselled sash, and buckled shoes; above this display of consequence, his austere Cape Malay face was unbending, like proud mahogany. As with many of the Cape families, he bore our name; he was Simeon Marais, the eighth of the line, as my father was the eighth of his. Slave forbears meant nothing to either side now, and perhaps they had never done so.

'Well, Simeon.'

'Miss Kate is a day late,' he said, with a slight relenting smile. As he spoke, his hands moved, like a conductor's, motioning other servants

74

to unload the luggage. Various dogs bounded up, plastering my white linen slacks with yellow dust; at the edge of the terrace, one of the bad-tempered peacocks screeched and spread his tail like a rainbow fan.

'We went racing, Simeon.'

'With good fortune?'

'Yes, for a change. . . . This is Mr. Steele.'

'Sir,' said Simeon. His face grew austere again; like Julia, he exhibited a long-term jealousy where I was concerned; he had been warding off unworthy suitors for twenty-six years, and there was a clear assumption that he would continue doing so. 'You are staying tonight, Miss Kate?'

'Yes.'

I led Jonathan indoors, slowly, happily; across the screened *stoep*, one of the world's nicest drinking places, and then into the *vorhuis* with its frieze of blue Batavian tiles. Here, as in the other rooms, and all over the house, the polished elegance of the past still reigned; the sun fell benignly on satin-wood and ebony, *imbuia* and burr walnut; on the brass locks of a huge linen press, on *kists* of yellow-wood and oiled teak; on Delft-ware brought out from Holland by Andries Marais himself, and blue-and-white Nankin china commanded from the other side of the world, when the Dutch East India Company was young.

Our feet fell softly upon silk carpets, exquisitely patterned, but worn thin by generations of dancing slippers, riding boots, *veldskoen*, the high button shoes of my great-grandmother, my father's shooting boots, and now by our own twentieth-century rope-soled *espadrilles*. A trio of Famille Rose wine-servers caught the sun afresh on their ancient glaze as we passed the dining-room door.

Of course, so much of all this was going to waste. . . . My long-dead and adored mother had graced this house like an angel; when she died and my brother was killed there also, the heart went out of it for my father, and he was now a rare visitor to a place which, though uniquely lovely, held too many poisonous memories for him. As I had told Jonathan, an agent ran the winery, another administered the estate as a whole; for the rest, it was a focal point for Cape sight-seers, and a week-end dormitory for me.

We returned to this matter of desertion later, after a walk round the estate, a hand-in-hand tourist's view of the main vineyards, the slopes with the young vines, the 2,000-gallon vats in the vast cool cellars, the 'slave-quarters' which now housed a hundred happy families. At lunch in the high-panelled dining-room, our view through the top half of the 'stable-door' was a lovely square of sunlight, a vista of red and yellow leaves, jacaranda, proteas, chincherinchees, framing a pathway leading off into towering oak trees; a view occasionally notched by the two pointed ears, no more, of one of the inquisitive ridgeback hounds.

Everything, as usual, was just right, and I could feel the magic working inside Jonathan, see its reflection in his alert, watchful, surrendering face. At the end he sat back in his high-backed chair of Sumatran wood, eating our Hanepoot grapes, drinking our own *vin rosé*, loving me, utterly content.

But, being Jonathan Steele, he had a sociological problem to discuss.

'It's the most beautiful place I've ever seen in my life, Kate,' he said. 'But a tremendous responsibility. . . . Why don't you live here, really?'

'I'm the urban type,' I told him, 'and I prefer the urban effort. I like the sort of work I'm doing now, and I don't want to do anything different.'

'But don't you feel you ought to stay here, and help to run the place? Or contribute in some way?'

'No.' I overcame a slight guilty touchiness at the word 'contribute' He had strayed into another area which didn't concern him at all; but for anyone who was seeing Maraisgezicht for the first time, it was still a fair question. 'It's being very efficiently run as it is. I couldn't do better, and even to do as well I'd have virtually to go back to school, learn estate management, learn the wine trade. Why should I?'

His voice was tender, but quite firm. 'Because it's yours.'

'It's my father's.'

'And after him?'

'It will be mine, of course. But on the same basis. I will enjoy it, other people will make it work.' I smiled at him. 'That's what we call the Kate Marais division of labour.'

'But in Johannesburg you said they were "your people".'

'They are, and they will be. Always. I'll see to that, at least.' On an impulse I got up (the servants had left the room), came up behind his chair, and kissed the back of his neck, where what we called his 'writer's hair' grew in literary profusion. 'Oh Johnny, don't probe too deep today, don't make us think, or go into mourning. Maraisgezicht is tremendously sad in spite of everything, and we both know it.'

'How can it be sad?'

'Because there's no one to take it over after my father dies. . . . It would all be different if Theunis were alive.'

'Theunis?' He stumbled over the unfamiliar name.

'My brother.'

I kissed him once more, briefly, and sat down on the nearest chair, still holding his warm hand.

'What happened to him, Kate?'

'He was killed, quite close to the house, about two years ago. It was a useless, senseless thing. He was caught under a tractor.'

'How horrible.'

'Yes, it was.' I wanted to tell him the story, in spite of us, in spite of our deep content. 'There was no need for it. One of the boys got the tractor stuck in a big irrigation ditch, and Theunis tried to get it out. It was the sort of thing he loved doing. . . . It rolled back on him.'

'Were you here?'

'Yes. It was a Saturday, a happy Saturday.' The terrible afternoon came back to me; for the first time, I wanted to share it with another person. 'When they carried him in, my father was asleep on the *stoep*; he woke up, and saw all their faces, and he shut his eyes again, trying to make it a dream. . . . Ever since I can remember, whenever father told him not to drive too fast, not to ride like a lunatic, not to swim too far out, Theunis always said: "You should have had more sons". . . . Would you like to see his room?'

'If you would.'

'I always go.'

Theunis' room was as we had agreed to leave it, without even mentioning the fact, for the past two years; untouched, unchanged, a monument to handsome, hopeful, bright-painted youth, a requiem for the last of the male line. It was an undergraduate room, somewhat spare in furniture—he had never cared for our show pieces. There was a rack of guns; rods piled in one corner; eighteen pairs of boots and shoes, all worn, some muddy; a rowing-machine that he was too lazy to use; girls' photographs.

'He had lots of girls, bless him,' I said. 'He drove them all crazy. He didn't give a finger-snap for any of them.'

'How old was he, Kate?'

'Twenty-six. Two years older than me. He used to look after me. He used to make me think that incest wouldn't be such a disgusting sin, after all. . . . Is it awful to say that?'

'Yes.' But Jonathan was smiling gently, his arm round my waist. 'I know what you mean.'

'He was terribly good-looking, and kind, and clever. He got a cricket blue at Oxford, much to our disgust.'

'Why?'

'Afrikaners think cricket is just a little too English to be bearable. . . . Actually we were quite speechless with pride. My father and I flew to England for the match.' Suddenly I had to complete the story. 'The boy who put the tractor into the ditch starved himself to death.'

Jonathan stared, as I had known he would. 'Why, Kate?'

'For African reasons.'

Suddenly the foreboding scent of death was heavy around us, and Jonathan caught it. He turned me round until I was facing him, close-pressed, enfolded.

'But we are alive, Kate.'

'Yes, thank God.'

'And I love you.'

'Yes, thank God.'

'Forever.'

'Forever is a very long word, Johnny.'

'Not too long for us.'

We slept that night in the bed in which I had been born; a huge bed, canopied, with the Marais arms on the carved satinwood headboard. (Said Jonathan at one point: '*These* are the only Marais arms I'm interested in.') There were no question-marks in our love-making now, no area of hesitation or shyness; we frankly adored one another, and we did our candid best to prove it.

It should perhaps have shamed me to sleep with Jonathan in my own home—my mother, indeed, had once mentioned this as the ultimate in misconduct; as it was, it seemed the most natural thing in the world, and when at a certain moment a leap of flame from the dying fire briefly picked out the crimson canopy over my head, I only thought: lucky girl, to be twice sheltered.

Then, much too soon, it was Monday morning, and after break-fasting enormously off fish-kedgeree and sugar-cured ham, we were driving back into Cape Town again. We had no plans, except to be in love, but the world was falling into step once more

When we were near the city limits:

'What are you doing today, darling?' I asked Jonathan. 'Are you going to work?'

'I don't think so. Are you?'

'Yes. I have to.'

'Don't, Kate,' he said, to my surprise.

'But I have to,' I repeated. 'I've taken a whole week off already. I really must start up again.'

'All day?'

'All day and every day.'

'But I'll be so lonely without you.'

'Me too. But if I don't work, things will only start dropping to pieces. I wish it weren't so.' I realised that this wasn't quite true, and I added: 'It's my *work*, Jonathan. It's the way I spend my time. I like it.'

There was an edge of sulkiness in his voice as he said: 'What about us, then?'

I laid my free hand over his. 'Darling, don't be a baby. You're writing a book. I'm running an office. Neither of those things even begins to come between us. Why should they?'

'But it means we can't be together.'

I realised at that moment that one could be swamped with love, and yet disappointed at the same time. Jonathan's attitude seemed curiously frivolous; moreover it appeared to contradict his expressed 'admiration' for what I had done with my life so far, which would have amounted to nothing at all without persistent concentration. As we inched our way city-wards along De Waal Drive, thick with the morning traffic, I thought that this was a point worth making.

'Darling, if I were the sort of girl who played truant from the office whenever she felt like it, I wouldn't have any kind of career, and you wouldn't think much of me, would you?'

'It depends.' But he was relaxing again, aware perhaps of a thread of discord which was his own responsibility. 'Look, I know I'm being selfish. I just want you to myself, for as long as I'm here.'

'You've got me.'

'Out of office hours?'

'Just that. . . . Mr. Steele, how much more proof do you want that I'm wild about you?'

'Give me some more at five this evening.'

'At half past four.'

79

'I'll try to make that half hour significant.'

I was to remember that conversation months afterwards, as a distant signal I should have recognised, like a faint swinging lamp in a bank of fog. But that morning, it only seemed to reflect a rather endearing masculine tantrum, with a distinctly flattering basis. . . . Jonathan spent the rest of the week at my flat, pottering about, going for walks, or scribbling notes, while I took up my own pattern again.

It was odd to think of him installed at home, while I worked downtown; indeed, it took some getting used to. Julia thought it *very* odd. . . . But it was fun to come back to a guaranteed loving welcome, and the nights of course were wonderful.

Then, at the week's end, we made another promised journey together, to see my father.

CHAPTER EIGHT

M Y father was still the wisest man I knew, and in many ways the most admirable. Psychiatrists customarily split their sides when a woman tells them this; it means, of course, the very worst. But in simple truth, he had been, and was, a great man; and lucky is the girl who has a great man for a father. Basically he was a mining man, of the older, tougher generation; family background had given him a running start, hard work and integrity had taken him to the very top.

He would have been a great deal richer if, in the bad old days of not so very long ago, he had been a more accommodating character—in brief, if he had played it crooked. But he had played it straight, as a life-long habit, and was now, alas, only a moderate millionaire.

At the age of sixty-five, he was already in semi-retirement; he had no wish to be any richer, and my brother's death had made most other pursuits and interests pointless. He spent a little time each year at Maraisgezicht, to enjoy the harvest; a little time in Johannesburg, where a dozen boards claimed his intermittent attention; in the autumn he shot buck and guinea-fowl, in the spring he watched his horses lose two or three of the top classics; the rest of his itme he spent by the sea, and most of that in simply watching it.

The house he had built for our family holidays was near Hermanus, a small fishing village now grown somewhat sophisticated, about eighty miles east of Cape Town. When we drove down on Friday night, it took about three hours, by a mountain road which gave us, in the early moonlight, a matchless view of the whole Cape Peninsula. Jonathan and I were very happy, as usual, and my father, bless him, was happy to see us.

He came down the front steps as soon as he saw the lights of the car; a bluff square figure, a little shrunken now, the lamplight falling on a face deeply carved, full of thought, full of time. I had not seen him for four months; he seemed greyer, but not less commanding, not less dear. He must have been very good-looking as a young man; now it could only be traced by the eyes of faith and love; the bony symmetry had shed its flowering, leaving only a gaunt outline of the happy past.

He knew already that Jonathan and I were lovers, since I had told him when I telephoned earlier; observant without being in the least inquisitive, he would have divined it anyway, and it seemed better manners on my part to volunteer the information. It also simplified the housekeeping. As an Afrikaner, he would have made Jonathan welcome in any case; since I was involved, however irregularly, and he loved and trusted me, he made a special effort of hospitality.

After he had kissed me, and I had inhaled his admirable male blend of cigars, brandy, bay rum, and the after-shave lotion (by Gourelli) I had given him for his last birthday, he turned to Jonathan, holding out a firm hand.

'Welcome to my house!' he said. It was the old-fashioned, traditional phrase I had never known him leave unspoken, with any newly-arrived guest. 'Did you have a good drive?'

'Yes, thank you, sir,' answered Jonathan. In the half-light, he was looking at my father in the way that most young men did: impressed, slightly awed, ready to be dutiful and attentive. On the journey down, he had remarked, à propos of nothing: 'I hope the old boy likes me.' This was the proper evaluation of that somewhat off-hand phrase.

'You've not been here before?'

'No, never. It looks beautiful.'

'It *was* beautiful,' corrected my father, an opponent of all progress which did not relate to deep-level mining. 'Now it's nothing but crowds, and new houses, and bottle-stores, and damned women playing bridge all day and night in mink coats. Hermanus used to be a simple place. Now it's a resort!'

He said the last word with special emphasis, as if it were his private pseudonym for hell.

'You don't see much of them, Daddy.' I reassured him.

'No, thank God! The best thing about this house is that it's got twelve acres and a good high wall. . . . Let's go in. You must be ready for a drink.'

Presently, at ease in the comfortable living-room, furnished sea-side fashion with the shabby overflow from Maraisgezicht, he nursed his drink, and said:

'I'll call you Jonathan, if I may. . . . Do you two want to fish tomorrow, or just do nothing?'

'Fish, I think,' I answered. 'Has it been any good?'

'The yellow-tail are running, I'm told. I've got you two gillies, anyway.'

'I'm not getting up at the crack of dawn,' I warned him.

He smiled, looking from Jonathan to me. 'I wasn't expecting any enthusiasm for outdoor sport before ten o'clock, at the very earliest.' But he said it without undue innuendo; it was part of his enormous capacity for strength and comfort that he never offered advice unless it was asked for, nor passed judgement until the appropriate curtain fell.

He knew that I had had lovers before; face to face with Jonathan, the incumbent, he might well have been discomforted, or disapproving of an idea scarcely conceivable to his own generation. But it did not show now, and it would never show unless, some time in the shadowy future, I perhaps asked him: 'What did you really think? . . .'

It amused me to see that, of the three of us, only Jonathan was embarrassed by this exchange. Indeed, on the pretext of looking at the view, he now wandered out onto the *stoep*, from where, I knew, the track of the moon on the water would be like a broad silver arrow pointing at the house.

'An Englishman, eh?' said my father in a gruff voice.

'I'm afraid so.'

'Your poor mother. . . .' But he was smiling. 'Be happy, girl! Life doesn't go on for ever.'

I kissed the top of his head. 'I *am* happy. Will you come fishing with us tomorrow?'

'You don't want me hanging around playing gooseberry.'

'But of course we do!'

'I always knew there was something wrong with Englishmen,' he grumbled. But he was pleased. 'I'll see. . . . I'm getting a bit old for scrambling about the rocks.' He heaved himself out of his chair. 'Now I'm off to bed. Don't stay up too late.'

'We won't.'

He winked, and said: 'I don't expect you will, somehow.'

'He's wonderful, Daddy,' I said, in necessary extenuation.

'He'd better be,' retorted my father, and stumped off to his room.

Punctually on cue, Jonathan wandered in from the balcony. 'It's a heavenly night,' he said. 'The moon is enormous.'

'It's all right,' I told him. 'He likes you terribly.'

'How can you tell?'

'If he didn't, he'd still be here, just to annoy you. . . . He once sat up for *four* hours, until my current young man lost heart and went home. I was furious.'

'Is that meant to make me jealous?' asked Jonathan, putting an arm round my waist.

'Yes.'

'It has succeeded.'

'What happens when you're jealous?'

'The same as when I'm not jealous. . . . I love you, Kate.'

'It's mutual, like the insurance.'

'Strong, like the box.'

We had lots of silly jokes already.

We slept deep and lovingly that night, and awoke to the sound of the surf pounding the beach below the house. As often happened in the Cape Province, the wind had got up swiftly during the night, whipping the long Indian Ocean swell to a fierce tumult; on our treacherous coastline, it was not a day for fishing, unless one wanted to end up as a statistic under the traditional headline: '*Fishing Party Washed Off Rocks at Hermanus.*'

Instead, we slaked our breakfast appetite with paw-paw and red snapper, assumed the customary Hermanus uniform of khaki slacks and rope-soled shoes, and prepared to loaf in the sun for the next forty-eight hours.

We started by being happy. It happened that the household needed

83

a new wash-girl (the last one had done something criminal to one of my father's shirts) and we were commissioned to quarter the locality until we discovered one. 'Find me a slut,' had been my father's directive, and so we drove round Hermanus in search of this commodity.

Despite the wind, it was a bright day, warm and encouraging; and Hermanus, as usual, was a good place to be in. My father had been right in saying that it was becoming overcrowded, overbuilt, and far too social for the simple tastes that had led us all there in the first place; but that could not spoil its basic attractions, which were sunshine, colour, and a superb position at the sea's edge, nor affect its air of village affability.

I still knew most of the people on the street; pausing here and there in our curious task, eating ice-cream, buying oranges and young asparagus, we were greeted by everyone from the local librarian (who, alas, had never heard of Jonathan Steele) to the courtly, devout, and high-principled cleric known to one and all as the Venereal Arch-Demon.

We found our wash-girl, after a number of false alarms: 'There's a slut!' exclaimed Jonathan at one point, only to add, a moment later: 'Sorry—no good—she has a tiny slut at breast.' But, in the usual Hermanus pattern, somebody's houseboy knew someone else whose girl-friend was 'going to be busy by and by' (the Cape-Coloured euphemism for pregnant) and would welcome the extra money; we finished up among some hessian shacks on the outskirts of the village, interviewing and then engaging an ugly sad-eyed girl who, if the three children playing at her feet were anything to go by, must have been fairly busy, on and off, for the past few years.

Then we drove home, happy for a variety of reasons; and then, after lunch (which saw an agreeably heavy intake of martinis, our own white wine, and Van der Hum liqueur) things started to come unstuck.

As so often in South Africa, the touch-stone was political. My father had no politics to speak of; as an Afrikaner, he was fiercely proud of our people's past, and their separate, valiant emergence as a nation; but he was also anti-Nationalist, and quite ready to concede that South Africa owed her nationhood to a genuine, twin-elemental grounding, and that neither side, Dutch or English, had had a monopoly of brains, guts, and endurance in the past.

However, he had his tender spots; and one of these was the late

General Smuts, whose special repute in South African history he thought overblown and undeserved.

Jonathan, as an Englishman, did not; and he was foolish enough to argue about it, well beyond the point where argument becomes sullen disagreement.

I don't think he would have done so if, in some curious, unassimilated way, he had not made up his mind that he disapproved of my father. Of course, there was no compulsion upon him to like rich people, nor any reason why he should be attracted by my father's special brand of effortless self-assurance. As a poor man, he must have found Marais-gezicht, and also the Hermanus house, somewhat daunting; jealousy was therefore involved, as well as the careless spur of alcohol.

In a much more subtle way, however, I believe Jonathan was shocked that my father did not object to our liaison—an example of upside-down English piety which at any other time I might have found funny. But whatever the mainsprings of his discontent, it emerged as a sort of cocksure argumentativeness, with which, alas, my father was just the right man to deal.

It would be dull to retail the whole course of their argument, which covered virtually everything, from the Battle of Slagter's Nek during the Anglo-Boer war to the inaugural session of the United Nations at Lake Success in 1945. In my country, it was a familiar theme and a familiar division of opinion; whether a newish, immature country like South Africa could afford the luxury of a 'world statesman' of Smuts' calibre, when the real need was for honest and capable politicians working on the home front.

My father, of course, was in no doubt about the latter point.

'I knew Smuts well,' he said at one stage, when Jonathan, already rather irritable, had tossed off some phrase about 'the verdict of history'. 'I don't really feel I have to wait for the verdict of history, as far as his effect on this country is concerned. He was a good chap, basically, and shrewd, but he was vain—vain as one of my peacocks! He was immensely flattered at the attention he got overseas, particularly in England; he never recovered from the idea which that rogue Lloyd George originally gave him—that he was too big for South Africa, and that his real parish was the whole world.'

'But that was perfectly true,' said Jonathan shortly.

'Nonsense, my dear boy!' said my father, with his customary self-confidence. 'Lloyd George simply wanted to flatter us country bumpkins into tagging along behind England, and Smuts was the bait.'

'He was a great man,' said Jonathan stubbornly.

'Oh, I agree! He was just the kind of man South Africa needed—but we needed him here at home, not throwing his weight about at the League of Nations and the U.N. If he'd given half the attention to South African politics—particularly race relations—that he gave to buttering up those damn' half-baked banana republics in South America, we wouldn't be in the mess we are today.'

'But he put South Africa on the world map,' said Jonathan. 'In fact, he was about the only man who could have done it. No one had heard of the place before he came along.'

'He put South Africa back fifty years,' rejoined my father, ignoring Jonathan's last astonishing sentence. 'We didn't especially want to be on the world map, as you call it. It was much more important to set our own house in order, and earn a *solid* reputation, slowly and honestly.'

'Well, of course, if you'd rather South Africa had remained a sort of farmers' republic, stuck at the end of nowhere——'

My father regarded him with his usual courteous attention, but there was steel underneath. 'There are worse people than farmers, Jonathan,' he said, 'and worse countries than old-fashioned, simple, honestly-run communities that don't bother over-much about their world reputation. Smuts worked and lived and thought completely apart from this country; and we just couldn't afford to have a man like that going to waste. When he died, he left his own political party in a mess, he left his country half-organised and very vulnerable, and he left a thousand things undone that were worth all his attention.'

'Of course,' said Jonathan, with some insolence, 'I suppose most Afrikaners are bound to be jealous of him.'

'I hope I shall never be jealous of self-conceit.'

And so on. . . . It did not end in direct collision, which my father's code of hospitality would never have allowed; but it was a somewhat grim host who presently went out into the garden, and a distinctly angry Jonathan who was left to me.

'You *are* a bloody fool,' I told him, without hesitation, as soon as we were alone. 'What did you want to get into that silly argument for? He knows ten times more about it than you.'

'Does he?' asked Jonathan, forbiddingly.

'Yes. And it's his house, too. It's so rude to behave like that.'

86

'He was rude to me.'

'I wish he had been. By now, you'd be lying in about eight separate heaps.'

'Those people are all the same—self-opinionated—blind—running in blinkers——'

'What do you mean, *those people*?'

'Afrikaners.'

'*I'm* an Afrikaner.'

'But you're not a real one. I mean, you were educated in England, and you've travelled——'

This point of view—that only an English education had saved me from utter degradation—always infuriated me, and it did so now. I got up from my chair, and from there looked down at him.

'For Christ's sake,' I exploded, 'do you think you're doing me a favour by including me among the English? You and Lord Muddley ought to get married. . . . I'm an Afrikaner, like my father, and we both know a bloody sight more about South Africa than you ever will, if you stay here until you're eighty.'

Jonathan, less angry now, looked at me in the most annoying way he could devise. 'Such language,' he murmured. 'I always say, an oath on a woman's lips——'

I produced another oath, which startled both of us. 'And I meant that, too!' I went on. 'If you want to give a lecture on South African politics, don't choose this house to give it in.'

Sulky once more, Jonathan said: 'I'd certainly prefer a more literate audience,' and retired to the sideboard for another drink.

We kept up this sort of thing for most of the rest of that day; it ended, indeed, after a very trying dinner, with myself going off to bed early, and telling Jonathan to go and sleep somewhere else, when he tried to come into our room. From the doorway, in his dressing-gown, he looked at me rather forlornly, and said: 'Oh well, that's the way it goes—chicken one day, feathers the next.' That made me laugh at last, and laughter, presently, made us lovers again.

I hated quarrelling with him, and I hoped that this was the end of it. But as it turned out, we had only just started.

If, on Sunday, we had been able to fish, perhaps it would have been all right; South African 'sport' fishing, for yellow-tail or mussel-cracker up to forty pounds, and sharks up to a hundred, was often extremely strenuous, and left people far too tired to argue about anything except the right time to go to bed.

But the gale still persisted, keeping the rocks all round the bay perpetually gleaming and sluicing with sea-water under its attack, and we were thus under-employed. We tried to sunbathe, but there was too much wind; we played canasta, and got bored with it; we drank rather too much at lunch-time, and thereafter embarked on a royal row which put an end to the whole excursion—and to a lot of other things as well.

Perhaps I should have made some allowance for Jonathan; he had agreed to apologise to my father during the morning, and possibly a quarrel with me was his way of assuaging a climb-down which, for someone of his temperament, must have been morbidly undignified. (I was coming to realise that he was a much more complex character than I had supposed.) But I made no such allowances, because I chanced to be in a brusque sort of mood myself; and the result was an argument of very considerable scope.

Basically, it was a continuation, an expansion, of the one we had had, driving into Cape Town on that earlier Monday morning. As on that occasion, I wanted to get back into town; Jonathan, however, wanted us to stay on in Hermanus, and tried to persuade me that it would make no difference if we did so. But this time, he was rather more direct about the whole thing.

'But, Kate, how on earth could it matter?' he asked, when I told him it was out of the question for me to stay. 'One day, two days, even a week—the world won't come to an end if you take a holiday. It's so lovely here, and——'

'Of course the world won't come to an end,' I answered irritably. 'I'm not claiming that it would. But I've got a job to do, with a lot of people depending on me, and I'm not taking any more holidays until I'm due for them.'

'I thought you were the boss.'

I stared at him. 'I'm the boss, just *because* I've got that sense of responsibility.'

'Oh darling, don't be so pompous!'

That annoyed me. 'Look, you can take all the holidays you want. You can loaf for six months without visible loss to anyone. I can't, and that's the difference between us.'

'It's not the only difference.' Clearly he thought I was sneering at

88

him—as perhaps I was—and he grew angry in his turn. 'You may earn ten times as much as I do, but my God! what you become in the process!'

'What does that mean, exactly?'

'Tough!' he answered immediately, with a certain crude relish. 'You just don't give a damn for anyone but yourself, do you?—I saw that, when we made that silly trip to Teroka. You won't even try to do anything with Maraisgezicht, because you can do much better for yourself as the queen-bee in an advertising firm.' He really *had* been laid low by that thing with my father, I realised, and now the score was being evened up, at my expense. 'All that damned nonsense about "my people"—' he mimicked me savagely, '—you wouldn't lose an hour's sleep if they all dropped dead tomorrow!'

It just wasn't worth answering this sort of thing in detail.

'Listen,' I said crisply, 'I *know* that I'm the bad character, and you're the good one. We established that, a long time ago. I'm not arguing the point. I happen to like achievement, power, money— whatever yardstick you care to use—and I'm going to continue on those lines. So you go on with the good works, I'll concentrate on the selfish materialism, and we'll both be happy. . . . And we're going back to Cape Town this afternoon.'

He shrugged. 'Suits me. This whole atmosphere is pure poison.'

I looked at him. He was smoking one of my father's larger Laranagas, and drinking five-star Martell.

'Well, don't choke on it before you get your money's worth.'

It was a sulky, silent drive back; the mountain road and the scenery did not help at all, and I had plenty of time to think as I drove. We were both still furious with each other, but Jonathan was something more.

For the moment, he was almost vindictively independent. He had been goaded by something—jealousy, my father's neat disposal of him, even the idea (somewhat late in arrival) that he was 'betraying his ideals' by associating with me—into a mood of separation which he was going to carry through, at all costs. Our love, our love-making, our recent delight in each other—these were not factors tending to bind him; indeed, they were the measure of his corruption, and thus to be abruptly purged.

There must have been many strands to this determination; there was even the physical fact that he had been making love to me, with fair persistence on both sides, for fourteen days and nights, and could do with a rest. Jonathan on the sexual ascent was one thing; but Jonathan satiated was a take-it-or-leave-it seller. . . . These were not pretty thoughts; they were deeply disconcerting also; and they guaranteed that I remained angry and uncommunicative, during two hours of frustrated Sunday driving.

But it was still a shock when, thirty miles out from Cape Town on the Somerset West road, he said:

'You can drop me off at the airport.'

Until he rang me up from Johannesburg, late that same night, it was hell. I hadn't argued with him about leaving; indeed, I had let him go in contemptuous silence, sloughing off both him and his luggage as if the car had become far too crowded anyway. But in the intervening six hours, the wheel had come round full circle again; I missed him so much, with such hungry abandonment, that I actually tried to charter a plane to fly me to Johannesburg, only to be side-tracked by some technical rigmarole about night flying regulations.

My mood involved a total surrender which might cost me dearly in self-esteem, later on; but that evening, alone in a flat which was full of him, between sheets which smelled achingly of his body. I would have given him the earth, on a plate balanced on my bowed head.

I didn't care what he did; he could insult my father, call me a mercenary bitch, show his utter contempt for my preoccupation with my job, be as English as Nelson, give everything we owned to the destitute poor. But he wasn't to stop loving me.

He hadn't stopped, as his charged voice over the long-distance wire from Johannesburg told me, at eleven o'clock that night. Indeed, I was instantly, triumphantly aware that he matched my mood of hunger and loneliness exactly; we made up our quarrel with a rush of endearments in which love, longing and reminiscent sex were almost alarmingly mingled. Good luck, I thought at one point, to anyone who might be listening in. . . .

We both apologised abjectly, swore it would never happen again, vowed we couldn't exist without each other, promised a whole range of compensatory delights when next we met, kissed and murmured like infatuated doves. We might have been seventeen years of age. It was heavenly.

90

'I'm wearing the top half of your pyjamas,' I told him, when, in tune again, we were saying good-bye.

'A nice thought. Moving, like the pictures.'

'Loose, like the living. . . . When are you coming down to collect them?'

'Soon.'

'Make it *really* soon, Johnny.'

'But you're so busy.'

'I won't be, I promise.'

'Soon, then.'

Alone again, but happy and reassured, I found myself wondering where we would actually go from there. We had left it in the air, because at that stage neither of us knew. And I really *was* busy. . . . My last ridiculous decision before I went to sleep was to take Jonathan onto my staff as a copy-writer, and make love to him every lunch hour, in the big dark cupboard next to the water-cooler.

CHAPTER NINE

A FRESH start to a fresh week suddenly made a great deal of difference.

It began with some self-conscious reminiscence, of a not-too-reassuring kind. Taking stock of the past fortnight's confusion, in circumstances ideal for such clear-headed appraisal—the office of Kate Marais Advertising, on a Monday morning—I had to admit that I had been behaving very oddly by my own standards, though almost normally by other people's. Common sense told me that lots of girls had lovers, lots of girls quarrelled with them, lots of girls, emotionally bereft, made it up again; every fifth book, every second TV drama, every single film, endorsed this corny pattern, and my own professional researches confirmed it.

But it was precisely because everyone else did it that I had never wanted to follow the fashion; and now, brushing free of the same classic web myself, I felt bound to dispose of my case with the equally classic: 'Not guilty—but don't do it again.'

For it *had* been confusion, fifteen solid days of it; there had been nothing like it, in my ordered life, for years. . . . Sitting at my desk in a room on the fifteenth floor of Cape Town's highest building—a room whose view of the harbour and its perpetual cross-thread of shipping was always severely rationed, in the interests of concentration, a room whose austere, polished elegance placed it midway between an executive office and a suite in the *Queen Elizabeth*—I examined the astonishing reverse side of the medal.

It had been a holiday, of course; the most heavenly holiday so far; but still a holiday, a break with custom and reality. I had treated myself to it because I had fallen in love; and love, as usual, had proved intractable, hard to handle. Jonathan had been a wonderful lover (a cautionary voice asked: *How and why? Years of practice? A professional performance?*) and a prickly person at the same time (the identical voice demanded: *Why? Accident insurance? The door left open for the neat get-away?*). During a whole fortnight he had disrupted my schedule, and had raged and sulked when I had refused to have it disrupted indefinitely. Though it had been mostly wonderful, that was *not* to be the pattern of our future.

Thinking of it, remembering it, feeling in my blood the intense languid well-being of a girl full up to here with love-making, possessed by a warm tenderness as well, I knew it had been worthwhile. It would be worthwhile again, when I could return to it; but in the meantime, office-life went on, and it was still my favourite kind of life, not to be exchanged for climactic partnership on all the inner-spring beds in the world.

Naturally I wanted to combine the two elements, to be a working girl and a playing girl; but on Monday morning it was the turn of duty, and that was going to be true (I determined) for most of the Monday mornings in the future.

As though to point this tardy moral, there was a knock at the door, and Mrs. Patch, my secretary, came in.

Mrs. Patch was one of those women who, for various unkind reasons, escape being a figure of fun by bare inches. She was large, severe, mannishly tailored, ugly; she affected scraped-back hair, blouses that buttoned up to her neck, shoes patently good for a ten-mile walk. Her massive bosom and rock-like jaw seemed to place her in a definable category; but these were coupled at times with a confusing, wayward coyness which made her a very odd personality indeed.

Looking at her, I and a lot of other people were bound to think:

Oh dear, she doesn't exactly enjoy being a woman, does she? . . . But she had been with me for four years, ever since the office opened, and she was an undoubted gem.

Originally she had been sent down by an employment agency when we were first staffing the office; I was shopping for the perfect secretary, and this was their unlikely answer—unlikely, to start with, because it would be her first office job, though her shorthand grading was marked as 'Excellent'. When I asked her what she had been doing hitherto, she had answered gruffly: 'I was a nurse in an institution,' and had added: 'But I felt like a change.'

An asylum attendant with 180-word shorthand seemed just what Kate Marais Advertising needed, at that stage; I engaged her on the spot, and I had never been sorry.

She did everything for me; kept my appointment book, dealt with my mail, juggled with my cheque-book, told social and commercial lies, made excuses, made airline reservations, made coffee. To say that I would have been lost without her would be a mis-statement; it would have been far worse—I would have been unbecomingly crippled, as at the loss of half my fingers.

Of course, one recovered from such crippling, and learned alternative ways of doing things; but the process of re-education in this case would have been painful and frustrating. Without Mrs. Patch, I would have had to do a hundred things each week that bored me to distraction. They didn't bore her, because she was that very rare creature, a devoted subordinate.

Of course (as was true of Julia) such devotion, and its complementary dependence on my part, carried with it certain privileges of behaviour; and some of these became apparent during the next few minutes.

According to custom, we dealt with routine matters—appointments, dead-lines to be met, follow-up letters stemming from the last trip to Durban. From the moment that she spoke, I had the idea that she was keeping something in reserve; but this was nothing new. It was Mrs. Patch's odd habit to bring things to my attention in inverse order to their importance; she always trotted out the office trivia first, and then, with a proper sense of drama, worked up to our bankruptcy, or the bleeding body in the waiting-room.

On this occasion, she obviously had something significant to tell me (I thought it was probably an indiscreetly-worded telegram from Jonathan, opened before I arrived), and, in line with habit, I waited.

Mrs. Patch and I always played the same childish game; I would refuse to ask what was on her mind, she would disdain to volunteer anything —until finally the thing got too much for her, and out came the tremendous news-item, good or bad. To anyone who says that women are nuts, I am prepared to nod my head.

Mrs. Patch, almost on the point of going, suddenly seemed to recall something.

'Oh yes—those air charter people rang up,' she said.

I smiled to myself. So that was it. . . . 'Yes?'

'It was the chairman. He said he was very sorry about last night.'

'It doesn't matter.'

Mrs. Patch frowned down at me. 'It was a mistake, wasn't it?'

I could play this game, too. 'No, it wasn't a mistake.'

'But he said he was sorry they couldn't fly you up to *Johannesburg*. Last *night*.'

'I'm sorry too.'

'But, Miss Marais—*are* you going to Johannesburg?'

'No.'

'Then it *was* a mistake?'

'No.'

Mrs. Patch sighed a massive sigh, from the very heart. 'I don't understand.'

She had confessed defeat. 'I thought of going up to Johannesburg,' I relented, 'but I changed my mind.'

'To Johannesburg *again*? Is there anything wrong?'

'No.'

'Did Mr. Sachs ring up?'

'No.'

'But you were there only a month ago.'

'Yes.'

Mrs. Patch gazed at me, displeased, reserving judgement only with a great effort. 'I'm beginning to wonder what the attraction is.'

She probably knew, or guessed, I thought; there was plenty to go on—the unexpected holiday I had taken, one or two long-distance calls, even local gossip she might have picked up. When she knew for certain, she would be horrified, of course; and then presently she would decide, as usual, that whatever I did was right, and she would defend me valiantly against all comers. It was nice to have loyal supporters, even if they were such odd creatures as this.

94

'I'm very fond of Johannesburg,' I said, insincerely. 'I just felt like going. Then I changed my mind.'

'That's very unlike you,' said Mrs. Patch severely.

'Yes, isn't it?'

We left it at that—or rather, I broke off the fascinating topic and steered us both back to work. But something in the conversation sounded yet another cautionary note; a note rather nastily echoed later that day at a cocktail party, when two extremely bad-behaved girls, who shared their assorted lovers as freely and as briefly as cigarettes, greeted me with such novel, sisterly *bonhomie* that I realised I must have slipped several points in the market already.

This disconcerting acceptance, by second-rate people I thoroughly disapproved of, confirmed me in my view that it was time to take a tug, and that love, like the vista of Cape Town harbour, must be rationed. As the blood cooled, as the office made its customary demands, this outline became sharper, and the order of priorities more obvious.

I was lonely, even miserable, without Jonathan; and yet (looking back on it) rather ashamed of myself when we loafed and loved together. In a contest between misery and guilty joy, I was long accustomed to opt for the former—and to cure the misery in the process.

With something like relief I settled down once more to the vestal world of business; and then Jonathan started ringing up.

It was exciting to hear 'Johannesburg wants you' again, and at the beginning our words were as loving as ever; but when it happened every night, when the proprietory air grew progressively more obvious ('Where have you been? I've been ringing since nine o'clock!'), and above all, when (however they began) the conversations all ended on the same note of discontent, I realised that I was being pressured, in a way I didn't like. For the burden of the telephone calls was invariably the same; I was to drop everything, and come to Johannesburg.

'I can't,' I told Jonathan a dozen times. 'I have to work. Why don't you come down here?'

'I have to work, too.'

'I know, darling. But you're so much more mobile.'

Silence over the humming wires. Then: 'You mean, my work isn't as important as yours,' he would say. 'Mine can be interrupted, yours can't. Is that it?'

I had to deny the vague basis of truth. 'No, it's not that at all.'

'Then you don't care any more.'

'Darling, you know I adore you!'

'Then come to Johannesburg.'

It would have been possible for me to do so, of course; as in any efficiently organised business, I could leave things to run themselves for quite a long time; it was the implications I didn't like.

'Johnny, I can't come to Johannesburg for no reason at all. I just don't live like that. I've got a working schedule.'

He didn't like the implications either.

'Won't you make *any* alteration for me? *Any* sort of effort?'

So it went on, for many nights.

Commanding: 'Darling, come up to see me. It's your turn.'

And pleading: 'Darling, I'm lost without you.'

And insulting: 'You've got someone else down there. I just *know*!'

And blackmailing: 'There are lots of women in Johannesburg too, don't forget.'

And tantalising: 'Remember what it was like? You know you want me to do all that again.'

And heckling: '*Why* won't you come? *Why? Why?*'

And coarsely wounding: 'You bloody teasers are all alike!'

And pleading again: 'I'm sorry, sweet. It's just that I'm so miserable and lonely. And starved! *Please* come.'

'All right,' I said at last. All right. *All right!*'

CHAPTER TEN

IT was a disastrous expedition. Perhaps, having been over-persuaded I wanted it to be.

Jonathan lived like a pig, in a shabby one-roomed flat off downtown Eloff Street. It was an old-fashioned warren of a building, dirty, dilapidated, suspiciously busy; the crazy lift ground up and down all day, cleaning-boys skylarked on the stairways; nearby radios blared out endlessly the world's dreariest listening-fare—the *boere-musiek* which a succession of third-rate accordion orchestras had somehow unloaded onto latter-day Afrikaners as their cultural birth-right.

The room was tiny, a mere slit of a place shaped like a wedge of cheese; it had a narrow bed, covered with a tartan rug and doubling as a sofa; a scored wooden table, and a curtained-off corner for a wardrobe; an airless kitchen smelling of fried grease; and an intrusive lavatory recalling (as Bruno van Thaal once remarked) the last act of *Tristan*—too loud and too long. The view from the single window was a grimy brick chasm below, wireless aerials and washing far above.

Into this paradise Jonathan bore me, protesting somewhat (since I had booked a suite at the Carlton), after meeting me at the airport in his embarrassing little car. I was already prepared for the worst; and the worst—in one area—happened immediately.

He was nervous, and, I suppose, sexually triggered; I was neither. He made love to me within a few moments, on the creaking, none-too-clean iron bed; as was bound to happen, he was finished almost immediately, leaving me not even frustrated (one cannot get frustrated in thirty seconds), just cheapened and angry. Hypersensitive, I felt that he had tried to prove something by this swift disposal; or once again, perhaps I had wanted it to happen like that, and thus to set the pattern—what was left of the pattern.

There were footsteps and laughter in the passageway outside as we completed our idyll. Then he started apologising.

'Oh God, Kate, I'm sorry!' he said, his breathing still constricted. 'I just had to have you. . . . I'll try to——'

'It doesn't matter,' I told him—and that was the very truth. All the posthumous manipulations of love—the smoothing out, the buttoning-up—suddenly seemed inexpressively sordid; I lay there feeling that I would be sick if I opened my eyes.

'I'm terribly sorry,' he repeated. 'I was afraid it would be like that. . . . You were too good for me. . . . It's been so long without you.'

I felt him get off the bed, walk into the bathroom. I lay still, trying to stun myself into deafness. The water gurgled and roared. Then he reappeared, and as I opened my eyes, he was wiping his hands on a grubby towel.

'Do you want to——' he began, looking down at me.

'In a minute. . . . Jonathan, give me a drink.'

'I've only got beer, I'm afraid.'

'Give me some beer.'

97

From the kitchen, he presently called out: 'You were wonderful, Kate!' I could not utter a single word.

When he came through, glass of beer in hand, he said again: 'I'm awfully sorry, Kate.' But he was brighter already, recovered, relaxed. Presently, with unbearable good humour, he set himself to entertain me.

We made love again an hour later, and it was better this time—possibly because the room was dark, or because I now wanted him, or because he took trouble about it, the trouble with which he had swamped and spoiled me in Cape Town. But though afterwards I lay by his side, tenderly spent, thinking: Perhaps it's going to be all right, perhaps I do adore him after all, perhaps I was right to come up here—yet this was not a lasting mood.

I had sent him out for some whisky, and this we now sipped, in a silence not quite easy; as far as I was concerned, there had been something about the act of taking £2 from my handbag, and giving it to him for his errand, which recalled horrid race-memories from the gigolo world of Antibes and Eden Roc. . . . It might have been this which prompted me to ask:

'Who looks after you, Johnny?'

'A boy. The faithful Alfred. He's not bad. . . . I told him not to come today.'

That seemed to have a slightly vulgar connotation, recalling my doubts, recalling the first, near-brutal, split-minute lovemaking which had felt so much like a cut across the face. Shying away, I said:

'But can you work here? It's so shut in.'

'It's good enough for what I want. It's only a base, after all.' I felt him smiling by my side. 'I know it's not quite up to your standard, Miss Marais.'

'We have the same standard, Johnny.'

'No. You're slumming, and we both know it. Don't think it isn't appreciated, though.'

We seemed destined to rub each other the wrong way. 'But *is* it appreciated? Don't forget I've cancelled half a dozen appointments, and flown an uncomfortable thousand miles, just to curl up with you.'

'I hope it was worth it.'

'That's what I'm meant to say to you.'

'My dear Kate, this little *matinée* hasn't cost me a thing. I'm just taking an afternoon off.'

'What would you be doing if I weren't here?'

'Probably staring at the wall. What would you?'

'Oh—dictating letters—seeing customers—looking over layouts—listening to other people's ideas—ironing out contracts.'

'Making money?'

'Making money.'

He stirred and sat up, moving perceptibly away from me. 'You have to do that, don't you, Kate?'

'How do you mean?'

'The profit motive. Looking for suckers, and squeezing them for all they're worth. . . . Lying in wait in the jungle. . . . You'd find the world a very dull jungle, with no one to eat, wouldn't you?'

I frowned, not agreeing with any of this. 'It's not like that at all. . . . Johnny, you just don't know enough about it; you're guessing, and they're children's guesses. Running an advertising business doesn't consist of looking for suckers, as you call it, and taking them for a ride. We wouldn't last a month if that was the project. . . . We try to give people their honest money's worth, in a highly competitive, highly specialised——'

'Come off it, Kate!' he interrupted. 'The answer is in the plural, and they bounce. . . . Listen—we are alone. You needn't make it sound like the faithful reciting the Rotarian creed.'

The magic languor of love-making had, I found, now largely worn off. Indeed, it was quite easy to remember that most of it hadn't been so magic, anyway.

'Let's go out, Jonathan,' I said. I pulled the fraying string which lit the ceiling light over our heads, and the room sprang into drab, shoddy life again. 'Let's have dinner at Fraternelli's.'

'Can't afford it, darling. I'm a writer. Remember?'

'I'll stake you.'

'Not in Johannesburg. Not any more.'

'Well, let's go out anyway.'

'No.' There was something in his manner which recalled an old, cruel, half-forgotten governess working off her spite; saying '*Just for that, no circus*. . . .' 'No,' repeated Jonathan, smiling at me over the rim of his glass. 'Let's stay at home. Just you and me, Kate. It'll be wonderful.'

In the night, strange creakings, shouts, traffic noises from the streets below; sometimes footsteps on the stairway outside, slurring, drunken, too close. In the room, oppressive heat, kitchen smells, cockroaches peeping and scuttling under the rug. In the frowsy narrow bed, brief joy, briefly achieved, like a small erotic dream, and then a night-long, wakeful, sweating discomfort. In the dawn, the brown flaked ceiling above my head making cracked patterns, puzzle-pieces shaped like animals, shaped like leaves. In the morning, a slatternly servant plodding out from the kitchen, leering stupidly at me, saying: 'Missis hungry, I bet.'

Turning from the telephone, Jonathan announced: 'Eumor says, can we have lunch with him, and if so, will Krug do?'

'Krug will do,' I said. 'But a magnum. . . . Let us accept.'

Fraternelli was delighted to see me (and why not, indeed?); he managed to enunciate: 'So soon again, no?' and then his English took the head-long nose-dive which meant that he was trying to extend a special welcome. Later, the veal *à la Zingara* spoke the necessary volumes for him. Eumor, on the other hand, started off by being sombre. He had a complaint.

'You come up here *secretly*?' he asked, as soon as we had greeted each other. 'You don't tell me?'

'I was going to ring you,' I reassured him. 'It was all spur-of-the-moment stuff. How did you find out, anyway?'

'My friend at the airport. . . . But he does not know *where* you are. The Carlton does not know where you are, either. They are sad. Then I ring Jonathan. But where are you?'

I indicated Jonathan. 'With my friend in Eloff Street.'

Eumor started to say something, then changed his mind. 'And how is the making of love?' he substituted.

'Ask my friend.'

Jonathan, sipping a six-to-one martini, inclined his head. 'Very satisfactory.'

Eumor looked from one to the other of us. 'Such enthusiasm. . . .' Then his face assumed a certain Balkan leer. 'You are tired, perhaps?'

'I'm tired,' I said. 'No perhaps.'

'That is better. . . . I tell you a story.' He was eating palm-kernels in oil, one of Fraternelli's minor specialities; he gestured with one of the small pointed weapons. 'It is a saying in Greece. If you take an empty bottle, and put into it one penny for every time you make love with a certain woman——'

'Not quite so loud, Eumor.'

'For every time you make love during the first two years—you follow me?'

'Yes. But why a penny?'

'Sixpence will do. Or a pin. Or a match. Anything.' He was not going to have his story spoilt. 'You do it for two years, and after that every time you make love, you take a penny out.' He paused.

'Is that the end of the story, Eumor?'

'Comes the point now! If you do that, the saying is that the bottle will never be empty.'

We digested this in silence.

'That's a rather sad story,' I said at length.

'Not for the first two years,' said Jonathan.

Fraternelli, who had been listening under the pretence of pouring out more martinis, said something in Italian to Eumor, and they both laughed.

'What was that?' I inquired. 'If a lady may ask.'

'He said, what happens if you take the bottle and go somewhere else?'

'You end up by getting shot in the back,' said Jonathan, 'leaving in your will the finest collection of bottle pennies south of the Sahara. By the way, Eumor, have you ever tried taking a penny out of a bottle?'

'It is a saying in Greece,' said Eumor. 'Do not be so literate.'

'I can't help being literate,' said Jonathan. He glanced at me. 'But I must say that, even this morning, I'd much rather keep putting those pennies in.'

There was something in his manner I had never seen before, and which I didn't like at all; a sort of gamey self-importance, unbecoming, proprietory, smug. Thus, no doubt, the plush hypocritical Victorians talked of their mistresses, stowed away snugly in discreet villas in Notting Hill Gate. . . . I was not in the mood, that morning, to be the object, even indirectly, of such comment.

'I'm hungry, Eumor,' I said.

'Then we eat.'

'Even I am hungry,' said Jonathan.

We walked back together, Jonathan and I, down the busy length of

Eloff Street, in the afternoon sun. The meal had been wonderful; I was feeling infinitely better; but still, within the area of total enchantment, not quite good enough.

'I think I'll move into the Carlton,' I said, when we were near it.

'All right,' said Jonathan.

'There isn't really room for both of us at your place, is there?'

'I suppose not.'

'They'll send round for my suitcase.'

'It will be waiting.'

We stood on the hotel steps, just out of the main stream of people passing in and out; Pratt the head-porter, a very old friend of mine, came to the alert, ready to go into action in any of the half dozen ways controlled by his baton.

'But come up, Jonathan,' I said, looking into his face for the first time that day. 'You can help me unpack.'

'I don't think so.' He returned my look readily enough, but his was veiled, withdrawn; he was contracting out of this moment, and he was not going to tell me why. Nor (I knew) was I going to ask him. 'I've got one or two things to do.'

'All right. Come round at drinking time, then.'

'Well . . .' Now he *was* slightly embarrassed, and I knew that something unusual must be coming. 'As a matter of fact, I promised to have dinner with Father Shillingford tonight. Down at the mission. Wouldn't you like to come along?'

'It doesn't sound quite my cup of tea, Jonathan.'

'I suppose not.'

'I'll be here, then.' I was going to say: *When you want me,* but I couldn't quite bring myself to that forlorn peak of availability. Instead I said: 'Give me a ring.'

'I'll do that.' He hunched his shoulders, buttoned his coat, preparing to take off. Then he added, in a much more concise voice: 'Kate, you do realise, don't you, that that room of mine is a lot bigger than most *families* have, in places like Teroka?'

'Sheer heaven, darling!' said Bruno van Thaal, licking the last remaining drops of strawberry juice laced with Curaçao off the tips of his fingers —a display of honest greed which in anyone else would have looked merely piggish. 'And that wine was *fully* as nice as my aunt's gooseberry Sauterne. . . . I must say that now and again even this *hostile* hostelry can produce the perfect meal.'

We had dined that evening in my suite, on a scale suitable to Bruno's appetite and my own need for reassurance; behind us lay a pleasing vista of cold Vichyssoise, a small Spanish omelette, and breast of guinea-fowl, topped off with the delicate strawberry dish which was currently exciting Bruno's enthusiasm. I felt much better now, and certainly there had been room for improvement.

'Why hostile, Bruno?' I asked idly, pouring his coffee, and then moving towards the couch. 'I'm very fond of it here.'

'Haven't you heard yet, darling?' His innocent blue eyes opened in a thoroughly untrustworthy way. 'I had an *altercation* in the bar here last week. They asked me not to come back unless I could behave *quite* differently. So strict!'

'But what were you doing, Bruno?'

'Just discussing things in a general way.'

I decided that I was likely to get a much more accurate version from someone else, and I cast around for an alternative subject. It became apparent that there was now only one. After an evening spent in talking of everything under the sun except what was in the forefront of my mind, it was high time to be serious.

I was not sure how to effect the change, since we had been exclusively frivolous so far; but Bruno, who, as well as being very good company, was one of the most perceptive people I knew, anticipated the switch of conversation. Making himself comfortable in a deep armchair opposite me, he suddenly said:

'And now, dear, how are things between you and that *pest* of a man? Still utter magic, I hope?'

I had to smile. 'Not quite utter, Bruno. . . . Do you ever see him?'

'Be your age, dear! Our *backgrounds* are so different. . . . Why haven't I been favoured tonight, by the way?'

'He was busy. As a matter of fact he's having dinner with Father Shillingford.'

'How very cosy!' But Bruno was regarding me with genuine surprise. 'Kate, surely you came up here in order to pursue love's torrid dream every single moment of the day and night?'

'More or less. But he did have this date with Shillingford.'

'Of course, Steele is like that,' said Bruno, who could not have been displeased with what I was telling him. 'So dedicated. . . . He turns every room into a seminary. . . . I picture him scurrying through the streets at dawn, famished and devout, tearing himself to ribbons in the confessional and then administering *soup* to the black poor. . . . Of course he's not a Roman Catholic, but he's *bosom* pals with Father Billingsgate, and if you made inquiries you'd probably find that he comes from a *long* line of priests and nuns. . . . However, please don't get the idea that I dislike him.'

'Of course you don't like him, Bruno. Why should you? It was me that fell in love with him.'

'In the past tense?'

'It wasn't, until—oh God, I don't know! *Our* backgrounds are different, too.'

'Love conquers all, I heard somewhere.'

I had to tell the story, and Bruno was the man to tell it to. 'Love was wonderful, Bruno,' I answered him. 'The most wonderful thing that ever happened to me. But basically there's almost everything wrong with Jonathan, from my point of view. He's so poor—I know that sounds awful, but it's silly to say that it's not important. He's *good*, in a very annoying way. He's been trying to change me. He lectures all the time. . . . He makes absolute chaos of my work. And if I get in any deeper, I know I'll be absolutely dependent on him for everything.'

'Darling, he sounds *perfect*!' Being Bruno, he had to say that, but he reverted swiftly to kindness and sympathy. 'Kate, you know I shall never understand love. I just take it for granted that if people feel it, they feel it, like the heat. But you and Steele together are really Siamese freaks. . . . Couldn't you just write it off to experience? Heavenly, no doubt, but just an *episode*, a *mad* moment?'

'I'm not like that, Bruno.'

'You're not like *this*.'

'True.'

Then the phone rang.

What followed must have been deeply instructive to all concerned, though Bruno, a fascinated eavesdropper, heard only an incomplete version of it. I said: 'Hallo?' and then: 'How was dinner?' My next sentence was: 'Come back and sleep here,' and then, after a long pause: 'All right, then.' Thereafter I rang off, and that was all.

Bruno, regarding me closely, began: 'If I may read between the lines——'

'He won't come to the Carlton,' I said briefly. 'Because I wouldn't stay at his place, I suppose.'

'Perhaps he's afraid of the house detective.'

'*I'm* not afraid of the house detective.'

'Well, of course,' said Bruno, 'if you *will* form a liaison with Hopalong Chastity——'

I was thinking deeply, and only half hearing anything else. I had a feeling that Jonathan was doing all this on purpose; he was once more applying pressure, in a novel, almost reverse way, and for reasons I could not comprehend. But whatever they were, there was an aspect of punitive therapy involved. . . . As if from a long way off, I heard Bruno say:

'Darling, this is all *so* unlike you. You *can't* want it as much as this. . . . Why don't you take the bull by the bull, and sack him?'

Everyone has some deep-seated personal infection, some disease which they will never lose. For myself, it is a taste for entertaining; for Eumor, it is horses, and for Bruno, gossip. For Jonathan, astonishingly, it turned out to be poker. But I only discovered this in the most mortifying fashion possible.

True, he had mentioned the fact before, at some happier time, and though I had thought it an odd enthusiasm for his kind of person, I also thought (being newly in love) that it could not conceivably have any sort of significance, as between myself and him. He played poker, he had told me on that occasion, every Saturday night, with the same six other people; Eumor was one of them, the rest were mostly stockbrokers.

My girlish trouble now was that I hadn't realised that today was Saturday.

When Jonathan told me what he had in mind, over the telephone, I was first incredulous, then furious. Dinner with Father Shillingford, coupled with a wasted night (as we both might have termed it, a few weeks earlier), was one thing, but this was really too rich for my blood.

'Jonathan,' I demanded, straight away, 'what are you trying to do?'

'Nothing, Kate,' he answered, wonderfully innocent. 'I told you before. I always play on Saturdays, with the same school. I can't let them down.'

'You can't let *them* down?'

'But we always play. I told you.' There was an edge of nervousness in his voice, as if he bore in mind the idea that he might be going too far, and yet was determined to persevere. 'I can't just not turn up, can I?'

'You could have let them know days ago.'

'But it's been a regular fixture for months. . . . Darling,' he went on, 'I'll be finished by two o'clock at the latest.'

I was now quite furious. 'What do you mean, finished by two o'clock? What the hell's the point of making all that fuss about my coming up here, when you're just not available when I arrive? And why poker, anyway? If you've got any spare time, you know damned well you ought to be working!'

'But I *am* working. I never stop. This poker-game is part of working. Poker—oh, you just wouldn't understand, Kate! It's one of the reasons why I love it so much. It's exciting, and sometimes expensive, but it's a lesson in psychology all the time. I learn more about people from playing poker with them——'

I dismissed that idea with a single word. Then: 'You're meant to be writing a book, or so you told me. Why don't you get on with it?'

'What do you know about writing?' he asked edgily.

I laughed. 'Writing happens to earn a large part of my living for me. And one thing I *do* know is the first rule: you have to *write*.'

'I meant writing books,' he said loftily. 'For that, you have to think as well. That's *my* kind of writing.'

He would never be arguing with me like this, I realised, in the silence that followed this particular piece of effrontery, if he were not satiated, if he had not slept with me enough times to risk a rain-check. I remembered an odd phrase of his from a past conversation: 'If you achieve something, whether it's a woman or an appointment as ambassador, you don't really want it any more.' Because of this 'achievement' he was prepared to take chances with my good humour which he would never have dared before.

He would probably be sorry later. I was sorry now; and, being sorry, there was only one thing for me to do. It only involved putting down the receiver, but (being a woman still) it cost me a special, angry, satisfying heart-ache to do it.

Joel Sachs rang me up about an hour later. I had never heard him so tense.

'Kate, what's going on?'

'This isn't a good moment to ask me that, Joel.'

'But I thought you were in Cape Town! George Barnaby flew down yesterday specially to see you.'

'Oh dear!' Barnaby was head of the principal cinema chain in South Africa. We had been after their account for years. 'I can still see him,' I told Joel.

'No, you can't.' It was the first time I had heard Joel anything but soft-spoken, fundamentally controlled. 'He just rang me up. He's sailing for the States tonight. You know what he's like. Now he says he doesn't want to make a change, after all. . . . Kate, I've been working on this thing for three months. It was almost sewn up.'

'I know, Joel. I'm terribly sorry.'

'Kate.' He was speaking from the same inner, first-time pressure. 'I may as well tell you. There's a lot of talk going round the town. About your coming up here so suddenly, and—and everything. What's going on?'

'Nothing, Joel.'

'Why are you here, then?'

'It's not important now. I'm going back in a couple of hours.' I tried a laugh. 'If it's costing us money, I'm damned well going back!'

'Well, that's good news.' Now he was softened, more like Joel Sachs again. 'Kate, if you have to come up again at short notice, if you *have* to see somebody. . . . I mean, just let me know.'

'I don't have to see anybody.'

'Well, that's good news,' he said again. 'But just let me know, all the same.'

'I'll let you know,' I promised. 'But at the present rate, it'll only come as a suicide note. . . . Joel, I'll ring you up from Cape Town.'

'Good girl.'

I might have spent hours in mourning, and perhaps that would come later; at the moment, being disappointed, angry, ashamed of myself and my feeble feminine heart, I was in the mood for quick decisions. Our swift rise, our astonishing ebb, would later puzzle me, keep me awake at nights; now they were just the twin triggers for a final definitive blast.

Playing poker, by God! I thought on my way out to the airport; if Jonathan didn't spend his spare time in bed with me, he might at least apply his manhood to his typewriter. What a hopeless, loafing amateur. . . . It annoyed me that it had taken a whole forty-eight hours to learn my lesson; to find out that, if two careers in one bed was a difficult proposition—indeed, almost unworkable—one and a half careers wasn't worth an hour's trouble, a moment's indecision, a single missed heart-beat.

I must, I decided, have been slipping. But I wasn't going to slip any further.

CHAPTER ELEVEN

HE wrote. I didn't answer. He rang up. I wasn't in. He sent messages, which I tore up, and flowers, which I gave to hospitals. He came to Cape Town to try to see me; I heard of it in time, from my spy and ally Bruno van Thaal, and took off for Durban. This time I had made up my mind, and nothing was going to change it. This time, I was doing the walking-out, not Jonathan, and the *fiat* was going to stick.

Accidental strands of evidence, kind contributions from friends, indicated that it first made him angry, then it made him sad. I had been both these things, in the course of our short love-affair, but now I was calling the tune, putting on the record myself, controlling the volume. The sense of power was important.

Of course, I was sad, too. . . . The items I held against Jonathan— that he interrupted my work, that (like every other man in the world) he was determined to change me, that he was poor and proud and prejudiced—these things were valid arguments, well-chosen words and sentences to satisfy the cool mind. But they didn't make allowance for feelings, they were no good to a girl in bed. I couldn't take the phrase: 'He was all wrong about race-relations, too,' and make it keep me warm at night.

Sexually, to begin with, I missed him very much indeed; to have been celibate so long, and then ecstatically abandon it, and then to impose celibacy again, was one of the hardest, saddest, loneliest, most miserable things I had ever tried to do.

I must admit that I cheated a bit, at the start; not with other men—

I didn't seem to want that, exactly, or perhaps the available candidates didn't, after Jonathan, make much sense—but in the realm of self-solace, borrowed from the adolescent past.

It was something I hadn't done for years; but the awakened, troublesome flesh had to be assuaged somehow, and this did not seem a particularly grotesque outlet. Of course, it was within the scale of sin, it was naughty. . . . I remembered a phrase from the nursery past (not, so far as I know, invoked in this connection): 'The Devil finds work for idle hands to do'. How very true. . . . But since I was not as good a lover as Jonathan, it presently faded and died.

Thus tided over in one area, I still mourned him in another. Jonathan had been very good company; we disagreed over lots of things, but he could be very funny when he felt like it, and behind the fun was wisdom, and behind that, compassion. . . . I had no compassion; he had enough for two; it had been exciting to borrow it for a space, to see one's fellow-men through eyes which did not invariably find them ludicrous or contemptible.

Perhaps this was the most searching bereavement, the worst aspect of doing without him. I got used to it in the end, like the other thing, but the self-denial was difficult, and took a degree of determination of which I came to be quite proud.

After a week, I was still hungry, in bed and out of it; after a month, I was reconciled to both areas of loneliness; after three months, I was restored enough (and busy enough) to feel only an occasional twinge. Life went on, I found—perhaps the saddest, and also the happiest, residue of a lost love. It was all one with the fundamental lesson of living as well. If you lost your eyes, you did not lie down and cry. You learned to be blind, and thus you learned to see.

Certain things still hurt, I found; even after months and months, they still had power to pierce and to wound, however briefly. These were the first-hand, accidental things: like sleeping in the great bed at Maraisgezicht, and reaching out unawares, and finding no one there; like my father not asking questions about Jonathan, yet knowing I was bereft; like lunching at Fraternelli's, and glancing at the table where I had first seen him, and finding it occupied by quite different people—fat, gobbling, base.

Once I did catch sight of him, at a charity concert in Cape Town; he was with a woman I did not know, quite old, grey-haired, somewhat over-intense; he was talking to her with great concentration. It was disturbing, even after six months, to discover that he was in the same city; but what I really wanted, for thirty forlorn seconds, was for him to be talking to me, with the same wrapped-up air, the same lean power. And for the whole of the next day, I was glad that the woman was old.

There were other things that Eumor, a faithful correspondent, told me from time to time. Jonathan was much the same, he wrote me in one letter, dictated to a secretary who probably took an iron hand in the re-phrasing—'but he does not seem to care so much about what happens. He is working, you will be pleased to hear—or will you be pleased?—but he gets into trouble rather easily. First he was drinking too much, and I told him not to, and he said it was in order to forget you, and it would soon be past, and I warned him that such things are hard to stop, once you start them, whatever the reason that made them begin.' Here Eumor's secretary, no doubt breathing hard, had imposed an arbitrary full-stop and a fresh paragraph. 'He wanders out at night, and sometimes he has bad adventures. Then there are politics. You probably read about the protest march.'

I had indeed read about the protest march, the first occasion (so far as I knew) that Jonathan Steele had achieved the status of a news-item. He had been foolish enough to come into collision with two basic South African laws, accompanied by considerable fanfare; firstly, by taking part, with Indian and Native speakers, in a public meeting which had been banned by the police, and secondly, by marching in a Johannesburg protest demonstration which ended up in a free-for-all riot outside Marshall Square police headquarters.

Subsequently, in the magistrate's court, he had been sternly lectured ('Disgrace to European Community') and fined £5 ('paid by supporters on the spot'). Rumour, which I took the trouble to confirm, said that the dossier recommending deportation had got as far as the Ministerial desk before being allowed to fade out again.

'After that,' wrote Eumor, 'he went to Natal with Father Shilling-ford, and sat down on the ground with some Indians.'

There Eumor's letter, tantalisingly, came to an end; but it seemed to paint quite enough of the picture. It confirmed, for me, Jonathan's fatally amateur status; he wasn't a writer at all, he was just one of those café exhibitionists of the school of Paris and elsewhere, who did every-thing to books except write them.

They talked about them, read bits of them aloud, spilled Pernod on page one, practised their dialogue on passing whores, boasted of how good they were going to be, what mastercraftsmen, how much better than Proust and Sartre and Victor Hugo. But, like professional 'lovers', all they did was talk; when it came to the pitch, they were as scared to put pen to paper as a gigolo to put Figure A anywhere near Figure B.

If Eumor claimed that Jonathan was working, then he was probably trying to be kind. It was possible that he was trying to be kind to me. But by then it hardly mattered at all, except for statistical reasons. All I wanted to do was to file him away at the back of the right drawer.

Bruno, in the line of duty as my Johannesburg contributor to the column, was another source for keeping me up-to-date, using a special, spiteful kind of exaggeration no doubt intended to cheer my desolation, to show me that in losing Jonathan I had lost nothing. About mid-year, on his way to England, he stopped a night at Cape Town; and there, after dinner at my flat, he unfolded a curious tale.

'Darling, your little chum is *definitely* operating in our area,' he told me. 'I haven't sent you much about it, because it's so dull anyway, and I didn't really think you'd want to print anything about that *monster*. But he has *not* been idle.'

'You mentioned Di Magnussen in one letter,' I reminded him. 'Surely she's been covering a great deal of carpet lately?'

'I think it must be her geo-physical year.'

'Who else, Bruno?' The idea of Jonathan making love to other women still made me want to be sick; I hoped that Bruno would exaggerate, tell lies if necessary, twist the knife and make a wound so gross that it would no longer hurt. . . . 'Tell me the worst.'

'He seems to like *older* ladies,' announced Bruno, with relish. 'Belle Yorke, Nancy Hughieson—all that nest. They pass him from hand to hand like a *ferret*, and compare notes afterwards. He told Martha Parker that she was too acrobatic for his taste, and my dear, it was all over town next morning! She took it as a compliment!'

'Bruno, does he really go to bed with those old sacks?' All the women he had mentioned were certainly prime South African performers, but they were also collector's items of another era, which should have dated them fatally. Their hospitality, for example, towards visiting convoys during the war had astonished even United States sailors. 'I should have thought he would have shown better taste.'

Bruno tossed his head irritably. 'The only sign of taste that *criminal* ever showed——' he began, and then stopped. 'Let's put it another way,' he proceeded smoothly. 'Whatever he was like when *you* knew him, he's back in the zoo now. My dear, it's just a continuous performance! I think he must be re-writing a sex manual.'

'Who else?' I asked.

He gave me half a dozen names; some I could have forecast, others were a surprise. Then he said: 'You remember Lyn Elliott-Smith?'

'Oh, *no*!'

Bruno nodded. 'I always think of her as the kind of woman who gives adultery a bad name.'

This was indeed true. Lyn Elliott-Smith's husband had really become a classic figure of fun; he put up with Lyn because he had to (being a senior civil servant for whom divorce was unthinkable), but it cost him dearly in the process. It had reached the stage now when he was afraid to walk into any room unannounced, for fear that Lyn would be in bed with his best friend, on the sofa with a casual caller, on the mat with the butler. Thus, as he moved about, in his own house or in any other, the poor fellow whistled and sang from morning till night; he coughed in every corridor, shuffled his feet outside every door. But it was no good; he still kept tripping over his best beloved in every conceivable attitude of abandon.

Just for once, I hated the idea of Jonathan in bed with this curling snake of a woman; and I hated him more for betraying me thus far.

'What happened with Lyn?' I asked.

'I understand it was rather hilarious,' answered Bruno. '*I understand*' usually meant that he was embroidering, if not lying outright, but now I chose to believe him. 'They say that George Elliott-Smith came home, positively *booming* out the 1812 Overture, as usual, and Lyn called out: "For Christ's sake stop that bloody singing!" and he thought she must be alone, and he trotted upstairs rather too fast, and Jonathan had to skip down the fire-escape with his trousers gaping in the breeze. . . .' Bruno, pleased with his recital, stood up, preparing to take his leave. 'If he'd only stopped to think, he really needn't have bothered. George would always have zipped them up for him.'

That night, when Bruno had gone, I actually roughed out a piece for the column, starting: '*Jonathan Steele, now in strict training as South Africa's guided muscle*——' and then I tore it up. If it were all true, the thing either hurt too much, or it didn't hurt at all—in slight sad confusion, I couldn't make up my mind which. But either way, I wanted to bury it; and anything except a silent disposal seemed silly and unworthy.

CHAPTER TWELVE

IT must have been about five months later that Eumor rang me up from Johannesburg.

It was an office call, about ten o'clock in the morning, a product of one of those rare occasions when Eumor and I were in business together; he had acquired four hundred tons of Bulgarian caviare which he wished to unload upon a defenceless public, and mine was the glowing prose which was going to do it. ('*So* different from ordinary caviare!' was our eventual, utterly truthful slogan; we polished the whole lot off in about six weeks.) When we had finished the business side of our talk, and were gossiping (at eight shillings a minute) Eumor suddenly said:

'By the way, Kate, have you heard about Jonathan?'

'Jonathan who?' The query was almost a genuine reaction; I had not seen him casually for half a year, nor thought about him for weeks.

'*Sans blague!* Jonathan Steele!'

'Yes, I've heard all I want about Jonathan Steele.'

'But about his book?'

'Yes, I've heard all about his book, too. I just *can't* wait.'

Eumor seemed somewhat mystified. 'You mean, you want to read it?'

There was something in his tone which communicated interest, and indeed alertness. 'Start again, Eumor,' I said. 'What about his book?'

'It is a success already,' said Eumor importantly. 'It has been chosen. And in America also.'

This was difficult to translate. 'You mean he's finished it?'

'Certainly he has finished it! Some few months ago. Now it is chosen. By the Book Society. And it will be a serial story in America. I have read it. It is wonderful, Kate. So wise. But I told you he was good.'

'Who's serialising it in America?' I asked, slightly knocked over in the rush.

'A magazine. To do with the Pacific. But not about the sea.'

'The *Pacific Monthly*?'

'Exactly!'

That really brought me up short, in spite of a prolonged, cast-iron refusal to be impressed by anything that Jonathan Steele might do. If Eumor had his facts right, it was sufficiently astonishing that Jonathan had produced a book at all; and a 'choice' by the Book Society argued (if nothing else) a respectable standard of saleability, as well as a positive guarantee that the book was not trash. But the *Pacific Monthly* was something else again. Unique in America, its consistently high standard, and crotchety insistence upon quality, meant a total absence of the second-rate; quaintly, it only hired writers who could coax the right words into the right sequence; having nailed the word 'literate' to its masthead, it kept it there, in all its baffling nudity. If Jonathan had made the *Pacific*, then he had made a lot of other things as well.

There had to be some mistake, if only to keep me happy.

'Are you there, Kate?' asked Eumor presently.

'Yes. I'm just being astonished, that's all. . . . Eumor, you said you'd read the book. Do you mean, in manuscript?'

'No.' Eumor struggled with the technicalities. 'It was printed. But with brown paper.'

'You mean, page-proofs? In a brown paper cover?'

'Yes. They have printed five hundred copies like that, to send to people in advance.'

This was another whole series of surprises, which I appreciated even less. It meant that Jonathan must have finished the book at least two months ago. It meant that, in spite of the oddest evidence to the contrary, he had been working all the time. And a page-proof distribution of five hundred copies indicated that his publishers were behind the book, and the author, in a very big way indeed.

I wasn't feeling guilty yet, but I had an idea that it would not be delayed very long. I fought valiantly against the process, which would leave me self-convicted as a damned fool, and a solitary one also.

'What's it like, Eumor?' I asked, as grudgingly as I could. 'It isn't really any good, is it?'

'It is beautiful, Kate.' His voice had a sudden warmth. 'I told you it would be, a long time ago—do you remember? It is about politics, and the locations, and people in Johannesburg, and how to live together. It is about a young man who comes to South Africa. There is a girl like you in it, too.'

Eumor was slowing up, struggling once more with the exact sense of what he wanted to say. 'Kate, I have lived here thirty years. I have watched everything. I am not blind. But I tell you, this book taught me twice as much. And all the same, it is more like poetry than a book.'

'Why did he give you a proof copy?'

'I am his friend.'

I don't know why I found the satellite phrase moving, and shaming at the same time; but it was so, in swift and almost unbearable measure. Eumor was his friend, I was not. I had withdrawn my patronage, for all sorts of perfectly good reasons; but I had withdrawn it. Nearly a year had passed since we had been lovers; during all the happy time together Jonathan must have been working faithfully, and during all the time since then also—unhelped by me, dismissed as a poor man and a liar. . . . I had been working too, of course. . . . I had made £9,000, and enjoyed myself a great deal. . . . It wasn't going to be possible to formulate any of these ideas properly, until I had read and assessed the book; but however disinclined I might be, however sulky and proud, a childish refusal to be impressed was no longer a plausible reaction. Every ostrich, sooner or later, came up for air—fresh, fantastic, mortifying air. If this, incredibly, were to be my astonished-ostrich phase, I had better face it, with all the grace that God allowed.

'Eumor,' I said. 'I'd like to read that book. Can you organise it?'

'Immediately! I send it down.'

'But, Eumor—don't tell him.'

'Ah,' said Eumor, meaningly.

'All right—ah!'

I still envy anyone who reads *Ex Afrika* for the first time.

As all the world knows, it is not a long book; by a remarkable feat of compression (bearing in mind the huge canvas of Southern Africa, the byways and digressions that beckon all the time) Jonathan Steele had kept his story down to 70,000 words. I remember one critic who remarked on that fact in a particular sense: 'Seventy thousand words,' he wrote, 'and not one going to waste, not one which does not do the work of ten, in sheer magic evocation.' Disallowing that terrible word 'evocation', used nowadays for everything from cigarette ads to old horse-race commentaries, the man was exactly right. Jonathan had watched, thought, felt, and lived his book for a year, and then distilled his story down to a concise, poetic brief, which had, for almost everyone who read it, a shattering reality.

I am not sure what I had been expected to read; I had been led to forecast a phoney book, and part of me, indeed, was hoping to be proved right. Even as recently as Eumor's telephone call, when he said: 'It is about a young man who comes to South Africa,' and added something about there being 'a girl like you' in it, I had been anticipating some atrocious by-product of the confessional; a subject piece, conceived in the guts, sucked from the thumb, and stuck together with self-regard.

It would be, I thought, a sort of 'What Awful Africa Did to Me' diatribe; one of those exhibitionist sagas which really belonged in the realm of indecent exposure, along with all tomes written by poets' widows with left-over lives to kill, women whose husbands died of throat cancer, reformed drunks, unreformed society whores, and ladies exposing for sale their many-splendoured things.

I had been wrong, all wrong. *Ex Afrika* was a beautiful book, and a discerning one; when Eumor, once again, had said that it taught him twice as much as he knew before, I was ready, after reading it, to sign my name under the same testimonial. I read it in one gulp—there was really no other choice—and then went back again and started breathing and licking it in, word by word, picture by picture, in purest self-indulgence.

It was Africa in little—people, places, and things seen in their customary raucous confusion and then reduced to order and sense by a craftsman's eye. It *was* about a young man who came to Africa; a young man who could look around him with a childish sense of wonder and an adult capacity to drink deep without getting drunk; who saw what the people were doing to each other, and why they were doing it, and when it had gone wrong, and how it could go right—if. . . . The 'if' was love, I suppose, or commonsense or decency or terror of bloodshed.

But the book was not a sermon. It was better than a sermon. It was a piece of mankind held up for inspection—inspection from all conceivable angles, like a jewel of many polished facets, none more flawless than another; a jewel of a book, indeed, presented in all the dimensions which skill, love, and pity could encompass.

There was one astonishing thing about it, which only dawned on me slowly. I kept meeting sections of it with a sense of partial recognition, thinking subconsciously: *But it wasn't quite like that* or *I didn't quite mean it that way* or *He's right, only he is still unfair*. I then realised that I had played more than one part in the book; not just as 'the girl like me', a sometimes flattering, sometimes bitchy portrait which I had to admit was extremely well done; but in the more unexpected realm of politics.

The book, where it bore on race-relations, was wise and compassionate; and where it condemned things-as-they-were, it—I was going to say, it pulled its punches, but that wasn't quite the tactic; rather did it concede (astonishingly for a red-blooded radical like Jonathan) that there might be two sides to this gory question, that all white men in South Africa were not automatically dolts or brutes, and all black men were not God's elect and mankind's undoubted masterpiece.

Father Shillingford, for example, was there, but not as Jesus Christ cycling sadly through the Transvaal; rather as a good but baffled man, who might, with the very best will in the world, precipitate a series of horrifying disasters, simply by up-grading the facts to suit his own generous heart. (In a location riot, for example, the 'Father Shillingford' of *Ex Afrika* was responsible for at least four extra deaths, because he gave asylum in his church to a negro thug who, if he had been a white man, could never have excited a moment's pity or even common tolerance.)

It was these 'second thoughts' of Jonathan's that I found fascinating. They proved that he *had* been listening, a year earlier; he had been listening to everybody, however unlikely—myself, Eumor, Bruno, Lord Muddley, Gerald Thyssen. . . . The book was brilliant, anyway; and it made wonderful sense, instead of being the slick-talking trash I had feared—or, at one ignoble stage, hoped.

But it was also balanced, in a way I would never have conceived possible, bearing in mind Jonathan's surface fixation about the rights of man (Sub-division 'Black, Enslaved'). The things that I and the others said in defence of 'our side' had taken root; sometimes they were laughed at, sometimes they were out-argued, but at least they were there, they were given a chance. The result was a novel of

African life, as exciting, sane, and rounded as it could well be. It was also the rarest thing of all, in any book about South Africa: it was hopeful.

When I had finished *Ex Afrika* again, at the second reading, I thought afresh: so he was working all the time, after all; he was working when he was happy with me, and when lonely and unhappy without me, and playing poker, and talking to Father Shillingford, and getting into police trouble, and wandering poor and proud. . . . No wonder he had been preoccupied and unaccountable; to him, the book was all, and (like myself and my own job) he wasn't going to have it sabotaged by any heavy-treading third party.

He had been telling the truth all the time, putting to shame all complaints and suspicions. I wished above everything that I could have been more help—for notwithstanding what I had given him, it was fair to say that he had written the book in spite of me.

It was now desperately important to find out if it were too late.

'Desperate,' I found, was an appropriate word to use. I finished *Ex Afrika* on a Friday afternoon, and it happened that I was going to the ballet that evening. Thus it was a foolish piece of erotica, as well as the magic of the book, which impelled me to ring Jonathan up, after nearly a year of silence. During a not-very-good *Lac des Cygnes*, I became conscious, for the first time, of the ill-concealed endowments of the male dancers, which seemed to be exhibited, in extraordinary prominence, especially for my discomfort.

It was very unlikely that any of the saucy young gentlemen on the stage would have wished to cause me a moment's worry in this department; but I knew one who would, and, in an overwhelming invasion of sexuality, primitive and undeniable, which took me out of the theatre at the interval, I knew that I had to have him, and it, and those, immediately.

I excused a frantic hankering by assuring myself that love would be there also.

I rang up Johannesburg as soon as I got back to my flat. After a long delay, when I feared that the continuous ringing at the other end was going to make me cry, there was a sudden click, and a native voice answered:

'Master not home.'

'Don't ring off!' Instantly afraid, I almost shouted the words; it must have given him the shock of his life. Then I remembered his name: 'Alfred?'

'Yes, missis?'

'Where is the master?'

'Master not home.'

'But where is he? Is he out?

'Master out, yes.'

'When will he be back?'

'Don't know, missis. Master gone away.'

It was a bad moment to hold an African conversation.

'Where has he gone to, Alfred?'

'Cape Town, missis.'

'Cape Town!' I really must stop shouting. 'Whereabouts in Cape Town? I'm ringing up from Cape Town now.'

'Yes, missis.'

'Did he give you a number, Alfred?'

'Master out, in Cape Town.'

I tried four hotels in as many minutes, and I found Jonathan at the fourth one. He sounded surprised, and rather sleepy at the same time. At least, I hoped it was just sleepy. It was very important that he should not be in the least drunk.

I said: 'Drop everything.'

I could almost hear him smile; it had been one of our accustomed signals. 'I will if you will,' he answered.

'I'm dropping everything now,' I said.

I was trembling already, damn it.

'At the very most, you have twenty minutes' start,' said Jonathan.

It was a wonderful re-encounter. Indeed, approximately four million people learned exactly how wonderful it was, because he used the whole thing three years later in a disconcerting novel called *Wrap-Around*, and I was readily identifiable. But even if I had foreknown that particular piece of exploitation, I would not have minded, nor hesitated. Girls are grateful creatures, and suddenly all that I was, was a girl.

We had some catching up to do, after the first wild wordless home-coming; but amazingly little, bearing in mind our total separation of nearly a year. Exquisitely relieved, we revelled in the happy parallel of getting up-to-date. First there was the book—now, in a sense, a top priority of both our lives.

'It's wonderful, Johnny,' I assured him. 'I was amazed when Eumor told me about *Pacific Monthly*, but I'm not any more. . . . And you were actually working on it all the time. That's what's so incredible!'

'Why?' he asked, seeming to be genuinely puzzled. 'I told you I was writing a book.'

I kissed him. It was a very great pleasure. Much of my body was woefully exhausted, but my lips and my heart were not.

'All right, you told me. But you weren't very convincing about it.'

'Have faith. . . . Just because I don't walk about looking like Charles Dickens and talking like one of those angry young men, it doesn't mean I'm not a writer.'

'You're a writer, all right. But Johnny, it *did* seem as though you were wasting your time. There were lots of other things, weren't there?'

'What other things?' He had got up, and was replenishing our glasses, while I lay still on the bed; but he had a way of communicating alertness, even with his back towards me, even with words of no tension whatsoever.

'Oh—drinking.'

'I was sad. Very sad. More sad than you'll ever know.'

'And that awful thing with the police.'

'I didn't waste it, did I?'

'No. But then, all those women.'

'What women?' He had turned, glasses in hand; except for the slip of white skin round his loins, he was very sunburnt, and well-muscled, and male—all the things I wanted to keep for myself, and hated to share. 'I haven't had any women.'

'But darling, the rumours. . . .' I reeled off a few of the atrocious names that Bruno had given me. 'It couldn't all be just talk.'

'Of course I met most of them. A fragrant nosegay indeed. . . . They're part of Johannesburg, aren't they?—a fairly sordid part, but a part none-the-less. I wanted to see what they were like at close quarters. Now I know.' He gave me my drink, kissed me in four or five important places, and lay down beside me. 'Except for one woman —I'll tell you about her later—I haven't gone to bed with anyone. I didn't want to. It wouldn't have cured anything. I discovered years ago that the answer to losing one girl isn't another girl. It's no girl.

'Who was this one woman?' I asked, cut to the silly heart.

'Later, Kate.' He had grown up; he was in command; he laid down the terms; I did not mind. 'But I'll confess some other things to you,' he said—and it sounded a strong phrase, not a weak one. 'When you walked out on me, I drank like a maniac, to try to forget how utterly miserable I was. And I went around with lots of women too, creating the maximum uproar in the process—basically, so as to make you jealous, because I knew you'd hear about it, sooner or later. But my particular torment, all the time, was the idea of you in bed with someone else. *Have* you?'

'No, Johnny. Not once.'

I was so glad that this was true.

'Thank God for that. I couldn't have borne it. . . . Kate, what are we going to do?'

'You tell me.'

'I've got to go back to Johannesburg. The book has been sold to America—I only heard about it this morning—and there's a possibility of a film. . . .' He was not boasting, he was not even parading his riches for me; but he was quietly excited, deeply pleased. 'I must stay in one place for a bit, so that I can keep in touch. But when the rush is over——'

'It's never going to be over,' I told him. 'With a book like that, and all the indications of success, you're never going to stop.'

'I mean, when the immediate negotiations and contracts and translation rights and things——' he waved his hand vaguely; he was still a bit lost, he had not yet learned even the words.

'Have you got an agent?' I asked him, pursuing this last thought.

'Yes. In England. And in America too, now. They're busy working on all those things. . . . But, Kate. You and me. I've got something at last. The Book Society. The *Pacific Monthly*. The American contract. Do you know, the book is already certain to make more than four thousand pounds?' He pronounced the modest figure as if it were at least half of the National Debt. 'What are we going to do?'

'We're going to be in love, and stay in love.'

'But everything's different now. I adore you. Not just like this——' he smoothed his hand over my waist, familiar, faintly exciting again. 'I mean, I've got something to offer you now.'

'You've written a wonderful book, and it's going to make lots of money.' There was a proposal coming, I knew, and I had no idea what to do about it. I recalled my mother's words, reproving, authoritarian, when I had made fun of some hard-breathing, carpet-creeping suitor: *Never forget, Katherine, it is the greatest compliment that a man can pay to a woman*. I wanted the compliment, and I wanted him; but marriage, marriage, marriage. . . . As well as a proposal, there was also a shift of balance already peeping over the horizon: a transformation of us into Jonathan Steele the pipe-smoking good provider, dictating the budget and the full life together, and Kate Marais the little woman, waiting at home in the flowered house-coat, basting with joy the modest shoulder of pork.

Lying beside him, trembling once more under his hand, I was ready to abdicate all things; but I would not tremble for ever—even sensations-by-Steele must have a stop, and when my heart-beat slowed to normal, I might just be me again.

And which *was* me, anyway? The ridiculous indecision that had marked almost every moment of our affair, changing me first from an individual to a dependent, then back again, and now forward once more to classic female subservience, came flooding in afresh, making me almost morbidly dissatisfied with myself, even in the midst of the very joys of being a woman. I had been overthrown by a man, in the first place; now, apparently, it only took a book. . . . It was high time for me to mark out a path, and stick to it. Chop-and-change must really come to an end.

I cheated that evening, and for some evenings afterwards. I said: 'I don't *exactly* want to talk now,' and presently his body pressed and warmed and merged with mine, and when next we uttered, it was only cries and moans and mouth-to-ear endearments. We both knew that I had not answered him; but since I was crowned with exhausted happiness, he, in his humility, was content to be content.

He *was* humble. The smash hit was coming; I knew it, and he guessed it; from now on, he could hardly fail to be the kind of writer that all other writers envied, whether honestly, secretly, or bitchily—a writer successful at a level of achievement which no one could deny. But it had not touched him yet, and he was still, in this area, the child of innocence. I had a striking, disarming instance of this when we first talked about publicity for the book.

We were in Johannesburg, where I had followed him after a few days; we were camping together in a borrowed flat, a compromise between my taste for comfort and his insistence that, in a world where people were dying every day like tortured flies, the man of good-will should die a little with them. Talking of the future—his future, still, not ours—I said at one point:

'Of course, you really ought to have a publicity agent.'

'Publicity agent!' He repeated the words as if mimicking, monkey-fashion, some totally unknown language. 'What on earth for?'

'Work it out, darling, You've written this terrific book. It's going to be a success anyway, and it might be an absolute earthquake. Things like that need organisation. They need handling. You don't want to make any mistakes, at this stage.'

'Handling?' Jonathan jumped on the word that had, for him, the most sordid connotation of all. 'What do you think I am—a boxer? One of those starlets with all their brains crammed into their bosoms? I've written a *book*, Kate! It's going to be serialised, and published, and perhaps filmed. But it's still a book, not a hunk of merchandise, and I'm a writer, not a touring whore from Italy. What has *handling* got to do with it?'

'But darling, it's such a story! Don't you see? You've had this terrific success——'

'It hasn't even been published yet.'

'After starving for years and years——'

'I've lived quite comfortably, and I've only been writing for three years.'

'It doesn't happen every day,' I insisted. 'It doesn't even happen every year. It's a once-in-a-life-time thing. You need someone to make the most of it, so that not a single aspect of it goes to waste. And not just here, but all over the world. Johnny, I tell you there are people, experts who understand these things.'

'Well, I'm not one of them. Of course, I'm glad that a lot of people are going to read *Ex Afrika*, and even more glad to earn some money from writing at last—enough not to have to worry for a year or two. But not to make a *production* out of it——'

We compromised. I gave him a big send-off in my column, the following Sunday, and all the local papers picked it up, crowded round for interviews, and produced quite a splash. The line was 'Sympathetic South African Novel Due for World Success', and my stepped-up estimate of £10,000 in earnings made a good sub-headline.

Johnny, to my surprise, was momentarily like a little boy over the whole thing; he carried the cuttings around with him for week fantastically pleased, ready to show them whenever the conversation flagged, like a sentimental sailor far from home, bulging with faded snapshots of the missis and the kids. So oddly affected was he that once I was impelled, though amusedly, to protest:

'Darling, don't get drunk on the thing. It's just something in the newspapers, after all.'

Fingering the tattered cuttings, beaming with a novel expansiveness, he answered:

'But I never realised my name *looked* like that.'

He was not often so childish; indeed, it was a rare descent. If he was like a small boy with his newspaper cuttings and his zest for seeing his name in large print, he was certainly a man in bed, and a poet with new authority when he spoke. There came a time, as the good news came flooding in, and I had spent three weeks of blissful happiness with him in Johannesburg and my office was falling into ruins, and I did not care, when he suddenly said, in bed but wakeful:

'You haven't answered my question, Kate. *The* question. But before you do, let me tell you two stories of Africa. They haven't any connection, really. Not with each other, and not even with us. But they are part of your country. I just want to tell you. Then I'll ask you again.'

CHAPTER THIRTEEN

ONE of the most horrible aspects (*he told me*) of life in the locations is that even there, in all that squalor and misery and hopelessness, the people who should be brothers actually prey on each other, to all the limits that evil can devise. You would think that people permanently condemned to dirt and near-starvation would help one another; but they don't. . . . There isn't a location in Johannesburg that hasn't been poisoned by racketeering.

Rent rackets, protection rackets, drink rackets, threats of murder and rape and beating-up—that's the inescapable background, all the time. It's fairly quiet during the day, when most of the men are away and the gang-agents go round in relays, leaving messages that the boss wants this and that, or else. . . . But at night the pressure is put on, the executioners move in.

There was a man called Ambuko, a Zulu, who came to live in the location of Teroka with his new wife. He was a strong man, of the middle years, but his wife was young. He built a new house, of iron sheeting and sacks and old planks and barrel-staves, but well-built, a house to be proud of in Teroka. Then one Sunday evening a thin man with a face like a meanly-made spear came to his door, and said:

'I am from the Lions.'

Ambuko had heard of the Lion-men, a gang of thieves and robbers who made a hard life harder still for those in Teroka, and he said nothing, but went on smoking his pipe. Only, not liking the eyes of the Lion-man, he motioned to his wife Amara to go to the back of his house.

'I am from the Lions,' repeated the Lion-man. 'There is a new thing called roof-protection, and you must pay it.'

'My roof is new and strong,' said Ambuko. 'I need no roof-protection.'

'None-the-less,' said the Lion-man, 'strong roofs can be taken away by the wind in the night, or perhaps they may catch fire. It is better to pay.'

'How much is this roof-protection?' asked Ambuko.

'Ten shillings a week.' The Lion-man looked at Ambuko. 'It is agreed, then?'

'No, it is not agreed,' answered Ambuko. He stood up and came towards the Lion-man; and though Ambuko was a man past fifty years, he was strong and well-made, and the Lion-man fell back a pace. 'Be gone, hyena,' said Ambuko. 'I pay no roof-protection.'

'Your roof may catch fire,' warned the Lion-man.

'I will put the fire out.'

'But you are away by day, working in the city.'

'Then my friends or my wife will put it out.'

'You will have no friends on that day,' declared the Lion-man. 'As to your wife, I do not know. But remember one thing—you are away all day working in the city, and your wife is young and beautiful.'

At that, Ambuko came towards him, and the Lion-man ran away, shouting: 'We will come again, you will see.'

Ambuko and his young wife Amara talked long together that night

—talking, indeed, when they would rather have lain in each other's arms, being full of the joy of new love. Ambuko was a strong man, blood-relative to the chiefs of his tribe, not the man to pay roof-protection to a gang of thieves and murderers; but in fact, he could not pay even if he had wished. His wage was three pounds a week, and with the rent of his small piece of land, and the long bus ride into the city, and the cost of food and clothing, there was no ten shillings a week left for roof-protection, nor one shilling a week either.

'Do not fear,' he said at last to Amara. 'I will not pay, and I will look after you.'

On the next day, a Monday, Ambuko came back from the city, to find his wife in tears, and no food to eat at the end of the day's weary work.

'They upset the cooking-pot,' she told him, sobbing and fearful, 'and they called me names, and said terrible things. They said'—her face grew pitiful—'that ten shillings a week was no sum at all, that I could earn it on my back while you were away at work.'

'Who said these things?' asked Ambuko, his face full of pain and anger. 'What men were they?'

'Lion-men,' answered Amara. Then she said: 'You must pay them.'

'I will pay nothing.'

'I am afraid,' said Amara.

That night another Lion-man came, when it was darker, and said, as if speaking something new: 'There is a thing called roof-protection. Ten shillings a week. A kind of insurance, like the Europeans pay. Will you pay, Ambuko?'

'No,' said Ambuko. 'And I am astonished that you dare to come here, woman fighter, when I am at home.'

'We will come here any time. Tonight, perhaps.'

That night there were strange noises, and singing, and shouting, outside the house of Ambuko, and a small fire was started at a corner of the roof. Ambuko beat it out before it could gain hold, and stood on guard all night, wakeful, though he had to leave his house at five o'clock to go to the city. When he left, Amara said: 'I am afraid, Ambuko.'

When he returned that night, which was Tuesday, Amara was weeping and trembling. 'We must pay,' she told him. 'We must pay, or we must go.'

'What happened?'

'They came, three men. Two held me, while one touched me here and here. Then the other two took their turn to touch me, while I was held fast. They said—' her voice faltered, '—they said that this was a tasting for them, like a first sip from a cup. They said, next time they would enjoy my cup to the full. They said also, it might be that I would myself have pleasure from it, much more than from lying with an old man whose strength was gone.'

'What did you do?' asked Ambuko, distraught with rage and shame because of the love he bore her. 'Did you not call out for help?'

'I called out, but none came, though there were many near. They were afraid. Perhaps they were glad that the Lion-men chose me, and left them alone.'

'This is a bad place,' said Ambuko. 'Some are hyenas, some are cowardly dogs. None are men.'

'I beseech you to pay,' said Amara.

'I cannot and I will not.'

That night, when they lay together, giving comfort to each other, a voice at the foot of their couch suddenly shouted: 'Enjoy her, Ambuko! Tomorrow will be our turn!' But when he sprang up, the man was gone.

The next evening, which was a Wednesday, a third Lion-man came to the house of Ambuko. All he said was: 'Roof-protection. Ten shillings a week.'

'I will not pay,' said Ambuko. 'Woman fighter.'

'Tonight we will fight both of you,' said the Lion-man, and walked away.

'I must go to the police,' said Ambuko.

'Do not leave me,' said Amara.

'The police will help me.'

'They will say: "Go away. Fight your own battles. Do not bother us." Perhaps they will put in prison for making a complaint.'

'None-the-less,' said Ambuko, 'a man with no friends must go to the police.'

He left his house, having embraced Amara and told her to stay hidden and to take care. It was an hour's walk to the police-post, and when he got there, the fair-haired policeman with the great shoulders kept him waiting for half an hour, though doing nothing, and then said: 'What is it, eh?'

Ambuko told his story, and said at the end: 'They held my wife, and touched her.'

'Where?' asked the policeman.

'Here and here,' answered Ambuko, ashamed.

'Which of you is complaining?' asked the policeman, smirking. 'Is it both of you, or just you?'

Ambuko said nothing.

'We'll look into it,' said the policeman finally. 'Where's that house again?'

Ambuko described it to him.

'Those damned shacks are all alike,' grumbled the policeman. 'Ought to be pulled down, the whole stinking lot. . . . All right, we'll keep an eye on it.'

'Tonight?' asked Ambuko.

'Maybe. You're not the only kaffir in this bloody location, you know.'

Ambuko walked back. He had been away three hours. There was a crowd outside his house, idlers and gossipers, who parted to let him through. In the darkness, he could not see Amara, and then he stumbled over a form beside the door, and it was she, and she was cold and lifeless.

When he had wept, and shivered, and thought for some time, he came to his door again.

'You,' he said, to an old man in an old army coat, 'what happened?'

'They used her, and then stabbed her,' answered the man indifferently.

'Did she not cry out?'

'Very loudly,' said a young man, almost laughing.

'And none came?'

'Who would come against the Lion-men?' said the old man.

'The men of my tribe would do so,' said Ambuko.

'Then keep your tribe away, for the love of Christ!' said a woman, a thin slattern with a thin child at her back. 'And pay your roof-protection, old fool! Do you think we want the Lion-men here every night?'

There was nodding and head-shaking among the crowd, and many said: 'The woman is right. Pay your roof-protection. Let us have peace here, for God's sake.'

Ambuko withdrew into his house, and did what could be done, in simple decency, for the body of his young wife Amara. Then he waited.

At midnight, a man called loudly from outside: 'Ambuko!'

He answered: 'What is it, woman fighter?'

'Now is the time to pay roof-protection,' said the same loud voice.

'I will not pay.' He walked to the door, and saw under the moonlight not one but twelve men, ringed about his small house. 'Murderers!' he said. 'Woman killers, I will not pay.'

Four torches blazed suddenly, and then the roof over his head took fire at its four corners. The twelve men moved close to his door, as if to prevent his leaving. But he did not try to break past them, nor to put out the fire.

'Pay,' said the leader. 'Pay before it is too late.'

Ambuko sat down on the floor of his hut, beside the body of his wife, and bowed his head.

'Pay,' said the leader, somewhat taken aback. 'Come out, and pay.'

'I will not pay, and I will not come out.' The fire began to leap and roar, and sparks fell upon his glistening shoulders. Suddenly he shouted: 'People of Teroka, watch how a man can die!'

'Come out, fool!' called the leader. 'We will let you out.'

'Men of Teroka!' shouted Ambuko, in agony amid the blaze. 'Watch how a man of my tribe can die, rather than pay roof-protection to these stinking jackals!'

He drew his blanket over his head, sitting like a crouching statue in the roaring flames. At the moment before the end, he called out: 'Remember me!'

Then the roof fell upon him, and the fierce flames sprang up and then died down, and the crowd walked away from the smouldering pile that had been the house of Ambuko. They muttered among themselves, and some looked sideways at the band of Lion-men; but it did not seem that they now had much more spirit than they had had, an hour earlier, and it was easy to guess that it would all be gone before morning.

'Bloody old fool!' said the policeman to his relief, later. 'All that commotion, just for ten shillings a week. . . . I tell you, man, these kaffirs have no brains.'

When Jonathan had finished his story he lay on his back, apart from me, his eyes closed, as if dreaming still. It was nearly dawn; the light was coming through the curtains, the thin pure Johannesburg air which promised us another day of dry sunshine.

129

'You really do love everybody, Johnny, don't you?' I said presently.

'You first,' he answered, his eyes still closed. 'Then everybody else.'

'Was that a true story?'

'Yes.'

'Why didn't you use it in *Ex Afrika*?'

'I suppose I was keeping it for you.'

'It makes me want to cry.'

His eyes opened unexpectedly, and he was smiling. 'For no particular reason, it makes me want to make love to you.' Without warning, his voice suddenly changed, taking on a low-pitched, almost ferocious intensity. 'Though I'm looking at the ceiling, Kate, I can see all your body perfectly. It's beautifully formed and wonderfully slim, and it will be mine again in a moment. . . . Your eyes are watching me, and the rest of you is getting ready—small movements, accommodations— we've learned them all, thank God. There's actually a second heart-beat where I'm going to be in twenty seconds from now.' He still had not moved; it was just his voice, his spring-gun concentration; already I was hypnotised into readiness. 'Open your arms, Kate,' he commanded, withdrawn yet imminent. 'So that you'll be absolutely ready for me. Are you ready?'

I could hardly breathe. 'Yes.'

'Three two one zero. . . . Steele.'

A long and languid and drowsy time afterwards, I said: 'What about the other story, Johnny?—the second one?'

He had returned—gently, lovingly, gratefully—to his relaxed position, his ceiling stare. 'It's about me and that girl. So it's closer to home. . . . Do you want to hear about it now, Kate?'

'Yes, I do.' He must have known what my answer would be; the preparation had been fantastically adroit. 'I'm ready for that, too. Tell me.'

'She was a whore,' he began, without preamble. 'If you don't know it already, it's just as easy to fall in love with a whore as with anyone else. . . . She was small and slim and very good-looking. She'd done a certain amount of posing and modelling, and she had a lot of character, of a sort. I must have loved her a bit, and I certainly slept with her a bit, because she was extremely good at it. But basically I thought I could reform her, help her to make something out of her life.' In the light which was by now nearly full daylight, he grinned ruefully.

'Writers and artists are always trying to work that particular, self-deluding swindle, aren't they? Toulouse-Lautrec, Maupassant. . . . She'd had an incredible life, Kate. She simply adored men, she just couldn't say no to any of them. During the last three or four years—she was only nineteen when I met her—she had been having a really fantastic sexual gallop.

'If the men paid her, well and good. If they couldn't pay, she put it on the slate. She's had abortions without number. She'd had operations that you only hear about by accident, from the police-court news. She'd had Fallopian pregnancies. She'd had her tubes blown from here to Cape Horn. She'd been barred from clubs, even golf clubs. She'd been cited in divorce cases. Men had left her. She had left men. Revolvers had been fired, mirrors broken by flying scent-bottles. . . . She'd had at least two tries at suicide. Once she had to have an abortion, and she hadn't got a penny in the world, so she agreed to sleep with the doctor for a fortnight—that was his price—and he was a repellent, diseased Hun with a suppurating thigh, and he gave her another baby.'

Jonathan lit a cigarette, took a sip of his decadent dawn whisky and soda. It was difficult to tell if he were moved at all by what he was saying; he was telling the story as if it were a skeleton plot for his next novel. Perhaps it was—and that was a comforting thought, for a girl just below the surface of extreme jealousy and hate, as I suddenly was.

'Well, as I said, I thought I'd reform her,' he went on. 'Silly Steele. . . . I stopped sleeping with her, so as to give her a flying start. I paid her rent for six months in advance, so that she wouldn't have to earn it by internal revenue. I put her through a modelling school, and a radio school, and then an acting school. At least I tried to, but nothing happened, it never jelled; her average enrolment anywhere was never more than a fortnight. You see, she didn't really want to model, or broadcast, or act; it was just a shop-window for her pretty little mouse-trap.

'She took a typing course, but she didn't like the feel of an office chair. Too vertical. . . . She was a doctor's secretary for a while, but he turned out to be a specialist, like all the rest. I even tried her at home economics. God, she was a lousy cook. . . . But *nothing* was any good. She *had* a lot of character, but it was all bad. She always crept back to whoring, only now she didn't have to charge anything, so she gave all her old chums a free ride. She adored me, I think, and she *was* grateful—but I was always catching sight of her in terrible night-clubs, obviously on the verge of climbing into terrible beds—soft-goods buyers, rotten wrestlers. . . . Once, when she was drunk, she let me see her diary. On the back page were a hundred and sixty pen and pencil strokes. They were men, by God! . . . When I said: "But that's an awful lot, isn't it?" (she was still only nineteen, remember) she answered: "But darling, that's for the *whole* of this year."

'It wasn't her fault. She couldn't help it. She was a sexual egg-beater. She had the itch, and I mean that literally. Because she died of it.'

'Oh, Johnny!' I said, torn by every kind of frantic emotion, but chiefly a late-coming, grisly happiness. 'She's dead?'

'Oh yes. Last month. That itch was real. She had some kind of internal growth, which had to be continually appeased, like a second, famished mouth. . . . She went into hospital for an emergency opera-tion, but it didn't take, it was too late. Darling Kate, that was the very saddest funeral I've ever attended. It was pouring with rain, and I held the umbrella over the priest. You know why? Because there wasn't anybody else to do it. After all those men, all those hundreds of customers, there wasn't a single person except me and the priest and the grave-diggers, within a mile of her coffin.'

We were married four days later.

My dear friend Mrs. Marchant lent me her house; my father made a speech; Eumor, who was in England, sent a telegram full of esoteric references to bottles and pennies, to which we replied austerely: 'They don't make bottles big enough for us.' But it was a delightful wedding, by civil ceremony—possibly the least civil ceremony ever staged in Johannesburg. All the better-known drunks shouted insults at their wives or toppled into the swimming-pool; many of the wedding presents were stolen; two Cadillacs were pulverised in the driveway. The bride wore pink, in elegant compromise.

Bruno van Thaal turned up for breakfast next morning, at 7.45 a.m., and when I objected, from deep beneath the bedclothes, he patted us both fondly on the bottom, and said: 'Don't exaggerate so, dear—this is a day like any other day.'

We were very happy; and then presently things began to happen to Jonathan, and thus to me, making us happier still, and the future brighter than a hundred suns.

BOOK TWO

THE PINK SAFARI

CHAPTER ONE

I COULD hear the Segovia record, from downstairs, all the time I was shaving, and bathing, and dressing, and I wasn't at all happy about it. It was not a tonic sound; the guitar, muted, exquisite, and melancholy, was for us an instrument of bad omen. If Kate were going on another Segovia kick, it could only mean one thing; she was brooding, she was sad, she was walled up again.

After six years, of marriage, I knew all her moods, and all her music too. Chopin was love, Brahms was deep feeling, Mozart was pleasure, Dixieland was the spark for rowdy fun. The classical guitar, of Frescobaldi and Fernando Sor, was music of mourning. This must be the boy's death once more, and the muddy stream of time, and me.

Since I was dawdling over dressing anyway—my lunch wasn't till one-fifteen—it seemed appropriate to take the hint and change ties, from a sparkling Jacques Fath to a brown, subdued Dior. It would be wrong to waste a Jacques Fath on a foreboding day like this. Perhaps later that afternoon. . . . And I still hadn't told Kate about the poker game, either.

Knotting the tie, I glanced over the edge of the mirror at the scene outside the window. The top floor of a twelve-storey building did not, in New York, allow anything spectacular in the way of long-range vista; competition from the forty-storey monsters nearby took care of that. But the view faced south, across the patch-work roofs of 76th Street and down to the low sixties; there was a glimpse of Park Avenue trees on one side, and the bare spaces of Central Park on the other. A February sun, pale and welcome as an honoured ghost, was doing its best with the overcast sky. It was, as I had thought many times before, not bad for New York; and so, at $800 a month, it damned well ought to be.

The extension telephone in my dressing-room rang, and I waited, lazy-like, to see if anyone else would answer it. But the guitar was claiming Kate's attention, and Julia, even after six years in a part of the world where the phone rang twenty times a day, was still afraid of the instrument and never picked it up if she could possibly avoid it. (She still used the Cape-Coloured phrase: 'The telephone wants you,' as if bearing a message from a living tyrant. How right she was.) So I answered it myself.

'Good morning!' said an exceptionally eager voice, a girl's voice, bright and confident. 'Is that the man of the house?'

I said that it was.

'Well, how are *you* today?' asked the girl, as if she were my closest living relative.

'All right,' I said glumly. I knew what was coming.

'Well, that's just fine! Because I have a wonderful surprise for you!'

'I don't want a wonderful surprise.'

But already, even at this early stage, she was no longer listening; she had launched, at break-neck speed, into her pitch.

'This is a personal and private call from the Steps of Heaven School of Dancing. Your name has been selected for one whole hour's dancing lesson, entirely free, without any obligation on your part. No matter whether one is a beginner, or a seasoned performer, we can all benefit from a lesson, can't we? Especially a free lesson in strict privacy.' She drew breath, for the first time, but not long enough to risk interruption. 'This is not a sales promotion; it is a complimentary offer to a few socially prominent persons and busy executives such as yourself. You can come in any time, morning or evening, and an experienced instructor—and mighty pretty too!—will devote sixty whole minutes to you and you alone, in a sound-proof studio in New York's most luxurious academy of the dance. New steps, such as the Cleopatra Cha-Cha, the Mashed Potato, and the Merengue can also be demonstrated. Now isn't that a wonderful offer, and may we expect you real soon?'

She stopped abruptly, running out of breath and material at the same time; the line hummed expectantly between us, waiting for an answer which must at least match so glorious a burst of generosity. I used to find this sort of thing sad, because behind every such call must be a girl backed into a contemporary corner of hell, trying to scrape a living from the forlorn barrel of life; now it was just a damned nuisance, a scuffling sound from someone else's trap.

'I'm a seasoned performer,' I said at length.

'Pardon me?'

136

'I don't want a dancing lesson. I don't need one.'

But I had pressed the wrong button; now she was off again, at the same romping pace. '*So* many people think that way, but it is not so.' I could almost hear a fresh piece of paper, labelled 'Sales Resistance', being shuffled to the top of the pack. 'Our files contain countless testimonials from so-called expert dancers who have been absolutely amazed at what the Steps of Heaven Dancing School was able to do for them. In many cases it transformed their entire lives. Modern ballroom dancing is the key to social success, and social success has no ceiling. There is absolutely no limit——'

I was now fully dressed; I was thirsty; this had therefore gone on long enough. I could have cut her off by abandoning the telephone, but I always did my small best to discourage such intrusion. Obviously she could only be stopped by a shout, and so I shouted.

'What was that awful noice?' she asked, after a startled moment of silence.

'I didn't hear anything,' I said. 'I was changing a record.'

'A record?'

'You people really must bring your files up to date,' I said coldly. 'If you knew anything at all about dancing, you would know that I have been a senior instructor at Arthur Murray's for fifteen years.'

Childish Steele, I thought, clamping down the receiver; silly Steele, baby Steele. . . . But I felt better, all the same; a blow for Steele was a blow for liberty. I was ready for that drink, ready for Segovia, ready for my difficult and darling wife. I shot my cuffs, like any other ham actor, and went blithely down the stairs to the day-time section of our apartment.

It was an elegant mess of a room. A New York decorator with a schizophrenic taste for wrought-iron grilles and long silk tassels had done his worst; and then Kate had moved in and tried to civilise the joint. The result had been a draw. There was still enough deep-pile, oyster-coloured, wall-to-wall carpeting to defeat the average power-mower, and the vast zebra-striped sofa had that come-on look associated with old filmstars' beds; but there were also some elements of taste and reason—a bookcase with actual books, a set of Hepplewhite chairs which could be sat in, a modest Modigliani—enough to show that we were just folks after all.

Kate had wanted a London drawing-room, I had wanted a show-off springboard for parties. We had compromised, with a room which we both liked well enough to leave alone—and that, I suppose, was life. It was certainly marriage. I worked across the hall, anyway, in a north-facing, functional office which didn't pretend to be anything else, and which caused peeping visitors to murmur: 'So dedicated. . . . They say he actually writes five hundred words *every day*!'

It was true enough, if you counted cheques.

Segovia signed off, with a generous shower of grace-notes, as I came in, to be succeeded by the wailing signal which daily reminded New Yorkers that the world of togetherness was still fissionable. Twelve o'clock. . . . I passed close to Kate on my way to the bar, but she did not look up; she was still listening to private echoes of the guitar, she knew I was alive. Two ounces of vodka, three ice-cubes, top up with orange juice—the restorative screw-driver took shape and, after a moment, taste. It was excellent, proving once again that the wage-earning man did appreciate a good breakfast. On the road back to health, I turned to look at her.

You do not see a woman, even the most beautiful, after a couple of years of her company; like a stolen picture, a missing limb, you see her if she is *not* there. I had not really seen Kate, nor she me, for a long time; six years had taken its customary toll, misting the eye, blunting the many edges of appetite; the only important thing about this was not to be surprised by it. Of course, she was beautiful—and she was beautiful now, lying back on the sofa, dressed in a pale grey Cashmir sweater and the kind of black tailored slacks presumably designed for homework only. The competition from the zebra stripes was formidable, but Kate still emerged as the glowing winner.

She was slim, she was lovely, she was impeccably groomed; we had been married for six years. Today's face, though beautiful, was sad, to match the music; and at the moment it was a face many miles away from me. She had gone into mourning again, and I knew by now that I was no longer the man to bring her out of it.

Children die, and it is more moving than grown-ups; but it is only death, after all—the Fell Sergeant catching up with his statistics. I had mourned our son, bitterly and briefly, and then put him out of mind; if it was heartless, that was because I *was* heartless—the small fingers had not had time to entwine, the grown-up spirit could not become forever bound, in the space of eighteen months. I had work to do instead, and I had done it.

Kate had been different, and she still was; for her, those eighteen months had fashioned a beloved individual, and now a mordaunt memory. She had blamed herself—'Any cow can have a baby,' she had said, in brutal self-contempt: 'you have to be smart, smart and loving, to keep it.' Of course, none of it had been her fault; it was just one of those things, the kind which made you feel, if you were an on-and-off believer, that God after all was barbarous, or asleep, or dead; but she had kept this conviction of guilt locked within her, for more than three years. Sometimes she took it out and looked at it, as she was doing today.

That made it a good time to be somewhere else, to miss the big, big scene. The man who could not help was the world's most superfluous object.

It was not only the child, anyway.

The guitar music started again, soft, insistent, plucking at more than the strings. This time, it was Castelnuovo-Tedesco—I knew all these records by heart, in the catalogue sense, though once again the heart itself was absent. I took another nourishing sip of my drink, and gave Kate a civil good morning.

She looked up at me at last, smiling the faint disengaged smile of wives between breakfast and lunch. She waited for a phrase of the music to finish, and then said:

'You were late.'

I came forward, to sit on the arm of the sofa. 'I had to break off for an hour, to do the show. Then we kept on having one more round. Dealer's choice. Then I couldn't get a taxi, so I walked home.'

'You'll get held up, one of these days.'

'They wouldn't have got much out of me.'

She nodded to herself, as if recognising a cue. 'How did we do?' she asked. The 'we' was because, by tradition, she got ten-per-cent of my poker winnings, and was thus entitled to the stock-holders' report.

'We didn't do so well.'

'How much did we lose?'

'We lost two thousand, one hundred, and eighty dollars.'

'Oh, Johnny!' She was startled, as I had known she would be. 'You can't afford that.'

'That's a very fair statement.'

'Who won?'

'Hobart.'

'Good God!' Hobart Mackay was my esteemed publisher. 'Hasn't he made enough money out of you already?'

'Not recently. . . . It was mostly one hand, damn it. Four jacks bumping four kings. Very expensive.'

'Why don't you give it up for a bit?'

'Never.'

She frowned, but as usual she did not try to follow up. Though she disapproved of my poker-playing, which most years took steady toll of all the spare money I had, she had never fought it or nagged about it. I didn't like some of the things she did, but I didn't try to alter them either. It was a fair exchange, a truce to mutual abrasion, and if it made two people grow a little apart, then a little apart was where they ought to be.

I finished off my drink, went back to the bar, and poured another one. Kate was watching me, without saying anything. She had never struck an attitude about drinking, either.

When I was within her orbit again, she said: 'How smart you look. . . . What's this lunch?'

'Jack Taggart, and a man called Erwin Orwin.'

'Who's he?'

'He produces musicals.'

'Oh, that one. . . . What are you and your agent doing, lunching with the likes of Erwin Orwin?'

'I don't know. Jack set it up.'

'He must have said why.'

It was too early, for all sorts of reasons, to give her any details. 'Just that Erwin Orwin had an idea.'

'Good for him.'

I reacted to the tone. 'Oh, come on Kate! He can't help being called Erwin Orwin.'

'Didn't he do that awful Napoleon thing?'

'That awful Napoleon thing is still running, after two years.'

'So is Lassie.'

I wasn't going to be irritated, or have the lunch spoiled, or even the current drink. 'She's got all those feet,' I said. 'Unfair to people.'

But Kate, for a change, was not to be side-tracked; poker, and Erwin Orwin, and a sense of exclusion, had triggered something important. 'I don't know what you and Jack Taggart are cooking up,' she said, with sudden energy. 'But if you want the advice of an older woman, keep out of it.' Her voice told me she was not fooling, in spite of the fooling words. 'Don't let them tie you up again, Johnny. . . . Don't get involved in writing the script for a musical. *Don't* sign on for any more TV. *Don't* make a speech at the Academy Awards. *Don't* go back to Hollywood. *Don't* take off for London.' She had rehearsed all this, I thought, or lived with it for too long a time; her words were too ready, even for Kate; and the next slice of expensive dialogue supplied the key. 'You're half-way through a novel, and you're a writer. The best I know, in spite of all the nonsense. Do us a favour, Steele. Finish your book. Think about it. Concentrate on it. Polish it up. Write it all over again, if you have to. But finish it. It's the only thing worth your while.'

I took the next-to-last sip of my drink, considered the idea of pouring another one, and decided to have it somewhere else. Like many another day, this was not my day for arguing. I knew what I was doing, and I was ready to climb over all the broken bricks and crumbling concrete, all the rubbish-tip of other people's ideas, to do it. If Kate, as part of the current drama, were in mourning for my life as well as her own, it wasn't going to be contagious.

'And in the meantime?' I said.

She knew what I meant; this was even older ground, fought over abandoned, recovered a dozen times; littered with tiny grave-stones captioned in red ink. She listened for another moment to the music, the dying music of someone else's sad story; and then:

'All right,' she said flatly. 'End of exercise. Go away and make some money.'

I had to admire a text-book withdrawal. It was just what I planned to do.

CHAPTER TWO

Downstairs, Joe the doorman, an imperfectly feudal retainer, said: 'Hi there, Mr. Steele!' and then, braided cap in hand, saw me out through the swing-door into 77th Street. The sun was still trying to shine, but the contrast between eighty-degree steam heat and forty-degree fresh air was too marked for comfort. I stood under the red-striped canopy, buttoning up my top-coat, while Joe looked towards Park Avenue in search of a cruising taxi. Waiting, we exchanged some traditional dialogue.

'Saw you on TV last night, Mr. Steele.'

'Did you? I hope you enjoyed the show.'

'That's the one we always watch. But my wife keeps asking, what's he really like.'

As usual, I resisted the temptation to say, 'Bastards don't come any bigger,' and answered: 'Oh, he's quite a character, once you get to know him.'

'That's what we thought. I liked the bit when he mixed up the commercial.'

A taxi, answering Joe's raised hand, drew up alongside. As I got in, Joe put on his cap, gave a windmill salute, and said:

'Take it easy, now.'

The master-and-servant charade was over; the one that followed it, loosely labelled 'All New York Cab-drivers are Characters', now took its place. Sometimes the credit-title was true, and on a long run, say from Kennedy Airport into town, one could really enjoy a salty monologue on the state of the nation; more often than not, nature's lovable cab-drivers turned out to be just another New York myth, and the reality was crude and disobliging, preoccupied with a radio tuned to the most raucous local station of all, which was raucous indeed. This morning, I had drawn a candidate from the majority, a surly spitting man who spent a full half-minute filling in his time-sheet before throwing over his shoulder the words:

'Where to?'

Though I knew the omens were not promising, I felt like getting my money's worth for the ride. Why should cab-drivers be the only people licensed to behave like barbarians? Just as if it were normal, I answered: 'The Court of the Sixteen Satraps.'

His head on its thick furry neck came round a fraction. 'How's that?'

'Don't you know a restaurant called The Court of the Sixteen Satraps?'

'Jesus!' He spat out of the side window, which should have been closed and was letting in a frigid draught. 'What are they going to call 'em next?'

'Thirty-eighth Street,' I told him. 'Between Madison and Fifth. You're meant to know that sort of thing.'

He braked roughly to a halt for the first traffic lights, hawked and spat once more, looked at himself in the mirror, and asked: 'What was that name again?'

'The Court of the Sixteen Satraps. Haven't you heard of it? It's been open about a year.'

'If I had to remember every nutty joint in town, I wouldn't be driving a hack. I'd be out of my skull.'

After that, he only spoke once more, when we were stopped by the lights at 60th Street, and he jerked his head at a policeman standing on the corner. 'See that lousy cop?' he growled, out of the corner of his mouth. 'He's the meanest bastard in town.' I said: 'Don't give up so easily,' and he glared at me in the mirror; and after that, we rode in welcome silence, and I was free to enjoy—and did enjoy—the descent into the grand canyon of this city.

After a season in London, we had lived in New York for the past five years; we had liked it from the moment we first went there, for the publication of *Ex Afrika*, and clinched the liking when we came back for the opening of the film. (I still recalled the trio of charming, watchful, look-alike Jews who went everywhere with us on that occasion, on a twenty-four-hour, round-the-clock, escort basis. I had been much impressed by the film company's thoughtfulness until Kate said: 'It's only to make sure we don't get drunk before the *première*.') After that visit, we had made the move a permanent one, leased the duplex apartment, and settled in to relish all that our bouncing home-town could offer.

It was a lot, even on an anonymous basis; and riding the crest of a book which stayed on the best-seller list for one hundred and four weeks, followed by another which lasted a full year, we had a wild and wonderful time. New York, we found, had open arms; and if sometimes they needed to be pried open first, that didn't affect the ultimate welcome. Oysters were just the same, and just as wild and wonderful.

There was an endless amount of things for me to do—in fact, too much for a writer who wanted only to write; I had to compromise, or rather I had to accept the fact, which was no hardship, that a book every three or four years was the most I could do, if I wanted to be a recognisable, available, quotable man as well. It happened that I did want that. . . . I had made, and still did, a lot of television appearances —all the old shows and all the new, from Dave Garroway down to Johnny Carson, via Sullivan, Paar, John Daly, and David Susskind. I did a lecture tour which, at the cost of staring down upon assorted seas of millinery, from Boston to San Francisco, four times a week for three months, netted me fifty thousand dollars, and a permanent distaste for Chicken Pot Pie and pineapple salad.

I made a trip to the Congo for *Life Magazine*, and another to London to sniff and then distil the fragrance of the Ward-Profumo-Keeler circus. I went to Hollywood to do *Wrap-Around's* screenplay, and then to Cuba for one of those sober assessments of the Castro regime —and swiftly out again as a suspected CIA saboteur. That didn't do me any harm, either.

It was part of a self-projection, consistent, long-term, and highly effective. Kate didn't like it, I did. As its result, *Ex Afrika* earned a swift quarter-of-a-million dollars before it started to ease off; its successor, *Wrap-Around*, bolstered by a monumental film deal, had already made half a million more. As far as I was concerned, there weren't any other kinds of book, and there weren't going to be.

$900,000 in six years was the current score, and it would top the million mark before this year was out. We still never seemed to have any money, but it was an acceptable kind of poverty; and here, as if to point the fact, was the gilded entrance to The Court of the Sixteen Satraps, home (so the ads declared) of the Gourmet Who Looks East.

A man dressed in a jewelled turban, scarlet leather jerkin, and golden-hued Turkish trousers, and flourishing a colossal two-handed scimitar (for which, I happened to know, he needed a police permit) stood sentinel outside, waiting to open the cab doors; and he was still only a minor clue to what lay in wait within.

The Sixteen Satraps, which was very much the 'in' restaurant that year, was predominantly Persian, with overtones from other vanished empires nearby; the bar was a copy of the Blue Mosque of Isfahan, the main dining-room shaped like a Persian walled garden, complete with lattice work and a control-system of falling rose-petals; the checkroom and cigarette girls wore transparent veils, cut-out velvet hearts in strategic places, and were known as Persian Lambs.

Vast tapestries covered the walls; vast punkah fans waved to and fro overhead; on the tables (shaped and coloured like shining half-moons) the place-mats were small Persian rugs, the plates inverted bronze shields, the knives miniature scimitars, the spoons miniature slippers, the wine-coolers miniature war-chariots. The waiters wore Turkish trousers, silk sashes, white turbans, and gold slave-bangles; all the men behind the bar sported false yet formal beards of curly gold thread, copied from the tapestried warriors above. The man in charge of them was called Xerxes.

The menus were enormous, printed in Persian (small italics) translated into English (18-point Roman); at the head of each was the Omar Khayyám quotation, '*A Loaf of Bread, a Jug of Wine, and Thou*', and underneath: 'You bring the Thou, we do the rest.' The *maître d'hôtel*, a remote personage, was known as the Head Shah. The food, leaning towards shish-kebabs on flaming daggers, stuffed vine leaves, and melons foaming sherbet at every pore, was atrociously expensive, and very good indeed.

I gave my coat to one of the Persian Lambs, a forward-looking girl of large and lavish build; indeed, her configuration, whether true or false, always seemed an architectural impossibility. If this was a lamb, it was no wonder about support-prices. Accepting the coat, she said:

'Hi, Mr. Steele! Saw you on TV last night.'

'So late? You should have been in bed.'

'Oh, I was!'

The look in her eye would have stunned a statue. I backed away prudently towards the bar, elevated none-the-less. Somebody loves me, after all.

'Hi, Mr. Steele!' said Xerxes the head barman, a small foxy man whose fake yellow beard made him look like a starving actor—which he may well have been, after office hours. 'Saw you on TV last night.'

'Good for you.' One day, someone was going to tell me they had read one of my books, and I would break down altogether. 'Did you like the show?'

'I liked it when he was on every night.'

I wrestled with this *non sequitur* for a moment, but it wouldn't come out. 'That's good,' I said. 'Now I'm feeling thirsty.'

'Farah Dibah?'

'Farah Dibah.'

A Farah Dibah was a martini with a stuffed date instead of an olive.

Sipping it, I looked round the Blue Mosque bar, and through its entrance to the walled-garden restaurant, and wondered, not for the first time, what strange tribal signal brought certain kinds of people to certain kinds of places at certain times of the year. The Court of the Sixteen Satraps, being the current 'in' eating-place, was naturally the current expense-account haven, particularly at lunch-time; it was as if someone had sounded a moose-horn in the heart of New York, and commanded: 'All right, boys. Four Seasons, out! Twelve Caesars, out! Sixteen Satraps, in! Get going!' And here they all were, the March of the Charcoal Greys in person.

Ad men, TV men, film men in from the coast; producers and directors from the Broadway musicals; agents from all over—they had all suddenly arrived at the Satraps, brandishing their meal-tickets from the Diners', Hilton Carte Blanche, and American Express; and you couldn't tell one open-handed freeloader from another. It was a curious and grisly fact that whether a man sold Chanel or Chryslers, soap or cheese, women or men, he shared this uniform look—spear-headed by the Madison Avenue brigade, all with the same cropped hair-cuts, the same never-still eyes, the same contempt for the customer, the same oldest young faces in the world.

Even their clothes had become a uniform. This season it was narrow-shouldered suits, cuffed sleeves, cream shirts, pointed black shoes, and those awful little hats with no brims. Next season it would be something quite different. But unless you wore the whole outfit, you were improperly dressed, like a soldier with a missing epaulette, and you suffered the same fate—the big black mark which defaced your conduct-sheet for ever.

I was improperly dressed myself, and it was a pleasure. But I was not ashamed before my own clan. At these prices, there weren't any other writers.

A hand fell on my shoulder, a gritty voice said: 'Hi, Tolstoy!' and I turned to face the man I was waiting for, Jack Taggart, my agent.

He was a large, not too talkative, somewhat unfathomable man who, in the jungle world of agency, sometimes seemed more like a game-warden than anything else. Agents could not afford to have split personalities; Jack Taggart came as near to it as any other man at the top of his heap. He was a born ten-per-center, a driving salesman who took whatever I sent him, judged it, categorised it, and then sold it in the precise market which suited it best, to the nearest five dollars. Yet he managed to remain curiously uncommitted; accepting without praising, acting without involvement, selling without ever declaring his critical hand.

146

He had loved *Ex Afrika*, and done his formidable best for it; he had not liked *Wrap-Around* at all, and never said so, and never pretended that it was anything more than the hottest piece of merchandise that had ever come into his office. But he had gone in to bat for it with the same tough skill, and come out of the game with $500,000 for me—and still no pretence of admiration.

He did not flatter me, he did not bolster me; he did not play either God or Uriah Heep. He was my agent; not my mentor, not my fool. For all sorts of reasons, some of them stemming from conscience, some not, I was very fond of Jack; and one day I would recapture his regard. But that day was not yet, and we both knew it, and we never said a word on the subject, because neither of us was going to yield, nor change our rules, nor relent.

Now I gave him a greeting of equal and agreed falsity—'Good morning, Svengali,'—and we settled down at the bar. No Farah Dibah for him; plain whisky, plain water, plain ice, plain glass. It was all he needed to say, or would ever say, about stuffed dates and sawdust people.

Jack Taggart wasn't wasting any other kind of time, either.

'Before he comes,' he said, as soon as his drink was poured, 'I'd better bring you up to date. I think we have a deal, if you want one.'

'I want one.'

'O.K. Like I said the other day, it involves you as well.'

'What do I have to do?'

'Write the book. Give the cues for songs, and what they should be about. You might have some ideas of your own for lyrics, but it's not necessary—and of course no music from you.'

'Who does that part of it?'

'I don't know yet. He's probably got a team lined up already—maybe the best—but he won't say until he's sure of you and *Ex Afrika*.'

'Sounds all right. I know how much of the story I want to use. What about the money side?'

Jack Taggart sipped his drink, as I did; the small pause before the vital statistics.

'It'll be a percentage deal,' he said after a moment. 'A cut of the box-office gross, after some of the production-costs have been taken care of. It's complicated, but I'll work all that out with the lawyers. Will you want something now, on account?'

'Yes,' I said. 'This afternoon.'

He grinned. 'I don't know what you do with your money. . . . All right. How about this? Fifteen thousand for saying yes to the idea. Fifteen thousand and expenses for writing all the non-musical side of it. That'll make a thirty thousand advance, against your percentage of the box-office. If it works out properly, and the show goes, that will mean a four or five year income.'

'Tell me again,' I said, mock dreamily, 'about *My Fair Lady*.'

'I doubt if there'll be any sort of parallel. But you never know.'

'How about an outright sale?'

Jack looked at me in surprise. 'You don't want an outright sale.'

'I might.'

He was dubious. 'You'll lose on it. I doubt if he would go to more than fifty or sixty thousand, for all the rights, all your work, everything. You know what it costs, to put on a big show like this. They like to cut down on the authors. . . . My way, you ought to make a couple of hundred thousand, spread over the years. It isn't worth doing on any other basis. You'll just be giving it away.'

I did some figuring, and agreed. 'All right. What you said the first time.'

'Good.' Jack Taggart looked over the rim of his glass towards the door. 'There he is now,' he said, and got down off his stool. 'Just one thing, Johnny.'

'What?'

'He's very keen on this. Try and take him seriously.'

' "*Follow that Lord!*" ' I declaimed. ' "*And look you, mock him not.*" All right, Jack. I'll mock him not.'

'That's my boy.'

Close to, it needed very little time to see the point of the warning. It was not easy to take Erwin Orwin seriously, unless you were utterly dependent on his grace and favour; if I had wanted to produce a caricature of the world's idea of a Broadway big wheel, this was the way I would have written him. Vaguely I had known he would be like this, since he was very much in the public eye, and his current musical, *Oh My Darling Josephine*, which Kate called 'that awful Napoleon thing', was just completing its second year on Broadway, and looked all set for a third. But the great man himself, in the flesh, was still a surprise.

To begin with, there was a lot of flesh. Erwin Orwin was an

148

enormously fat man, and he made a cult of it; he positively barrelled into the restaurant, wheezing and snorting, scattering other customers like so much chaff; when he shed his coat, it was like an elephant shouldering its way out of a circus tent lined with astrakhan. He was obviously well known to the Satraps; at his approach, fingers were snapped like castanets, waiters scurried like ants on overtime; even the Head Shah came down into the Persian market-place to greet this rival potentate.

He boomed out a welcome to me: 'Mr. Steele, it's *my* pleasure!' and then he laughed uproariously, for no reason at all, and it was like a thunderclap; his jowls shook, his vast stomach heaved and swayed. I was reminded of an inverted proverb which Kate once made up: 'Inside every fat man there's an even fatter man trying to get out.' Erwin Orwin seemed intent on making this come true.

At the table—and he occupied one entire *banquette*, while Jack and I sat opposite him, on mere four-legged chairs—he went straight into his act. His own personal bottle of whisky, which bore the extraordinary title 'Colonel Wilberforce's Entire Old Sour Mash', was brought out with a flourish, and sent away again with an even bigger one when he changed his mind about his particular-mood-of-the-moment; he finally elected for a vodka martini with three drops—'No more, God damn it!'—of Pernod.

Ordering lunch was an equally tremendous business; while I settled swiftly for grilled marrow bones and an odd, rather whiskery fish which I had enjoyed before, Erwin Orwin inspected dozens of dishes, from *bouillabaisse* to rack of venison, and consigned them all to outer hell before ordering a sixteen-ounce blood-red steak from a certain ranch in Texas where, he claimed, he had once worked as a chuck-wagon cook. (Too much TV, I thought; but it could have been true —he had the build, and the gall to match.) So it went, anyway; as well as the build, he now had money, crude showmanship, and current success; and there wasn't a man, woman, child, or dog in the Court of the Sixteen Satraps who wasn't made blindingly aware of all three facts.

I might have been embarrassed or angry at being mixed up with all this nonsense, but I was neither. Some children behave so outrageously that, as long as they do not hack one's own shins, they are funny. This was one of them. Appalling as he was, I liked him.

He liked me. 'Mr. Steele, I want to make you a rich man,' was his opening declaration, when the main uproar had subsided, the table-hopping by other extroverts dropped off, and we finally got down to business; and when I answered (feeling the need to put my own point of view) that I was a rich man already, he said: 'And you deserve to be, God damn it! You're a genius!' in a voice that rang through the building. It was irresistible, I suppose it was meant to be, but I didn't mind that, either.

Already he had lots of ideas about a musical version of *Ex Afrika*. 'Let me tell you how I see it,' was how he started the discussion, and I would as soon have interrupted Moses' first *précis* of the Ten Commandments. But the principal surprise was how closely his ideas sat with my own.

I also had done a lot of thinking, in the past week; I had roughed out the shape of the thing, what we would have to lose, what we would have to spotlight, what we were trying to say—in short, what the author should do to the show, and what the show should do to the customer. Erwin Orwin, between gulps of raw meat and absurd commands to the waiters, produced a pattern remarkably like my own.

At one stage of this, he said solemnly: 'It's a work of art, of course, but I think we can lick it.' That was the only moment when Jack Taggart, for the most part a silent witness of our exchange, looked anxiously in my direction. But I answered, with equal solemnity: 'That's the only way to stay in the ballpark,' and Erwin Orwin, after a brief flicker of a stare which showed that he knew he was being mocked, laughed with such all-embracing violence that a lamp over his head went out, shattered beyond repair.

It was a good match, in a lunatic sphere of endeavour, and for that single moment I didn't mind whether I won or lost, and neither did he.

But such moments were not meant to last. With coffee and brandy, he asked suddenly: 'What about money?'

'As long as there's plenty,' I said, 'I'll leave all that to Jack.'

'That's what I like,' said Erwin Orwin. 'The artistic approach.'

Jack Taggart leant forward, entering, as I knew he would, exactly on cue.

'Johnny agreed to my idea of a small advance,' he said. 'Against a percentage of the box-office. I'll work out the main details, and bring them along tomorrow.'

'What's a small advance?' asked Erwin Orwin.

'Thirty thousand. Half now, half on delivery.'

Erwin Orwin made a pretence of clutching his temples in agony. 'My God!' he said. 'Brandy!'

Jack Taggart grinned. 'Oh, come on, Erwin! It couldn't very well be less, not at this level. For that, you get the name of the book and the name of the man. *And* all the work he's going to do on it. Don't forget, you said he was a genius.'

'I didn't know he was a genius at this. . . . All right.' His eyes gleamed. 'It's the percentages we'll be arguing about, anyway.'

I drew on my cigar, aloof from this sordid chaffering. A woman, old, seamed, grey-blonde, with the death's head look of an abandoned whore and a mink coat which, in this context, had died in vain, approached our table, and was waved away by Erwin Orwin, with the brusque dismissal: 'Not now, damn it!' There could in this wonderful world, be losers as well as winners. . . . I said:

'Who's going to do the music and the lyrics?'

'Same as for *Josephine*,' answered Erwin Orwin. 'Teller and Wallace. O.K.?'

'Very much so.' I was beginning to like all of this, and now it didn't matter if I showed it. 'I'll have to get together with them, before too long.'

He nodded. 'They'll be ready. I want this thing to get rolling as soon as it can. My idea is, you work out your part of it—doesn't matter how rough it is—so as to give them something to build on, then you can meet up for the real working sessions. Might be a good idea if you all came to stay at my place.'

I said: 'Yes,' not too enthusiastically. I had heard about his place, a vast, split-level, ranch-type hide-away up in the Catskills, with a barn converted into a fifty-seat cinema, and bathrooms labelled 'Guys' and 'Dolls'. 'Yes, that's a good idea.'

'You could bring your wife, too. I hear she's very beautiful.'

I shook my head, Chinese-like. 'She has some pretensions to good looks.'

'That's not the way I heard it.' But he wasn't really interested in anyone else's world, good or bad. 'We've got to find a name for this thing,' he said. 'That's going to be very important.'

'Something with Africa in it,' I said. '*African Song. Song of Africa.* Something like that.'

'I thought of *X is for Africa*,' said Erwin Orwin.

'Or a word with *African connotations*,' I said, shying away speedily.
'Spoor. Jungle. Safari. Drums.'

'*Safari Song*,' said Jack.

'*Notes from the Jungle*.'

'*Jungle Drums*.'

'*Jungle Bells*.'

'*Black and White Notes*.'

'*Black Melody*.'

'*Black Tracks*.'

'*Black Safari*.'

It didn't matter which one of us was speaking; we were gradually
losing ground. The process of just thinking aloud was reaching its
usual murky depths. Presently Erwin Orwin, a man of practice at such
sessions, looked at his watch.

'Well, back to the salt-mines,' he declared. He levered himself up,
quickly enough for so vast a man; when it was time to move, he moved.
'Mr. Steele, I'll be waiting to hear from you. Jack, call me tomorrow
morning. We can probably do this by phone.'

Jack smiled. 'I would doubt that.'

'Well, we can try on a few hats.'

We left the Sixteen Satraps on a swirling tide of other people's
good will. The Head Shah bowed to us—or rather, he bowed to
Erwin Orwin, gave me a distinct if distant nod, and ignored Jack
Taggart, an anonymous man who doubtless had hardly any money at
all. In the foyer, the Persian Lambs closed in, coats and all else at the
ready. Largesse was distributed like over-size confetti. Erwin Orwin,
laughing loudly once more, was whisked away in a chauffeured Rolls-
Royce which had the word 'HIS' embossed on the near-side door; and
Jack Taggart and I were ushered into a taxi by the Turkish-style
doorman, who bowed, touched his finger-tips to his forehead, flourished
his scimitar in formal farewell, and said: 'Come back real soon.'

Riding back up town with Jack Taggart, whom I was to drop off at
his office in Rockefeller Centre, I was well content. Lunch had been
excellent, the drinks very adequate, the company just right for the
occasion; if all lunches were as good, with a cash bonus of $30,000 at
the end, this would be a happy life indeed for the dedicated man of
letters. . . . I threw away the last of my cigar, and gave the credit for
all this where it really belonged.

'Thanks, Jack. Another win for the old pro. . . . I liked Orwin, in spite of all the snow. He ought to be an easy man to get along with.'

'Don't fool yourself. When he gets exactly what he wants, he's as sweet as pie. Otherwise—' he gestured, '—a heart as big as all indoors. He can be the toughest man in this fair city.'

'Will there be much wrestling about that box-office percentage?'

'No.'

'It didn't sound that way.'

Jack Taggart smiled. 'Oh, that's just part of the act. I know what he'll give, he knows what I'll take. The figures happen to coincide. End of drama.'

I sighed. 'Thank God I don't understand any of this.'

'Now don't go into *your* act. . . . That was good news about Teller and Wallace. They're right at the top of their form now. It must have cost Erwin a fortune to get them. Which means that he's really serious about this.'

'How will they be to work with?'

'Strictly professional. You'll have to run to keep up. It's Erwin who takes his own sweet time.'

'How so?'

'He likes other people to work fast. Then he looks at the result, and tears it all apart, and sends it back for repairs, again and again. It's the only thing he ever wastes money on, and he can afford to, with what he's got going for him. He breaks all the rules. I've known him take a year producing a show. *Josephine* was nearly five months in rehearsal. But that doesn't mean *you* can dawdle. Your rules aren't breakable.' Our taxi was slowing for the lights at 49th Street, and Jack Taggart leant forward. 'I'll get out here. . . . How's the book coming alone?'

'Oh, fine.'

'Shouldn't it be finished about now?'

'It's turning out longer than I expected.'

The taxi was stopped. 'I don't want to hurry you, Johnny, but Hobart Mackay shouldn't have to wait for ever.'

'Has he said that?'

'No. He would never press you. But it's in the air, just the same.' Jack decided not to get out, and the taxi moved on a block, caught in sluggish traffic. 'It really is time for that third novel.'

It was now my turn to say: 'Haven't they made enough money out of me?'

'I'm not arguing on that. But they did advance forty thousand, and that was two years ago.'

'This musical will take care of the rent.'

'I'm not arguing on that, either.' The taxi was stopped again, between streets, and he opened the door, prepared to make the necessary suicidal dart for the sidewalk. 'But we want to take care of you, too. You're a writer, with books in your head. Remember?'

I sighed again, more genuinely. 'You and Kate. You ought to set up as Authors Anonymous.'

He laughed. 'Give her my love, and tell her I'll sign up for that, any time.' The door slammed, and he was lost to view, in the moving cars and thronging people of Fifth Avenue.

'Your friend just fractured a city ordinance,' said the cab-driver, a nice young man, a spectacled Negro with a copy of the *Saturday Review* clipped to his sun-vizor. 'But I see no evil. Where to, now?'

'The Sherry-Netherland.'

I was not quite ready to meet the other charter-member of Authors Anonymous.

CHAPTER THREE

IT was half past five before I got back; one thing had led to another, and not by accident. I had not hurried home, because I had enjoyed the session at the Satraps, and did not want it spoiled too soon. I had not hurried home, because if there were lunch guests, as there usually were, I probably wouldn't like them, and preferred to have them out of the way. I had not hurried home, Immortal Bird, because hell! I had something of my own to celebrate.

It was nice and quiet upstairs, as I stepped out of the elevator and let myself into the apartment; quiet, private, un-invaded. Generally, we lived in crowds, Kate and I; they were not always of my choosing, and I suppose—to be fair—my own crowd was not always hers. She had retained a taste for two categories of people whom I found a pathetic waste of time: for those very smart women of the kind who thronged the Colony at lunch-time, twittering like love-birds on the loose, all hat and no head; and for chic, elegant, pastel young men who kept her boredom at bay without introducing anything so crude as the battle of the sexes.

The women I could avoid, and did; the young gentlemen I was trying to freeze out, and it was a long process. (I had been reminded of this by a stop at an equivocal 'Men's Bar' on the way home, where, at my entrance, a trio of emaciated fruits had paused in discussing their affairs, given me long appraising stares, and gone back into committee again. I was only there because I had become thirsty on that particular street-corner, and I hoped they knew it.) But I was always likely to find a nest of such soft-skinned snakes at home, curled up on cushions at floor-level, entertaining Kate with song and story.

At one time the invasion had been spear-headed (to use the term loosely) by a man I specially disliked, Bruno van Thaal, on a visit from South Africa. That had turned out to be a very long visit; indeed, there were moments when it seemed that he might infest us for ever.

Kate loved having him there, for obvious reasons which I could understand; he was first-hand news from home, he was amusing in her own, not-too-generous fashion, he spoke that dialect of the language of South Africa which reminded her of warm sunlight, warm entanglements, warm words at superior social levels. He recalled to her, in a series of quick snap-shots, spitefully focused, what she had 'given up' by marrying me; the aura of success, the pleasures of manipulation, the fun of being Kate Marais in a world small enough to fit a juggling hand.

He had brought a message from Johannesburg, which she had dearly loved, to New York, which she was beginning to find false, and perhaps daunting. Johannesburg and Cape Town had been just the right size for her—conquerable size, made to measure for such slim fingers, speculative eyes, influential comment. She had had the inside track there. In New York, there was no such thing; not for a female stranger, anyway. The city was too big, too alien; it was not to be breached and therefore not to be loved.

Bruno van Thaal had reminded her of the glowing time when she had called the tune.

Perhaps that was the main reason why I had worked to get him out again. He was disturbing: not to me—and I needed no ghost from the grave of Freud to instruct me in the possible mainsprings of anti-homosexuality—but to Kate. Our marriage had given us a year of enthralment, a year of intense happiness, and a year of search and dilemma; the rest, dating from *Wrap-Around*'s fire-stoking success, had been resolutely neutral. I did not want any free-lance archaeologist probing this delicately balanced structure.

But there was no doubt that Bruno had been amusing, in spite of all the things I disliked or found embarrassing (he was now too obvious altogether, and in the freer air of New York he walked with a limp even more pronounced than I remembered). Once again, he had brought her news exactly angled to her own nostalgia. Talking about her gossip-column, and what had happened to it since she left, he said: We do miss you, Kate. The girl who took over wouldn't hurt a fly. In fact, she wouldn't even mention such a rude thing.' It had been just what she wanted to hear, and phrased in her own brittle language, by way of dividend.

No wonder that he had been hard to detach, that he had sparked a tremendous seminar of quasi-residential queers, that there rose from our apartment what Tennyson innocently called the murmuring of innumerable bees.

No wonder Bruno, noting my expression as I broke in upon this honeyed, inter-twining hive, had once exclaimed: 'My dear, we're driving you *out*!' and I had answered: 'Wait and see.' No wonder I had not rested until I got rid of him, and some of them, and celebrated this first win in a crucial tug-of-war by buying Kate the longest, widest, pinkest mink stole ever seen this side of Cinerama.

Too confusing, not important now. . . . I slammed the door shut behind me, dropped my coat in a chair, and marched towards the sound of the ice-cubes.

I was heading for that benign first drink of the evening, to which I was now, by the clock, entitled; the sedative, remedial gin-and-tonic. It was not until I had dropped the cap of the bottle into the poured-out gin, and started to splash tonic-water into the waste-paper basket, that I realised what a long day it had been. Another Jonathan Steele first. . . . (The previous record for relaxed behaviour had been when I lost my balance and plunged an elbow wrist-deep into the wedding-cake at a reception, attended by royalty, at Claridge's in London. Then, I had overheard an austere compatriot murmur: 'Pity about

Steele,' to which his companion, equally austere, had answered: 'I do not agree.') Rocking slightly, I now rectified today's glaring social error, and bore my fresh drink across the hall and up the stairway leading to Kate.

At the top of the stairs, a guardian wardress stood in the way. It was Julia, another person who, fantastically, did not approve of me. She was standing there, silent, watchful, thin as a mahogany rail, her brown brow sullenly opposed to all such uncouth invasions. I said, in her own funny tongue: '*Hoe gaan dit*, Julia,' and moved to get past her. But I had not given her the acceptable password. All she answered was:

'Madam's resting.'

Momentarily I was inclined to think that this might suit me best. Though I bore good news, it would not be good news for Kate; why should I exchange the dusk of contentment for the burning noon-day of the inquisition? (That lunch had really been extremely good.) But then I heard Kate's voice calling me, and suddenly it suited me better still to tell her my story there and then. We would not be different people tomorrow; I would not have a readier tongue, nor she a softer heart. The prudent man who laid down that there was a time to fish, and a time to dry the nets, was concerned too much about the weather.

Smiling at Julia—who was not an enemy, only an ally in a different uniform—I passed her by, and walked through into Kate's bedroom.

I had crossed this threshold many times, on many a diverse errand; most had been pleasurable, some dubious, a few lit or dulled by rage or spite or despair. But they had always had some meaning; as long as she was there, it was never a walk into an empty room. There was some meaning now, as I came in, and saw her lying on the bed under a light silk coverlet, with the lamp-light falling softly on a face full of quality, and beauty, and grave assurance. There was no doubt that she was a person, and—as soon as I could get her into reasonable focus—a damned good-looking one as well.

Kate had been reading; now she laid the book, still open, face downwards on the bed, in the way which enrages bibliophiles and does not worry writers at all, and smiled, and said:

'Sorry I was so low, Johnny.' Then she saw me closer to, in more detail, and added: 'But as long as you've been making up for it.'

'I was celebrating.' I sat down, as I often did, at her dressing-table, and started fiddling with bottles and sprays and manicuring what-nots. When I knocked over a lamp, it made a wonderful clatter, and then went out, like a lamp over Erwin Orwin's head. 'God damn it,' I said, not worrying at all. 'I could have sworn that was a fixture.'

'We will make it so. . . .' She was staring at me, without rancour, without surprise. I was the man she had married, give or take a swindle or two; I was not Caliban drunk, nor Galahad sober. As I took a deep refreshing draught of my gin-and-tonic, she asked: 'What was there to celebrate? Or was it just lunch?'

'More than lunch.' I was looking down at my feet, because that was the way I sometimes liked to tell her things. 'We're just thirty thousand dollars richer than we were at noon, that's all.'

Her voice broke a silence. 'How did that happen?'

Rather drunk, rather pleased, I said: 'They're going to make a musical out of *Ex Afrika*.'

When I looked up, I saw to my surprise that her eyes were closed; the lamplight now fell on a face as lovely, blank, and impenetrable as a sculptured mask on the grave of Helen. I had a coward's moment when I feared to know what those closed eyelids might be concealing —whether anger, or tears, or the insult of laughter; and then I thought: To hell with this guest-charade—it is *my* scene, and I said:

'Well, say something, if it's only goodbye.'

'I could say goodbye.' Her eyes opened, and I saw then that she was absolutely appalled; she was staring at me as if I were something precious lying dead in the gutter. In a fainter voice, she asked: 'What's it going to be like?'

I had been sufficiently warned, but this was still my scene, my very own creation; I was not going to be robbed of any of it. 'Something like the book. But basically it's going to be funny.'

'And called?'

I had decided this, too, the perfect title; it had flashed itself upon a spectral screen, right before my happy eyes, just as I was negotiating the swing-doors of the Sherry-Netherland.

'*The Pink Safari.*'

There was no applause; and when I looked for it, I found that the audience itself had turned away. Kate's head had fallen sideways onto the pillow, like a weary child's. It was as if dead Helen had become one of her own mourners—but a mourner remote as the very ghost of grief, drained dry of tears before they had time to fall. 'Oh, Johnny,' she said, in the most desolate of all the voices I had heard in many a year. 'What's happened to you?'

She was always asking me that, and I could not have been more sick of the question if it had been the key phrase in some absurd oath of loyalty, administered every hour on the hour for six dictatorial years. God damn it, I thought, what more did a woman want from a man, apart from his guts and brains and liking and love and loose cash? There was only his doubt and sorrow left to give. . . .

People always changed; Kate had changed herself, in a thoroughly odd way; why should I be the exception, the Man Who Never Wavered? But this, it seemed, was what she was expecting of me; and in this process of encouragement towards the grail of perfection, it had been a long time since she had approved of anything I did.

What Kate had never seemed to understand was the weird lure of great success; how the man took the bait, and the bait took the man, and no one could say which was the captor and which the prize; how this was a mutual love affair, a pact between doomed and generous equals; and how, unless a man kept pace with the coursing stream in which he swam, he would be no better than any other landed fish, first gasping, then stunned, then dying, then gutted, sliced, and powdered for the pigs to root.

Fish, flesh, fowl, or good red herring, I was not going to finish up on that side of the trough.

Where she had changed most strangely was that she *had*, at one time, understood this process perfectly well. The cult of success had ruled her completely, when first we met; and I had despised, even while I acknowledged, her skill at it. It had then been I who struck the moral attitudes, and laid about me with a sword labelled '*Right, Justice, Truth, and Brotherhood*'—one of that year's longer swords. But presently, when I lost a skin or two of this pristine innocence, and exchanged the sword for a dagger labelled just as Erwin Orwin's Rolls-Royce was labelled, she had turned pale with grief and begun to intone the Credo.

It had started with *Ex Afrika*, that freak of nature—the book of quality which sold like the *News of the World*. Kate had loved it, and perhaps loved me more because of it, and had taken enormous pleasure in its success; and when they made it into a really good film—produced in England, winner of the Golden Lion at the Venice Festival, a

159

perennial stand-by at the 'art houses', and a financial flop in eight assorted countries—she had been happier still. But from then on, I began to fall in her regard.

Chiefly it was the things I had to do, involving the public face of Jonathan Steele; the lectures, the television shots, the glittering life of New York, the 'being seen' in public when she thought I should be crouched in private over my desk, patiently writing books as good as *Ex Afrika*, and nothing else. Even to that stage, I could not afford this shadowy seclusion, and the sort of writing it might produce; the habit of high living—from which Kate herself did extremely well— had us firmly hooked, and the bills were coming in.

Whatever I wrote next had to be a 'property'; worth a minimum of $100,000 before a line of it was set in type; tailored just right for a club choice or a condensed book contract; certain to be read in galley-proof by half-a-dozen competing film companies, and snapped up by the one who got there first with the most. So I wrote *Wrap-Around*, succinctly labelled by one reviewer—the kind of reviewer who waited, his tiny razor a-gleam, for the second novel of people like myself— as 'Sex on the half-shell'. It was about love in idleness.

It was supposed that I had dashed it off, all 700 pages of it, over a couple of high-class week-ends at Palm Beach, with my literary conscience in one hand and a glass of champagne in the other. In fact, *Wrap-Around* was re-written four times, polished and re-polished until the very back of my brain was shining in sympathy, and delivered two years from the day I first tapped out its opening sentence. It left me with what a psychiatrist would call—or should call—the ivory-tower syndrome. Whenever any sniffy practitioner of the profound pro-claimed that it was only too easy to turn one's back on artistic integrity and produce a rip-roaring best-seller, I always invited him to lay aside his current masterpiece, which only his mother would love, and try his luck in my vulgar market-place.

The curious idea that anyone with a typewriter and two reams of quarto white could write books which millions of people wanted to read, died very hard; but it certainly died on my doorstep.

Kate was different; I could not preach this doctrine to her; she wanted me pure and undefiled—and maybe poor and edgy again. I could name the very moment when she took off in final flight from this traditional odour of corruption: a brief and tremendous row over one particular bit of the promotion of *Wrap-Around*.

In the course of their many-hued campaign, Mackay Jones, my American publishers, had sent to every book-seller in the United States a small, foot-square decorative towel, with the message: '*Wrap this around your head, while you count the take from WRAP-AROUND.*' As a matter of courtesy, they sent one to us.

Kate was absolutely furious. Adjectives such as 'cheap', 'corny', 'vulgar', 'crude', and 'insulting' flew through the air like whirling darts; she called up Hobart Mackay to give him a monumental earful, and she hammered on my door at ten o'clock in the morning to deliver a red-hot slice of the same message. I wasn't that sort of writer, she declared, with all the appropriate gestures; I didn't need that sort of promotion; if I had to write bad books, they didn't have to be sold as if they were cut-price salami. Unless this kind of exploitation stopped immediately—and so on.

I couldn't take her very seriously, and I didn't pretend to. Books were things which competed with each other, as well as with all the other merchandise in the show-case; people didn't buy books, in preference to records, theatre-tickets, television sets, and magazines, unless the idea was pushed at them forcefully, right in the flap of their wallet, not with a whimper but a bang. In this field, Mackay Jones knew exactly what they were doing, and I was delighted to leave it all to them.

In the event, *Wrap-Around* had appalling reviews and tremendous sales, particularly as a paperback; the film version won five Academy Awards, including a little one for me; and Kate and I were still merrily spending the half-million dollars it had pulled in. Neither financial flow, inwards or out, had ever ceased.

We needed that money, the way we lived, travelled, and entertained. Taxes came very high; so did chinchilla, and Balenciaga, and Mercedes station-wagons with fitted bar-refrigerators. Kate hadn't suffered too much. . . . We needed that money; and I could not forget that I had worked like a ditch-digger to make it.

I got no credit for that, either; no 'E' for effort, no award of any sort. What I got instead was a sort of running emotional invoice, expressed or implied, for all that she had 'given up' in marrying me; for betting on me as an artist and finding, on the contrary, that I was a pro in a rather rougher league. Of course it was a lot for her to lose; when Kate Marais of Johannesburg, advertising queen-bee in her own right, was transformed into Mrs. Jonathan Steele, little brown hen (with mink accessories), faint second fiddle in a thoroughly noisy *duo*, it was not exactly her fairy god-mother's work.

But she *had* volunteered for it, she *had* chosen marriage in preference to that solitary life on her own self-erected pinnacle; and though she might now feel cheated, the rules were the same as for any other bet on any other breed of animal; those losers who wished to cry into their beer had to pay for the beer as well.

If, suddenly, I was not what she had expected, it was her own fault, her own bad guess. I had become what I thought she wanted, I had copied all that I once admired in her. She had been tough, I was now tougher. . . . I had grown tired of saying: 'But you used to do things like that yourself. Don't you remember?' and of hearing her answer, in appeal or despair: 'I didn't want you to change.'

Thus now, when she asked: 'What's happened to you?' I did not turn baby-blue and shake all over, struck speechless with guilt. I knew what had happened to me. She had.

Yet I loved her, and so had obligations, for many precious reasons; obligations to do something, however reluctant or bad-tempered, when this sort of thing happened. Part of the chronic blackmail of love dictated that I must not leave her out on a willow-limb, weeping. But I did not have to be wildly enthusiastic about the rescue operation.

'Nothing's happened to me,' I answered, cue-ing in an old and sometimes scratchy record. 'We're making a musical out of *Ex Afrika*, that's all. It's got to have a name, If you can put *Pygmalion* to music, and call it *My Fair Lady*, why not *Ex Afrika*?'

'There are hundreds of reasons.' Her voice had dropped so low that I could hardly hear it, but there was no doubt of the tone and feeling; we were playing a tragedy, and I was the foul fellow brandishing the mortgage. 'And I'm not talking about the title, specially, though that may be the most awful part of it, in the end, because it's a sign of what you're prepared to do to the book. *The Pink Safari!*' She made it sound pretty terrible, I had to admit; a great little actress, my wife; scornful, imperious type. 'Why not *Africa on Ice*?'

'Chocolate ice,' I said, beginning to be nettled. 'Let's be really cute, while we're at it.'

'Oh, you'll be cute enough. . . . It was a special book, Johnny.' She was not going to give up on this, nor be turned aside; she had only just started. 'It's still special. And so are you, whenever you choose to be. That's why you shouldn't do a thing like this to *Ex Afrika*. It's not that sort of book, and this isn't your sort of work. How can you write a musical, anyway?'

'Easily.'

'But you're a *novelist*!'

'I wrote the screen-play of *Wrap-Around*,' I said, without too much humility. 'Take a look at the Oscar. It's downstairs.'

'So?'

My humour wasn't getting any sweeter. 'It made a damned sight more money than the film of *Ex Afrika*. I can do that sort of thing, that's all. I can put *Ex Afrika* on the stage, in a different version, and I want to do it.'

'It doesn't need a different version. It doesn't deserve to be treated like that. It's a work of art.'

'I'm sure we can lick it.'

'Oh, don't be such a clown.'

'Well, don't be such a Kate.' The reference, long established, not often used, was Shakespearian; there was a family tradition that I would never wish to tame this shrew. I did not feel so sure of that now. My drink was finished, and I wanted another one; but I could not quit this field, at such a moment. Now she was actually stopping me drinking. . . . 'Why the sudden tenderness about *Ex Afrika*, anyway? That book had nothing to do with you. I wrote it *against* you.' These were old wounds, hopefully covered, often forgotten; they came to ugly life at moments like this, when anger reddened the scars, and the naked eye could trace them again, and the raw flesh could feel. 'You left me flat, just when I needed you most. Remember? You very nearly destroyed that book. I had to write it alone. And drunk. And sad. You did your best to wreck it. Well, you're not going to wreck it now! Not any part of it. Not this new part, especially.'

I had spoken more bitterly, more destructively, than I might have chosen on a clear day under friendly skies, and Kate's face showed it; she was always surprised when my temper proved short, and she was surprised now. Well, she had started it. . . . Her eyes had become huge, like the children's eyes one sometimes saw in pictures of famine, or flood-disaster, or gross cruelty; they were all I was aware of, across the room, under the circle of lamplight which divided us one from the other, two people sundered by an unforgiven past.

For a moment I felt ashamed of the crude stroke I had dealt. The

163

man who swung the sword must always feel this pang, at the moment of impact; even if it were a pang of triumph and release, it still involved an instant of true communion with the victim. So I was sorry for Kate. But I still could not forget the time, the murderous gap in our joint lives, when she had not been sorry for me. Not cured of anger, nor purged of bitter feeling, I listened unrepentant as she asked:

'Is that why you're doing this? Some kind of revenge?'

'There's no question of revenge.' I was not absolutely confident of the truth of this, and I moved on, to ground I was more sure of. 'All I know is that I can't afford to pass this thing up. It's too good an idea, and I need the money too much.' I wasn't feeling apologetic about that, either. 'Do you realise how much we've spent, in the last six years?—nearly six hundred thousand dollars, and all the rest has gone in taxes, and we still haven't a cent, and I'm overdrawn from here to London and back again, and I owe Hobart Mackay forty thousand dollars on a book that's stuck at page fifty-four.' I paused, for the needed breath. 'It's just a matter of plain arithmetic. Unless I make some money soon, this whole thing will collapse, they'll move in on me, and I'll finish up with an apple in my mouth.'

She shook her head from side to side. 'You'll be no worse off than the day I met you. And you don't need to rip through money like that. It's childish. It doesn't prove a thing.'

'It's fun. And you've had your share of it.'

'I don't want that sort of *share*. Johnny, why don't we simplify this whole thing? Why don't we——'

'I don't want to simplify!' Now it was my turn to shake my head, and I found that I could do it just as well as Kate. 'I haven't climbed up this mountain, just to slither down the other side. I haven't worked up to the hundred-thousand-dollar-a-year mark, in order to creep around like a mouse that's had an illegitimate baby. *The Pink Safari* is going to make lots more money, spread over lots of years, and this time I'm going to hang on to it.'

'But you ought to be *writing*.'

'My delight is in the well-turned cheque. . . . This *is* writing, Kate. Different format, that's all. *Ex Afrika* is still a valuable property——'

'It's not a property, damn you! It's a book, and it's time you stopped being a——a sort of literary gangster, and wrote another one.'

'I can't afford to write books. . . .' I tipped my chair, and leant back against the dressing-table; the lamp crashed down again, like the theme of the very music she was now doomed to hear, the opening chord of a weepy Wagnerian twilight. 'Don't you understand that I don't want to reform the world, free the slaves, carve a niche in the hall of fame, contribute to permanent literature, or be a man of letters, with a beard instead of a tie and a book every fifteen years. All I want to do is write whatever I take a fancy to next, make a steady hundred thousand a year, and enjoy everything to do with the process.'

'But you've shown that you can do all that. Why not write your very best, like the man said.'

'Who cares what the man said?' This had been Hobart Mackay again, gently preaching the virtues of a literary conscience. 'Honestly, if I have to listen to another higher-thought expert talking about the duty of the artist towards his environment, I'll stuff the whole thing up his jersey! *I have to make money!* And I can do it, too.'

'I know that.' She also had her theme, and was equally doomed to repeat it. 'But we don't need money. Not on that scale. We don't have to live like this.'

'I want to live like this! You taught me, and I love it!' Once more, I felt I had to batter out all the old arguments, to which she never listened—to which I scarcely listened myself, since I knew them by heart and was convinced of them. 'Look, you think I'm a mercenary, or prostituted, or whatever the word is nowadays; more of a publicist than a writer, more of an institution than a man. That's all very well for you—you've never been poor. Well, I have. Kate, I've had a tough life. I've been damned hungry. I put up for years with the most lonely, dreary kind of poverty, before I got it off my back. . . . You don't know what it's like, to have that whole load lifted off you.'

'You didn't find it a load, in those days.'

'Well, I would now. And I'm damned if I'm going to take it all on again. Because I've conquered it, and it's going to stay conquered! Once and for all, I'm not going to turn back. It gives me enormous satisfaction, self-conceit, whatever you like to call it, to run one of the biggest one-man businesses in the world; to have the Mercedes and the boat and this apartment, as public symbols of success; to stay at Claridge's or the Plaza Athenée, go round the world when I want to, waste money, show off. . . . I know all my faults, and I don't give a damn about any of them. I've worked a long time for this, and I'm going to keep it.'

'And you haven't changed.'

'Maybe I've just grown up.'

While I finished speaking, she had been drawing the coverlet up to her chin, as if to keep the sordid world at bay, to preserve herself spotless from this poisonous fall-out. I stood up, and came to the foot of the bed. I was used to being unpopular, and it was time for that missing drink. Watching me, she said:

'Now you're leaving.'

'I'm going downstairs.'

She nodded solemnly, recognising a symptom. It wasn't too difficult: I could have given her a hundred like it, without cracking a book. 'You're always going downstairs, Steele. Or walking out of rooms. Or holing up in your study. Wrapping yourself in a cocoon. Insulating yourself.' It was a sad recital, not an accusing one; she was listing the forlorn facts of our life, from her own end of the microscope. 'All you want to hear is someone agreeing with you, and writing a cheque. . . . What's happening, Johnny? Why can't people reach you any more? why can't I?'

'I've just been telling you,' I said, 'in richly-coloured and expensive prose. A dollar a word, at least. None of it was new, I know, because the message is the same. There are things I want to do. I'm going to do them.'

'Without compromise? Without even talking about it? I turned my life upside down for you.'

'I think you were very wise. . . . My God!' I said, near to irritation again, 'all this three-act drama, just because I want to write something, and you don't happen to like it.'

'It's more than that. Otherwise we wouldn't be like this. In love in vain.' The strange phrase caught my attention, and I sat down on the end of the bed, ready to be my sweet and reasonable self once more, in spite of all the opposition. But it was not very likely to work. 'You've gone away from me. You've gone away from almost everything. *The Pink Safari.*' This time she said it, not like an insult, but like a repeated note of mourning; like '*I was desolate and sick of an old passion,*' like '*O Absolom, my son, my son.*' She really *was* low. . . . '*The Pink Safari.* You used to care about places like South Africa. You used to feel and suffer with them. Now you just use them for jokes, like a Jewish comedian making vicious fun of the Jews. Yet your own son died, because there was dirt and poverty in a place we were using as a playground. Have you forgotten that?'

Arguing with a woman. . . . The man who compared it to trying to fold an air-mail copy of the *Times* in a high wind had been dead right. I realised now that there had been two ways of resolving this current division, at least for the moment, and that I had picked the wrong one. I had tried talking. The tongue had been my unruly member, and it had proved very much the second-best weapon.

With a vague idea of correcting this, even at so late a stage, I wormed over and stretched out on the bed beside her. She did not move then, nor when I pulled aside the coverlet and sank down into her dear and disapproving arms. Presently it became evident that this was not the cure for either of us; and I realised it before committing myself too shamingly, and began to fall asleep instead.

Just before I faded out, I heard Kate say, from a long way away:

'I don't think I can bear to watch you doing this.'

'This' was not *this*, and I knew that also, and there wasn't a thing in the world, either waking or sleeping, that I was going to do about it.

By one of those rare chances which come to the aid of the maritally afflicted, it turned out that she would not have to watch me doing it, after all. A couple of days later, when I had barely progressed beyond sharpening a few pencils, and Dorothy Kilgallen's column had reported: '*Jonathan ("Ex Afrika") Steele readying a musical of his best-selling tome for Broadway biggie Erwin Orwin.... Don't get lost in that jungle, Johnny,*'—a couple of days later, Kate came into my study. Her face was serious, which was nothing new, and devoid of make-up, which was. I made ready for another crisis, and I was not disappointed.

'That was Gerald Thyssen on the telephone,' she said, without any other lead-in. I had heard the phone ringing, and, as usual, had left it to more willing, female hands. 'You remember him.'

'Yes,' I said, not too enthusiastically. I had enough enemies already, without importing them from the southern tip of Africa. 'Is he in New York?'

'No. He was calling from Johannesburg.' She came round the corner of the desk and, to my surprise, put her arm tight round my neck. 'My father's ill, Johnny.'

'Oh.' I never had the right words ready for other people's woes, but I tried my best. 'I'm so sorry, Kate. Is it serious?'

'It sounded like it.' Her hands, restless and strong, were now pulling and kneading my neck, communicating a desperate anxiety. 'I'll have to go. I'll have to go immediately.'

'Of course.'

'Can you fix it all up for me?'

'Yes.'

Lucky Kate, I thought, as I reached for the telephone and the receptive ear of American Express. Lucky Kate, to have a rich husband, and be able to fly off to South Africa with a single snap of the fingers, for a mere $1,600. Lucky Steele, to be able to spread this jewelled cloak for his beloved. . . . Of course I could not help being sad about her father, if she was sad herself; it was not possible to be neutral— no man could become so detached an island, however hard he tried. But her father's illness was not exactly a sword-thrust through the bleeding heart of the world-famous author.

We have never liked each other, the old man and I; and the kind of relationship which she maintained with him—close, loving, dependent, interested—had occasionally irked me. No girl should need such a father, with such an all-capable husband on hand. . . . But who would argue the finer points of family loyalty, at such a moment? Faced with a crisis which would take her from me, and towards him, I was still terribly good with American Express, and they with me.

'Tell them, two tickets,' said Kate suddenly, while I was busy on the phone. And as I turned to take proper stock of this: 'I want Julia to come with me,' she said. 'It'll be so much easier.'

I nodded, while the man on the other end of the telephone reeled off alternative connecting flights from London, Lisbon, and Lagos. I had not really thought that there was any question of my going with her, but I was glad to be sure.

'Don't let Julia get caught down there,' I warned her. 'As a Coloured fugitive from the glorious republic, or something. Hang on to her passport. You know the trouble you had, getting her out.'

'I can fix it again. Or Gerald will.'

'Two bookings,' I said, back on the phone again, making a swift choice, like any hot-shot executive with a sales'-graph spearing his vitals. 'Pan-Am to Lisbon, B.O.A.C. from there. It'll save five hours.'

Later, when Kate was choosing what should be packed for her journey that night, and I was sitting on the window-seat in helpful indolence, she asked:

'What about you? Will you be all right?'

'Oh, sure,' I answered. 'I want to work, anyway. I'll get somebody to come in. Or I can go to the Pierre.' A patter of raindrops beat against the window behind my head, and when I turned, I did not like the look of New York at all. It was damp, it was grey; no guaranteed sun shone here, nor would do so for many a long week. 'Actually,' I said, on an impulse, 'I think I might take off into the blue myself. I can work anywhere, at this stage.'

'Why not?' She was preoccupied, sorting shoes, underwear, jewellery, furs—all the secure armour of womanhood. 'It'll do you good to get away. Where will you go? Florida?'

'I think Barbados.'

She came to, at that, and raised her head and stared at me, across an armful of clothes which would no doubt have kept the traditional family of five moribund Koreans alive for a year. 'Oh Johnny—what a fantastic idea. Do you really want to go back there?'

'I liked it,' I answered. And then, since this was for many reasons a particularly crude thing to say, I added: 'I could do with some sun, too. And I want to look at Negro faces.'

She had turned away again. Woman's basic dilemma, I thought. She had to pack, and plan, and worry about her father, and the house-keeping, and what to wear at a possible funeral; there was scarcely time for the big-scale, raw emotions; scarcely time for battle.

All she said was: 'Don't you remember what the faces were like?'

'They alter,' I said. 'Like people.'

It was clear that I needed a complete change. We both did.

CHAPTER FOUR

I DROVE down from New York, taking four days on the trip and then leaving the car at Miami; it was only 1,300 miles, and the slow approach, the gradual melting of the winterised spirit, the warming trend from bleak New York to a Florida which really was doing its damnedest as the Sunshine State, was much more fun than any quick flip by jet. The soft sell was the one which best suited escapist authors.

So I loitered by the way, though the way—mostly U.S. Highway No. 1 —was not invariably enchanting.

There were some curious contrasts on that journey, the contrasts of two or more Americas. There were the rich and rolling grasslands of Virginia, and the bare, scratched, exhausted earth of South Carolina. There was poor drab Georgia, suddenly blossoming into rich, well-kept Florida within the space of a few yards of highway. There was the magnificence of Palm Beach, which must command some of the finest houses in the world, compared with the vulgar stucco horrors of Daytona and Delray. There were Spanish mission-churches four hundred years old, and then the miles of garish motels, and the snake-pits and monkey glades and alligator farms, and the temples erected to pecan fudge and peanut brittle, and all the orange-juice you could drink for ten cents (children, fifteen).

Above all, there were the signs—signs by the million, all the way from the New Jersey Turnpike to the last screaming mile of the main street into Miami. There must have been a clear thousand miles of exhortation—to eat, to drink, to sleep; to spend, to save, to invest; to visit, to explore, to sing, and dance, and pray; to ride, walk, swim, fly, and sail; to mount elephants, to crawl along the sea-bottom, to catch tuna and tarpon, to wrestle with alligators and shoot the rapids in the Tunnel of Love and send a peach-fed ham home to the folks. There were twenty-seven flavours of ice-cream, and a flavour of nothing at the same time.

I would like to read the journal of the Man Who Did Everything. But it would have to be posthumous.

At the beginning, I started to 'collect' odd signs, and then the spirit of research faded and I gave up. With the sun warming my hibernated bones, and the Mercedes going like an elegant bomb, I wanted to enjoy myself, not probe the sociological horrors of tourist travel. But a few of them stuck in the memory. They ranged from whimsical motel signs: 'MADAM, YOUR SLEEP IS SHOWING,' and 'OUR HONEYMOON SUITES ARE HEIR-CONDITIONED,' to the sinister: 'SAVE AMERICA— IMPEACH EARL WARREN,' and the cynical: 'SOUVENIRS OF ANYWHERE'. But after I encountered 'IT'S PARADISE IN THE GARDEN OF EATIN'', I lost heart. There was a limit to what one creative writer could take from his competitors.

As soon as I was air-borne, however, the voyage itself took wing. The only available plane, on the day I wanted to leave, was an island hopper, reaching Barbados by a wayward route which included Jamaica, San Juan, St. Croix in the Virgin Islands, Antigua, and Martinique; and the idea of taking off and touching down six separate times, instead of sampling one shot of each manœuvre, seemed to involve lending several extra hostages to fortune.

I had never really enjoyed flying, since the day when a plane from New York to Washington, with me in it, developed a high-pitched scream in one of its engines and had to make a forced landing at Newark, New Jersey. The magnificent array of fire-engines, ambulances, police-cars, television equipment, and undertakers' touts which awaited our arrival on the runway had turned me a dull shade of green at the time, and remained in the memory ever after. Since then, if I flew at all, I flew fortified.

I was fortified now, on a rum basis, and continued to be so for the best part of twelve hours, as we zig-zagged our way south. It was not at all an ordeal. With each stop, it grew sunnier and warmer, and greener, and friendlier; it was a pleasure, every time, to dip down upon a new island, and emerge from the plane into the benevolent air, progressively shedding topcoats, and other coats, and waistcoats, and eventually ties, as the air grew more benevolent still, and the bars cosier, and the drinks longer and cooler.

I made several life-long friends in the course of that journey, all for the right length of time—about an hour; and there was always something to watch, even if it was only staid citizens buying funny island hats, and being self-conscious about them, and then gradually growing to look as if they had worn them all their lives. As far as Puerto Rico, where we were bereaved, there was a most ravishing stewardess on board; about eighteen, hopelessly incompetent, quite lovely. All the male passengers were turning handsprings and putting up with terrible service, just to catch a glimpse of those shy young breasts, that delicious puzzled face.

'Regular Madonna of the airways,' said the man next to me, with absolutely no warranty, practically sobbing into one of his martinis. But I wasn't going to argue a technical point. She had just bent over me, and beamed her breathless smile, and murmured: 'I declare—I'll forget *myself* next!' When we finally lost her, we lost a certain zany element, and no more coffee was served in Old Fashioned glasses; but we lost a lot of the *décor* as well.

Her place was taken, as a focal point of interest for the observer, by a quintet of people who, on the next leg of the journey, honoured us with their presence. They were five largish, fattish, oafish young men, distinguished by an enormous self-assurance. They broke all the rules enforced upon ordinary travellers; they stood up during take-off and landing, wandered in and out of the pilot's cockpit, clogged the aisles, monopolised the pint-sized bar, talked loudly and determinedly about recent air disasters, exhibited an embarrassing gallantry towards any woman travelling alone, and generally impeded and annoyed the paying passengers to the point when a lot of us wished we had gone by sea.

They were delegates on their way to a convention of airline public relations officers, enjoying a free ride with the aim of popularising air travel.

But all things pass, including such thick-skinned idiots as these; and next, between St. Croix and Antigua, we were entertained by a genuine drunken nuisance. He was a great bulging hulk of a man, wearing a ten-gallon white Stetson which might have been Texan, and could have been Albertan—or any other part of the world where the men look like bulls and the bulls look ashamed of it. He had a load on when he came aboard—and who was I to comment?—and he improved on this at a phenomenal rate; the process involved, apart from a fresh drink every ten minutes, a servile and scurrying attention from anyone for whom the bell might toll.

Above all, he was argument-prone, and proud of it; everything was wrong, from the buckle of his seat belt to the ice in his drinks; it was clear that he had assumed a God-given right to be where he was, and for all others a God-given duty to minister to his needs. He was up, we were down; he was rich, and everyone else was poor.

Such men were only funny if, in the end, they were defeated; and eventually this one was. But before that happened, we had a long way to go, and a lot to endure. He got into one tremendously vulgar row with one of the stewardesses, a nervous Jamaican girl who was doing her best in exceptionally trying circumstances, and who was finally dismissed with the bellowed command: 'If you don't want to be a hostess, for Christ's sake change your job! If you want to keep it, bring me another martini-on-the-rocks. Pronto!'

Later, after Antigua, there was another rancorous scene when the vacant seat next to him, over which he had spread his coat, hat, brief-case, camera, and feet, was needed for an incoming passenger. He rounded out a noisy refusal to give way with the ringing declaration: 'If these cheap trash are first-class passengers, then we're using the wrong words.' After that, the captain was called, a man of a different calibre, and the culprit—dispossessed, deflated, and dry—subsided into mundane sulks.

There were plenty of ways, I thought virtuously, to be drunk on an aircraft, without using this one.

Then suddenly it was the dusk of a long day, dusk at Martinique. As we climbed back on board for the last lap of all, the burnt smell of the tropics mingled with flower scents—of hibiscus, and bougainvillea, and wild orchid—to make the bowl of night a perfumed blessing. A row of scarlet poinsettias, standing sentinel at the edge of the tarmac, caught the lights overhead, and gleamed darkly, and shimmered, waving us farewell.

By way of mundane contrast, while we were waiting for our final take-off, the captain came out of his cockpit, walked purposefully down the length of the passenger compartment, gathered up a handful of air-sickness disposal bags, and went back into his lair. But the incident was funny rather than foreboding; at this stage, it did not seem to matter much—and in the event it did not matter at all, since the short flight was rock-steady all the way, and no disaster threatened. By logical deduction, I worked out that he probably wanted to wrap up some spare sandwiches for home consumption.

We flew low, across a dark sea just restless enough to shiver when it caught the track of the moon. The stars came up to bear us company; the Dog Star for mariners, the far-away Southern Cross for romantics, the winking Pleiades for decoration. Presently we picked up the glow of Bridgetown Harbour, and the ribbon of lights along the shore-line; I took my last legal swig of rum at the company's expense; and then we touched down in the warm, welcoming air of Barbados.

It was eleven o'clock on a velvet night; twelve hours from Miami, and the forsaken world; a gentler pace altogether, a release from care, a private accommodation.

The reporter, a small, earnest young Negro who had never seen me, nor anyone else, on television, but had actually read one of my books, asked:

'Mr. Steele, what do you think are the chances of the novel surviving, as an art form?'

173

Though this was not something which worried me to distraction every waking hour of my life, I was ready with the answer. It began: '*From Vanity Fair* to *The Shoes of the Fisherman*, from Flaubert to Steinbeck, the novel has always been——' and ended, four paragraphs later, with: '——in a stronger position than ever.' It was a good answer, and I hadn't used it for more than four months, and never in Barbados; it came out as smooth as hot chocolate sauce. The young man scribbled industriously, while I watched the waves bending the sunlight as they broke over the edge of the reef, fifty yards away. Bliss, literary bliss. . . . The reporter crossed his question off the little list he had prepared for the interview, and then propounded the last one:

'What do you think of the prospects of a new West Indian Federation?'

I began again: 'I think it's a very hopeful sign that——' and then I thought: *What the hell*, and broke off. We had had a good hour of this, and an hour, though no hardship, was enough; it would make a full half-page interview anyway, topped off by a photograph of the distinguished author gazing seawards, manuscript in hand, cigar in mouth, creative gleam in eye. Therefore, instead of pontificating, I answered: 'I honestly don't know. I've only been here three days. I'd prefer to wait a little longer before giving an opinion,' and then stood up.

It was dismissive, but not, I hoped, too brusquely so. He had taken a lot of trouble with his questions, which were a vast improvement on those of his average American and British counterpart, who didn't read books, not even their titles, and only wanted to know how much money one had made in the current financial year. And (I thought, as he took his courteous leave) when I had said: 'I honestly don't know,' it was, though an evasion, somewhere near the truth. I didn't know the answer, aside from guesswork and *cliché*, and basically I didn't care. Barbados, God bless it, bred this sort of indefensible neutrality.

It was in the air, the climate of disengagement. Every morning, when I awoke, it was to one of those dawns which only a very clever painter, and no photograph, could ever reproduce; lucid as water itself, fresh as virginity, soft as the feathers on the wings of sleep. One woke to this pale, yellow-green light with quick pleasure, instant awareness, and clear-headed in spite of all past and current excesses. The new day beckoned, and could only be answered by a matching readiness.

I would dress, scruffily and swiftly, and pour a drink, and go out to meet it.

Pouring a drink was no blasphemy. Once you were installed in the West Indies, rum did not count as alcohol. A whisky-and-soda before breakfast might have meant all sorts of deplorable things; neat rum at dawn was nothing, nothing at all. Already I would have felt eccentric without it.

My cabin was on the shore-line itself, a few feet from high-water-mark and a prudent distance from the main core of the hotel, a sophisticated log-palace dedicated to the belief that North American travellers wanted nothing so much as to feel that they had never left home, and were prepared to pay $50 per person per day to achieve this immobility. I spent the minimum of time there, and the maximum in the sun, my back turned to plush civilisation, my face to the sea.

The beach, though freshly manicured each morning and evening, was still for beach-combers; and wandering along it, as I did every day at first light, was a boyhood exploration. It was never a rich harvest; there were no pieces-of-eight, no doubloons or jewelled pectorals, no over-spill from Captain Morgan's vanished cache of loot.

But there were other things, trophies of a minor chase; tiny scurrying crabs, and flying fish which had strayed off course, and strange shapes of driftwood, and beautiful shells, called Auroras—double-winged, delicate, shading from orange to palest blue or pink; and fingers of coral, and the bleached skeletons of gulls, and fronded weed-tresses, and sand wrought by the grind-stone of a million years, as fine and white as sea-salt itself.

I would plod a slow, meandering, bare-foot course, or bend to look at new treasures, or stand still, staring over the blue-green lagoon to the deep water beyond, listening to the waves growling as they washed across the reef. On the far horizon, the sails of the flying-fish fleet dipped and swung and held taut against the North-East Trades. . . . It was at such moments of trance, in this rum-soaked, sun-blessed, sea-circled paradise, that there was a temptation to contract-out for ever; to cast off and sail—by island schooner, by dug-out canoe, by catamaran, by raft—anyhow and anywhere, as long as it was far enough away; to let the lousy argumentative world go by, and dis-appear without trace, and emerge five years later with the best book ever written about *bêche-de-mer* or Gulf Stream flotsam; with a skin the colour of rubbed mahogany, with no answers to any questions except to say: 'It was heaven.'

But heaven, I knew, must wait, perhaps for ever; it did not sit with

175

reality, with top-heavy bank loans, with books about crowded people; it could not enthrone Erwin Orwin. And now, here was the argumentative world again, on my own salty doorstep—a small oared boat which had been fishing close to the reef, and was now hauled up in shallow water, surrounded by people like quarrelsome gulls, market slatterns arguing the price of fish. . . . I would leave them chaffering over their prey, and wander home again, and breakfast off pawpaw and fried dolphin and slightly-spiked coffee, under the eaves of my own humble cabin—rented at tourist-trap rates, panelled in satin-wood, vacuumed not less than once every morning.

Already I had loafed for three days, and it was nearly time to work, and I was ready for it.

Three days had been enough to take the temperature of the island, and sample its offerings, and appreciate the difference between the life of the side-walk and the life of sand between the toes. The resident queers were wearing white shorts that year, which possibly gave a new hazard to the inquiry: 'Tennis, anyone?' and the steel bands were banging out a devout offering called '*Jesu Joy of Man's Desiring Bossa Nova*'—a translation which had excited a certain amount of local protest, but was no more offensive than the close-harmony monks and hit-parade nuns of our northern paradise.

I had lunch with a doctor friend at the elegant, old-style Barbados Club, and picked up the essential gossip. (On a small island, the grapevine on who-was-sleeping-with-whom was, if anything, more hotly debated than on Lower Broadway.) I had a swim at the Yacht Club, and paid other regulation visits: to Sam Lord's Castle, to the Garrison Savannah race-course, to the oddly-named Bathsheba beaches, to the thriving inner harbour, patrolled by policemen straight out of *H.M.S. Pinafore*, and still called the Careenage.

I ate Inside Soup, and callalou, and grilled flying-fish, and pepper-pot stew. With very little urging, I sang a perennial calypso favourite, '*Back to Back, Belly to Belly*', at a night-club where, to destroy the edge of pleasure, they cooked the steaks in rancid coconut oil. I donated a transcribed first page of *Ex Afrika* to the local museum.

I bought a tartan dinner-jacket, made of Madras silk, unwearable except among sympathetic friends, behind closed doors, south of the tropic line.

I visited, on impulse, a small grave.

It was high on a southern hillside, overlooking the sea; as I pushed open the creaking gate of the cemetery, and walked the criss-cross pathways of stubbly grass, and came at last upon the miniature plot, all that now remained of '*Timothy, beloved only child of Jonathan and Katherine Steele, aged 1 year and 6 months*', my mind went quickly back.

The coral headstone was green-moulded already, and shabby, and weathered by sun and wind; I remembered when it had been shining new—and when there had been no headstone at all, but only a small gash in the ground, and a pile of fresh earth waiting to fill this fatal hollow.

I remembered Kate, on that bright and terrible morning, turning to bury her face against my shoulder, in hopeless grief; and my own face, still and frozen, in a mask only wearable because a man did not cry. That had been Timothy, beloved only child of privilege and protection, tripped and tumbled just as he had learned to run, brought to his first and last stillness by enteric, which only killed poor people in dirty houses—and there was another memory there, of Kate crying: 'No one dies from that any more!' in frantic disbelief.

But within an hour of her saying it, someone *had* died; and within a day, for tropical reasons, the someone was buried where I now stood.

At that moment of remembrance, I missed Kate, with astonishing sharpness, with a lonely hunger. Later that night, lonely still, I thought of writing to her, to say—I did not quite know what. But the mood passed. I had lived alone a long time, in the old days, and I could encompass it still. And the trigger of this weak relapse was three years rusted. . . . I put a different piece of paper in the typewriter, and went willingly to work.

Once started, it ran smoothly and steadily, because I knew exactly what I wanted to do, and could thus control the wandering child. A week for the skeleton, two weeks for the lightly-fleshed form, and I was well on the way to the complete 'rough outline' for which Erwin Orwin had asked, as a starter. I enjoyed the writing; when I re-read bits of it, they made me laugh quite a lot, though I could not guarantee that this was a good sign.

I grew very sun-burnt, from working on my patio at the water's edge, and a little sleek round the middle, and a little dreamlike, on and off, from the steady intake of rum and pressed limes. People— passers-by, hotel guests, local spies—bothered me at first, and then they gave up. The word went round that I was working, and furious if disturbed; and though people often regarded this as a social challenge, a long-haired myth to be disproved at all costs, I managed in the end to make my point.

When the customary Canadian business blockhead—florid, complacent, stupid as the ox behind his eyes—plunked himself down in my spare chair, with the words: 'I wish I could afford to just sit and scribble, ha ha ha!' and was sent away with a metaphorical flea in his ear and a literal kick in the pants, my isolation was pretty well established.

The pile of typescript grew; now the pages were numbered. Presently I could sit back, and clasp my hands behind my head, and stretch my legs and wiggle my toes, and think: *This meal is really on the fire*. I had reached the stage when I was rewriting and touching up, rather than conjuring magic spellings out of the warm Barbados air.

Then I became aware, as a man does when he has time to wiggle his toes, of a very beautiful girl, a resident of my district.

She was not staying at the hotel, but further down the beach, at a lesser establishment which catered to younger and slimmer people; and she was there all the time. The good news was a matter of gradual release. First, I came to realise that there was a long-distance, pretty girl around; then, on a morning paddle along the edge of the water, I saw her closer to, and found that she was far more than pretty. At much the same time, she became aware of me, and before long we had established a mutual observation society. About her, I learned a little more each day, and I imagined that she was doing the same as I.

She spent her time, for the most part, alone, either reading or sunbathing. She sat under a shabby beach umbrella, with a towel, a mesh-bag full of oddments, and sometimes a drink; but under the umbrella the girl was far from shabby. She was tall, and not too slim; she had beautiful legs; she was generously breasted, and her hips—for want of a better word—were as full and rounded as a strong man could wish for.

Sometimes she wore dark glasses, and robbed the world of a pair of large, decorative eyes. She had very fair hair—model's hair, done in a different way on different days; sometimes like a beehive, sometimes like a shower-cap, sometimes close to the shape of her head, which was very good. I liked that version best.

She wore a sun-suit, red-and-white striped; or a plain black swimsuit; and once a bikini, designed, I would have said, for a smaller frame. She swam well, and walked as a tall girl should. She did not have to tell me that she knew I was there. We both understood all about that.

She would look at me, and I would look at her, and we then would agree to give our eyes a rest. Once she smiled, but it was not really a smile for me. So far, it was just a smile, though with a teasing quality, more than enough to trouble the blood, if ever the blood were willing. She really was lovely.

In fact, she was a rare beauty, in this Barbados wasteland of over-stuffed tourist femininity, and of haggard resident harpies, run out of England for God-knew-what brand of public harlotry in the middle thirties. It was a pleasure to know that she was on deck, to be sure that the beach would be adorned, for most of the daylight hours, by this handsome and glowing creature. I could always just see her, far away, from my working platform; and during the last week, when I was working less, I saw her more and more.

She was beautiful, and mostly alone. I did not really want to do anything about it, and then suddenly I did.

It was six p.m. The sun was dropping down, the sky fading from pale blue to pale green; the coral reef, bared by low tide, had fallen silent. Anticipating dusk, the bats were already weaving overhead, trying out their radar. In more sophisticated climes, it was the hour of the assignation; of the quickly-swallowed cocktail, the very late nooners or early, top-of-the-bedspread love-making; the confederate world of *cinq-à-sept*. In Barbados, for various reasons, the transition from work to play was not so sharply divided; we had no offices to leave early, no patient wives to keep waiting. But there was still no doubt that these twilight hours intensified the playful urge. Perhaps, in spite of an island simplicity, we were all still city boys at heart.

It was six p.m. I had done enough work for that day, and was restless for something else; I did not even specially want another drink. The girl, I could see, was still at her post. It was high time for us to meet.

She saw me coming, and looked away, no doubt in utter confusion. I could even divine her thoughts, or make them up for myself, which was even more satisfactory. (Who was this lone romantic figure, wandering along the beach, coming nearer with every passing moment? Could it be? Yes, it was! It was the mysterious stranger of the last ten days, the pale despairing loiterer, the lover of her secret dreams! Ah, pray Heaven that he would speak! She would die if he did not, she would surely die. Be still, betraying heart! Down, fluttering bird!)

When I was level with her small encampment, I walked up from the tide-mark, until I was standing by the beach umbrella. She looked up, and said: 'Hallo,' in a matter-of-fact American accent.

She was wearing her black swim-suit, and observing it I said the first thing which came naturally to mind. 'You mustn't catch cold.'

'I was just going in,' she said. 'But sit down.' As she spoke, she swung a yellow beach-robe round her shoulders, obscuring a view which really had been as lovely as I had guessed. 'Are you through work?'

'For today.' I sat down beside her, not too close, not too menacing; there was a delicate balance here, to be preserved for at least the next five minutes. 'How do you know about my work, anyway?'

'Well, I know who you are,' she answered. 'Somebody told me. And I saw you typing.' She smiled suddenly, changing a lovely face into an open-house invitation. 'Jonathan Steele. Easy.'

After that, everything else was easy.

'What's your name?'

'Susan Crompton.'

It sounded vaguely professional, but I could not yet identify the profession. 'How long have you been here?'

'About three weeks.'

'All alone?'

Her face clouded briefly. 'Sort of. I was with some people. But they had to go home.'

'All alone now?'

'Yes.'

'Are you hungry?'

'Not yet. But I will be.'

'Would you like to have dinner with me?'

Her face was grave again. 'Yes, I think I would. Where?'

'Let's start at my place. About eight o'clock. I'll send a car.'

Her bright hair caught the last of the sun as her head turned. 'That sounds wonderful. Can I dress up?'

'I think that's a very good idea.'

We dined by candlelight, under envious eyes. My hotel was staging some sort of gala dinner that night, involving floodlit coconut palms, long trestle tables laden with serve-yourself food, a steady stream of tourists gorging and screaming, and two orchestras, count them, two —a steel band playing calypso, and a smaller dance group filling in the awkward gaps. We managed to withdraw ourselves a little from this bacchanalia, and sat at a side table under the trees, where we could watch if we wanted to, and ignore when we chose; we were served as rich men squiring beautiful women should be served, in any democratic society. At $50 a day, I wasn't going to carry any plates, not even for this one.

The girl really had dressed up, and the result was something for me to be proud of, and the rest of the mob to covet at a distance. I had been sure that she would wear black, the addiction of young things who wanted to look like women of the world; in most cases, they might as well be wearing their school uniforms. But Susan Crompton had settled for white, the badge of chastity. It was fair to say that, in this case, only the colour looked chaste.

The white dress revealed, in benevolent detail, a figure remarkable for its invitational candour; and above the expectant bosom and the creamy-brown shoulders, her face—young, alive, ready to laugh, ready to melt—had a beguiling beauty. She sat there, a few feet across the table from me, with the candlelight linking us and winking on the wine-cooler; the trees arched over our heads, and above them was a far-distant sky, black, star-pricked, the canopy of our intimate night. But I only looked at her. Thus close to, she seemed as feminine as perfume, as available as the next bed, and I could not take my eyes off her.

I had to admit to being overthrown. I was out of practice in this area, of course, and vulnerable for other reasons, other frailties of armour. But even so, even so. . . . If the food had not been so good, I would have started eating her there and then.

She was something of an eater herself, which I welcomed; so many girls in this category of looks seemed to believe that the ideal of beauty was the kind of skinny lesbian known as a 'top model', and nibbled accordingly. This girl was hungry, and didn't care who knew it, and was going to do something about it. . . . The moment of this discovery was also the only moment when she seemed really young, almost touchingly so, in spite of all the glamour and elegance. While we were ordering, she read the menu from beginning to end, with many a sigh, and then asked:

'Do you think I could have caviar?'

'Yes,' I said. 'Next question.'

'It's *so* expensive.' She looked up, almost as if gauging my mood; she might have been an orphan at a convent picnic, wondering what the nuns would stand for. 'Can I have steak as *well* as lobster?'

I could not guess whom she had been dining with lately, but he sounded economical. 'You can have two of everything, as far as I'm concerned. . . . Susan Crompton, you look absolutely wonderful!'

I wanted to practise her name a bit, just in case. Sometimes, in moments of stress, one used the wrong one.

'Thank you,' she said, and gave me her ravishing smile. 'I feel wonderful. For a change.'

I ordered dinner, and the champagne I now felt like, and then asked:

'Why? Haven't you been enjoying yourself?'

'Not much. Something went wrong.'

'What was that?'

'Oh, just something. . . . You're married, aren't you?'

'Yes,' I said, readily enough. If she wanted to make the point at the outset, she was welcome to it. This thing was not going to stand or fall on a technicality. It was not even in the lap of the gods. It was in hers and mine, and as far as I was concerned I could feel it there already. Either we would, or we wouldn't, and the key to this traditional puzzle was not going to have much social connotation. Freedom alone would not get us into bed; nor would the stigma of adultery keep us out, if that was where we were headed. 'Yes, I'm married.'

'Where's your wife?'

'In South Africa. Six thousand miles away.'

She nodded to herself, accepting the answer, unsurprised; as if all the people she met had 6,000-mile wives, as if there weren't any other kind of marriage, nor breed of men. We listened to the music, which already had an agreeable, insistent beat; and then the caviar arrived, and after that the evening started swinging.

She lived in New York, she told me, between hearty mouthfuls of everything in sight. Doing what? Having fun! And for a living? Oh, all sorts of things.

She had started, at the age of fifteen, as a movie-theatre usherette, but had soon given it up. 'It was too dark,' she said, and her eyes grew wonderfully dark at the thought of it. 'And I was embarrassed, anyway.

The things they asked you to do in the back row!' She had acted as a doctor's receptionist, and sold magazine subscriptions on the telephone, and been elected 'Miss Representation' at a used-car dealers' banquet in Miami.

She had walked on at the Met (gypsy-girl in *Carmen*), and off again at a ski-school in the Adirondacks, where the Austrian instructor insisted that they all lie down before they even learned to stand up. She had demonstrated lots of different things at exhibitions—potato-slicers, stain-removers, floor-waxes, sewing-machines.

'I can do monograms on a sewing-machine,' she said importantly; and when she saw me grinning: 'Well, it's not so easy,' she went on, smiling also. 'It took me two whole weeks to learn. And I used to model at fashion shows, till I put on too much weight.'

'Weight?' I said. 'Oh, come on! If you're too big anywhere, I'm Napoleon.'

'But it's true,' she answered. 'They don't want girls like me. You have to be as thin as a stick, so they can hang any sort of clothes on you and get away with it. They've all got a thing about little boys, anyway. I used to go through agonies every day, trying to keep my weight down. I starved! A few pounds here and there can make a terrific difference.'

I poured out some more champagne. 'I'm ready to confirm that,' I told her. 'And three cheers.'

'Oh, it's all right for *that*,' she said, leaving me to wonder. 'But professionally it's terrible. I used to do TV commercials too. But then you get identified with the product, and that's no good, either.'

'What was the last product you were identified with?'

'It's all very well to laugh. I had *a whole year* as one of the silhouettes for Playtex.'

Mostly, I realised, her story was keyed to the phrase 'I used to'; there had been little clue as to what she was doing now, and how she had come to Barbados, and why. I was going to raise the point, when she said, out of the blue:

'I'm having a wonderful time tonight. I do want to thank you. And I like that coat.'

'It's terrible,' I said. The switch of subject for some reason, had been rather moving: like a very pretty child remembering its manners. 'But what the hell? I'm a writer. . . . Why did you suddenly say that?'

She was playing with the stem of her wine-glass, waiting for the next course, which was the much-desired steak. I watched her twining fingers, and pictured them elsewhere, like any dreaming boy. The music wove its pathway round us, soothing and sensuous at the same time. She saw my eyes on her bosom, and she said: 'You like me, don't you?' and before I could answer she went on: 'I thought we'd been talking enough about me, that's all. You're so important. I know that. People keep saying things about you. . . . Do you always drink so much?'

'Yes.'

'I just wanted to know.'

'I'm used to it,' I said. 'And champagne doesn't count, anyway.'

'It counts with me. . . . Do men really say they're "investing in a girl"?'

'Well, yes,' I answered, brought up short. 'I suppose they do. In certain circles. But why?'

'I heard it somewhere.' She smiled, and this time it was for me. 'In certain circles.'

'How old are you?'

'Nearly twenty.'

'I'm thirty-four.'

'Why, Mr. Steele,' she said demurely, 'thirty-four isn't *old*,' and we both burst out laughing.

The steak came, and was steadily demolished by both contestants. This girl was excellent for all the appetites. A couple I knew vaguely at the hotel—they were English, the woman as leathery and loud as an old sergeant-major, the man positively pop-eyed at the first waft of female youth—tried to crowd our party, and were eased out, not too subtly. (But writers had absolutely no manners, it was well known.) Susan Crompton, sighing still, disposed of the last few licks of the *filet*, and asked: 'Can we wait a little before the strawberries?' as if loath to forfeit or even to hurry a single strand of the night's enjoyment.

She was on the right lines, and I was willing her to stay there. I poured from the fresh bottle, and went back to something which had stayed in my mind.

'Why didn't you go on with television?' I asked her. 'I know all those commercials are damned stupid, but there must have been plenty of other things to do. Like ordinary acting. The way you look, there should have been lots of work for you.'

'The way I look,' she answered, frowning for the first time, 'there was lots of work for me, but it was never in front of the cameras.

184

Honestly, Johnny—' it was a great pleasure thus to hear her say my name, '—you've got no idea how those bastards operate. . . .' Her face had now taken on an entirely novel look, of dislike, of reminiscent contempt. 'To start with, every single man expects you to sleep with him, as a matter of course, as part of the deal. Whoever they are. Assistant producers. Cameramen. Dialogue writers. Every stinking little hanger-on who's remotely connected with show-business takes it for granted you'll lie down for him, before he'll do a damned thing to help. It got to the point when I thought, if that's the way it is, I might as well——' She did not finish the sentence; instead she took a sip of her drink, and started another one. 'It's the same everywhere. I actually did take a screen test once—or very nearly—and that wasn't for free, either.'

'What happened?'

'Everything,' she said crisply, looking back on it with grim disdain. 'It was one of those nights. . . . I was in Chicago, doing the cabaret at a lawyers' convention, and afterwards I got in with some film people, and they said, you look so gorgeous, why not come and take a screen test tomorrow? You could be famous overnight. They have screen tests in Chicago. They have everything in Chicago. So I said, O.K., I'd like that very much. Then the party broke up, and I went to bed. In the middle of the night, there's a knock on my door, and it's one of the film people from the party, and before I knew it he pushed me inside and just jumped on me. He had this robe on, and underneath he just had his woollen underpants, and they had moth-holes in them. . . . He worked me back to the bed, and he said: "How about it, baby? I didn't want to say anything earlier on, I didn't want to take advantage of my position." His position!' She expelled a long breath, through lips which suddenly had a vicious twist in them, older than the oldest victim of betrayal. '*His position!* He was one of those jerks they have hanging round the studio, slapping two bits of wood together and saying, "Take one". And you know—' she was now almost breathless with indignation, '—that's exactly what he did say. He said "Take one, baby", and then there he was, lying on top of me.'

'Good heavens!' I said, genuinely appalled, both at the picture, and at the bitter edge to her voice. 'What then, for God's sake?'

'I was eighteen,' said Susan Crompton, 'but I still had my strength.' Already, in the space of seconds, she was something less than bitter; her lovely brow was clearing; this was danger escaped, and therefore not too awful to remember. 'I brought my knee up hard, the way mother teaches you in survival school, and then I called the front office, and kept on calling till they sent someone up. I don't know who he was; one of the girls said they keep this guy they call the rape clerk, but I don't know. Anyway, he said, like, we don't want any scandal in this establishment, do we, and then he said, could it have been your own fault, and then by golly *he* wanted to settle down and talk things over quietly, like two reasonable people! Men!' She ended her recital, with a sharp toss of the head which made her hair glint in the candle-light. 'You really are a wonderful bunch, you know.'

'Don't look at me,' I said. 'What happened about the screen test?'

'That *was* the screen test. They sent word down next morning, they'd mixed up the dates and couldn't fit it in. And that was all I ever heard. I think that was the day I decided I was doing all this on the wrong basis.'

'How do you mean?'

Her eyes lighted up suddenly; but it was for the strawberries, which did indeed look luscious. 'Oh, I don't know,' she said. 'But all the wrestling, all those propositions. . . . And what did I have to show for it? I was getting less famous every day.'

This was still not clear. 'Was that what went wrong down here?'

She laughed. 'Heavens, no! That was something else again.' She was now busy eating, at ease once more, and certainly resigned to most of the current hazards; it seemed that she had forgiven us all, because we could not really help it. 'Men,' she said again, on a gently chiding note. 'And it's not as if I was just dumb and stupid. After all, I practically graduated from college.'

'I wish I had enrolled at that establishment. Where was it?'

'Well, it was a sort of finishing school. In San Francisco. The first day we were there, they told everybody: "Go away and write an essay called *Who I am and why I came to college.*" One hundred words. Then they worked out what courses we ought to take.'

'What did they choose for you?'

'Courtship and Marriage.'

After that we danced, because it was by then high time that I had at least an arm-and-a-half round this ravishing creature. A man could spend just so much energy on the twirling capework; thereafter, honour and appetite combined to make a definitive engagement essential.

There were certain young women of whom you knew, as soon as you touched them, that their next word—even their next movement —would be 'yes'; and for me, Susan seemed to be one of these. She was a close dancer, supple and generous; we had circled the floor only once before I felt as if I knew her all over. My terrible tartan dinner-jacket was thin, and through it I could feel both the shape and the warmth of those delicious breasts; when our thighs touched, hers lingered closely and frankly before moving aside. The moving-aside was not exactly a bereavement.

Yet I knew very soon that my overall guess was going to be wrong. For all her compliance, she seemed to have made up her mind to remain cool; cool to me, cool to the music, cool to the fact that my body was growing patently ambitious. She must have known what was going on —she would have to have been wearing armour-plate, to think other-wise; but she was not really joining in, so much as riding out a storm which she hoped would be brief.

Her own pressures were skilful and receptive, yet they remained friendly; and at this particular moment I was not looking for a friend. I did not need to be psychic to realise that no measurable or mature progress was being made; this message, for some reason, was being relayed swiftly, continuously, and finally, by a body which, though almost frantically sensual, belonged only to her.

At the age of thirty-four, one did not become bad-tempered when facing this particular *cul-de-sac*; and when we went back to our table we still liked each other, and the evening was still much more fun than any other social occasion was likely to be. Indeed, when I cooled down a little, I was intrigued. There were some odd pieces in this appealing pattern; and unless it was a simple teasing operation, which I doubted, they combined to make up quite a puzzle

What was she doing in Barbados, solitary, beautiful, and probably broke? What was the thing that had 'gone wrong' down here? And that remark about 'investing in a girl'—what was that meant to be? A caution? There were plenty of other things. The vivid and disgusting picture of the near-rape had been frankly revealed—but to what end? Enticement?—or warning? And the other remark about doing things on the wrong basis. What was the right basis, and was she using it now? And what was this thing all about, anyway? If it was a seduction, who was doing it to whom, and what was holding it up? And if it was a stand-off, why had she started the exercise in the first place?

She could have been lovely. She might even have been hungry. But having told me so much, she would surely have told me this also.

I did not ask her any of these questions; by now, we both wanted, by mutual agreement, to enjoy what there was, not what there might have been. All I did was confirm the fact of exclusion.

When the music re-started, about half an hour later, I said: 'We try again?' and she answered: 'Help yourself,' with a smile and a look which told me that she knew what *this* was all about, also. I had not been mistaken; the rules remained the same. Though she nestled in my arms agreeably, and such pretty witch-crafts as a chance visitor might feel were enough to set up a thriving pulse, yet her whole body was once again saying No.

Later, we sat and talked on the patio outside my cabin, and we held hands, because—with moon rhyming with lagoon, and night with delight, and sea with you-and-me—it would have been silly to do otherwise. Later still, we walked back, barefooted, along the beach towards her hotel; and when we were near it, we stopped and kissed candidly, our toes in the water, our faces in moonlight, our bodies one single shadow on the sand, and, in the flesh, warm and confluent.

At that moment, I wanted her, with the most urgent need of all the evening; and at that moment she put her refusal, at last, into words.

'No, Johnny,' she said, her arms still twined round my neck. 'Not tonight. I'm just not in the mood.'

'You could be,' I said. 'And I presume you already know about me.'

'Oh, I know you want me,' she acknowledged. 'And of course it could be mutual. It just isn't, that's all. I can't really explain why. I'm just not too keen on men, at the moment.'

'How long will that last?'

'I don't know that, either.' But she was not being tough, nor even unkind. 'I'm sorry,' she said softly, and turned within my arms, brushing my whole body, as a loving girl should. Her hands, it seemed, were ready to move obligingly. 'And I know what it's like for you. . . . Can I take care of anything?'

'No,' I answered. She really was an astonishing character; as knowledgeable, understanding, and generous as a man could wish for, if he had to make a second choice. 'No. Though thanks. Top prize only.'

'Good night, then, Johnny. Lovely evening. And no hard feelings?'

'Well,' I said, 'that's one way of putting it.'

We laughed together, and on laughter we kissed again, and on laughter we parted. I was left to cool my ardour with champagne, under the wheeling stars, staring sombrely at an ocean as restless and alone as myself. The champagne and the night were both beautiful, but they were not her. Nothing was her, and I knew it for many hours afterwards, hungrily aware of what another man in another part of the forest had called divine discontent.

She was still not too keen on men, the following night, but at least she told me why.

The daylight hours had passed as they usually passed in Barbados; dreamily, gently, happily, under a tropical sun whose burning edge was eased by trade winds traversing three thousand miles of surging ocean to console us. I had worked most of the morning, cleaning up the masterpiece, which was now almost ready for other eyes; then, after lunch, I had given Susan a long-distance wave, and joined her in a swim out to the reef and back, and a little collecting of sea-anemones, and some frank admiration of a body which, when dripping wet, was as good—as very good—as naked.

Then we drank at our ease, and talked the sun down, and kissed a temporary goodbye, because there was some obvious mutual pleasure in kissing. Now we were keeping our second formal appointment.

First we had gorged ourselves afresh. Already, traditions were springing up around this particular contest, and that night they involved a procession of caviar (again), grilled dolphin, chicken off a turning spit, and *crêpes suzettes*, with (God bless us every one) a lime-sherbet as a chaser. Susan justified this atrocious menu with the words: 'It's good for you to eat'; in the circumstances, it was one of the least disinterested remarks I had ever heard.

Afterwards we went for a slow drive through the Barbados maze of winding inland roads; lost ourselves in mid-island; had a brief wrestling-match in a sugar-cane field ('Not here,' she said reprovingly; 'don't you know, everyone does it in the cane-fields?'); made our way back to the coast by star-navigation; and finally settled down in a beach night-club, a few miles out of Bridgetown. If there was one thing I had to do, it was to put my arms round her again, in legal circumstances and permissive surroundings.

Our surroundings were certainly permissive; the place was impenetrably dark, the *décor* chiefly palm branches and bamboo partitions, the dance-floor thronged by entirely motionless couples, from whom an occasional moan was the only evidence of life. But if one was in the mood, it was just right. I was in the mood.

She was looking very pretty that night, as always, in a green dress of off-the-shoulder, liberal design; though her hair, which yesterday had been smooth and closely shaped to her head, was now a top-heavy, *bouffant* swirl, like a small pitch-fork of hay. I did not like the effect at all; but perhaps, I thought, it would come undone later. There was no harm in looking ahead.

It was a night and place for confidences. I played with her hand on my knee, and told her all about being a writer; she leant back in her chair, superbly aware of a ravishing display, and told me all about being a girl. Presently, when we had groped our way round the dance-floor, and finally given it up (we were really too old for this branch of the Tunnel of Love), she began to answer the questions that still intrigued me, and by degrees her story was out.

She had come down to Barbados with a man. 'You probably guessed that already,' she said softly, her fingers stroking my wrist. 'It's not the surprise of the year, is it? Not for me, anyway. . . . I never have any money, I couldn't afford this sort of trip myself. . . . You know how men offer you trips and money and things, as soon as they know——' she left that one in the air, as she sometimes did, and finished instead: 'Well, anyway, that's what I do sometimes.'

'How many men has that involved?'

'About twenty.'

'*Twenty!*' I had not meant to react so swiftly, nor to grimace, but she must have seen my face in the half-darkness, for she went on:

'Well, it's not like every day and night, is it? It could have been *hundreds*. . . . I told you, it just didn't make sense, doing it for phoney screen tests and interviews with agents and things like that.'

'Well, all right,' I said. Naively, I felt bereaved, though I guessed that the feeling would pass. She was that kind of a girl; the girl who was eternally forgiven, forever kissed and taken back; and if not by the same man, then by another man prepared to adore her in spite of all transgressions. 'But it still seems a lot of people.'

She was frowning. 'I thought you'd be more——'

'More what?'

'Understanding.'

'So did I.' That was true, and I came round to the realisation even as I pondered it. 'And so I am. But tell me more, Susan. Who was the one down here?'

'He was a mistake. He was terrible.' She was sitting back again, staring squarely at her miscalculation, and not liking it at all. 'He seemed just right in New York, and then it all went wrong. It's always guess-work, and this was a bad guess. But what can you do about that? If you say yes, and they make all the arrangements, you've got to go through with it. To begin with, anyway.'

'What actually went wrong?'

'Well, as a starter, he turned out to be mean.' This must have been the first time she had talked about it, and she was very ready to take the chance. 'Mean like an expert. . . . I told you, he was perfectly O.K. in New York. He spent all sorts of money up there. I suppose that was the investment bit. Then he must have begun to add it all up, and he was a very slow counter. . . . First there was the mink stole. He promised me a mink stole. He didn't have to. But he did.'

'And?'

'He kept making excuses. In the end he *rented* one. In Washington. With my initials on it, but only for a month. He said, let's not lose our heads over this, by the time we get back it'll be warm weather again.'

'Frugal,' I said.

For once, she wasn't listening. 'That was just the beginning of it. We went to lousy motels all the way south, and he'd argue half the night about the price of the room, and if there was one where we could share a bathroom with someone else, he'd take that. . . . We used to go the whole day on coffee and doughnuts, and then for dinner he'd go out and buy *one* chicken-in-a-basket and *one* carton of French fries, and we'd sit down and share the feast, watching complimentary TV. Then we came down here, because he had a free pass or something, and after that it got really bad.'

'No wonder you're so hungry,' I said. But it was not at all funny, and I squeezed her hand, ashamed that I had tried to make a joke out of it. 'Sorry, Susan. . . . What did go wrong here?'

'The whole bit,' she answered. 'He was just a pig, and soon he didn't bother to pretend anything else. . . . He was dirty. He never took a bath, or shaved, or changed his shirt, or anything. And he was horrible to share a room with. You'd think he'd never lived in a house before. He used to do it in the wash-basin.'

'*Do it?*'

'You know—wee-weed.'

'Oh.' Visions of truly bizarre behaviour evaporated, in favour of mundane eccentricity. 'Lazy as well. . . . But the thing I can't understand is, how you picked him in the first place.' I squeezed her hand again. 'You know, you're truly one of the most beautiful girls I've ever seen. Why give it to a man like that?'

'I told you—it was just a bad guess. Back in New York, he was just another Joe, with a nice car and plenty of spare money and a few good jokes. . . . I suppose that was the advertising front. He was in advertising. He was quite good-looking, too. . . . What worries me is what you do if you actually marry a man like that. It could happen! I mean, suppose you wake up and find you're tied for life to a man who absolutely revolts you.'

'You usually spend more time choosing.'

'I'd like to believe that. . . . Well, anyway, there I was in Barbados, with a mean man who behaved like a dirty animal. . . . I can't tell you what he was like, Johnny. He used to scratch himself for hours. And he had enormous yellow toe-nails. Like tusks! He never cut them. . . . It's not funny,' she said, seeing my expression. 'They slashed me!'

'I'm sorry,' I said. 'Some of the hazards of the profession are new to me.'

'It's not a profession,' she answered. She brooded for a moment. 'At least, I don't want it to be. . . . I suppose that's really why I walked out. He was disgusting, and it wasn't any fun, and I had a little money left, and I was still me. So I said, that's all, my friend, thank you, and he went back to the States with the mink stole, and I stayed on here, by myself.'

'When did all this happen?'

'About two weeks ago.'

'And how much money left now?'

'Not much. But enough. And I've got my ticket back to Miami.'

It was the end of her story, and it had been sad, and moving, and somehow important. The thing which struck me most forcibly was the terrible vulnerability of a girl like this one, as soon as she had opted for a life set in this pattern. What started out with glamour and hope and excitement, tailed off into rented minks, French fries, intrusive toe-nails, and just enough money to get half-way back home. . . . If this was what could happen to the pick of the candidates, how fared the ugly and the old?

Of course, I was probably being naive again. The fiasco—and all comparable set-backs—were entirely her own fault; she could just as easily have chosen to be the world's most beautiful waitress, and her worst hazards would then have been gravy-stains and fallen arches and ten-cent tips. But, stern commonsense apart, I still could not help feeling sympathetic, and vaguely protective.

There was, I found, no residue of distaste. There was quite a lot of jealousy, but that was something different. . . . Above all, this girl, who had put herself in the public domain, still kept intact her own private quality; she had remained a free spirit, and she had not feared to cut loose when she fell out of step with what she was doing.

It seemed to me that she would never weep, nor blackmail, nor beg for favours, nor move in and try to clean up the masculine half of the human race, no matter how brutally she might be brought up short by its imperfections. She would shrug it all off, and start again.

The two of us had been silent for a long time, while the music beat its pathway through the gloom, and the smoke shrouded the dubious stationary figures on the dance-floor. It was Susan who spoke first.

'Thinking?'

'Just a little.'

'You want to go?'

'Yes, if that's O.K. with you. Let's breathe some fresh air.'

'I hope that wasn't meant for me.'

'No. No! Actual oxygen. I've had enough of this zoo.'

She did not argue about that, either.

That evening's farewell, on the beach outside her hotel, was far more gentle than the night before. It was not that I wanted her less; there was, as I now found out when I kissed her, only one thing which would slake that particular thirst, and it wasn't lime-sherbet. But I had discovered quite a lot more of what she was thinking and feeling, in the course of the evening; I recognised her reasons for withdrawal, and they were good ones. She had been man-handled, in several disgusting sequences, and she was still showing the scars.

If she needed time to clean the decks, and forget the taste of ordure, then time she could have.

In all sorts of ways, she was now, more than ever, just what I wanted.

But this tender and forbearing *courtoisie* was not the sort of thing that lasted—not with Susan Crompton, nor with me. She didn't need time, I decided next morning, as soon as I awoke, refreshed and ambitious once more; she needed encouragement. I walked along the dawn-deserted beach, and ate breakfast, and downed the first medicinal daiquiri of the day, with a total recall of appetite. Faced by man's most momentous challenge, I felt lion-hearted, and lion everything else. Today was going to be the clincher, or else.

All other urges apart, I was in a wayward mood of benevolence, the sort which, in northern latitudes, encouraged men to hand out chinchillas to comparative strangers while the martinis ran out of their ears. I made a quick trip into Bridgetown, and came back with the best example which the modest town afforded, in the realm of diamond bracelets. Then I changed back into Tropical Alert, and walked along the beach again, my little present in my hand, like any dutiful envoy; and there was Susan, just spreading out her wares under the beach-umbrella.

It was bikini day, and I wasn't quarrelling with that, either.

I sat down, and put my hand firmly round her ankle, by way of making the first shy contact.

'That was a message from your sponsor,' I said. 'Good morning, out there in TV-land.'

'Who are you?' she asked. 'My fraternity doesn't have that grip.'

'The man of the moment.' I proffered the jeweller's case, unwrapped, brash as a bare chest. 'I was just passing the flea-market. . . . This is for you, Susan. I thought you deserved it.'

She opened it, and gave the traditional gasp of surprise. Then she looked up, her eyes shining. 'But Johnny—it's beautiful!' Swiftly the bracelet was out of the case, and swiftly clasped round her wrist; she turned it this way and that, allowing the sun to set up a very respectable sparkle. 'Is it really for me? It must have cost a fortune!'

'It cost about the same as a small car, and I don't care who knows it.'

'Oh,' she said, watching me, but smiling, 'it's like that, is it?'

'Just like that.'

'You don't have to give me presents.'

'That's all I want to know. . . . How about coming on a picnic?'

'I'd be a fool to say yes.'

194

'I'll get the hotel to set up a lunch for us. A shaker of daiquiris and some wine and lots to eat. You like chicken-in-a-basket?'

'Now just a minute!' she began.

'It's all right,' I said. 'I'll make the jokes, you—er—make the coffee.'

Suddenly she put her hand on top of mine, which had left her ankle and was thoughtfully playing scales up and down her leg. 'Thank you, Johnny,' she said softly. 'I was afraid I'd scared you off.'

'Afraid?'

'Just that.'

'I think we'll have smoked salmon and cold grouse and some of that Brie, don't you?'

'You mustn't put yourself out.'

'The very opposite.'

'Hey!' she said. But she was laughing. 'So early in the morning.'

'Actually,' I told her, and I almost meant it, 'I thought we'd just wander off somewhere in the car, and enjoy ourselves.'

'I'll have to change, and get ready.'

'Come like that,' I said, eyeing the bikini.

'Absolutely not.'

'The bracelet will stop the sunburn.'

'Slacks and a shirt,' she said, 'for a very minimum.'

'All right,' I agreed. 'I'll pick you up. Twelve o'clock. "*When the bawdy hand of the dial is on the prick of noon*." Romeo and Juliet.'

'You're full of alibis this morning!'

'Yes,' I said. 'I'm taking over that department.'

It was cooler inland, on the high ground which formed the spine of the island, as we jogged along in the minute hired car which was all that was viable for the Barbados road-system. Susan's idea of clothes suitable for a picnic turned out to be lemon-coloured stretch-pants, and gaping scarlet shirt with bare black foot-prints stencilled on it, and a nutty kind of frayed straw hat such as I wore myself, and gold-strapped Roman sandals; this unabashed get-up did not improve my driving, though it did no harm to the scenery. The clink of bottles from the basket on the back seat made music for our holiday mood.

After a lot of local inquiry and back-tracking—Barbados was sign-posted strictly for those who knew their way around already—we found the place I was looking for. It was an elegant ruin of a former plantation house, transformed alike by time and by a film company which had tried to make it over into Hollywood's image of British colonial magnificence; but the later excrescences—fake plaster colonnades, a garden staircase with false magnolias stapled to the balustrade—were now becoming happily overgrown, and the superb shape of the old house, of pink coral stone weathered to a honey-gold, was beginning to assert its mastery.

We wandered hand in hand through a succession of bare, echoing rooms, and kissed in strange places—larders, slave-kitchens, a vast oval ballroom whose ceiling had sagged down in one corner to meet a floor itself buckled and rotted out of shape. Some of it was sad, but we were not sad; if we had a vanished past, it had vanished in favour of a buoyant, impulsive, living present.

We were followed round, all the time, by a small ragged smiling boy, who might have been the official guide. I gave him some money quite early on in our tour, but he continued to cling to us, wide-eyed, watchful, interested perhaps in human nature for its own sake. True to artistic integrity, we did not censor the show on his account.

Then it was time for pastoral delights. We found a place for our picnic, on a high bluff of rock with a magnificent view eastwards to the sea; far away, caught by the sun, the marching lines of gleaming white breakers advertised the surge and assault of the great Atlantic. I broke out the bar with a flourish, and we drank to scenery, and sunshine, and us; figured against a pale blue sky, Susan looked very lovely, and I told her so, with words always at the command of a writer with half a tumbler of rum cocktail in his hand. She seemed pleased, but admitted to being hungry as well.

'You be cook, then,' I told her, pointing towards the picnic-basket. 'If they haven't been nice to us, I won't pay my hotel bill.'

'Is that place very expensive?' she asked, already rummaging.

'Yes. Much too. It's like all these Caribbean paradise hideaways. They start by being simple and unspoiled and cheap, and then five different airlines decide to run a daily jet service from New York and Toronto and London and Paris, and the prices go up through the roof. What they sell you here is only what they got for free in the first place—the sea and the sun and the climate. And that hotel of mine is only a sort of Dog-patch Hilton, anyway.'

She spoke indistinctly, through a smoked salmon sandwich. 'Why do you stay there, then?'

'It's comfortable,' I said, munching also. 'And I can ring a bell when I want anything, and they leave me alone. It's been a very good place to work. That's getting to be the most expensive thing in the world— privacy.'

'It must be wonderful to be a writer,' she said, traditionally.

'Now don't you start. . . . You haven't got a manuscript you want me to look at, have you?'

'I used to keep a diary.'

'And you'd like me to turn it into a book, and go fifty-fifty on the proceeds.'

She laughed. 'Is that what people say?'

'It's one of the things.'

'What else?'

'They say: "If only I had the time, I could write a best-seller." They say: "*My* life has been much more interesting than that girl in your last book." They say: "Do you plan it all in advance, or do you wait for inspiration?" They say: "Why don't you write a book about my uncle? He's been round the world *twice*." They say: "Do you write with a ball-point pen?" They say: "You're not at all what I thought you'd be like." '

'What did they think you'd be like?'

'Dignified, I suppose.'

'M'm.' She was thinking, and of course eating at the same time. 'Johnny?'

'What?'

'*Do* you wait for inspiration? I've always wondered.'

I laughed, and rolled over on my back, and stared up at the flawless sky, with the sun hot on my face, and the earth under me warm and sustaining. 'No. You sit down and start writing, and if you don't sit down you starve. Inspiration is for people with rich old aunts. . . . I'm waiting for you to have inspiration,' I told her. 'In the meantime, I couldn't be more content if I was up to my socks in Krug.'

'What's that?'

'A superior brand of champagne.'

'I'm so glad. . . . Why do you want me?' she asked suddenly.

I addressed the listening sky. 'Because you look like a million dollars and you make me feel like a man.'

'Didn't you feel like a man before?'

'Not specially.'

'What happened to you?'

There was a faint echo there, and I knew what it was, and turned deaf to it again.

'I got in with a fast crowd. They go for canasta.'

'I was just interested,' she said, rather far away. 'I wondered what made someone like you want one girl more than another, or want to change suddenly. . . . If we made love, would you tell me?'

'If we made love,' I said, 'I wouldn't have to tell you.'

'Oh, tra la la!' she said, suddenly light-hearted again. She pretended to search through the picnic-basket. 'I can't find it. Don't tell me you forgot to bring it.'

'What?'

'The violin.'

'Now just for that,' I said, 'I won't play my piece.'

'It probably needs a rest.'

It was good to be mocked, when mocking promised such sweet certainties as these.

I think we were both feeling happy on the same secure plane, and sun-drugged, and dreamy—the things which accorded with the spirit but not necessarily the act of love, especially not the first act. We found this out a little later on, when the cool wine was finished, and all the food; we smiled at each other, and presently took to the woods, but it was in search of shade, not of cover.

There was a grove of trees nearby, mostly pine and spreading oak, topped by a lone cork tree which might have served as the banner for my other field of endeavour. We lay down under this interlacing arch, withdrawing into the dappled, speckled shadows, like prudent animals. We kissed, with good average intensity, and Susan was freer with her body than she had ever been, and we saw in each other's eyes that, by mutual accommodation, the animals need not be prudent.

But it was siesta time, not love-making time. I did not especially want to make love to her then. *We* did not want it. Though we were moving towards our rendezvous, and we both knew it, we knew also that it would hold a little longer for us. Ours was not to be a cane-field free-for-all, nor love among the pine-needles; no lemon-yellow stretch-pants were going to be involved, either. We were waiting for the most liberal licence of night.

So before long we smiled again, and moved gently apart, and went to sleep instead; and we slept untroubled, like babes-in-the-wood who knew their way both round and out, until the sun went down and the cool relief of twilight returned to our earth.

When we awoke, yawning, thirsty, bone-happy, we clasped hands and wandered once more out of the forest, as good as when we went in. Perhaps there were not many people in the world who would have believed us; and there was one on hand who patently did not. This was the small attendant boy. I gave him some more money as we climbed into the car; but—unfair, suspicious, prurient boy!—he watched us go with shadowed eyes, seemed rather shocked, like Cupid who feared he had only been serving as Pandarus after all. The gulf of doubt between the generations had never seemed wider than at that moment.

The way back was the way onwards. It was eight o'clock by the time we had regained coastal civilisation, and after a brief parting to put on some clothes more suitable to the conformist trend (it was a long time, a very long time, since I had thought;: *The next time I take these off. . . .*) we dined once again at my hotel. Tonight it was a quieter retreat; the revellers had gone somewhere else, and we could sit in private solitude, under the trees which were once more our own, and talk without intrusion, without raising our voices above a companionable murmur.

Susan had chosen to wear red, that night, and she had chosen right; no matter from what angle—and she afforded them all—she seemed to sum up the very shape and colour and texture of desire. When she saw me staring at her, in admiration and all sorts of other things, she said: 'This is the third of my three dresses,' and I answered: 'Then they've just lasted us out,' and she mimed the violin-playing motion, in mockery again, yet in collusion.

She was wearing the diamond bracelet also, and making unashamed play with it, as if the time for secrets—whether between us and the world, or between herself and me—was now coming to an end. It was a very agreeable way to be given the good news.

After dinner we walked along the beach, in and out of the shadows, in and out of the mounting tide, and when the mood took us we stopped and coupled and kissed. This time the kissing was different. It was as though she were saying: You are hungry?—so am I. Women can be as hungry as men. . . . I had never known—or had forgotten—that there could be such willing and wanton co-operation, in so simple a thing as an open-sky embrace.

The word 'professional' slipped into my mind, and was quietly buried again. If one single fraction of this was assumed, if she was doing any sort of a job on me, I didn't want to know about it.

'Why so sweet to me?' I asked her, at the end of one memorable bout.

'I suppose because now I like you enough.'

'What made that happen?'

'Just the way I am. Just the way you are. . . . You're strong tonight. Strong all over.'

'That's consolidated Steele.' We had reached the furthest margin of the beach, under a rising moon; the only way back was now homewards, and I was ready to take it. 'I would be very sorry,' I confided, 'if any of it went to waste.'

'We mustn't let that happen, must we?' She was looking round her, at the moon, the lapping tide, the line of palm-trees along the foreshore; then she rose on tip-toe to kiss me, and she was all warmth, all yielding softness. 'What a beautiful night to make up one's mind. . . . It's no good at my place, Johnny.'

'Come back to mine, then.'

'Won't they object?'

'Not if we're absolutely quiet.'

'Keep reminding me about that,' she said softly. 'I could forget.'

She was extraordinarily talented, as I had known she would be; from the moment when, naked in the half darkness, she allowed her face to take on the divine, surrendering silliness of love, while her superb body lay waiting for my capture, she had not ceased to tremble, to excite, to move like warm quicksilver, to kindle and to assuage. I forgot all else, first in wild enjoyment of this invasion, then in a more lingering *reprise* which presently achieved the same rank end.

I could not be quite sure that she shared this abandon. Sometimes, in those moments of acute awareness which illumined our long night, I thought I could detect in her a sort of detachment, as if she felt it was not her province to enjoy, only to serve the tender necessities of love. I never had to caution her to be quiet; indeed, it was she who at one moment laid her fingers gently on my lips, and whispered: 'You'll wake the baby,' in amused, reluctant discipline. She was keeping her head, and it was just as well that this was so, since I was intent on losing mine.

I did not find out, till much later, the reason which lay at the core of this faint detachment; and I was not at all disposed to raise the topic, at such a moment, though my motives were entirely respectable—I wanted to return all her lavish courtesies, in the same measure. But she was not complaining; she was moving like a wild stream, she was clenching my exultant body as if it were the last prize left on earth. . . . I need only take delight in the fact that she was there, to hold and to have, exactly when she was wanted; and being beautiful, agile, and utterly unconstrained, she was, on that first night and for many nights thereafter, wanted a great deal.

Some time after dawn we walked back to her hotel together, plodding across the sands with the relaxed, wandering gait of all disbursed lovers at five o'clock in the morning. She was notably pale, and so, I felt, was I; but she looked very beautiful, very languid, very much mine, with that recognisable air of set-back which could only be a source of pride to the executioner.

We stopped to kiss half-way, but it was very much a token salute; if the entire band of the Royal Marines had struck up their *fortissimo* version of *Anchors Aweigh!*, I could not have hoisted a butterfly net. At her hotel steps, we played a subdued balcony scene.

'Thank you for all that, Susan.'

'Thank you for all *that*. . . . People are dead wrong about the English. Refer them to me.'

'I'll do nothing of the sort. . . . Are you going to sleep now?'

'Yes. And I can recommend it. Aren't you really tired, Johnny?'

'I might snatch a brief nap. But towards lunch-time . . .'

'We'll see.' She reached up, and kissed my cheek briefly. 'That's for now. . . . Tell me something, How do you like me to do my hair?'

'Normal. Smooth. Simple. You've got a beautiful shape of head. It doesn't need to be churned up.'

'All right,' she answered, with a curious air of gravity, as if she were agreeing a treaty which would bind us both for a hundred years. 'From the next time I see you. Good night. Good morning.'

I walked back even more slowly, scuffing the wet sand, observing what seemed to be an entirely different kind of sunrise. Perhaps it was because I wasn't collecting sea-shells any more. I was conscious of the usual male *tristesse*, and accepted it, and took good care to discount it.

This had been the first time, damn it, in six long years. A substantial record had been broken, a citadel of sorts breached and overthrown.

A little while ago, I would have been very surprised. Now I was not, and that also was a measure of decline.

But beyond this small moment of mourning, the pangs of conscience could not and did not pierce very deep. Susan had been much too exciting.

She never stopped being exciting, not even when she moved into the cabin next door to mine, and the engagement became continuous. (My hotel, true to form, turned a benevolent eye on this arragement, when I proposed it; perhaps they had very little choice—its general discouragement would deal a fatal blow to the industry.) She never stopped being exciting, and I did not cease to exploit the fact, on all possible occasions.

We seemed, in those days of dream and desire, to have everything going for us. The sun was constant in a cloudless sky; the sea washed us clean and innocent and as good as new, each morning; the afternoons were gentle pauses in time, yet full of subtle reminder, promising us all that we wished, and very soon, and then and there, if we had a mind for it; the nights were cool, and secret, and ours. At such signals, manhood returned with the full flood of virility, and a pounding eagerness to prove it.

This revival of mine had been instant and inevitable; I had only to put my arms round her to be reminded of a whole range of forgotten tastes and savours. It had a good deal to do with the feel of a different body, which, as always, made for the total renewal of many urges. Susan was taller than Kate, and put together differently, and, at twenty, a full twelve years younger; however little one wanted to make comparisons between the old love and the new, they were being stated all the time, by the response of one's own body, one's own instinct and appetite.

When we made love, it was a sensual contact between two people new to each other, never yet explored; and it was rendered wildly exciting by this novelty. She could drive me nearly frantic by a certain movement, or sometimes by a certain lack of it; it was as if she could invent, with her body, things I had to have, things I had to do; and she knew this, and she practised the fluent magic like some goddess-conjurer, dispensing gifts from her liberal store to those who had divined the right answer, and promises to those who had been tricked or blinded.

Sometimes, when in post-operative mood I tried to analyse this to her, and perhaps became over-involved in the *minutiae* of speculation, or clinically dull, she would smile like an indulgent teacher, and then contribute a chiding, realistic note: 'You know, one of these days you're going to talk yourself out of bed. *The reasons for things don't matter!*' And if the tide was right she would show me straight away that they did not matter, and indeed they did not.

She was a funny mixture of a girl. Many of the things I had expected, she was not. I had met beautiful girls, by the raftload, during the last few years; and beautiful girls were not my favourite characters, except to stare at when I had nothing better to do.

For the most part, these creatures grew unbearably spoiled; living on their looks, monstrously proud of them, scared to death of losing them; turning like animated toys towards every mirror in sight, as if to springs of water in the desert; absolutely self-centred, only happy if everyone in any given room was concentrating on them and them alone; and liable to turn into sulky bitches if this were not so

Susan was not at all like this, though—in the category of good looks —she was well entitled to be. She did not seem to give a damn who stared at her, or who did not, or what was happening to the current of her career, or how well she was doing in society, or in love, or in the span of life itself. She was generous, and out-going, all the time; she could give her undivided attention to another person, and enjoy the process, instead of demanding the same concentration upon herself, as of sacred right.

She seemed content with whatever took place next, good or bad, hopeful or daunting; if she were broke one day, then tomorrow would be better—and if not better, then different anyway, and worth a girl's living, a girl's welcoming smile. She had to be very disappointed, or misused, or angry, to take a stand against fate in the form of man.

She knew that I was a celebrity of sorts, she thought that I had a lot of money; naive or not, I was ready to believe that this had made little difference to her, in the realm of seduction, and none at all in its lavish catalogue of sequels.

'Everyone has the same income in bed,' she once said, at a moment to match the metaphor. 'A rich man doesn't feel rich. He either feels good or bad, gentle or rough, sweet or mean.' She listed, in her customary specific language, some of the other things which money could not replace. 'What I like about you,' she concluded, 'is that you always do it with *you*.'

I suppose she had admired this element in a lot of men, that it was what she was always looking for, that this was why she had sacked the odious character who had brought her down to Barbados in the first place. Generally speaking, she was very fond of the male animal, by inference as well as by candid confession; and this was another thing which surprised me, for a particular reason.

It became clear to me, before very long, that in spite of apparent ardours, in spite of a leaping sensuality, she never actually turned the trick; and no divining rod was needed to establish this, once I started watching her progress in love, once I began to take some trouble. At the start, I did take a lot of trouble with her, because I was deeply grateful for all she was giving me, and I thought she deserved her return; and there were also the customary promptings of vanity which, if they did not separate the men from the boys, at least gave them all the same target to shoot at.

It did not work, and presently, in deep well-being and content, I grew lazy about it, and thought: 'Hell, I don't have to bother—it isn't that sort of transaction.' I tried to raise the question once, but all she said was: 'Johnny, don't *think*!' and gave me, with prompt co-operation, something to take the place of thought.

I did not know whether she was being unselfish, or if this was all she wanted; I could not guess what impeded a consummation which, by her look and feel and touch, she might have been invented for. Before very long, I began to forget all about it, as she seemed to wish me to, and simply took the darling hand which had been dealt to me, and had a wild time with it.

If Susan really minded, if she missed something, if I was failing her in any particular way, she never showed it, never once withheld her cunning accommodation, and only spoke of it once again.

On a warm Barbados afternoon, when Susan lay asleep behind our slatted blinds, and I was trying to make the choice between waking her up, shaving, finishing the heel of a bottle of rum, or falling asleep myself, a letter came unexpectedly from Kate. It gave me a faint jolt —nothing worse—and then some news to which I lent all that I could muster in the way of dreamy, detached attention.

She was, she wrote, still in South Africa, in Johannesburg, where her father had now gone into hospital. He was very frail—'*hanging on*' was the term she used—and terribly depressed about politics, and she was not too hopeful of his recovery. He just didn't seem to believe that he had much to live for, any more. She would of course stay for as long as was necessary. She sent her love, and (here came a neatly loaded phrase) so did a lot of other people whom I used to know.

She ended with the cryptic message: '*There are some disgusting things going on here. More when I see you.*'

I read the last paragraph with wry recognition. Kate had no monopoly. There were some pretty disgusting things going on here, too.

Suddenly it was time for me to leave. The signal, which I had been hoping never to hear, was relayed by the booming voice of Erwin Orwin, telephoning from a city, New York, which seemed as nebulous and as far away as China or Peru. But I could not really pretend that his world of hard fact did not exist. Not any longer.

'Mr. Steele, I need you!' was his opening chord, thundering above the minor squeaks and whines of Barbados' overseas hook-up. 'And I hope you have some good news for me. How's my book coming along?'

'It's finished,' I answered, caught off-guard. It was nine o'clock in the morning, and I had been summoned to the hotel lobby, with the utmost discretion, straight from a bed which was a sad one to leave at any time. I back-tracked a little, using the social courtesies as a screen. 'Hallo, Mr. Orwin,' I said, with great heartiness. 'Nice to hear your voice again! How's New York getting on?'

'New York's all right,' he said, 'if you like rain, and a big row with Equity. How are things down there? How are all those babes in bikinis?'

'Barely visible,' I said, straight from the joke book.

The onslaught of his laughter could almost have been heard without the aid of science. I held the phone away from my ear till the paroxysm died away.

'That's good!' he shouted. 'Keep that one in . . . Did you say it was finished?'

'Pretty well.' I could not really tell him otherwise; I had been gone for six weeks, and writers with contracts and professional commitments did not throw away six weeks, nor any other span of time. 'I've just been polishing it up a bit.'

'I'd like to see what you've done,' he said, rather more formidably. 'I want to get things moving. And so do Teller and Wallace. They don't like hanging about doing nothing, even on my pay-roll. When can you get back? Tomorrow?'

'No,' I answered, conscious of a slightly chill breeze in the warm morning air. I remembered Jack Taggart telling me: 'Your rules aren't breakable.' This must be the translation. 'That's too soon,' I went on. 'I doubt if I could get a reservation.'

'I'll fix your reservation,' he said, 'if that's all it is. What airline are you using?'

'Don't you bother,' I told him. 'I know the people myself. I'll organise it.'

'When?'

The wires and the air-waves hummed and throbbed between us. I had to make up my mind, to this and a lot of other things. 'In a couple of days,' I answered. 'But I left my car down in Miami, and I'll have to drive it up again. How would it be if I sent you the manuscript? Then I can be back home in about a week, to go over it with you.'

'I guess that's O.K.,' he said grudgingly. 'But don't forget, I need you as well as the book. And Teller and Wallace will be needing you too.'

Everybody needed me.

'All right,' I told him, 'I'll mail the manuscript tonight, and start back on Wednesday.'

'We'll be looking out for it. And for you.' But once he had his promise, he seemed prepared to relax. 'You know, I envy you creative writers, Mr. Steele. A few hours in the sun, and the work's all done. I'll bet you didn't even have to get yourself a desk.'

'I can't afford a desk,' I said. 'And I've been working like a—like an African field-marshal.'

'Now then,' he said, starting to wheeze. 'No editorial comment.'

His laughter roared and crackled over two thousand miles of defence-less air, as the call faded, and I hung up. But it was not infectious; I wasn't feeling much like laughter myself. I had given Orwin a promise which I did not in the least want to keep, which vaguely I had hoped to stall for another two weeks at the minimum. Yet now I could not do so. One of my dies was cast.

There were several others already lining up, and as I went down the coral-stone steps into the hotel garden they began to crowd in on me. Under the towering palm-trees, the pool was still deserted, and I sat down at the water's edge to try to sort the thing out. I had known for many days that I would soon have to wake up, and that when I did so, I would be waking to a simple, central problem. The problem had arrived. I must make up my mind about Susan Crompton.

It was not going to be easy, whatever I did. Though she was not yet on my conscience, which was elastic, she certainly would be, as soon as I picked up and left her. It was going to be almost impossible to walk out, and still face the mirror in the morning—or, if that was too much of a *cliché* from the Boys' Book of Priggery, it was safe to say that I would feel all sorts of a fool if I quit so early.

Much of that feeling could only be selfish; I simply did not want to bid her goodbye; she had become an endearing as well as a desirable member of our cast, and I wanted lots more of the same. Why should we part now? Why should I leave this feast, when the feasting had hardly begun?

There were other reasons, more admirable—or more arguable, by a man looking for arguments to justify what he was going to do next. There were all kinds of ways in which I could help Susan; there was so much that could be made out of a girl like this, if she were given a new compass and a fresh start; all it needed was a rescue-operation, and a little non-opportunist love.

I felt splendidly capable of this, particularly at nine o'clock in the morning after a night of wakeful endeavour, in bed with the object of charity. But if this romantic relief-work had Cinderella cast in a dual and somewhat dubious role (one wave of my wand, and we turned into a motel), yet the results might still be just as good as if the Fairy Godmother herself had mapped them out.

Susan had been snared, by her startling good looks, her generous heart, and by the most potent man-trap of all—man. If she 'went on like this', it could only be downhill, and she would end up as an old woman in a back-alley, performing standing services for sailors. It did not have to happen, and it would not, if she were helped now, at a time when she had so many assets, so much promise, so fine a life to live.

There was an ancient, skinny Negro circling the pathway round the pool, dressed in a tattered white under-shirt and a pair of blue jeans faded to the colour of a rain-washed sky. He bore a rustic implement resembling a wire-mesh spoon on the end of a pole, and with it he was cleaning the surface of the water. Leaves, weed, patches of scum, palm fronds, dead insects—all were lifted out, piece by piece, one by one, with delicate, dedicated care.

Each time he passed me, he grinned, and raised his straw hat, and bowed. But while the greeting was automatic, the other thing was not; it was, on this bright morning, his life's work. He was giving his whole soul to his act of purification.

There was a far-fetched lesson here, and I prepared to take it, nodding my head sagely like a man seeing the light—the light he chose to see. It was suddenly tied with something else, something more remarkable, which had only just occurred to me.

Years ago, when it had been desperately important that I marry Kate (and I would never have denied, nor reversed, that urgency), I had made up a story about a girl in Johannesburg, a traditional harlot with a heart of gold, who lived for love, and died of it. It had been a good story, designed to catch Kate's attention at a crucial moment, and it had worked; along with some other things, it had injected just enough jealousy to propel her into marriage.

One of the points of my story had been that, with a mixture of motives, I had tried to set this girl up as something better than a corporate bed-fellow.

My heroine had started life as fiction, and now she was not. Suddenly she had arrived on my own doorstep, as Susan Crompton, with something like the same problems and all of the same appeal. The fairy-tale girl herself had taken flesh—and no one could deny that she had made a delicious job of the transformation.

All at once, duty seemed clear, and pleasurable at the same time— the way that all duty should present itself. I had to take this thing on. I could not do less for the fact than I had done for the fancy.

I jumped up from my chair, on swift impulse, endangering the balance of the old man, who was nearby. But he recovered, and raised his hat, and bowed again. He was not to be turned from his endeavours. . . . There were obvious dangers and complications ahead, if I did take Susan to New York, which was a small town in certain ways, and a most resonant sounding-board for the faintest whisper of gossip, particularly at the café-society level.

But the reasons for taking her back with me had suddenly grown bigger than the reasons for leaving her in Barbados, or saying goodbye in Miami, and I was walking down the garden path to tell her so.

Armed with the stiff drink which the occasion demanded, I crossed to her cabin, and peered inside. She was still asleep, curled up under the covers of our work-shop; but the shapely mound was still recognisable as a girl. I patted the mound where it was most appealing, and she raised her head, and opened one sleepy eye.

'Hi,' she said. She blinked, and frowned, and pushed her hair out of her eyes. 'Aren't you the man who was here? What happened to you?'

'A phone call.'

'Tell her you're all tied up.' She was still fathoms deep, and not too keen to come to the surface. 'Don't call us,' she mumbled. 'We'll call you.'

'It was from New York,' I said. 'Erwin Orwin.'

'What he want?'

I took a drink before I answered: 'I'm afraid I've got to go back.'

'Oh. . . . When?'

'Wednesday?'

She yawned cavernously, but the news had already broken through; both eyes were open now, and she was peering doubtfully up at me, as if the warmth of our bed were no longer sheltering her from the much colder world outside. 'I've lost count,' she said, though I did not think this was quite true. 'What day is today?'

'Monday.'

At that she really woke up, and sat up too. The view was charming, and if I had had any thoughts of changing my mind, I lost them then and there, in a stalwart determination to rescue everything in sight.

'Why so soon, Johnny?' she asked.

'They need the play, and it's ready for them. I can't really stay on here any longer.' I drew a long breath, the breath of determination. 'But when I go, I want you to come back with me.'

Her face grew suddenly wary, and guarded. 'You mean all the way to New York?'

'Yes.'

'I don't know.' She shook her head, flicking the small bright curtain of her hair across her shoulders. 'Give me my robe. I can't think when I'm naked.'

'I'm not surprised. And while I remember, thank you for last night.' But something in her face told me that she was not in the market for this kind of reminiscence, and I picked up her silk robe, and put it round her, with a kiss on the top of her head for luck. Then I sat down on the edge of the bed, and waited.

'I don't know,' she said again. 'Maybe we just ought to——' she was back to her old habit of not finishing sentences, and this time I could understand it. Her expression had grown more careful still. 'I mean, we've had a lot of fun already.'

'There's more to come.'

'Maybe. But I didn't want this to grow into a problem. . . . Look, I'm going back to Miami anyway. Why don't we just leave it like that?'

'What happens to you in Miami?'

'I'll get by.'

'I don't want you to *get by*. It's not good enough. I want us to go back together. Then when we get to New York, we'll do something about you.'

'What about me?'

I tried not to make it sound too noble. 'I want to help you somehow. I really do. It shouldn't be too difficult. It just means a fresh start.'

'I don't need a fresh start.'

'That's all you do need.'

It was almost pathetic to watch her face as she considered what I was saying. I was reminded once again of an earlier thought—of how vulnerable was a girl like Susan, once she had stepped into this sleazy arena. Sitting on the bed, remembering last night and many other nights, I realised that I was not in the best shape for cold calculation. It was the sort of moment, the sort of potent situation, when one could be betrayed into all kinds of stupid decisions; decisions which, though grounded in pity, could flower into monsters of complication and deceit.

But I had, at the same time, a picture of her, standing outside the airport at Miami, waiting for the bus and the next pick-up, and I could not bear it.

As she said nothing, I spoke again. 'It *is* all you need, Susan. Give it a chance. Come back to New York with me, and we'll work out a plan.'

'What sort of plan?'

'I don't know. You could take a course at one of the acting schools, something like that. Or have another try in television. They're not all bastards, and I do know a few people who could help.'

'They *are* all bastards. . . . But you're being very sweet. Wouldn't

210

it mean trouble for you? I don't want to involve you in anything. I mean, being married, and tied up. That sort of thing never works out.'

'It's worked out all right so far.'

She shook her head, like a child refusing a treat for reasons it cannot really explain. 'That's down here. It could be different in New York.' Suddenly she faced the test question, the thing we were both thinking about, and not mentioning. 'What happens when your wife comes back?'

I didn't know the answer to that, and I didn't try to find it. 'One thing at a time. Let's get to New York first, and see how it works out.'

'I'll think about it . . . I'll think about it all morning. . . . I don't want to sound ungrateful, but it *is* difficult.' She stretched her arms high above her head, and the robe fell away from her shoulders, and she was a big girl again. 'It's nice to have a choice, anyway.' She was eyeing me, and I was doing the same, without disguise. 'Didn't they ever tell you?—it's rude to stare.'

'I just don't know where else to look.'

She leant back against the pillow, and asked, as she had sometimes asked before: 'Shall I get up yet?'

'I'll think about that,' I answered, copying her earlier tone. 'I'll think about it carefully, for all of the next ninety seconds.'

'Ninety seconds? What's happened to the great trigger-man?'

'He's getting old,' I said. 'But that won't last, either.'

Clearly, there were all sorts of dangers and complications in this idea of mine, and they might not be too far away. But once having made up my mind, I was ready to take them on happily. The death-wish, I thought, as I lay down beside her and prepared to show that I had not grown as old as all that, was not a novelist's tiny spark of invention; it was a real thing. And to be worth while, it had to be strong.

We drove back a different way, keeping more to the west and avoiding the atrocities of the Florida tourist-strip; it gave us one spectacular section, a scenic road called the Blue Ridge Parkway, which roller-coasted its way for more than three hundred miles from mountain top to mountain top, striding a loose-slung tightrope in the clouds, with fantastic views of the plain-lands far below on either side, and slow-circling hawks to keep us company.

We were in high spirits, to match this vantaged eyrie; later on, when we had to drop down to lower levels, across the blue-grass country of northern Virginia, we seemed to be bringing gifts from Olympus to the lowly earthlings. But happiness persisted, at whatever altitude; Susan was very good company by day, and, by night, a soft and sinuous pillow for a weary man.

When it grew cold again, in Washington, I bought her a fur coat, bringing comfort to her, and the total cost of the excursion to another well-rounded figure, $11,000.

Then suddenly we ran out of north-bound, home-going road, and it was April, and spring in New York.

CHAPTER FIVE

First I had to console Kate.

I was so very sorry to hear about your father (I wrote). *It must have been a horrible shock for you, even though you had some warning, and a little time to start to live with the idea. These can only be desolate days for you, and I hope you have some good friends at hand to help you. But I know how close you always were to him, and how he thought and felt about you, and nothing you get from other people is going to take the place of that.*

I've never found out if these letters of sympathy do any good; I would doubt it myself. Anyway, husbands don't send wives letters of sympathy; they send their dearest love, which is what I do now.

You don't need me to say, stay as long as you feel you have to. There are bound to be a thousand things to do at Maraisgezicht, and you are the obvious and probably the only person to deal with them. I suppose you will be selling the place itself. Anyway, all that sort of thing can wait its turn.

New York is full, and busy, and I am working very hard, living at the Pierre as you see, and occasionally sallying out for sessions with Teller and Wallace. Teller is the tall one, Wallace the small; I was never quite sure of this till now. They are fantastic people to work with, quick like foxes. Erwin Orwin's wife calls him 'lover'. When I got back to N.Y., everyone said: 'Haven't seen you on TV lately,' and that was about all they did say.

Now it is time to drop this twelve floors down the letter-shute, into the hands of the tiny postman who waits to catch it. They say he has never missed a single letter, in forty years. (He has a younger brother, who switches off the lights inside refrigerators.) My love again, and call me here if there is anything you want or anything I can do.

Teller was the big one, and wrote the words; Wallace was the small, and wrote the music. Together they made up a team which knew exactly where it was going, and the quickest way to get there. They had done four shows together, and in planning this, their fifth, they thought and talked a kind of shorthand which often spanned chasms of question-marks and produced the identical right answer at the same moment. They were, as Jack Taggart had warned me earlier, a very hard pair to keep up with.

When I met them in New York, I had only just made my first minimum contribution to *The Pink Safari*. So far, it had been easy— perhaps too easy; I felt there was bound to be something much harder for me to do, and I was not disappointed. All I had achieved at this stage was to produce a bare blue-print of the linking material for the music and songs of the experts. This was, as they speedily showed me, only a dot on a chart, a point of departure.

What I had done with *Ex Afrika*—and it was not by accident— was to simplify it, trim it down, switch on a few extra lights, and give it a transfusion of cheerfulness in place of foreboding.

It was still the story of white South Africans having fun on top of their volcano, and Negroes, even in degradation, having fun in mockery of the whites. But this schism was not the end of the world for either— my picture was of two contrasting cultures, two kinds of life, which, when they met and touched, did not inevitably blast off into a dark orbit of hatred and contempt.

The story-line was sad in parts, like life, and funny too; people struck noble attitudes and flourished weapons, but they also tripped over their own togas, and sometimes discovered that their weapons were toys from the wrong catalogue. Boy met girl, and made the most of it; and if, somewhere off-stage, something sinister was smouldering, the smoke was not too acrid, the smell not too noisome.

Life went on, for man, woman, and dog, and it was never entirely futile, nor disgraceful, nor unbearable, at any level.

'Keep it light,' Erwin Orwin had cautioned, when we said goodbye after our first lunch. 'We're not solving any problems with this one. We're setting them to music.' I had stuck to this directive, and he liked what I had done so far. But it was only the beginning. From now on, I had to be on call, ready with the vast improvements which everyone seemed to take for granted.

I enjoyed every moment of it, not least because—after many weeks of *dolce far niente*—it was just the sort of wit-sharpening process of which I stood most in need. We worked in a colossal barn of a studio, tacked onto the back of one of Erwin Orwin's run-down, off-Broadway theatres; and, at this stage, everything to do with the production was centred upon this echoing foundry.

There, Teller scribbled the lyrics, while Wallace hummed the tunes in a thin nasal baritone; a wireless man at a piano (he was actually Teller's mother's cousin) transcribed the result, and hammered it out for size. I was there myself, enjoying it all immensely, admiring the way these people could worry away at a bone until it was clean-picked and ready for inspection; but I was also there to be shot at, by anyone with my own kind of gun.

Sometimes Teller would say: 'We want some diddle-diddle music in there,' and Wallace, almost before the words were out of his partner's mouth, would go 'Diddle diddle diddle,' mimicking a violin, and the man at the piano would jot it down, and stick in a few grace-notes and *arpeggios*, and incorporate it into the score.

Sometimes, more alarmingly, they would both turn to me, and say: 'Hold it! That needs two more lines, and a joke about the spear, and a song-cue for *My Mother Bids Me Bare My Breast*,' and then they would wait, as everyone in the room would wait, from Erwin Orwin's secretary to the man who had come to look at the humidifier, until I produced the right answer. There was never any question of my saying: 'Let me think about it.' People didn't use that phrase any more.

Erwin Orwin spent a great deal of time at the studio, stamping and wheezing his way in, manœuvring his vast bulk behind a corner desk, and sitting down like an enormous spider come to inspect one of his chain of webs. I would have thought that Teller and Wallace might have objected to this invasion, but it seemed that they were used to it, and that this was the way an Erwin Orwin musical was always evolved, at this particular stage.

There was no nonsense about the isolation of the artist, or the paramount necessity for cerebration in an ivory tower; we were producing a public spectacle, soon to be dissected by a thousand probing eyes, and it was taken for granted that the more people who crowded in at this formative moment, the better were our chances of shredding out the rubbish.

If any other team worked like this, I had never heard of it. But that didn't make any difference. These were the rules in this particular establishment, and anyone who objected to them was free to join another circus. Erwin Orwin did it this way, and so did Teller and Wallace, and so, at the tail-end of the comet, did I.

Orwin came to see us; people came to see him. Stage-designers arrived with miniature sets; dress-designers brought sketches, and slapped them down on the table in a petulant act of salesmanship. Agents bounced in, bearing fabulous package-deals involving one girl-acrobat, one husband who played the bassoon like an angel, and one TV commitment which could be fixed. Mothers brought children, who stumbled through their tap-dance routines and were then hustled out again, to the sound of off-stage slaps and wails. Men came, and took off their ties, and sang; girls came, and shed their furs like snakes in spring, and danced.

The men would glower and flash their eyes, intent on projecting an image of the menace which a show such as this must surely demand; the girls, more realistic, darted fiery glances at Erwin Orwin, at Teller and Wallace, and even, as a last forlorn resort, at me. Men and women alike arrived in all shapes, sizes, and colours, since one half of the cast was to be Negro. But they all had one thing in common. They wanted to be in *The Pink Safari*.

That fact itself would have been flattering, if I had had any time at all to be flattered. But I was low man on this totem, and working, harder than I had worked for many a long year, at an entirely new job which fascinated me. It was earn-while-you-learn at its most compelling; and as long as the day lasted, I could bear nothing else in mind, and did not want to.

Gradually the show began to take shape, which made us all happy, and vaguely suspicious of our luck. But I could be happy in another way, without suspicion, since I had a dividend declared to no one else.

When our work came to a weary stop, at each night-fall, and the team cast its slightly withered petals, I still had Susan Crompton.

Like all intent romantics, we had settled down to the routine of our choice. Between six and eight each evening, depending on theatrical pressures, Susan would meet me, not too far from the studio, at a bar on 44th Street. There I would down the first recuperative drink of the day, and we would sit and hold hands, re-establishing the world of sensual contact. From then on, we would take the town for all it was worth.

The things I liked to do, in these off-hours, were luckily the same as hers—or, if they were not, if she were ever tagging along in mutiny and despair, it never showed. We both enjoyed eating, and New York was made for such a hobby; there was better French, Italian, or German cooking to be discovered here, than in large tracts of the respective homelands.

Of course, the sources needed tracing, but we were never in any hurry. We could afford to shop around, and we liked to wander.

Our range of choice was fantastic, enough to enliven any conceivable mood, though we had our favourites, and they also became traditional. If we were monumentally hungry, we went down town to Luchows, and gorged ourselves, like any Bavarian trencherman and his *frau*, on heavy slices of everything in sight, washed down by treacly draughts of Loewenbrau.

If we were feeling elegant and Gallic, the Maison Basque or Maude Chez Elle stood with open doors, ready with anything to be found anywhere within the *Dictionnaire Gastronomique* of Larousse. If we felt—or wished to feel—like bulgy Italian peasants on the spree, we would dive into Romeo Salta's, and there dive into the pasta.

The kind of uninhibited lobster-gorge which called for a bib and a succession of finger-bowls was all ready for us, down at the King of the Sea. If we wanted food cooked by blow-torch, or Chinese mounds of this and that, or the roast beef of Old England (via Argentina), or goulash, or *bouillabaisse*, or clams steamed in Hawaiian sea-weed, there were places for these, too. If we were lazy, or didn't care much either way, we stayed where we were, and nibbled hot pastrami and dill pickles, and looked forward to starting all over again, the following week, with renewed appetite and another seven different places to choose from.

Later we would be in the mood to listen, and to look on while other people sang the songs and made the jokes. I was anti-theatre at this time, or rather, I didn't want anyone else's dramatic ideas crossing up my own; we therefore kept away from other men's masterpieces, and enjoyed the best trivia we could find.

Every night, there were dozens of such offerings waiting for our inspection; 'club acts' at the smart places, off-Broadway reviews, places like Upstairs at the Downstairs or The Establishment, where wit was irreverent, and guaranteed, and very funny. Or we would go in search of music—our kind of music, which was usually jazz; Dixieland at Eddie Condon's, or wherever Wilbur de Paris might be ripping out with *Wrought Iron Rag*; or finding something cooler down in Greenwich Village, even if it was nothing more than a piano, a drum, and a clarinet wandering up and down one's spine, like an exploring hand; or meeting the edge of crudity on the edge of Haarlem—a quartet of hopped-up Negroes singing *That Chick's Too Young To Fry*; or watching George Shearing's blind hands on any keyboard in town; or (by way of somersault) joining the operatic extroverts at the 'singing tables' of Chez Vito, where jazz gave way to the melodic line, and barbershop to *bel canto*.

When the weather grew warmer, we used to walk a lot, particularly homeward bound at the end of our evenings, through the many villages which made up this huge city. Like London, New York was sliced into segments, endless in number, utterly different in character, and (if one wished) completely self-contained.

One need never leave the area of Sixth Avenue between 50th and 54th Streets; one could shop, eat, live, and love in a narrow band of the East 70s; one could settle down in the Village below 14th Street, and never come up for any other kind of air. Crossing such boundaries on our way home was like wandering the length of Europe, through a succession of open frontiers.

We usually finished up with a non-buying session in front of the glittering windows of Fifth Avenue, where Cartier and Saks were, at this time of night, available to rich and poor alike; and then we would move a little way across town again, past the doorway where lurked the huge blind man in the khaki Balaclava helmet, and into our last dive of all, the downstairs room at '21'; a retreat which, in the small hours of the morning, was not all tourists—and not all celebrities, either.

217

Here, as in many other places all over town, I was unlikely to be anonymous, and Susan was enough to turn a score of heads anywhere she went. But I had grown careless, during all this time of love and dreaming and desire; I wanted this girl, I had her on a single string, and I did not give a damn who knew about it.

At '21', give or take a few knowing stares, we would merge into the background, and sign-off our last public appearance with a drink, and a gossip with anyone we knew, and, if still hungry, with the eggs Benedict or oysters Rockefeller which custom dictated; and then, at one or two or three, we would saunter out again, night owls going back to roost; down the echoing street, up the wide deserted highway of the Avenue, and gently homewards, hand in hand, to bed.

'Home' was on 54th Street, where I had installed her in a very small apartment in a tall, run-down house which, if the traffic on the stairs were anything to go by, was tacitly given over to such arrangements. (My hotel, of course, was out; and, for various semi-admirable reasons, my own apartment did not appeal.) Susan had settled happily into this nest, and organised the milk and the groceries and the newspapers and the drycleaning, like any blinded bride. I had moved a few of my clothes in, and a work-table for my typewriter, and I spent a lot of time there.

I was getting to know her much better. What had started as a cheerful fling in Barbados had developed, imperceptibly, into a *liaison* of a different sort. It had a continuing, almost domestic quality, and I thus had the time and the chance to observe her more closely. In the process, I was finding out much more about Susan, Susan in depth.

I had never before been at close quarters with a girl whose beauty was so remarkable that it put her into the professional category, and it was strange to watch her as she went about the business of preparing to face the public gaze. Bathing, dressing, and make-up never took less than three hours, even if she were just going down the street to pick up a can of beans (which was her most likely local errand); her hair alone, although in the severe and simple style which I had voted for, and which she had continued, was good for half an hour of combing and patting, fingering and lacquering.

I remembered how surprised I had been, one morning, to walk into the bedroom and find her standing before the mirror, her whole head covered by an impenetrable gauze bag as she prepared to put on a mohair sweater.

'Good God!' I said, startled. 'No one told me it was Hallowe'en. What on earth is that thing?'

Her head came slowly out of the neck of the sweater, like some nightmare cork, and then she removed the bag, very carefully, and there underneath was a sleek head of hair and a brand-new make-up, all ready to go.

'It's my head bag,' she said. 'Haven't you ever seen one before?'

'No. Did you invent it?'

She shook her head. 'Models use them. They protect your hair and make-up and everything.'

'Why can't you put on the make-up *after* you put on the sweater?'

'It doesn't work out so well.'

I examined the bag, which was made, it seemed, of old nylon stockings tacked into the shape of a pineapple. 'Does everyone know about those things?'

'Models do. But you can't buy them. You have to make them yourself.'

'I *must* get the concession.'

As with her hair, so with a lot of other things. There were professional ways of dealing with whatever might go wrong—dresses that wrinkled, stockings that sagged, girdles that bunched, straps that showed, mascara that caked, *lamé* that might tarnish, sequins that might shed, furs that might mat themselves into tufts; and she knew all the appropriate tricks, and could put them to work wherever necessary.

She managed everything which concerned her appearance with meticulous skill; it was the sort of narcissic devotion which one could never quarrel with, nor grow impatient about, since the result, when at last she stepped out onto the street, or walked into a restaurant, or nestled into one's arms, was feminine perfection.

But I could not help noticing that only this end-result was shining clean and *chic*; the background from which it sprang was deplorable. Compared with Kate's spotless, laundered elegance, Susan was grubby and disorganised; her flower-like appearance was rooted in a positive farm-yard of untidiness, hit-or-miss housekeeping, and tawdry chaos.

The apartment—our warm and cosy little home—was like a neglected zoo. Lip-sticked towels littered the bathroom floor; rubber instruments of hair-raising complexity and dubious application swung to and fro behind its door. Soiled Kleenex decorated the dressing-table; cupboards or shelves unwarily probed might reveal anything—rejected underwear, torn brassières, exhausted deodorant sprays, miniature yet rusty razors, squeezed-out tubes of assorted lubricants; all the dirty jetsam of cherished femininity.

She made a bed in one swift movement; she left the bath just as it was, with a tide-mark of scented bath-oil clinging to it; the sitting-room was littered with every movable object—cushions, records, magazines, loaded ash-trays, used glasses. Neither bed nor bath nor sitting-room was ever more than fractionally mine.

She was a dear girl, and a wonderful one to sleep with; but I would have hated to share an apartment with her, on a long-term basis. She looked, in public, like a million dollars; but home was a real slum, and she an adorable, highly decorative slut.

Wonderful in bed she certainly was; it made up for almost everything else, as, at Stages One and Two, it generally did. When I came to know more about her, this talent of hers was possibly more surprising than anything else.

My main discovery in this area was almost accidental, stemming not so much from research as from my own vanity—or, as the couch-concessionaires would put it, my need for potency-reassurance. In bed, talking (as we sometimes did, without too much diffidence) of other men who had enjoyed these same favours, I had asked her: 'Who was best?' and she had answered: 'You, darling! You're fantastic!' so promptly that even a self-deluding male was bound to be suspicious.

Something in her answer had seemed automatic, and therefore odd; when I questioned her, in the loving-nagging way which women must often find unfair, she finally said:

'Sorry, Johnny. I didn't mean it to sound like that. But everyone asks that question.'

'Do they?'

'Sure.' She was smoking a cigarette, lazily, propped high on the pillow, surveying the world from her own languorous slope of Olympus. 'It's usually the first thing they say, afterwards. Sometimes it's the *only* thing they say, except "Look out!" or "Jesus!" '

I digested this, without too much appetite. 'Who *was* best, then?'

'My husband.'

Well, well, I thought: a fresh character; one learned something new every day. 'I never knew you were married,' I told her. 'When did that happen?'

'About two years ago. When I was eighteen, and miserable. But it worked out pretty well, for a time. *Very* well. He was a doll in his own way.'

'Mr. Crompton?'

'Mr. Crompton.'

'Who was he?'

'Oh, just a little guy, a drummer in a lousy orchestra. "The Five Bobcats". But he was all I had then. He was wonderful to me.'

'How wonderful?'

'He took all the trouble.'

'Trouble?'

'You know, preparation. And he used to talk all the time it was happening, Sort of dirty talk, but on purpose. It was the first I'd heard. It was very exciting.' She blew a smoke-ring towards the shadowy ceiling, and went off at a tangent. 'You know that joke about talking in bed? The psychiatrist says: "Do you talk to your wife during sexual intercourse?" and the man says: "Only if I can reach the phone." That was one of his.'

'But what happened to him? Are you divorced?'

'I don't think so. . . . Oh, he just got fed up with everything. Like, the trouble was too *much* trouble. And he used to think it was his fault that it didn't happen more easily.'

'Whose fault was it?'

'Mine.'

Then she told me all about it.

She had had a curious, even grotesque sexual history. She had been wild about sex, from the age of eleven; but it was sex pictorial, sex sniggering, sex self-practised. 'I'll beat the hell out of you,' her father had warned, 'if I ever see you within ten feet of a boy,' and he had beaten the hell out of her, once, and she had feared him, and boys, and men, for years afterwards. She was left to her own devices, and the devices had proved ruinous.

Secretly ashamed, secretly delighted, frantic and then downcast, she had become her own lover. 'It nearly drove me mad,' she told me, her eyes wide. 'But I *had* to do it, maybe ten times a day. I just couldn't stop.'

It had had a sadder effect than driving her temporarily to distraction.

Now, she could never 'get anywhere' with a man, unless this service were first provided for her; and even then there was no guarantee. It might take two hours or more, so deadening and abrasive had been that earlier process. What man had the patience? What man, especially, was going to pay for this dubious privilege?

And who cared, anyway? Girls were there to be used. . . . It had been her final misfortune that her first true lover had been a text-book athlete who also concentrated on his own progress, and never gave a shadow of thought to hers. Others of the same kind had followed; a girl so beautiful positively invited swift conquest, and swifter disposal.

Her husband had been the only man who knew of her problem, and had loved her enough to try to solve it. But there were limits to love of this sort; he had lasted no longer than any other radical reformer who tired of trying to persuade a dull electorate to rally to the poll.

The result was with her now, as a permanent disability. Though in body co-operative and lively, she remained alone, and untouched by any spark of appetite. In the act of love, the important part of her lay back, isolated, *dégagée*, munching mental peanuts until the brief storm passed.

'Men are so quick.' she said, explaining some more of this, as if she had to justify her inability. 'All that build-up, and then "Phtt!", and it's over.'

'It's sad,' I said, and in truth I meant it.

'Sad and silly. One misses the dwelling application of the soul.' When she saw me staring at her she giggled and said: 'It's all right. I read that in a book.'

Amazingly, she was still cheerful and undefeated, in this and, as far as I could see, all other respects. She was also vulnerable, and did not seem to care about that, either. One might have thought that this constructive frigidity of hers would have put her in a strong position, not a weak one; that she could have afforded to ration or withhold her gifts, in an area which meant so little to her.

But obviously she still liked men, and could not really do without them, and constantly invited a relationship which, in the carnal realm, amounted to no more than a cigarette, and much less than a square meal. It did not make much sense, but this only joined the long list of other things which, in the female world, did not make much sense, either.

She remained, when all was said, a wonderful person to make love with, and she was, for me at that moment, just right. Indeed, she was almost too available, posing no demands, requiring no effort. She was always there, always wide open and suggestible, always ready.

I suppose that, giving me thus nothing at all to measure up to, she was bad for me. But I felt I would survive such self-indulgence. This was all I really wanted: a girl who would lie down at the given signal, and was not the smallest trouble otherwise.

Even the 'rescue operation', which I had planned with such nobility of purpose down in Barbados, had been no particular problem. I found that I knew enough people in the middle reaches of TV to win her a re-entry of sorts, into that silly section of television which, for pretty girls, involved trotting out the prizes on give-away shows, and holding up audience-cues on cards designed by some nameless actuary to leave the chest and legs as principal features of the landscape.

In pursuing this line of endeavour, she had modelled furs, and been chased across the screen by small agile comedians, and had pretended to faint when kissed by Dr. Kildare, and been photographed winking at the late-night audience before composing herself for sleep. (She photographed very well, though she really was too big for the confinements of the 21-inch screen.) She had earned about $600, which delighted her, and spent it all on a nightdress and matching lace *peignoir*, which delighted me. It added up to a marginal living, the kind which gave her something to do, and kept her out of mischief. At least, so she assured me.

'No passes?' I asked her, when we were debating this aspect of her career.

'Not really. Nothing desperate, anyway. The policy seems to be hands-off.' She smiled across our dinner table, which was in one of the darker corners of a restaurant known to the trade as the Almost Inn. 'You're really quite important, you know.'

There were implications there which I did not welcome, but I let them go. 'So everything's all right.'

'Oh yes. I'm doing another of those quiz-shows next week. But——'

'But what?'

'I really want to act.'

'What sort of acting?'

'You know. Real acting. On the stage. But I don't know enough about it.'

223

'You'd better go to school, then.'

'Oh, Johnny!' She was delighted, and showed it with a smile which, if there had been enough light, might have ravished the entire room. '*Could* I?'

'Why not?'

She went to school, for three whole weeks, joining an establishment absolutely dedicated (according to its brochure) to the living theatre as an art form, an arm of the cultural crusade, and a fulfilling way of life. But three weeks was enough to determine that the omens here were not favourable.

'It's not for me,' she reported, dispiritedly, when we met after one of her afternoon classes. 'I'll never be any good at Shakespeare.'

'There are lots of other things.'

'Oh, I know that. But I don't think I'll learn them at this place. The students are all so damned dramatic! And they're such kids!'

'But you could still learn something useful, all the same.'

She shook her head. 'It's not for me,' she said again. 'The things I need to know, I know already. Let's face it. I'm never going to be Katherine Cornell.'

'So?'

'What I want is a *small* part, now.' She saw my face, which I suppose was disappointed, or preoccupied with the instability of the world of self-expression. 'But don't you worry, anyway. You've been so good to me already. I don't want to be a nuisance. Something is sure to turn up.'

'It's not so easy.'

'That's why I don't want you to worry about it.'

Of course, I did worry, a little. I hoped to make her happy, because she had made me so; and selfishly, because I did not want any frustrated actresses hanging round the foot of my bed, declaring that all they needed was *one* break—just *one*. I thought about the problem, on and off, for a day. Then I had a suitably unscrupulous idea.

Teller and Wallace and Steele were hard at work, at one of the things which was giving them trouble—a Johannesburg native-location scene which had to steer a delicate course between the maudlin and the murderous—when Erwin Orwin came into the studio. He sat down in his corner, as usual, and busied himself with the pile-up of papers which, however large it grew, never snowed him under for more than an hour of any day.

Clearing for action, I strolled over, leaving Teller and Wallace to weave a few more of their spells round the piano.

'Good morning, Erwin,' I greeted him. We had progressed to this stage of familiarity, after a formal period unusual in theatre. 'Is this your day for doing favours?'

He looked up, losing one enormous jowl in the process but not really altering his air of heavy-weight consequence.

'Don't tell me,' he growled. 'You've got a girl who wants a part in a play.'

Though I was used to his displays of intuition, which had made him a very rich man in an area where, above all, hunches paid off handsomely, I thought this was a superior example of the art. I tried to take it in my stride.

'Just that.'

'I knew it.' It was difficult to tell if he were in a good humour or not. 'I should have put something about this in your contract. . . . Well, let's hear the worst.'

I told him about Susan, using certain significant and glowing adjectives from my own field of achievement. 'I don't want to make anything special out of it,' I finished. 'I know you get ten of these things a day. But if you could possibly fit her in somewhere——'

'Can she sing?'

'She's sung at the Met.'

'Oh, come on!' he said. 'You don't have to overdo it.'

'But it's true. She was one of the gypsies in *Carmen*.'

'I knew there was a bull involved somewhere. . . . O.K., Johnny. I'll take a look at her, if that'll keep you happy. I like happy authors, provided they don't cost me too much.' He glanced at his watch. 'I'm leaving for the coast in a couple of hours. Is she available now?'

'In ten minutes,' I told him. Susan was, in fact, waiting round the corner, in our bar on 44th Street.

'Wheel her in, before I change my mind.'

It was funny to see Susan in the studio, and to watch, as a neutral observer, while she put on her act for someone else. She really did it very well, with the right amount of deference to the great Broadway producer, and the right show of leg for the man behind the label. When she had gone, with a wink to me and a smile for the general public so warm and lovely that even Teller's mother's cousin looked up from his piano, I closed in again to scout the prospects.

'What do you think?' I inquired of Erwin.

'I wouldn't ask that, if I were you. . . . Pretty girl, all right. Too pretty—she'll never be taken seriously. What do you want me to do for her? Something in a road company? I've got *Greensleeves* playing Chicago, and then going on west.'

'Well,' I said, 'that's not quite what I had in mind.'

'O.K., O.K. She's too delicate to travel. But there's not much here in New York.' He fingered the nearest of his chins. 'There's a bit part coming up in *Josephine*. The victory pageant scene. The girl who plays the Goddess of Plenty got herself pregnant again.'

'That sounds wonderful.'

'It's not,' he said, rather grumpily. 'It's a fill-in between Austerlitz and Waterloo. . . . Hundred-twenty-five a week, then. Why should I pay your bills?'

'Thank you so much, Erwin,' I said formally. 'It's very good of you.'

'I like happy authors,' he said again. His face cleared, as if, against all likelihood, he really did prefer to make people happy. 'Incidentally, when's your wife coming back?' he asked, and burst out into laughter so loud that Teller, who had heard the laughter but not the joke, looked up and called out: 'My God, Erwin! Let's keep that one in.'

I could have done without Erwin's last comment, though it was not much of a price to pay for having this thing settled, so satisfactorily, with a small wave of the wand. But of course his question had the truth at its core. I did not want Kate to come back yet; and I knew, perfectly well, the reason why. It was not entirely the obvious reason.

Apart from her tremendous sensual appeal, Susan was giving me something else; along with the generous girl came freedom from that close, cool, and penetrating inspection of love, which I could only sum up as Kate herself, and which had begun to unnerve me.

It was peace I really wanted; peace, and a long truce to the cold war which our marriage had in part become. With Susan, at last, I had established an uncomplicated, simple give-and-take, without deep engagement, without inquisition, without comment, without the cloying siege of love. With Susan, it was summer-time, and the living was easy.

Once again, that was all I wanted; and if it was more than I deserved, that was *my* dividend.

We worked all through a hot mid-year, in a town full of tourists,

226

Turkish-bath humidity, gasoline fumes, and crabby cab-drivers. By early September, *The Pink Safari* was finished, or as nearly finished as it would be before Erwin Orwin, that maddening perfectionist, started pulling it to pieces again on the stage; casting had begun in earnest, and rehearsals were due to start in about a month.

I had been paid my second $15,000, and had banked it, in the sense that it had been pushed through one bank-teller's wicker and had started to leak out at another. Erwin, had then asked me to stay on with him, on a salary basis, until the *première*. It was being forecast with true theatrical vagueness, that the show might start its out-of-town try-outs in January, and open in New York some time in April.

The smaller partnership of Crompton and Steele continued, with unflagging energy, or (not to be too boastful) with the energy appropriate to an affair which had gone on for seven straight months. It seemed that she was happy, in bed and out of it; professionally, she was still with *My Darling Josephine*, and had been promoted from the Goddess of Plenty to the Spirit of Paris, whose *décolletage* was lower. I had stopped paying substantial sums of money for not using my suite at the Pierre, and divided the time between Susan's modest lair, and occasionally camping out in the apartment.

I was beginning to wonder, at odd moments of the day, what was happening to Kate.

She had stayed where she was, down at Maraisgezicht in the Cape Province; regular letters arrived, saying how busy she was, how much there remained to be done in the settlement of her father's estate, how impossible it was to come back to New York at the moment, I believed her, but I had a curious feeling that there was a loose end somewhere, some item unidentified and out of my control. Or perhaps it was just that we could not talk things over any more.

I began to speculate on what she was really thinking. One of her recent letters, at least, had brought some substantial news: '*I have inherited, after taxes, about £600,000, but I still love you, just the same.*' I could credit at least half of this, and, perversely, wanted to believe the other half.

Then, in October, with rehearsals just starting, an unexpected courier arrived, bringing news.

I was at home—my home—early one evening, wandering about the silent rooms in a dressing-gown, after a bath which had done nothing much to remove the scars of a sticky day, when the phone rang. I very nearly ignored it, being in that nineteenth-century mood which was prepared to dismiss the telephone as the damned intrusion it was; but it rang for a long time, and finally I picked it up.

A voice said, very loudly: '*Enfin!*' and then: 'Is that Jonathan Steele, if you please? Is it?' The rasping tone and fractured accent could only belong to one man. It was my old and wily Greek friend from darkest Johannesburg, Eumor Eumorphopulos.

'Eumor!' I shouted, unreasonably delighted. 'What are you doing in New York?'

'Trying to find you,' he answered, promptly and sardonically. 'Where you live these days?'

'Here. But I was away last night.'

'Ha!'

'It's not "Ha!" at all,' I said. 'I was sitting up with a sick manuscript. Where are you staying?'

'At the Plaza. But I leave again tonight.'

'Where to?'

'Peruvia.'

'That's Peru, Eumor,' I told him. 'And it's in the other direction. But hop into a cab and come on over.'

'I bring bottle champagne?'

'I have bottle champagne waiting. Hurry!'

After a six years' interval, he really looked very odd—or perhaps I had forgotten how odd he had looked in the first place. He seemed smaller, older, and greener than I ever remembered; under the kind of wide-brimmed black hat which George Raft wore on very late-night movies, his face was more creased, more crafty, and more Balkan than ever. He advanced through the opened door at a run, threw his arms round me with a cry of 'My friend!' and kissed me energetically on both cheeks. I was not at all put out. I had always had a soft spot for Eumor, who had proved himself so good a champion in Johannesburg, and had been, I remembered, the first non-publishing character to read *Ex Afrika*.

When our outlandish greetings were done, he wandered round the room, fingered the curtain material, and asked 'How much?' as if he really expected an answer. Then, across brimming glasses, we toasted each other, and the happy past, and set to work to bring it up to date.

He was going to Peru to do something about a bauxite mine. Was he buying it? I asked.

228

'Or selling,' he answered, between swallows. 'These things very difficult. I have not yet made my mind. You know I am a millionaire again?'

'So am I, Eumor. But I spent it all.'

'*Mon élève!* You want some more money?'

'No. But I'll keep you in mind. What time does your plane leave?'

'Middle night.'

'We'll have dinner, and I'll drive you out to the airport. But can't you stay any longer?'

He shook his head. 'Have meetings in Peruvia. I stopped to see you. I promised Kate. But I come back in three, four weeks.'

'How is Kate?'

'*Fabelhaft!* Sends her love.'

'What's she doing, and when's she coming back?'

He held out his glass for a refill before answering: 'She is working hard. She doesn't come back till work is finished.'

'When will that be?'

He looked at me, his eyes calculating. 'Perhaps never, Jonathan.'

'Good God!' I said, startled. 'Why? What does she want to stay for? What is there to do?'

'Plenty.' He sat down, and began to speak more slowly and carefully. 'You know she has Maraisgezicht to look after now. She is very busy with that. She feels she cannot leave yet, because of her people.'

'But the place can run itself,' I protested. 'With a good agent. Or she could sell it.'

'She does not want to sell it. She does not want to sell anything. She wants to stay. Because of that, and because of South Africa.'

'Is that the real reason?'

'I believe so.'

'But what about South Africa?'

'It is terrible, Jonathan. Such hatred, such bad laws, such division of peoples. You would not believe.'

'I don't see what that has to do with Kate.'

'It has to do with everyone.' He looked up suddenly. 'It has to do with you.'

'No, sir.'

He was silent, and I felt that we were in danger of parting almost before we had properly met. I tried to soften my last firm reply.

229

'Of course it has to do with *everyone*, in a way. But you can't go on tearing yourself to bits all your life. . . . Be fair, Eumor. I did what I could about that sort of thing, with *Ex Afrika*.'

He nodded. 'Oh yes. I agree. A very wonderful book. How I remember when I first read it! You write another one like that?'

'No.'

'Why not, Jonathan?'

'Because I've done it once, and I'm not going to do it again. What do you want me to write this time? *Son of Ex Africa*?'

'You are son of *Ex Afrika*,' he countered, with, for Eumor, a rather subtle twist of phrase. 'Don't turn your back on your father.'

I had to laugh, since I did not wish to get angry, nor sad either. I wanted to enjoy my friend's company, and the grisly side of the grey world was going to wait till I had done so. I poured out some more champagne, and tried to convey my own mood of relaxation.

'Come on, Eumor,' I told him. 'We're not going to solve any of these problems tonight. I'm sorry if Kate's getting really involved, and we'll talk some more about that, but not just now. Hell, I haven't seen you for six years! Tell me what's been happening in the old home town. How's Skip Shannon? How's Fraternelli?'

We gossiped and drank for about an hour, touching nothing that hurt, enjoying a re-hash of South African wild life such as the tourists did not see. Eumor, who had been thoughtful, almost brooding, now seemed ready to join in this nonsense. Presently I looked at my watch, and at the two empty bottles, and said:

'I'm meeting a girl for dinner, Eumor. Let's pick her up, and then eat somewhere. She's got to go to the theatre about nine, so we can come back to all this later.'

His corrugated olive face assumed a well-remembered air of appetite.

'What girl is this?'

'She's beautiful, Eumor. You'll love her.'

'Tall?'

'Huge.'

'All right. She do for me. What about you?'

'I like food. I'll just watch.'

'You *voyeur* now?'

'Me *voyeur*. You Tarzan.'

As a compliment to the visiting potentate, we dined at a Greek restaurant, where Eumor, taking over completely—and who had a better right?—used the Grecian inside track to command one of the strangest meals I had ever seen, seeming to consist of large, unrelated portions of things from different ends of the normal menu.

Among other items, we had stuffed vine-leaves, and a *Moussaka* of *aubergines*, and skewered lamb, and most of a sturgeon, and piles of those elegant long fritters, perfumed with rose-water, called *Scaltsounia*, and honey-cake, and a jar—an actual *amphora* with the classic tapered base—of white Retsina wine which tasted, most agreeably, of pine-tree gum.

In sum, it was a prodigious meal, and it made my friend Eumor very popular with Susan.

This seemed to be mutual. Eumor always behaved, towards any woman who was not seriously disfigured, with such alarming gallantry that it was difficult to gauge his private scale; but there could be no doubt that this time he thought he had moved into Elysian fields of beauty.

There was no doubt either, judging from his increasingly complicated jokes, that he was taking my relationship with Susan for granted; and indeed, since at one point she absentmindedly said something about the laundry having ruined one of my shirts, not too much guess-work was needed.

We were a cheerful party, and when, at nine o'clock, Susan had to leave us, to make her triumphant second-act appearance as the Spirit of Paris, she was given a flourishing send-off, and Eumor kissed her hand so often and so hungrily that other diners cheered. But I did not make a date for her to meet us later. Eumor and I had left some important things unsaid, and I was now in the right mood of well-fed benevolence not to wish to shirk them.

Eumor came back from the door, whither his farewell enthusiasm had swept him, and sat down with gleaming eyes.

'More wine!' he said, and snapped his fingers, alerting the whole world of waiters. 'What a girl! I meet her when I come back, yes?'

'I'll warn her about that,' I assured him, and hoped it did not sound too ambiguous. 'You really liked her, Eumor?'

Having nothing else to kiss, Eumor kissed the back of his own hand, in private homage. 'I *love* her already!' he exclaimed, and snatched his freshly-poured glass of Retsina, and gulped it as no doubt it was meant to be gulped. 'How long has she been your friend?'

'About seven months.'

'Oh. . . .' He raised his eyebrows very high indeed. 'I did not realise. That's not good, Jonathan. That is too long a situation.'

I drank also. 'Why too long? She's a beautiful girl, and I'm very fond of her.'

'But seven months,' he said, and I felt he was ready to be serious again, and that we were moving to that part of the field from which I had coaxed him earlier. This time, it did not seem to matter. 'It's too long,' he said again. 'Too permanent. After all, she is only——'

'Only what?'

'*Poule de luxe*.'

I wasn't going to lose my head over a point of protocol. 'She's more than that.'

'Not for you, my friend.'

'Why not for me?'

'Because you have Kate.'

This was something else I was ready to talk about. 'That's been a long situation too, Eumor. Six years. Remember that joke you used to tell? About putting pennies in a bottle, and taking them out again?'

'It was a joke.'

'Jokes can be true.'

'And now you are putting pennies into this bottle,' he said, with sudden energy. 'What does that prove? Even I could put pennies into that one. At my age! But it is not marriage. Not marriage like you have.'

'Like I had,' I corrected him. 'It isn't the same now. Why should it be? These things always fade out, and it's silly to pretend otherwise. Or to expect it. I honestly believe there's a natural term for every marriage—five years, ten years, whatever it is—and after that it's over, except as a matter of habit, of social convenience, to keep the kids in the station-wagon and the neighbours in the rumpus-room.' I could see from his face that he was not agreeing, but I pressed on with an argument which, at that moment, across that dinner-table, armed by that particular glass of wine, seemed crystal-clear, and utterly logical. 'It's true, Eumor! Never shake thy gory locks at me! Marriage *can* be like that, a sort of hen-coop of togetherness. But because it comes to an end, that doesn't mean it's been a failure. It may have been wonderful, for its correct length of time, and then it finishes, at exactly the right moment.'

'My poor Jonathan,' he said, and there was real compassion in his

232

voice. 'Is this what you have been thinking, in your little tower of success? You cannot have changed so much! What you say is nonsense, and you know it. With Kate you have a wonderful marriage. With this girl—' he jerked his head towards the street door, '—you have just a ——' he used a word, presumably Greek, which I did not understand, and which I took to be biological. 'You cannot throw away someone like Kate, just because you do not wish to make love with her every day.'

'Twice every day.'

He was not to be turned from his argument: flippancy would not stem this flood. 'And now you have this girl twice every day, and you think it—' he waved his hand irritably, searching for the word he wanted, '—you think it *cancels* Kate? You are mad! Have the girl all you want, until you are tired and don't want her any more. Have her until you break the bed, or break something else! But do not leave Kate alone. Do not leave yourself alone. You and Kate need each other, and you have proved it.'

'How, proved it?'

'By being married six years, and missing her when she is gone.'

'I never said anything about missing her.'

'You do not have to. This girl is part of missing her.'

'Oh, rubbish!' I was sure this was not true. 'You've got it all wrong, Eumor. Susan isn't a substitute for Kate. She's her successor.' I did not quite like this idea, and I corrected it. 'I mean, she's a complete change, the very opposite of Kate, and just what I need. She doesn't give a damn what I——' This was getting too complicated, and confused, and I broke it off. 'Anyway, Kate's O.K.,' I said, after a moment. 'Apparently she wants to stay and look after Maraisgezicht. And she's got all this money. She can be perfectly happy by herself.'

'She does not want to be by herself. That I can assure you.'

It suddenly struck me that this was really why Eumor was in New York; he had come here on purpose to say these last two sentences of his; he was carrying out an appointed mission, using the weapons of wine, and friendship, and the dedicated look which belonged to the honest go-between. Though he was not the sort of man I could ever be angry with, I was irritated none-the-less.

'Perhaps *I* want to be by myself,' I said, shortly.

'You cannot afford to be, Jonathan.' He really was very involved in this, very earnest, very intense. I could concede that it was good to have such friends, and that at any other time, in any other area, it would have been wonderful to have this paragon of a doctor on hand, ready with the splints and the acute diagnosis and the brisk tonic which would set a man on his feet again, in no time at all. But just at the moment, I wanted to stay in bed, sick as a dog, and loving it. 'I tell you,' Eumor the paragon continued, 'you need her. And she still thinks it is a good marriage, in spite of everything.'

'In spite of what, exactly? The girl?'

'She does not know about the girl. And she will not hear from me.' He put his hand on my arm. 'Anyway, the girl is not important, unless you choose to make her so. Don't forget that. Girls in bed are cheap. In the end they are just like money, to be enjoyed, to be spent, to be forgotten. That is why they *cost* money. . . . But they should not cost anything else.'

'What did you mean, then, that Kate thinks our marriage is O.K., in spite of everything?'

'Because of how you have changed. You used to be serious. You used to care about such things as Africa, and write about them also. Now you do not.'

'Is that bad?'

'It is tragedy,' said Eumor, and looked as if he meant it.

I decided that I did not want another mourner at the bedside of significant literature, and I did not want any more of this, either. Once again, I could not quarrel with Eumor, and, particularly, not where Kate was concerned; he had been at our side on the first day we met, and on the night we fell in love; he was our god-father, our presiding angel; such men, such friends, were not expendable in any circumstances. But if this privileged, interior pressure went on any longer, the mould of concord was liable to break, and that would be the end of a lot of things I valued.

I said: 'O.K., Eumor. You've said your piece, and I've listened to it. Now let's press the button on this.' I looked up, at the clock on the wall behind his head. 'We have exactly one hour before we have to drive out to the airport. What would you like to do?'

He opened his mouth to say something, and then, like the rare man he was, changed his mind, and with it his whole expression. He tossed off the last of his wine, and smiled wickedly, and said:

'Strip tease! What else?'

Afterwards I drove him out to Kennedy Airport, and saw him off on his plane to Caracas, which was the first leg of his journey, and went slowly back into town, meandering along the Grand Central Parkway and over the Triborough Bridge. The lights of the East River seemed to unravel as I moved smoothly south again, like an endless skein of yellow-white wool falling gently apart as a dark hand divided it, and I found myself wishing that a lot of other things would unravel half as easily.

I was ready to acknowledge that Eumor had done his best. As an emissary from Kate, bringing a salutary shock from the world outside my bed, he had made his mark and sounded his warning. The message was simple: when Kate returned, *if* Kate returned, I would have to straighten up and fly right, because she would be leaving something she wanted for something she could not be sure of.

She would be doing a basic favour for me, and I would be in honour bound to match it.

Eumor had given me a lot to think about. The fact that I did not want to think about it could not be held against the man, nor the message, nor anyone but myself.

CHAPTER SIX

Eumor's visit had been like a stone briefly troubling the pool; I felt that if I waited long enough, the ripples would go away. But this was a Chamber of Commerce forecast, tailored strictly for the vacation trade. I was first made aware that the boat itself was beginning to rock, by an entirely new greeting from Joe the doorman.

I had been on television the previous night, as a guest-detective trying to unmask such diverse toilers as the girl who crocheted ball-pockets for billiard tables, and the man who ironed the newspapers at London's most august club, restricted to the octogenarian nobility. (I had guessed him wrong; I thought he was a pants-presser with a funny accent.) But Joe the doorman did not pass judgement on my performance; this time he broke precedent. He said:

'Hallo there, Mr. Steele! I was reading about you last night.'

'Reading?' I said, surprised. 'What have I been doing this time?'

'Oh, I didn't believe any of it,' he assured me, with a cheerful grin. 'It was just an item. . . . But I saved it for you to see.' He fished inside his coat pocket, and came out with a crumpled evening paper, a paper which, to put it mildly, I did not normally read. 'Keep it,' he said. 'I've been all the way through it.'

I thanked him, and put the paper in my own pocket, and went on up to the apartment, where I planned to spend a quiet day. I forgot it for about an hour, while I was going through the mail, and listening with half an enchanted ear to David Oistrakh, well-known communist infiltrator, playing his insidious violin. Then something made me remember the conversation downstairs, and I took the paper over to my desk, and looked for the 'item' which had caught Joe's eye.

It was not too difficult to find; he had folded the paper at the appropriate page. It was half-way down a gossip column headed 'Show Biz Confidential'.

Jonathan Steele (I read) *now toiling on the final version of Erwin Orwin's* Pink Safari *musical, based on Johnny's own block-buster*, Ex Afrika, *still manages to make the scene in his spare time. . . . He's all over town these days and nights with stunning Susan Crompton, who you can catch (if you're quick enough) as the low-cut 'Spirit of Paris' in Erwin's other opus, that ever-loving, ever-running darling*, Josephine. . . . *Nice casting, Johnny. . . . Meanwhile, back at the ostrich farm, current mate Kate Steele sits it out in wildest Johannesburg, her home town, counting the loot from a recent inheritance. . . . Better get your head out of the sand, Kate, or you'll wind up as the ex in Afrika.*

I was glad that I had a drink in my hand, at that moment; there was a sudden and urgent need for a different taste. I read the column again, more analytically, feeling a little sick and a little chilly round the conscience. Then I poured another drink, and turned off the hi-fi set, and gave the matter some serious thought.

The report was considerably dated, as far as history was concerned; yet, amazingly, this was the first time Susan and I had appeared in print as a team, explicitly or otherwise. I had always been expecting something of the sort, though not perhaps so viciously angled; but there was an enormous amount of competition in this area, from New York's perennial crop of public lovers, and writers as a class were of less amorous interest than Hollywood apes, French poodles, and imported English stallions.

So far, in spite of a less-than-discreet progress all around the town, we had been left off the form-sheet; we had remained technically anonymous.

It was difficult to judge if this anonymity had now been breached. Kate might never read the paragraph, nor hear about it; and if she did, she still might not take it seriously. It was, I thought suddenly, couched in her own kind of prose, the kind she and her gossip column had thriven on, in the distant past; and she must know that a lot of such 'revelations' were balanced on a very slender wire of fact, if they were sustained by anything at all. She might decide to take the professional view that fire and smoke, so often unrelated, were in this case part of the same mirage.

I was still speculating about this, an hour and several drinks later, when the phone rang. It was Susan, Susan in a serious mood.

She began immediately. 'Johnny, there was a terrible thing in one of the papers last night. Shall I——'

'I know,' I told her. 'I heard about it.'

'Who told you?'

'The doorman. Who told you?'

'People have been calling me up all morning,' she said excitedly. 'Well, three people, at least.'

'What people?'

'Girls in the show. Johnny, what do you think?'

'I don't think anything,' I told her, and after about twelve straight drinks this was fundamentally true. 'I think we've been damned lucky so far, that's all. Now we're not.'

'Are you angry?' she asked after a moment.

'Not with you. Why should I be? You come out of it all right, anyway. They said you were stunning and low-cut. What more do you want?'

'You *are* angry,' she said. 'Johnny, I'm so sorry. I wouldn't have this happen for anything in the world. Aren't people awful?'

'Yes,' I said. 'Everyone's awful but us.'

'Would you like to come back here and talk about it?'

'I don't think so. At the moment I'm in conference with a bottle of Comrade Smirnoff's best. Stunning and uncorked. I'll make out with that.'

'Darling, isn't there anything I can do?'

'Not a thing.' I gathered a few stray thoughts together. 'Susan, don't worry about this. It'll either blow up in our face, or it won't. Probably it won't. There are hundreds of these damned gossip items every day, and they're forgotten in twenty-four hours. Who reads the bloody paper, anyway? Doormen, and stunning old show-girls, and pimps, and truck-drivers, and Broadway drunks, and all our best friends.' I realised that my thought-gathering had not been too successful, and I tried to sum up, in a common-sense verdict. 'Kate may never read it, anyway. By the time she gets back, they'll be libelling someone else instead.'

'Do you really think so?'

'With every fibre of my being.'

'It *is* libel, isn't it? Can't you sue them?'

'Oh sure. Just let me get my trousers on. . . . Susan, it isn't libel, and no one is going to sue anyone, and with luck she won't hear about it, and that'll be that.'

'I wish you'd come over, all the same.'

'I'm lying low,' I said. 'Eliot Ness gave me the signal. Goodbye.'

When I woke up, it was with a wonderfully dry mouth, but in other respects I felt better all over. Already, the gossip item which had so downcast us was out of date; already, there must be another issue of 'Show Biz Confidential' on the stands, and people would be reading and talking about some other sordid couple. There was nothing plucked so featherless and forlorn as yesterday's love-birds.

Tonight, with luck, Susan and I would start to be forgotten again. And perhaps Kate, six thousand miles away, burying her head, counting her loot, would never hear about it anyway.

But that guess turned out to be wrong. Kate did hear about it; in fact she must actually have read the column; some prompt and kindly friend must have sent a helpful cutting winging southwards within twenty-four hours. Three days later, I had a cable from her:

'*Returning in about ten days. Who is stunning Susan Crompton, or can I do it? Love Kate.*'

It was a fair warning, a very fair warning indeed.

Waiting for her (and it was strange to realise, after so long a separation, that 'her' meant Kate), I went to several parties by myself, in a kind of reverse effort to stay out of the limelight. It seemed possible that if enough people saw me moping unaccompanied round the town, they would begin to think: *Poor old bachelor Steele—he must be pining his heart out.* . . . But the price of this ingenious stroke of camouflage was, for my own taste, rather high.

The six-to-eight cocktail circuit, as established in any city where more than a quarter of a million people huddle together for urban shelter, always seemed to me a prime example of the stupidity and self-delusion lying in ambush for group-behaviour of any sort.

It was as if someone, ignoring the law of diminishing returns, had worked out that if four people could enjoy themselves in one room, forty could have a real whale of a time, and four hundred could touch dizzy heights of ecstasy. And if one were really shooting for the moon, there was still the regal or presidential bash for four thousand.

The result, in cities like New York, or Washington, or London, or San Francisco, or Paris, or Rome—all highly civilised places where people should have known better—as well as in vulgar carbons such as Toronto or Johannesburg, was the conviction, deeply embedded, already sacrosanct, that a party could never hope for the higher ratings unless there was no room to move, no way of talking save to scream against the uproar, no time for anything but banality, and no way to survive except by burying the nose deep inside a glass, and dulling all the other senses as quickly as possible.

The idea that only an idiot would prefer to stand and shout when he could sit and read, or listen to music, or dine with six friends who were prepared to take turns at talking, seemed to have gone the way of the crinoline.

Yet I launched out upon this tormented sea none-the-less, and did my share of elbowing, and shouting, and grinning, and gulping, like any compulsive good-timer. The outcome, though negative for fun, was at least instructive.

I learned that no one seemed to give a damn what I was doing with my spare time, or which bed I was bouncing on, or where I hung my hat. A few friends asked: 'Where's Susan?' and a few others: 'Where's Kate?'; neither group used any special or distinguishable tone of voice, and neither group waited for an answer, which they could scarcely have heard in any case.

It was an effective illustration of the fact that, by and large, in spite of the grinding gossip wheels, other people's love affairs were really the dullest topic in the world; and that the type of exhibitionist whose peculiar pleasure it was to perch high on the head-board and crow to the world: '*Look at me—I'm loving the daylights out of Liz,*' had only his own pointing finger as the emblem of success.

However, there was one exception to all this, one chance-encountered man who did take a personal interest in how I was spending my time. This was Hobart Mackay, my publisher, whom I met at a literary-and-stage gathering in one of the big party rooms at the St. Regis.

Hobart went to a lot of such parties; he could not have enjoyed them, since he was essentially a quiet and studious character who did more thinking than doing. But he probably felt it necessary to keep an eye on other publishers and authors, to ensure that the former did not steal anyone from his own stable, and the latter, if they felt like straying, knew that they had a comfortable home to go to.

He was a small man, about fifty, with short sandy hair and a blue bow tie; he looked like a university professor who had not changed his basic style since his own student days. We saw each other by chance across the jam-packed room—he was not an easy man to see at such a party—and he raised his eyebrows comically, as if in despair of the company we were keeping. Then he was lost to view behind a massive man with a bushy white beard, who really did look like a writer, and then we finally came together, in an eddy of traffic beside one of the St. Regis potted palms.

'Hallo, Jonathan,' he said, with a slightly harassed smile. His glass was empty, and he could not have been further from the bar, which was at the opposite end of the room, and under fierce and continuous siege by crowds of much larger guests. 'It's nice to see you, but I wish you were a dry martini. . . . I didn't know you came to this sort of circus.'

'But I love them,' I said, insincerely. 'They keep me in touch with the world of achievement. And of course I've got nothing else to do.'

'I hope that's not true.' He was looking at me carefully, as he always did; to him, writers were people, not names or labels, and he liked to find out what sort of mood and shape we were in, though, as a spectator of the human comedy, he was rarely disposed to do anything about his findings. 'How's my book coming along?'

'Slowly,' I said. 'You know I've been working on this *Pink Safari* thing.'

'How's *that* coming along?' he asked, with markedly less enthusiasm.

240

'It's pretty well finished. But I'm staying on to help with the production.'

'Book!' he said suddenly. 'When do I get a book?'

'In the new year, I hope.'

'Really?' He was still watching me, with clinical interest. 'That's good news. Can you say when, in the new year? It's time we published you again.'

'I honestly don't know, Hobart.' I wasn't going to worry too much about this examination; I had been working hard on Erwin's musical, and did not feel guilty of waste of time or effort. 'You know how some things go fast, and then they go slow. The book got stuck, but one of these days it will come unstuck again, and land on your desk.' A waiter, squirming his way through the throng with a tray of someone else's drinks, passed close to me, and I reached out and abstracted two glasses of what looked like very strong Scotch and soda. I had been drinking vodka, but a thirst was a thirst. 'Courtesy of the house,' I said to Hobart, handing him a glass. 'Never say I don't look after you.'

'Oh, you look after people, all right.' He sipped the drink, and made a face, and stared at me intently, over the rim of his glass. 'This seems to be rye and ginger-ale. . . . When is Kate coming back?'

Unlike other inquirers, he was actually interested in the answer, and I told him as much as I knew. 'In a few days,' I said. 'She got tied up in South Africa, but that seems to have been straightened out.'

'I'll be very glad to see her again. You must have missed her.'

'Very much.'

'Seven months must have seemed a long time.'

'Infinity.'

He took another sip of his drink before saying, in a gently censorious tone: 'I'm sure it will be good for you to have her back in New York.'

There was no mistaking the subject of this, and though I did not resent his interest, since he was a good enough friend to be allowed the latitude, the idea of baring secrets and sharing the confessional made no appeal at all. I was not seeking a father figure, however small and discreet, even though I had taken a $40,000 advance on my patrimony.

I looked away from him, as any keen party-goer might, and glanced round the packed room. The uproar, aided by a low ceiling and a rising intake, had now reached a fearful level of decibels.

'If New York were all like this,' I said, 'Kate would be better off in South Africa. Luckily it isn't.'

Hobart had not quite finished.

'When she comes back,' he said, 'you must bring her to dinner.'

'We'd enjoy that.'

'Like old times.'

The phrase, in this context, rang particularly false; we always dined with the Mackays three or four times a year, and we would no doubt be doing so again. If this was a revival of 'old times', so was renewing one's driving licence. But in the interests of peaceful co-existence, I said again:

'We'd like it very much.'

'If you won't find it too dull.'

'Now why should I find it dull?'

He gave a very small wave of his hand, the only kind feasible with the amount of room we had to spare.

'Well, you know—the theatre crowd. I thought you might have developed a taste for fast living.'

I had had enough of this little contest. 'You've been reading the wrong papers, Hobart,' I told him. 'I haven't changed, and I don't intend to. Anything else is a cowardly smear circulated by my political opponents.'

With that, he seemed to be satisfied. He smiled, much more easily, and said: 'Time for me to go,' and promptly poured the rest of his drink into the potted palm, with the courage of small men who know what they want and what they don't. Then, without disguise, he slipped the empty glass into his side pocket.

'Only way to deal with it,' he said, noticing my expression. 'I give it to the doorman on the way out.'

I was still surprised. 'After that, anything I do will seem normal.'

'Mind you keep it that way,' he said, and with this cautionary farewell he made for the door.

I moved slowly after him, ready to leave also; I had done my duty for the night, and the small exchange with Hobart Mackay had been vaguely unsettling, the first hint of its kind from a man who had always seemed to view other people's habits, as distinct from their writing, with the blessed unconcern which one could bestow on other people's children.

Pressures, great and small, seemed to be building up, about to burst

242

in upon poor old Steele, who had only wanted a quiet life, and a big strong girl to serve the nectar. . . . Manœuvring my way towards the door, I heard a fruity, long-forgotten voice declare, as if pronouncing the ultimate in benedictions: 'Just looking round. I might even—ah—settle here,' and I turned swiftly towards the source, and by God it was Lord Muddley.

I had not seen him for years—nearly seven years ago, to be exact, during the strange early reign of Kate Marais. It was funny to come upon this early Georgian dinosaur, this genuine fossil from the vanished past, and to recall the last time we had met, over a flaming row in a Johannesburg night-club, with Kate—new Kate, cool Kate, unknown Kate—keeping the ring for us. But I did not expect our re-encounter to be unduly funny, otherwise.

Lord Muddley had not changed. The beefy red face was still matched by the small boiled eyes, like pale carrot-rings in a stew; the built-in condescension, the aura of fat insolence, were both unaltered. He had added a monocle to his *ensemble*, and, that night, a hairy checked suit which smelled very slightly of wet retriever. Otherwise, his lordship appeared to have remained his barnacled, stupid self.

He recognised me, after a long unblinking stare; it was like being inspected by a rather dopey foreign general. 'Ah, Steele,' he said, in the authentic plum-cake voice of Old England, 'I thought it must be you. I suppose this is actually your sort of party, isn't it?'

The man he had been talking to melted swiftly away, with a readiness I could understand, and we were left to the joys of each other's company.

'Ah, Muddley,' I said, not to be outdone. 'What are you doing among all these clever people?'

'I came with Baxter, our consul-general. You know Sir Norman?'

'No.'

'Pity. Quite a capable fellow. He might be able to help you.'

The idea of the British consul-general giving me a hand with the dialogue of *The Pink Safari* was not within the compass of my imagination, and I let the thought, regretfully, go by. Instead I asked:

'Are you living in New York now? I thought you were going to—ah—settle in South Africa.'

'But I did!' he declared promptly. The noise round us made it necessary for both of us to shout, and his answer rang out like a challenge. 'I should have thought you would have known that. I gave it two years! But it was hopeless, quite hopeless! South Africa simply isn't a white man's country any more!'

This was an interesting viewpoint. 'I should have thought,' I said, 'that it had become specifically a white man's country, and that a lot of the trouble stems from that.'

'No, no, no. That's just newspaper talk. After all, you can't count Afrikaners as white men, can you? They've been out there too long, that's their trouble! . . . My point is that it is not an *investment* country any more. There's too much unrest. It's impossible to count on a settled return. The politicians worry so much about their blasted natives, they can't do a decent job of running the economy. You can see this sort of thing all over the world nowadays. I mean, take the United Nations.'

'Tell me about the United Nations.'

'It's ridiculous!' said Lord Muddley. 'And I *know*—I looked in just the other day. Nothing but a blasted nigger-minstrel show! Damned committees of Africans and Buddhists telling us how to run our affairs. I mean, take a man like U Thant. What sort of a secretary-general could he possibly be? Fellow probably couldn't write his own name, five years ago.'

'I believe he is actually very well educated.'

'Nonsense! And if he is, it's our fault for doing it. Things were far better off as they were.'

I could see that the interior Lord Muddley had not changed, either. He had been a pompous old idiot when we first met, and I had allowed it to get under my skin. He was a pompous old idiot still, but now I could not bring myself to worry about it. Vaguely I supposed that there was room in the world for both of us; that this was part of nature's system of checks and balances, and that Lord Muddley was one of the checks; and that if he had not existed, it would have been necessary to invent him, to preserve the equilibrium, to inhibit the spread of commonsense, or stop the ants taking over.

There were certain mysteries in our universe which the wise man must come to accept. Otherwise, tortured by doubt and misgiving, he would never be reconciled to this or any other century.

During my silence, Lord Muddley had been staring at me, his little eyes as blue and sharp as corn-flowers. Now, when he spoke, it was in a different way, more calculating, more to the point.

'I believe I saw you on television a few days ago,' he said, as if television, from his single use of it, had now received official sanction. 'That's partly how I recognised you.'

'I hope you enjoyed the show.'

'I couldn't understand a word of it,' said Lord Muddley. 'Lot of gibberish, as far as I was concerned! However, I believe it's very popular with certain classes of people. . . . They tell me you're getting to be quite well known as a writer, these days.'

'Now who told you that?' I asked, intrigued.

He almost smirked. 'Oh, I pick these things up, you know. It's the sort of thing I hear about. Tell me, how much does a best-seller—isn't that what it's called?—make? In round figures.'

'About half a million dollars.'

'You're joking,' he said, incredulously. 'Why, that's getting on for two hundred thousand pounds!'

'One hundred and eighty thousand.'

'From a *book*?'

'From a successful book.'

'Good heavens!' he said. 'I must look into this. I used to do a bit of scribbling myself, in the old days. And I've had, as you probably realise, a very full life. I really had no idea it was so easy to make these large sums.' He was looking at me, now, as if I might suddenly have become eligible for one of his clubs, against all probability, all reason. 'Let me see—how many of these things have you written so far?'

'Only two.'

'Two best-sellers?'

'You could call them that. One big, and one small.'

'Ah. . . .' He made a ponderous pounce on what seemed to be a flaw in the balance-sheet of creativity. 'But how much does a small one make?'

'About a quarter of a million. Dollars.'

'Well, well. . . .' His tone told me that I was eligible for election once more. 'You were writing when we first met, weren't you—when we had that—ah—top-hole party in Johannesburg.'

'Yes.'

'I believe I met your wife, too.'

'Yes.'

'Is she here tonight?'

'No,' I answered. 'She's in South Africa. Her father died, and she had to clear up his estate.'

245

'Indeed? Was that—ah—a complicated matter?'

I told him what he wanted to know. 'About two million dollars. Kate got it all.'

'Well, well. . . .' By now his monocle was quite misted over, and he extracted and wiped it, looking at me the while with that pop-eyed stare which linked the angler to the fish. After a moment he said: 'Now that we've met again, I expect to see more of you. When does your wife return?'

'I'm not sure. Not for some time.'

'But you'll keep in touch with me, I know.' Some semblance of heartiness had come into his voice; it rang very strangely, like a plastic gong. 'Perhaps we can arrange another party, one of these days.'

'Why not?'

'I'm kept moving about pretty strenuously, at the moment. Looking round. But Baxter—the consul-general—will always know where to find me.'

'I'll remember that.'

'It's most agreeable,' he said, with true condescension, 'to meet a fellow-countryman so far from home. I think people like us should stick together, eh? Are you dining anywhere tonight, by the way?'

'Yes. I'm fixed up, I'm afraid.'

'Some other time, then.'

'Yes,' I said. 'Yes indeed. Some other time.'

He had been funny after all, I decided as I took my leave; funny, in a grisly sort of way. I felt that I had added to my collection of oddities without too much involvement. But what had been truly bizarre was to have the bad news of South Africa confirmed from so novel an angle. It seemed to rank as something almost incomprehensible to man, like Stonehenge, or a bird's-eye view of a bird.

It did not persuade me to burnish up my shining armour, pick out a spear, and go forth into battle for the current cause. In fact, the very reverse; it multiplied the pleasures of neutrality.

It proved, in this respect, to be very good practice for Kate.

Her plane from Lisbon was late, and it was past midnight before we were driving back from the airport, through a clear black December night, with Julia mounting guard over the luggage in the back seat. Kate looked beautiful; very sunburnt, very well, exquisitely dressed and accoutred; sixteen hours of flying, plane-swapping, and waiting

246

about might have been just what she needed, to groom her for our meeting, to bring her up to her own level of perfection.

We held hands all the way into town, with that kind of electric anticipation which only lovers on the brink could ever really feel; we were clearly delighted to see each other again, and we knew we had the means to prove it, as soon as we were under cover.

It was like that, all the rest of that night. She did not think much of the state of the apartment, but it was a loving kind of criticism; *I am here*, her glance seemed to say, *and I will set this nursery to rights by and by: but first I will deal with the chief inhabitant, my first-born favourite child. . . .* We went swiftly to bed, because we had that kind of feeling, instantly recognised, urgently shared; and in bed, as usual, all cares were smoothed out, all problems solved by simple sensual alchemy.

She had chosen to make it so. I had thought that she would come back armed with questions, even accusations, and insist upon plain answers before she even took off her gloves. But—though we both knew that a cloud hung in some corner of our sky, and would not go away until we had looked at it together—she did not want to handle it like that.

'All *post mortems* tomorrow,' she said at one point, when it had become clear that there was only one thing for us to do next, and that very speedily. 'We'll talk about your terrible misdeeds later. Just for now, I propose to be the only girl in the world.'

She was. Once again, it was the shape and feel of a different person which gave to desire that extra teasing quality, that mortal thirst which must be slaked at this very fountain, and at none other; and that night, something more had been added even to this: the delight of loving, anew, a known body, with all the subtleties and tender agreements of love which had been mislaid or forgotten.

Throughout our *rendezvous*, during all the deep headlong dive into the private compartment of our marriage, we always knew what the other was going to do next, with precise recognition. Alone among all the possible examples of foreknowledge, of routine, of exact response, it proved to be the most exciting part of love-making.

Six years together, seven months apart—who could say which was the spur of action, the actual word which cast the spell, the key to this most delicate of locks? Did it also, for me, owe something to the secret, all-but-lapsed pleasure of carrying another person along on this

247

delicious road? Was it bound up with the simple male pride of the man who could swing it? And what was it for her? Use or un-use? The accustomed persuasions of the past, the wildness of the present, or a wishful trust in the future?

We did not know, we could not really share this speculation, and we did not try to find the answer, since we did not need to. We only recognised that we had rediscovered the fiery simplicity of Eden, in ourselves, in each other, and that to lie together after a time of lying apart was sweet to all the senses, overwhelming to all emotions, and very exciting indeed.

Next morning, as so often happened, up and down the ladder of marriage—next morning was different.

Kate, taking her full entitlement, slept very late, while I pottered about my study desk, running off some letters which would later go down, via dictaphone belt, to one of the young ladies at the secretarial agency. Jack Taggart called, about some translation rights of *Wrap-Around*, and Erwin Orwin, about a rehearsal which he did not want me to miss. I was in a suspended mood, waiting, like Job or Oedipus, for the day's ration of bad news. All problems still remained, queueing up for solution; the postponement had been pleasant indeed, but this was the morning after.

I heard Kate's bell ring in the kitchen, and presently, through my open door, saw Julia making for the stairway with a coffee-tray. On impulse, I waylaid her.

'I'll take that up, Julia,' I told her, and when I had the tray in my hand I asked: 'Did you enjoy yourself in South Africa?'

'Yes, sir,' she answered. Her face, impassive at the best of times, was a positive mask of inexpression.

'Did you go home and see your family?'

'Yes, sir.'

'How were they?'

'Just the same.'

'What's your brother doing now?'

'He was away,' said Julia, with even less expression than before, and went back into the kitchen.

So much for those interminable travellers' tales. . . . Upstairs, I knocked on Kate's door, and called out: 'Room service,' and went inside.

She was sitting up in bed, with her hair falling loosely over sunburned shoulders; whether from her long sleep, or the aftermath of love, her face seemed completely and innocently at peace, smoothed out like a child's; she looked about sixteen years old. She smiled when she saw me, and said: 'What a funny hotel this must be.'

'Very versatile staff,' I said, and manœuvred the tray, which had snap-down legs like a hospital model, into its position across the bed. Then I took my own drink from it, and bore it away to the window seat. I remembered that I had sat there before, seven long months ago, when Kate had been packing for her flight, and I had surprised her by saying that I was going to Barbados. I wondered who was going to do the surprising now.

As sometimes happened, she got my thought. Sipping her orange juice, she looked at me across the room, and then she said:

'This is where we came in, isn't it? . . . How's the bottle going, Johnny?'

'Very well.'

'You've put on weight, haven't you?'

'About eight pounds. But it's all good stuff. I've been eating rather a lot, for some reason.'

'Eating? But you never eat anything.'

'It must be going around with Erwin. . . . You've got yourself a lovely tan, Kate. But I told you that last night, didn't I?' I toasted her in spiked tomato juice. 'You were wonderful.'

'Don't sound so surprised.' She had reached the coffee-stage now, and with it came the new line of thought, the one I had been waiting for; and with that, we were off to the races. 'Johnny, who's Susan Crompton?'

Answering, I used the light tone, but not, I hoped, too light; Kate was an excellent judge of such revealing falsities. 'She's just a girl in one of Erwin's shows.'

'It sounds very convenient.'

'It's not like that at all. How did you hear about her, anyway?'

'Somebody must have known I could read, so they sent me some material.'

'Who, for God's sake?'

'I don't know.'

'Oh. . . . What a lousy trick.'

'The master speaks.'

'Oh, come on, Kate!' I said, energetically. 'You know what those gossip columns are worth.'

249

'What's this one worth?'

'Absolutely nothing. I've met her a few times, and we've been out together.'

'And she's stunning, like the man said?'

'In a show-girl sort of way.'

'What sort of way is that?'

I took another drink before I answered: 'I mean, she's tall, and quite good-looking, and she's in a show. There are a million girls like her.'

'You must have been busy.'

I laughed. 'You can't do them all.'

'Some people try.'

'Well, not me,' I said, moving up for a bit of opposition. 'Good God, if you knew the amount of work I've been doing! I haven't had time for that sort of thing, even if I'd wanted it.'

'Why didn't you want it?'

'I just didn't. There wasn't any message. What's the opposite of chemistry?'

'Sophistry.' But she was frowning. 'When did you see her last, then?'

'About a week ago. Maybe a bit longer.'

'That must have been when I cabled.'

'I suppose it was, if you want to figure it out.'

'I want to figure it out. . . . Why did you stop?'

That seemed a good moment for a flash of irritation, and it needed no special effort to produce it. 'I didn't *stop* anything. We went out a few times, and that was it. I've been out with all sorts of people. Jack Taggart, and Hobart Mackay. I was at a party with Lord Muddley, the other night. Remember that character?'

'I remember Lord Muddley,' she told me, 'and I'm not too worried about you and him. I'm worried about stunning Susan Crompton.'

'You needn't be,' I said shortly. 'She's just a girl.'

'That's not the most reassuring thing you've ever said.' Now, in a curious move, she turned over on her side, and put her head back on the pillow, and addressed me via the nearest wall. 'Johnny, don't fool around. If you're involved with her, I want to know about it.'

'I'm not involved with her.'

'Were you?'

'No. It wasn't like that at all.'

'What was it like?'

'We went out a few times. I told you.'

'Where does she live?'

'Down in the fifties somewhere.'

'Somewhere? You mean you walk around till you suddenly meet her? Don't overdo it, my friend.'

'West Fifty-fourth Street.'

'That's better.' She turned her head, till she seemed even further away from me, her face buried in the pillow. I had a sudden, bitter, panicky thought that she was doing this because she had gone into mourning, for me and for us; because she did not want to watch my face when I was lying; because she knew the whole story, or thought she did, and would never be persuaded otherwise. Her voice muffled, she asked: 'Is it over, Johnny?'

'A thing can't be over if it never got started.'

She answered me with some words spoken into the pillow, which I could not hear, and I said: 'What?'

Her head turned, and suddenly she sat up to face me. 'I said, white man speak with forked tongue,' she told me, in a swift change of mood. 'Madison Avenue jargon joke. . . . Steele, I've had enough of Susan Crompton, and I'd like to be sure that you have.'

'Admitting nothing,' I said, 'I've had enough of Susan Crompton.'

'How old is she?'

'I don't know.'

'*Johnny!*'

'Twenty-something. Twenty-five, maybe.'

'I'll find out, you know.'

'Tell me when you do.'

We were fencing still, but it was not so serious now. Kate seemed to have accepted something; perhaps she had even begun to accept the actual facts, as I knew them and as she suspected; but if this were so, she could have decided at the same time not to be worried or deeply wounded by them, because the thing must assuredly be over and done with, a part of the buried past.

Perhaps, when she had used the phrase '*post mortem*', she had already been willing it so. . . . The topic seemed to have been disposed of, for this particular session; and in my relief I felt she was entitled to a remark she made later that afternoon.

We were downstairs, after lunch. When the door-bell rang, Julia answered it, and returned with the message that it was 'the electrician', and then Kate went out into the hall, where I heard a man's voice in conversation which I could not distinguish. When she came back, I asked:

'Who was that?'

She answered, very calmly, out of the blue: 'Just the man to see about the lie-detector.'

Good old Kate.

We had given half a day to one of the issues in contention; it had been quite long enough for me, and if there were loose strings still untidily showing, they were not enough to trip a strong and wary man. But it appeared that we had two such topics to discuss; and for the second, I presently began to think that the rest of her life might not be enough. At night-fall, after a dinner enlivened by lots of home-coming champagne, and one of Julia's nicest South African dishes, a sort of Cape-Malay version of stuffed egg-plant which they called *brinjals*, we came to Kate's chief concern.

The meal had supplied the clue. It was South Africa itself. As a matter of distraction, I welcomed the fact that it seemed so very important. But before long I realised that this welcome was likely to be overstayed.

She started with Maraisgezicht, her home, and why she had not been able to leave it for so long. It was, I had to admit, a sad story; and as she sat there, her legs stretched out on the zebra-skin couch, looking young and very pretty in a dress so elegant, severe, and simple that it could only have been available to an heiress, I found myself moved by both pictures.

Kate was the one I preferred. But in essence, she was not there any more. She was far away, staring up at the façade of her great house, wandering through its rooms, trying to take care of its people, her people.

'I couldn't just walk in, and then out again,' she told me. Her face was serious, and troubled; it was clear that this was a picture which had never left her, which she had brought back to keep her company and to grieve over. 'Dad had been ill for such a long time. I'd always thought that the place would run itself, even if he weren't there to watch over it, because it's been going for so long, more than two hundred years, in the same mould. But that wasn't true. It needed him, and if not him, then someone like him. Otherwise, it was just falling apart.'

'But what about the agents?' I asked. 'Weren't there two of them? What were they doing?'

She was frowning even more deeply. 'One of them died, and the other—' she paused, '—the other, I had to get rid of.'

'Why?'

'Because he didn't deserve anything else. He was an Afrikaner, of course; one of my own people. He used to be very good at his job. But he'd changed, like so many other Afrikaners. He'd become brutal, Teutonic, harsh—all the bad words. I was ashamed of him, and so were the people he was overseeing. Ashamed and puzzled, like when a friend suddenly becomes your jailer, like it must be when one's parents get divorced, or start hitting each other, or punishing their children for no reason beyond the pleasure of it. . . . Anyway, he had to leave. He could go and play Hitler anywhere else, as far as I was concerned. But not on my money. Not at Maraisgezicht.'

'But someone had to run the place. It must need a lot of discipline.'

She shook her head from side to side. 'Not discipline like that. Not like a private cage, with a long whip, and a bunch of mangy lions to use it on. . . . The big Cape Province estates have never been run like that, and they don't have to be. . . . Do you remember meeting Simeon? Simeon Marais, the major domo?'

I nodded. 'A proud man.'

'Not any more. By the time I got there, he'd become absolutely brutalised. Koopman—that's the agent—used to treat him like an animal, like a dog he didn't like. Simeon had never had to learn tricks like that—servile tricks, jumping and running with a man shouting out at him, hitting him. . . . But he'd learned them now. . . . *And he's an eighth generation Simeon Marais!*' She put her hand up to her temples, in despair, in remembered pain. 'It was like that all over, Maraisgezicht. It was disgusting, repellent! So I got rid of Koopman and the night he left they all came and thanked me, and I don't know if there were more people crying than laughing.'

'But you know an agent doesn't have to behave like that. You could get another one, a good one.'

She shook her head again, more vigorously. 'It's *my* house, and they are *my* people. How can I leave them to be handled by strangers? They need me, Johnny. Most of them knew me when I was a little girl. Some—a few—can remember my father when he first went off to school in Cape Town. On a red pony, they said, with a satchel of books, and a little shot-gun for luck. . . . I can't leave people like that. I have to take care of them, and of Maraisgezicht. With all that money, I can do it. It can be a great house again, with hundreds of people who can count on working there all their lives, working as *men*. . . . I can do it. But I have to be there, to make sure that things go right. *We* have to be there.'

This was fast becoming a fantasy, with tentacles which might stretch anywhere, with undertones of fact which I did not like at all. I tried to ward off my share of it.

'I don't think I'd exactly fit in there, Kate. Can you honestly see me helping you to run Maraisgezicht? Or lending a paternal hand with the labour force, with my little shot-gun in my hand? It's not my line, it never was, and it never could be.'

'You *would* fit in!' she insisted. 'But in a different way, an even better way. You could try to do for South Africa what I would try to do for Maraisgezicht.' And as I looked at her in astonishment: 'It's true. There's a desperate need for people like you.'

I laughed, in absolute disbelief. 'The jails must be full of them.'

'That's exactly it! All South Africa is going that way, and unless people who know the country, and love it, and want to change it, agree to come to the rescue, it's going to go down in ruins.'

She paused, but it was only for breath. She seemed ready to break over me with an even bigger wave, an avalanche of argument which truly took me by surprise. I scarcely recognised her tonight. She had left me a simple traveller, and returned as a messiah with a message.

'I was all wrong about South Africa,' she said after a moment. 'I was wrong, and you were right.' And as she saw me ready to disagree, she held up her hand for the floor. 'I mean it. I was wrong about not getting involved. One *must* get involved. Anything else is simply cowardice. Anyone who doesn't speak out now doesn't deserve to have a tongue to speak with.'

'But what on earth is the use of speaking out? I told you—you just end up in jail.'

'Then keep out of jail!' she answered forcefully. 'Keep on the right side of those monstrous laws. It's not too difficult, for a clever man. But you must still do something about them. It's not too late—I'm sure of that—but very soon it will be.'

Unwisely, I asked: 'What monstrous laws?'

'You read about them in the papers,' she answered, 'and often it doesn't mean much. You tend to think: people don't go to prison for nothing, people deserve what they get if they try to defy the law. It's not true any more! South Africa is becoming a colossal jail, for anyone who doesn't keep to one line of thought and one single conviction—that things are going to stay as they are for ever. If you show the least sign of resisting, you can be labelled a communist, or a criminal, or a traitor, and you might as well be dead. They just take you out of circulation. You can be imprisoned for anything! I found that out at first hand.'

That sounded like a brand-new item. Pouring out some more champagne—it seemed a good night to stay with the grape—I asked: 'What happened?'

Kate was very ready to tell me. 'As soon as we got there,' she said, 'we found that Julia's brother was in trouble. Bad trouble. Her mother hadn't told Julia anything about it, because she was afraid to write. He was in jail. He'd been there for eight months. Something to do with that fatuous treason trial. Treason!' She positively ripped the word out. 'He works on the railways—just a man with a hammer, some kind of maintenance work—and he joined a protest meeting up in the Transvaal, trying to improve union rights for coloureds, and the police stuck a communist label on the movement, and rounded everyone up, and suddenly Julia's brother was awaiting trial for treasonable activity against the republic. And he's still being held.

'We were in Johannesburg,' she went on, 'because ·Dad was in the hospital there, and that was where her brother was in prison, so I told Julia to try and see him, or get a message to him, in case he wanted anything—and the next thing that happened, *she* was in jail too. It was absolutely monstrous! They came and picked her up for questioning, one day when I was out. She was completely terrified, of course. She wasn't even able to leave a message for me. They asked her where she'd been lately, and when she said New York, they suddenly started asking her streams of questions about who she knew in America, and if she belonged to any clubs, and whether she'd brought any letters or messages over—things like that. They kept her there for three days, interrogating her all the time, trying to link her with what her brother was supposed to be doing, before they even let me know about it. Then it took another two days to get her out, and it would have taken longer if I hadn't put every lawyer in town onto the job, and all the newspapers as well.'

Kate paused, thinking, remembering what must have been, in the context of her settled life, her position in South Africa, a fairly shattering experience. I had been interested in the story, but not much more than that. Coloured railway workers who tried to drum up union agitation in South Africa were obviously due for the high jump; it was a fact of life, and Julia's brother must have known about it.

Of course it was all wrong, but so was a whole calendar of other laws—liquor laws, parking laws, obscenity and libel laws—which the prudent man steered round, or over, or away from. Keeping out of trouble wasn't the trick of the week, in South Africa or anywhere else. It was the commonest of commonsense.

But Kate was back to her story. 'As soon as I got Julia out,' she said, 'I sent her down to her mother in the Cape, because the old woman was pretty well shot by this time, and Julia needed a rest and a change of scene. Then I suddenly realised that I was being followed myself. I got a private detective to check on it, and it was quite true. The police were trailing me all over the place, even when I went to the hospital to see Dad. My letters were being opened. They were probably tapping my telephone, for all I know. *They actually came to Dad's funeral.* . . . And all because I raised the roof about Julia.' Her eyes flashed sudden fire. 'In South Africa! My country! Damn it, my family was there before most of those towns had names! And most of those jumped-up policemen and politicians too! Can you imagine what it was like, to be treated like a criminal in *Johannesburg*? My father opened five of the Reef gold-mines. He was a Marais, and I'm a Marais too. And now apparently I'm not a Marais any more, I'm a run-of-the-mill police suspect, with a bunch of those blond Afrikaner blockheads following me all over town.'

Her indignation was so fierce that I could not help laughing. The proud lineage had certainly taken a beating, and I knew, better than most people, what it must have meant to her. By now, I was beginning to suspect that this crusade of hers was grounded in something else beside political morality, that injured self-respect was playing a large part. But this was clearly not the moment to raise the point.

'Don't laugh,' she snapped irritably. 'You wouldn't have thought it funny if you'd been there, or if it had happened to you.'

'Sorry,' I said. 'You looked so indignant.'

'I was indignant. I was furious. And I still am.'

'Well, you're home safe and sound now, anyway.'

'And that wasn't so easy, either,' she flared out again. 'Do you know, I had the damnedest time bringing Julia back here with me? First they said, no, she couldn't leave, she had to stay there for further investigation. Then they said she could go, but they would impound her passport so that she couldn't come back to South Africa again. Johnny, it's *her* country! . . . If it hadn't been for Gerald Thyssen going into action, and getting them to drop it, Julia would still be there, being hauled in for questioning whenever the police felt like it. And she's still going to run into trouble, whenever we want to go back.'

'What did Gerald do?' I asked, curious.

'He's Gerald Thyssen,' she said curtly. 'He mines gold. It's the only thing those crooks understand.'

After a moment, during which I felt somewhat excluded from great affairs, I said again:

'Well, you're out of it, anyway.'

'But that's exactly what they want,' she declared. Apparently I was doomed, tonight, to produce all the wrong answers, the kind which only triggered a fresh fuse. 'They want people like me to get out, and stay out, so they can go ahead with their stinking little police-state. There's a terrible I'm-all-right-Jack process going on down there; whatever awful thing happens, no one does anything about it, as long as they're left alone themselves. It's like bullying at school; the victim takes the heat off all the others. . . . It just isn't good enough, not for any country, and particularly a country where the people being bullied are a five-to-one majority. Black South Africans won't stand for it much longer. They're sick of injustice, they're sick of being kicked around, and they're sick of running the elevators.'

I shrugged. 'Who isn't?' I was growing tired of this topic myself; all I had was a thirst, and it wasn't a thirst for facts, nor for causes either. 'Who *doesn't* want to step up in the world? We all do.'

But I had only lit another fire-cracker. 'Oh Johnny, don't say things like that!' she burst out passionately. 'That isn't even remotely the problem, for people like you. These are men and women who have *nothing*! All their hopes, all their real lives are being squeezed out of them. I saw it happening. That man Koopman was making a slum out of Maraisgezicht, and his friends are making a slum out of the whole country. We can't just ignore it; the bell is tolling for us. *All* cruel laws are wrong, whether they hit you or whether they pass you

257

by.' Suddenly she got up, and crossed over to me where I stood by the drink-cabinet; she seemed to be on fire with her determination. 'Come back with me, Johnny. Let's go together. There's so much for both of us to do, and we're just the people to do it.'

The plea was incomprehensible; it would have made more sense if she had been urging me to sign up as a space-pilot. I almost backed away from her, so startling was the lunatic proposition. Though I wanted to avoid an argument, there was a tide here which had to be stemmed, before it ran completely wild and carried me away with it. I half-turned from her, in physical disagreement, and busied myself at the bar. Over my shoulder, I said, as coolly as I could:

'How can I conceivably do that?'

'Why not?'

'Why not? There are hundreds of arguments.' I was untwisting the wires of a fresh bottle of champagne, and I gave this the attention it deserved before going back to my answer. 'To begin with, I can't afford to. I'm busy now, and I shall always have to work for a living, in the future. Work means writing. I can't possibly break it off now. It's ridiculous to ask me.'

'I'm not asking you to break anything off. You can work in South Africa.'

'Not if I get tied up in politics.'

'But that would *be* your work. Writing about South Africa, writing about race-relations, writing about the people there. You know so much about them already. You could do enormous good, even if you never touched active politics, just by being there and telling the rest of the world what was going on.'

'I've done that once already.'

After a moment's silence, I heard her voice say: 'Johnny, can't you even look at me?'

'Oh, nuts!' I exclaimed. I turned, irritated and impatient. 'What the hell is all this? Kate, you're talking absolute rubbish. I *can't* go to South Africa, or anywhere else where the very stones are crying out for justice. I live and work here in New York. I like it. This is where my life is, and this is where I'm going to live it.'

'It's not a life. It's a selfish holiday.'

I drank deep before I answered: 'It may be selfish, but it's not a holiday. I do work, damn it!'

'What at? Making a funny musical out of a deadly serious subject?

258

You're just wasting your talents. You're wasting your feelings. You're wasting everything that ever made you worth while, as a man.'

'So your courier said.'

'Courier?'

'Eumor. The cunning old Greek messenger of the gods, Eumorphopulos. He gave me an earful, too.'

She had crossed to the sofa, as if in retreat or despair, and was preparing to lie down again. 'Did you listen to him?' she asked more quietly.

'I listened. Then we went to a strip-tease show. I'm just not in the market for a reforming influence.'

She sighed, dropping her head back on the sofa arm. 'It's this damned town, I suppose.'

'It's not this damned town!' I said, with some spirit. 'New York is wonderful, if you allow it to be.'

'Look what it's done to you.'

'It hasn't done anything that wasn't there before.'

She shook her head. 'That's not true, Johnny. Basically, you're *not* phoney, you don't give a damn about status or money. You've just lost your head over this crazy sort of life. You're in the middle of a love-affair.'

'Now, now,' I said. 'No re-hash.'

'Oh, not *that* one. You're having a love-affair with New York. With the *idea* of New York, the idea of fun and games, and a wild time as a celebrity, and money to throw away on things that nobody in their senses would ever want. It's the very worst of the western world, a distillation of the whole damned idea of luxury, where they do more for the man who has everything than the child who has nothing.'

'I read that somewhere.'

'Then I wish you'd get it through your skull that it's the literal truth.'

And so on. Kate would not stop making her absurd presentation, and eventually I ran out of patience, and we went off to our separate beds, as sundered as we had ever been. I was angry with her, both for spoiling a perfectly good home-coming, and for interrupting me, with this picket-line parade of banners and slogans, when I was trying to concentrate on something quite different.

I *was* working, as hard as I had done for a long time, and this was the wrong moment for her to mount another crusade. There had been more than enough of that already. First it had been my awful writing, now it was my awful politics—or lack of them. Both campaigns were aimed at involving me in the fatal trap of participation.

I did not want to be involved, I did not want to take part. Though, long ago, I had believed that all artists should be thus 'engaged', that they owed mankind a duty to dismantle the flaws and cruelties and indecencies of our mortal house, and then to build something better with whatever sound timbers they could find, I did not think so now.

A writer, especially, had enough to do, scratching a living from the bare earth of invention. . . . I took to bed with me a fresh astonishment —the totally unreal moment when I asked Kate, in exasperation: 'Why *do* you feel this way about South Africa?' and she had answered, soberly and seriously:

'I learned it from you, and I shall always be grateful.'

That was really the low ebb of this weird little fairy-tale.

It was good to escape, each day, to another theatre, where I could play something like a man-sized role. There was more work for me now on *The Pink Safari* than there had ever been; Erwin Orwin was getting his money's worth, and I was glad to give it him, in a job which involved more question-marks, more sudden crises, and more quick thinking than anything I had tackled before.

Though we were now well into rehearsals, the show was still growing, and changing shape, and losing a bit here and adding a bit there; like a baby in the womb, the main format was traditional, but there were certain processes at work which would determine whether a fat boy, a thin girl, or a six-toed midget would presently emerge. If there was anything I could do, by way of last-minute jewels from my smoke-filled head, to ease the delivery, I was there to do it.

As an early Christmas present to me, Erwin had given Susan a minute part in the show. It was only a token appearance, involving a couple of those connective phrases which, in old musical comedies, used to be expressed as 'Girls! Here comes the Duke!' followed by glad cries, merry laughter, and a *reprise* of '*Welcome to Monte Carlo!*'

But it gave her an obvious pleasure, and kept her within the fold. Erwin, discounting my thanks, remarked: 'It saves trouble if you know where they are all day,' and that was perhaps all that he needed to say, about a situation which had settled down to a pattern of slightly pedestrian sin.

Following the prudent tradition of such affairs, Susan never called me at the apartment. We used to meet in the early evenings, after rehearsal, and go back to her place on 54th Street; this hallowed time-slot for love-making, between the office and the domestic dinner-table, was really all I could manage, without going too deep into lies and evasions. It had come to be enough.

The affair was now not very wild, not very anything. The new body was now the accustomed one; though beautiful as ever, warm and entwining as long grass under sunlight, she was no longer the girl I had to have at all costs. She was a girl who was there when I felt like it, the free pass which never lapsed, and that was a different thing altogether.

She was also, subtly yet perceptibly, a girl who was ready with the withdrawal symptoms, in case of need.

'Do you still sleep with *her?*' she asked me one evening when the matter of who-slept-with-whom was an appropriate topic.

'No,' I said. 'Of course not.'

She sighed. 'Men always say that.'

'Do they?' The bare-faced lie seemed a good mirror of our situation at that moment, and I saw no harm in it. 'Then it's probably always true.'

'Are you getting tired of me, Johnny?'

'No. Not in the least.' I rolled over and looked at her. I *was* tired of her, at that moment, but it had been a matter of mutual agreement. 'I thought I just showed you.'

'That doesn't count. . . . But I wouldn't want you to go on, if——' She threw the rest of the sentence away, as usual, and started another one. 'I don't mean you have to make up your mind, or anything. But this has gone on for a long time, hasn't it?'

'Nearly ten months,' I agreed. 'I haven't kept any other score.'

'It's been the longest ever, for me.'

'I'm glad.'

'You'd say if you were bored?'

'I'd say.'

'What's she like, really? What do you talk about? I hear she's beautiful.'

'Yes.' I couldn't get interested in any part of this conversation. 'You hear right.'

'And rich.'

261

'Loaded.'

'Johnny?'

'M'm.'

'You never say anything about her. Say something.'

'Curried shrimps *à la Créole*.'

'What *do* you mean?'

'I don't know. It's the thing she cooks best.' I reached out to touch the nearest place of Susan's body, which happened to be agreeably rounded. 'Knock it off, Susan,' I said, not too severely. 'You don't want to talk about this, and neither do I.'

'I don't really mind if you do sleep with her,' she said, and I felt that this was true. 'I just want to know about it, that's all.'

'Why?'

'Just so that I know where I am.'

'You're in bed with me,' I told her. 'What more could a girl ask?'

'All right,' she said. 'But don't say I make you do things you don't want to. . . . Wasn't that an awful row at rehearsal this afternoon.'

'It was just a row.'

'I don't know how people can behave like that.'

'They're actors.'

Her quick change of subject was typical, not only of her attitude towards us—a friendly, take-it-or-leave it permissiveness—but of what she was really interested in nowadays. Susan had become deeply intrigued with the small internal politics of the show, which I could never take seriously; for her, it really was exciting to watch, listen to, speculate upon, and endlessly discuss the private lives and public demeanour of every member of the *Safari* cast.

Such up-to-the-minute gossip had become of daily, hourly, engrossing importance to her; and in this she was only joining the throng, following a trend which was probably as old as the theatre itself.

It was a self-contained world, private, trivial and confined. One was aware all the time of the total absorption of theatre people, not in their art (which though dull would have been excusable), but in themselves. Their days were filled with tremendous, to-and-fro discussion about nothing—about make-up, diet, clothes, missed cues, dry-ups, other shows, flops, smashes, show-stoppers, good and bad reviews, and arguments in which they had demolished the opposition. There was occasional, grudging praise for perfection, and instant, spiteful comment on any observed weakness. It was like a nursery, full of boastful little show-offs stealing each other's toys.

Above all, these people, like most exhibitionists, were immensely vain. Happy when they were bitching about the rest of mankind, they were happiest of all when listening to single-minded homage of themselves. The old theatre chestnut: 'But let's talk about *you*. What did *you* think of my performance?' still remained the classic attitude.

At the beginning, when Susan joined the cast, I had feared that I might have to watch her being propositioned before my shadowed eyes; that, in this world of handsome, active youth, jealousy would find too much to feed on. I need not have worried. On a few occasions, I did observe the faint beginnings of a romantic approach. But it never lasted, it ran out of muscle well before the muscles came into play. These young men were actors, and their sole enduring love-affair was with themselves.

Buttressing this vanity was an immediate readiness to quarrel. There were perennial feuds between various members of the cast, devious intrigues whose currents altered each day, like the changing delta of a shallow-running river. As on the stage itself, everything had to be larger and brighter coloured and more dramatic than life. The most furious rows could change to vows of eternal friendship over-night, and veer back again at the drop of a mink stole.

This was the touchy world of the tiff, the hunched shoulder, and the smacked face, and if one did not join in and take sides, one was rated heartless or, worse still, conceited, and a fresh grouping, a mute stockade of set faces and meaning looks, very soon made one aware of the fact.

Some of our crises stemmed from having a cast more 'mixed' than in any other comparable operation in New York. We would have had our troubles anyway, but this was an extra guarantee of action. The tender area of race-relations (referred to by Susan and her friends as 'the black and white bit') ensured that when all other themes of discord ran out, there remained a rich lode of ill-will which had scarcely been mined at all.

The row that afternoon, which Susan had recalled with such pleasurable awe, had been typical of our brittle, tantrum-prone society. There were four leads in *The Pink Safari*, two black and two white; they all seemed to get along pretty well ('So they damned well ought to, for the money,' Erwin Orwin had growled, when I mentioned

263

this amiable circumstance), except for Dave Jenkin, the leading Negro actor, who, as a matter of professional habit, did not get along with anyone but himself.

Dave Jenkin was a promoted song-and-dance man who had progressed, by an admittedly rocky road which would have vanquished anyone with less endurance, guts, and gall, from small-time vaudeville player to Broadway personality and (when he found something to suit him) a very competent actor; in the process, he had also graduated, with outstanding success, from little bastard to big. Within the sacred grove of race-relations, however, no one was allowed to point this fact out. He was one emperor who, by statutory falsehood, was always fully clothed.

It as a curious piece of artifice. Here was a man who, if he had been white, would have been written off, by almost anyone who met him, as a loud-mouthed, uncouth, and conceited boor. If the question ever came up of his marrying one's sister, he would have been shown the door as a matter of family necessity. But Jenkin was not a white man, and so none of this could be true. He was black; therefore, he was a great coloured artist, and woe betide the first fascist swine who denied it.

He had been a pain in all our necks ever since he joined the cast. He was abominably rude to everybody. He argued all the time. He was late for rehearsal, late on cue, late everywhere except for lunch. He arrived each morning with a hangover, and left with a chocolate chip on his shoulder. He should have been sacked at the end of the first day, when he had started bragging about 'pepping up this turkey'; but that of course would have been a clear case of racial discrimination, shaming the democratic process.

There was also the fact that he was absolutely made for his part in *Safari*, if he chose to try. But the job of coaxing him to be a reasonable human being, let alone a good actor, was so mountainous and so unpleasant that, in happier circumstances, he would have been replaced over the week-end.

There we were, anyway, stuck with Dave Jenkin, the distinguished Negro actor whose best protection was his skin. It was he who had precipitated that day's quarrel, not the least in our long roster of confrontation. He had kept the stage waiting, at one important moment when he should have sailed in on cue; and apart from the irritation of this check, there was the additional annoyance that his voice could be

264

heard off-stage, in a deep-toned monologue which might have had a lot to do with Dave Jenkin but had nothing to do with my plot.

It was the stage-manager's job to rout him out, but before he could do so, someone more in the limelight took a hand. This was Sally Coates, the actress who was playing the 'white girl' lead, a cheerful and bouncing character whose reserves of energy and good humour had already done us many a good turn. It was she who had been held up and thrown out of stride, and she who, at last, felt compelled to point the fact out.

Standing centre-stage, in the slacks and shirt which were the universal rehearsal rig, Sally called out briskly:

'Dave! Wake up! You're on!'

There was a silence, and then Dave Jenkin strolled on-stage, at a pace which indicated his indifference to this or any other drama. His tightly-cuffed yellow pants and checkered shirt made a convenient focus for our dislike. He drawled:

'You want me, honey?'

Sally Coates had already had enough of this long day, and she reacted snappishly.

'No,' she shot back, hands on hips. 'I don't want you one little bit. But the play does. You had a cue there.'

'Well, now,' said Dave Jenkin, in the same insolent drawl, 'aren't we the funny one today. . . . Maybe if you spoke the cue louder, I could hear it.'

We were all waiting in silence—Erwin and myself sitting side by side in the second row, the director leaning over the piano onstage, the half-dozen other actors taking part in the scene, the usual drift of people watching or learning lines or hanging about—but now all staring in upon this unpleasant little tangle.

'I spoke loud enough,' said Sally sharply. 'If you'd stop talking for a bit, and listen, you could come in on time.' But she was not the girl to hold a mood of irritation. 'O.K., Dave—let's go!' She spoke her cue-line again. ' "*And if I do, I know just the man to take care of you.*" '

Dave Jenkin stood silent, sullen and frowning. Finally he executed an absurd little step dance, a cut-and-shuffle from his remote, soft-shoe past, threw out his arms, and said:

'What was that again?'

'You heard me.'

265

'I didn't. That's just the trouble, baby.' The whining insolence was even more pronounced than usual. 'I heard a mumble, that's what I heard. Can't hardly take that for a cue, can I?'

By my side, Erwin Orwin stirred. 'Dave!' he called out.

Dave Jenkin crouched and cupped his hand. 'Yes, sir, boss?'

'Let's get on with it.'

'Yes, *sir*! Any time I hear the call.'

Erwin drew a considerable breath. 'All right, Sally,' he said after a moment. 'Let's go back. Just give that cue-line again.'

Sally repeated: ' "*And if I do, I know just the man to take care of you.*" ' She then, being angry, improvised: 'And I wish to Christ that was true.'

Without a word, Dave Jenkin turned and stalked off the stage. His reputed girl friend, a small and lithe young dancer with the waist and disposition of a wasp, called out: 'That's the boy! You show 'em, Dave!' and was countered by another girl, less sympathetic, whose contribution was a crisp 'Shut up, you stupid bitch!' Hair was pulled, faces once again were slapped; Sally's husband, who had no part at all in the show and was in fact a night-club singer on holiday from Philadelphia, came down centre-stage and embarked on a long harangue vaguely directed at Erwin Orwin.

The piano-player, a man of long-term, all-absorbent resignation, began to play the overture, in a key so satirically modulated that it sounded midway between the *Danse Macabre* and Chopin in a mood of revolutionary despair. Dave Jenkin reappeared in his street clothes, and strode purposefully from left to right on his way to the exit. Sally's husband said something to him, whereupon Dave Jenkin, who had been a boxer before he became a tap-dancer, promptly knocked him down, and then continued his walk off-stage.

Sally started to cry, and Dave Jenkin's girl friend took a running kick at the prostrate man, missed him, and landed flat on her cushioned-ride behind. From this non-vantage point, she called shrilly after her departing lover: 'Keep going, honey! Don't pay them any mind! Don't even ignore them!'

Into this lively *tableau*, which had some affinity with the last act of *Hamlet*, Erwin injected his own personality. He suddenly stood up, and bawled:

'Break! Five minutes! And everybody off stage!' He then rounded on me, and snarled: 'It's all your God-damned fault!' and as I looked up, genuinely startled, I saw that he was grinning, and we both broke into laughter.

It seemed perfectly natural that, five minutes later at the end of the interval, the rehearsal continued as if nothing had happened. Only Dave Jenkin, coaxed out of the nearest bar by his female friend (who had been threatened with automatic dismissal if she did not bring him back), made anything more out of it. Pleading sinus infection, he had his dresser follow him round the stage with a nasal spray for the rest of the afternoon, applying soothing surges of medicament at the conclusion of every speech.

'I wish I had the use of that thing,' grumbled Erwin Orwin, settling down again. 'I'd try a different approach. . . . But he's good, all the same, isn't he? The son-of-a-bitch is really good!'

Surrounded by such intermittent flurries, Steele the stolid anchorman toiled, feeling at least a hundred years older than the assorted delinquents romping round his feet. But, trying for the long view, it was possible to feel optimistic. *The Pink Safari* had taken on a good hard outline, and a reasonably distinctive one. It had a book, a score, lyrics, a cast, eight different sets, a costume plan, and a schedule of future operations.

The time was now December. The play would be ready, even by Erwin's spendthrift standards, in about a month. It would then have its first try-out in Boston in January, and open in New York in the spring—the second spring of its life.

CHAPTER SEVEN

THE day started, like the first chapter of Genesis, on a note of novelty

'You have an old friend in town,' observed Kate, with that lack of emphasis which characterised a lot of the things she said to me nowadays. She tapped the newspaper which lay by her breakfast tray. 'But I suppose you know about it already.'

I had only called in to say goodbye on my way to work, and, already preoccupied with what lay ahead, I was paying no more attention than any other husband on the commuting wing at ten o'clock in the morning. Straightening my tie before her mirror, I asked:

'Who would that be?'

'Father Shillingford.'

'Well, well,' I said, taken by surprise. 'That *is* an old friend. Father Billingsgate. What's he doing at this end of the tottering globe?'

'He's at the United Nations,' she answered, in a short sort of voice. 'He phoned last night. He's appearing for South Africa.'

'*For* South Africa.'

'Oh, they didn't ask him to. . . . He was giving evidence before one of the committees, the one that's trying to get South Africa expelled. He spoke against it. Didn't you read about it?'

'No,' I said. 'The *Times* is terribly bad on foreign affairs, don't you think?'

'The *Times* is the best——' she began energetically, and then broke off. 'Don't joke about it, Johnny. People like Father Shillingford are killing themselves, working to get some sense into the world. If you're not interested, at least you might respect what they're trying to do.' She was frowning; it was a familiar pattern of disapproval. 'Anyway, he's here, and he's coming to dinner.'

'Tonight?'

'Yes.' She looked at me carefully. 'Please be here, Johnny. Don't run away from it.'

'I'm not running away from anything. I'm reviewing my social calendar. What's for dinner?'

She smiled, having won. 'Bread and water.'

'Cut another slice.'

I had, I hoped, shown the necessary co-operation, but in fact it was not at all the sort of interruption I wanted, at this stage of the *Safari* production, in the last two weeks of rehearsal; and, skimming the solid print in the *Times* on my way down town, and later on at the theatre, I felt even less inclined to give it room for manœuvre.

Father Shillingford was indeed in town. He had left South Africa a few days earlier, minus his passport, with a vague 'travel document' which was no guarantee of his return-entry; he had arrived at the U.N., and there begged leave to appear before a committee, chiefly African and Asian, which seemed at the moment solely concentrated upon the expulsion of South Africa on the grounds of her racial discrimination.

Once accredited, he had promptly, and to everyone's astonishment, brought all his skill and persuasion to pleading the cause of his country —the country which despised and rejected him. Don't throw South Africa out of U.N., had been his theme, in a passionate speech which had 'visibly moved' the delegates. Keep her inside, treat her like a misguided but not incorrigible friend, and try to persuade her to mend her ways.

As an example of 'other cheek' Christianity, it was memorably effective. The picture kept nagging me all day; I returned to thinking about it again and again, with foreboding, and with doubt about meeting him once more, and about dining in this elevated atmosphere. It got in the way throughout that day's rehearsal, which was enough to try the patience of another kind of saint; and was an appropriate prelude to one of the most absurd and uneasy meals I had ever eaten.

If Lord Muddley had been a fat ghost from the past, Father Shillingford proved a veritable skeleton from a cupboard I had thought long walled up.

He was there when I got home, talking to Kate, and it was strange to see the two of them together—the extremely elegant woman and the pale shabby priest, sitting side by side in our gilded cage. He got up when I came in, and greeted me very warmly.

'Jonathan! How very nice, after all these years! How are you?'

'All the better for seeing you.'

It could hardly have been less true. Close to, he looked pathetic; shrunken, cruelly tested, pitifully spent; the energetic and rather tubby little man I remembered from six years earlier had been worn down, by God knew what pressures and pains, to a wafer-thin figure of exhaustion. His face had that look of bony dejection which one sometimes saw in pietistic carvings of Christ on the cross. Of course, he had fashioned his own cross, and chosen to suffer on it, and perhaps was glorified by his ordeal. But one look at him, one brief clasp of his meagre hand, was enough to send me to the bar, almost at a run.

Dinner was very awkward. He caught me unawares by bowing his head to say grace, just as I was taking my first swig of wine; I said 'Cheers', and he said *'Benedictus benedicat,'* at the same moment; as a chorus, it was ill-matched, and Kate's face showed it vividly. We talked, of course, about South Africa; or rather, they talked, and I mostly drank. I was not really in on this party, and it needed no stage-direction to make the fact clear.

269

His old shanty-town of Teroka, he told us, had now vanished; the people had been dispossessed, the houses razed the area given over to a neat white suburb called, it seemed sarcastically, Pleasantville. The former population had been pushed still further out, and rehoused nearly twenty-five miles from the centre of Johannesburg, where they had to work.

'Of course, the houses are a little better,' he said quietly, 'and there is running water. But it has become terribly overcrowded already, and lawless, and dirty. And now it means travelling almost fifty miles to and from work each day, in those wretched buses. Some of the men have to queue up at four in the morning, to be sure of getting to town by eight. And the same thing at night.'

'That must mean a long journey for you, each day,' said Kate.

'About the same,' he agreed. 'I tried to move nearer to the mission, but I couldn't find anywhere suitable. But—' he smiled, 'I have a motor scooter now! Very dashing. So I am not really badly off at all.'

The picture of Father Shillingford, his cassock swirling in the breeze, hitting forty miles an hour on a Vespa along the dusty Transvaal roads, amused me, and I made an effort to become one of the party. I said:

'I'd like to see you riding that chariot. . . . Of course, they've always had those queues for the buses, haven't they? They must be pretty well resigned to it by now.'

'They are certainly resigned,' said Father Shillingford. His eyes, meeting mine across the candle-light, were unexpectedly searching, as if he was trying to discover my whole character at a single glance. I wished him luck, and sealed the wish with a libation. 'But that doesn't make these hardships any easier to bear.'

'It's wonderful what you can get used to.'

'I think it is more sad than wonderful.'

Kate, with a frown for me which made me suspect that I might well finish the evening standing in a corner, guided us somewhere else.

'I don't think I saw any of the Black Sash people while I was there,' she remarked, in a bright tone which seemed to invite, irresistibly, the label of Social Notes from All Over. 'Are they still operating?'

'Oh yes,' said Father Shillingford. 'But less than before, I suppose. Don't forget that the movement had been going on for nearly fifteen years, and some of the women—well, I don't wish to be ungallant, but they must now be well into their seventies. It takes a good deal of courage, and stamina as well, to engage in silent-protest picketing at that age. I don't think they have had much success in gaining new recruits.' He sighed, and his pale face seemed to go even further into mourning. 'There is curiously little feeling for that kind of politics among the young people. They simply don't want to be bothered. South Africa is very prosperous, the police are extremely efficient and energetic, so—' he spread his hands, '—so life goes on quite agreeably, and very few white people want to change it. Particularly as it might cost them their liberty in the process.'

'I think that's one of the worst things,' said Kate. 'The way the police lay down the rules, and everyone just says "Yes" and does what they're told.'

Julia came in with a fresh course, of chicken *Kiev*—dinner was really very good tonight, and it was a pity that one could not enjoy it in peace, instead of being driven inexorably to the bottle—and there was silence as we set to work. Presently Father Shillingford, who was eating with a sad kind of reluctance, as if food, though pleasurable, were an insult to the hungry, took up his tale again.

'The police certainly lay down the rules,' he said. 'I don't think there's a single thing which a man could say or do in South Africa, which could not somehow be brought within today's sedition laws. And once you become suspect, you have a police-dossier and you can be hounded quite unmercifully.' He smiled at Kate. 'You found that out yourself, didn't you? I remember reading about it, and wondering how a person of spirit would react to it.'

'I reacted, right enough,' said Kate. 'I hadn't been so angry for a long time. But that's another thing. I didn't *worry*, because I was safe, really. I was absolutely innocent, and so was Julia, and I had some influential friends to fall back on, and, I suppose, enough money to get the best kind of legal advice and protection. But what do other people do? What *can* they do?'

'Nothing,' said Father Shillingford flatly. 'They are powerless. They are also permanently afraid, whether they are black or white.' He brushed his hand across his forehead, wearily. 'I have lived with this for so long, it is sometimes difficult to realise how strange it is. How wrong. How *iniquitous!*' It was, for him, a very strong word, and he spoke it with extraordinary feeling. 'It reaches its worst point in wh-t they now call "house arrest", which must be one of the most wicked forms of punishment ever devised by a so-called Minister of Justice.

Imagine being told to stay at home, seeing no one, during all your free time. Imagine being ordered to travel straight to work, and straight back, and not to visit anyone on the way, except to report at the police-station, and not to have friends in your own home, at any time. Imagine a whole week-end like that, when you may not move beyond your garden gate, nor talk to anyone except a policeman. *Imagine that for the rest of your life!*'

He was obviously distressed, and his voice as he recalled these details was trembling. I took a sip of my wine, not knowing quite how the ideal host should react to this sort of thing. A kindly word? A change of subject? Finally I said, in as reasonable a tone as I could muster:

'I don't think I should like house arrest.'

For some reason this innocuous statement did not seem to sit well with Kate. She gave me another of her formidable frowns, and then, as if to draw attention away from her unworthy spouse, said to Father Shillingford:

'What I don't understand is, what you're really trying to do at U.N. Why go to all that trouble, if you feel as you do? Surely South Africa doesn't deserve to keep her membership.'

Father Shillingford, now more composed, shook his head. 'If she were expelled—which is what they are trying to do—I believe it would be nothing short of disaster. There would then be no form of pressure or persuasion left, except the threat of war, which is unthink-able. The very people who most need our help would be the first to suffer. They would be left to the wolves.' He looked from one to the other of us, seeking allies, seeking confirmation of his urgent hope. 'I have thought about this for a long time, and I am sure I am right. South Africa in isolation would go her own way, and a sordid and terrible way it would be. But South Africa as a member of a world body might still listen to reason, and be brought to reform. The United Nations is now a very sophisticated and powerful body. All the members are subject, whether they know it or not, to a sort of group civilising influence. It's far better for such a country to be a member, however unpopular, rather than an outcast. You cannot hope to reach a country, or a man, who has locked himself in.'

It was at that moment, faced with this barrage of marginal though lofty logic, that I was trapped by an uncontrollable fit of the gapes. At one moment I was sitting back in comparative ease, doing nothing except perhaps compare the flavour of our present company with the sharper tang of Rhein wine; at the next, a cavernous yawn split my face, just as Father Shillingford glanced in my direction. Kate also caught the tail end of it, and gave me a furious look. There could be no doubt that this was a social *gaffe*, and would be classed as such for a very long time to come.

I smiled at them, brave to the last. 'I'm so sorry,' I said. 'I've really been working very hard. I must have been saving that one up all day.'

'I'm afraid I've been neglecting you,' said Father Shillingford, with a contrite air which was really very irritating indeed. 'My trials and troubles must seem excessively dull. . . . Tell me about your play.'

'Well, it's a musical,' I began, readily enough, 'and it's funny, and it's about——' Suddenly, the words simply would no longer flow. It was not that I wanted to hide anything; it was just that I did not feel like another argument—and an argument it would become, as soon as the pair of them got busy on the suitability of certain themes for merriment. Why should I strip in this frosty climate? 'Oh, you don't want to hear all this,' I said after a moment. 'It's only a play. Mass entertainment.'

'About South Africa, I think I read. Based on that wonderful book of yours.'

'About South Africa.'

'I would not have thought,' said Father Shillingford, 'that there was a great deal of humour to be found in that particular subject.'

There it was, damn it, flat on the table in front of me, before I had a chance to dodge. I hunched my shoulders, not listening to his voice any longer. I did not want to talk about it. I did not want to talk to Father Shillingford. This inability to meet his mind, to face this strange little spectre of the past, might have shamed me; instead, it only goaded and irritated. It was a hateful reminder of Kate's own crusade, and the role of low-class, scarcely mentionable target which had been assigned to me, throughout the last few months, the last few years.

I was fed up with playing that part; and when Father Shillingford ended his small homily with the words: 'You should really be back there, you know, Jonathan,' I suddenly found that I had had enough, and was going to tell him so.

'I don't agree,' I said roughly. 'I'm not interested in South Africa. I don't want to go back there. In fact, I don't even want to talk about it any more.'

'Jonathan!' said Kate, with a look which might have snuffed the candles. 'That will do.'

'You're damned right it will do,' I told her. I surveyed them both, first over the top of my wine glass, then through its stem, then through its empty shell. What was there to be afraid of? I had long forfeited my chances of a good conduct medal. Surely, in the company of my dear wife and my old and sanctified friend, I could speak my little piece. . . . 'O.K., I'm selfish, I'm making a balls out of my entire life, and this is all part of Hate Steele Month. Sorry, Father,' I threw across to him, 'we're raking over a few very old ashes tonight.' Yet I was going to rake them, none-the-less, and not all the cassocks in holy church were going to stand in my way. 'But the fact is, I'm fed up with being made to feel like a criminal, just because I want to work at one sort of book rather than another.'

Father Shillingford was looking at me with infuriating mildness. 'Why should anyone hate you, Jonathan?' he asked gently.

'Because I'm trying to talk sense, and *live* sense!' I turned from one pair of eyes to the other; his were inquiring, hers were steely and unforgiving, and I did not give a damn about either. 'Come on, let's cut out all the nonsense! What are you trying to do? What do you actually want for South Africa? How do you want her to change? You think the natives can take over and run the country? That's complete rubbish, and you both know it.'

'Johnny,' said Kate, icily, 'I think we'll——'

'*Johnny, Johnny!*' I mimicked her, as savagely as I could. 'You going to send me off to bed? I'll try for a warmer one. . . . Let's hear some more about the great South African Negro republic! Who's the black Oppenheimer? Who's the new chairman of De Beers? What particular coloured boy from the Free State is taking over Gerald Thyssen's job?'

'You have a very fair point there,' said Father Shillingford surprisingly. 'And I would never presume to answer it, not for perhaps fifty years. There are *no* qualified natives in South Africa, fit to govern a modern industrial country. How could there be? But one day there *will* be, and we must make a start, perhaps a very slow start, on finding them and training them.'

'You make a start,' I told him. 'I'm too damned busy making money.'

Kate rose. 'Coffee, I think,' she said, in her loftiest voice.

I glanced up at her. 'I haven't finished.'

Father Shillingford was also standing up, and now he looked across at me. He seemed to be facing the fact that we had moved far beyond all acceptable patterns, that this was already part of saying goodbye; and he met it with dignity.

'You cannot deny the need,' he said, much more firmly than he had spoken before. 'If you do not wish to play a part in helping, that is your choice to make. But you should never discourage other people from doing their best. That is wrong. You know that there is misery. I am a priest, and I can do something—though a very little—to make it bearable. You know that there is political baseness and cruelty. You are a writer, and could do something to help in that area. Turn your back on it, if you want to. Deny your gifts. But don't pretend that a thing does not exist, because you are not there in person to witness it.' He smiled suddenly, an old worn-out smile, full of the compassion I had no use for. 'God bless you,' he said softly. 'Jonathan, my son.'

I smiled back. Then, with matching softness, I brought the palms of my hands together, and apart, and together again, in a round of restrained applause which saw them both out of the room.

I stayed where I was, gradually tipping the last of the bottle. Julia came in, and looked at me, and left again, wordless. I heard Father Shillingford saying goodbye, and the door opening and closing. I wondered what Kate would do and say now. I did not have long to wait. She appeared in the doorway, and stood staring at me as I lolled very comfortably in my chair.

'How could you, Johnny?' she asked presently. There was cold astonishment in her voice.

'Easily. Try me again.'

'But he's your *friend*.'

'I never saw him before in my life.'

We were silent. She seemed to be waiting, listening, hoping. Eventually I sat up, and said:

'You won't hear it, Kate.'

'What?'

'That third cock-crow. . . . Now leave me alone.'

She turned, with a face of stone, and walked out, leaving me indeed alone; alone with an empty table, and a full glass, and a perfect if subdued contentment with both.

. . . . .

I did not see Father Shillingford again—which could have come as no surprise, nor any great denial, to either side—but it seemed that I had not yet finished with Old Home Week. The pressure from the Good Guys was still upon me; for now Eumor was in town once more, *en route* from furthest Peru to uttermost South Africa. I supposed that this was an innocent re-appearance, but in my present mood I could not be sure of it.

I had suspected Kate's artful hand in the arrival of Father Shillingford, unscrupulously imported to put swinish Steele to shame; and now we had Eumor on the same stage in the same morality play. Perhaps he *was* making a chance land-fall, like some wizened snowgoose; yet somehow he seemed part of this matching frieze of disapproval. His visit, at that particular moment, was probably unplanned, but—like any other coincidence—it did not feel so at all.

However, after a cagey introduction, we enjoyed ourselves—a surprise benevolence, like a sprig of mistletoe in hell; and we spent a curious truce-like evening, which recalled that other night, long ago and far away, when Kate and I first met, and all known patterns were suspended. It was now near Christmas, and so we walked the Christmas streets, a-glow and a-glitter under the black winter sky, raucous with the hard sell of our Saviour's late disciplines, yet beguiling and heartening at the same time.

Strolling, moving with the crowds or stemming their formidable advance, we munched hot roasted chestnuts from the street-corner barrows, and gave money to poor strangers, and talked to Salvation Army girls rattling their collecting boxes, and went into bars and stood drinks to down-at-heel customers who had had enough already, and window-shopped at Tiffany's, and Bonwit Teller, and Doubledays, where a lone Pocket Book edition of *Ex Afrika* stood sentinel for global culture and my own solvency. Then it was time to eat, and eat we did, like happy, hungry humans who had no other care but appetite.

We chose Luchows, for a hearty Teutonic blow-out, and there we swam out upon a sea of Bismarck herrings and *sauerbraten* and dumplings and *apfel strudel*, fit to stupefy Santa Klaus, however long and hard his journey. Suddenly we found it easy to be merry; neither envy, nor evil, nor deceit divided us—we were three friends whose concord had survived a long apprenticeship, and the world after all was warm and kindly, and hell! it was Christmas. . . . We ate, we argued, we reminisced; we drank long draughts of Munich beer, bitter and sugary at the same time, and put on paper hats modelled upon the *pickelhauben* of the Prussian *corps d'élite*, and presently we grew sure, without voicing it, that the ancient Christmas miracle had once again flowered into substance.

Fantastically, it seemed that, for this easy hour, a world of innocence and love was being born again, with tidings of comfort and joy for all concerned.

At one point, Eumor became bawdy, and drew us along with him. He had a short two hours before his plane for Lisbon, and he affected an ambition to make a last conquest in North America, before, as he put it, 'unpacking the old bags of Johannesburg.'

'Get me a calling girl,' he commanded.

'You mean a call girl, Eumor,' I said.

He shook his head. 'Call girl not grammatical. Calling girl, please.'

'*Six calling girls, five French hens,*' sang Kate—and since it was Luchows, and Christmas, no one minded her small contralto contribution.

'I can give you a couple of numbers,' I told him, sophisticated like.

'Numbers? Do they not have names?'

'They're all called Lacy Faire,' said Kate.

We made up some more suitably silly names: Belle Ring, Inna Circle, Annie Moore (an Irish devotee), Cosie Van Tootie. Eumore translated some of them into Greek; they sounded authoritative and vaguely frightening, like Homer at his most majestic. As usual, my friend was having a wonderful, tonic effect on both of us; but this time I feared that the effect would fade out swiftly, as soon as he did, and I was right.

We saw him off in his hired car, towards midnight, under the solemn, shabby portico. He embraced me *à la française*, without embarrassment, and then he kissed Kate with his usual fervour, and said: 'See you before long,' which, for me, struck a small cold note of warning. Then she and I were left to ourselves, and, content enough, we began to stroll back up town, hand in hand, heading for home.

It had been a happy evening, a dividend of our interwoven past. But the small cold note had been the true one. Next day, the axe fell.

I had left the house early, for another long day at Erwin Orwin's salt-mine, and I did not get back till nearly seven. As I closed the front door

277

behind me, and stood in the hall, I seemed to encounter a curious waiting silence; there was no music, no radio, no visitors' chatter, no promising sounds from the kitchen, but simply a blank, as if I had stepped onto a bare stage into the wrong play. For a moment I thought that Kate had gone out; but then I saw her, standing by the fireplace, her back towards me and her hands clasped behind her head, staring at a vase of tall yellow roses.

They must have been newly delivered that day, and I came forward and said:

'Who's your admirer?'

'Your friend,' she answered, without turning. There was a sort of gritty enmity in her voice. 'Your protective friend Eumor.'

I heard enough in her tone to warn me to keep silence, but I still had to query whatever situation this was. It would not go away, whether in silence or not.

'Protective friend? Why protective?'

She turned at that, and I saw her face; and her face surprised me very much, being set in a mask of almost murderous determination. She looked as if she had waited a long time for this moment, and now that it had come she was going to play it like a pro.

'The clue is the roses. So good for a girl's morale. . . . I suspect that you two boys are sharing a secret,' she went on crisply. 'One of those male secrets which has to be hidden from the staunch little woman at home. . . . Does Eumor know anything that I don't know?'

'Lots, I should think.' I wasn't going to answer any such riddles this evening, nor any other evening. 'You name something.'

'It's just a suspicion,' she said, now almost savage. 'Did you tell him about that girl?'

'What girl?' Then I realised that this sounded silly, and I said: 'Yes, I mentioned her.'

'I don't want us to get these girls mixed,' said Kate. 'I mean, stunning old Susan Crompton, the girl you met in one of Erwin Orwin's shows.'

'That's the one I meant, too.' I was now making for the bar, and a little more protection than Eumor seemed to be giving me. When I turned, glass in hand, Kate had picked something up from the mantelpiece, and was staring at it with special, almost theatrical concentration. Before I could add anything to the general gaiety, she spoke, in the most brutally sarcastic voice I had ever heard her use:

'I did so enjoy our stay at the Bon Soir Motel in Richmond, Virginia. What a lovely time that was!'

She was stretching out her hand towards me, commandingly, and with a slightly sick feeling I took what she held in it. It was an over-size post card, ornate and glossy, from the motel she had named. '*Happy Christmas!*' it said. '*Come back real soon for another fine stay!*' It was addressed to 'Mr. and Mrs. J. Steele.'

I said the first thing that came into my mind. 'They shouldn't do that.'

Kate was watching me, very closely. 'A lot of people shouldn't do a lot of things.'

'Oh, come on, Kate—you knew about Susan.'

'Not from you, I didn't. . . . Of course I knew about her. Do you think I couldn't smell her perfume on you, when you came back each evening? . . . But now it's different. Now I *know!*' Before I had time to sort out this piece of feminine logic, she burst out, in sudden furious onslaught: '*You bloody liar!*' she stormed at me. 'She *wasn't* just a girl in one of Erwin's shows! Richmond is on the way back from Florida! This must have started weeks earlier than you said! You must have met her in Barbados!'

'All right,' I said. 'That's the way it was.'

'You took her there in the first place!'

'No. She was there already.'

'Waiting for the spring trade. . . .' But anger, which had boiled up so swiftly, now seemed to be ebbing, fading to a bitter mood of mourning. 'Oh, Johnny, why, why, *why?* What's this all about? Is it still going on?'

'Well—you know.'

'Jonathan!'

'Now and then, yes.'

She had turned away again, back to the fire place, back to the yellow roses which had given her so odd an extra joit. From there she spoke, sad, disillusioned, taken unawares; but the basic question was the same.

'I don't understand. What does it all mean? Who *is* this girl?'

I took a fierce gulp of the drink I needed, and tried my best.

'Kate, she's a beautiful, uncomplicated, rather loving whore. I bought her. That's all there is to it.'

Kate's face in the mirror had now become expressionless; it was

279

difficult to tell what she thought of this, or if she thought at all, or felt at all. Her only reaction seemed to be puzzlement.

'But why should you want someone like that?'

'For a change. . . .' And as this did not seem to register: 'She's sweet,' I went on, 'and no trouble at all. She wouldn't ever be.'

'Is that what you want? No trouble?'

'Yes. Or I did then. The other thing——' I did not want to hurt her, for all sorts of unaccountable reasons, but suddenly I was sick of the invasions and swampings of love, as well as the eternal pressure of its inquisition. 'Oh God, Kate, I just couldn't take the intensity any more! You never left me alone for a minute! At the beginning, it was like living in a Turkish bath, with hot Chanel instead of steam. And at the end——'

She had grown watchfully still. 'At the end?'

'You turned against me.'

'I never did that, Johnny.'

'Criticism. Whatever I was doing was wrong. You never left me alone there, either.'

'But we didn't get married just to leave each other alone.'

'I didn't know that.'

She sighed, a deep sigh of resignation. 'I once told you that "forever" was a long word.'

'The longest in the language.'

She went off on another, more immediate tangent. 'I still don't see what it is that I don't give you, that this girl does.'

There must have been several words for it, but I could only find one —or rather, two. 'Elbow room.'

With a flash of the old Kate, she said: 'Well, don't wear out your elbows,' and we both laughed, briefly and harshly, for the first and the last time of that exchange. From then onwards, the night divided us again, and grew bitter, and irritating, and utterly destructive.

Kate paused only long enough to switch subjects; then she was away once more, in full swing, and all I could do was fend her off, first with restraint, then with an answering toughness. It seemed that, having lost one strong-point, she must straightway build another one, and sally forth from that, armoured for battle.

'To hell with that girl!' she said, with sudden vehemence, sudden crudity. 'But that doesn't mean to hell with us! It's going to take more than your loving whore to screw up *our* lives, and that's a promise, from me to you! . . . Johnny, now is the time, for a whole battery of reasons. Come back with me now. Break this all up, and come back.'

'South Africa again?'

'South Africa again. I *must* go. I have to. But I want you with me. It won't make any sense, otherwise.'

'It doesn't make any sense, the way you suggest. What do I eat? How do I live? As a fake land-owner? As a tame pensioner of the rich Mrs. Steele?'

She had wandered to the window, and was staring out of it, as if somewhere down in the caverns of 77th Street she could find answers to everything, even to me. 'That wouldn't matter,' she said. 'That sort of thing never does.'

'Of course it wouldn't matter, to you!'

She sounded as if she were smiling. 'Would you care to elaborate on that?'

Her returning confidence irritated me. 'It wouldn't matter, because you'd have me back where you think I belong. Down in the cellar with a leg-iron on me. Your leg-iron. We'd be back to the same old round of high-low.'

'High low?'

'It's a zany kind of poker game,' I said, 'and a damned good way to lose all you have in the world.' I splashed out another drink, spilling half of it, and a slice of lemon for luck, onto our expensive parquet flooring. But I let the mess lie where it was. Someone else could clean up the world tonight. . . . 'In this case, it would be you high, me low. Well, I'm *not* going back to those good old days, Kate. I've grown out of them, whether you like it or not. And you never did like it, did you?'

She had turned round, for an inspection which took in me, and a certain wildness in my look, and the sticky spread of gin and lemon on the floor. But for once she did not summon domestic aid, nor dart forward with an assuaging dish-cloth. She had decided her priorities. 'Honestly, Johnny, I don't know what you're talking about.'

'Oh yes, you do! *I* have the limelight now, not you, and you've never been able to bear the idea. You want to change us round again, so that you're back in the centre and I'm somewhere out on the rim. Hauling me back to South Africa is just the first step in that process. Then I suppose you'll get to work in earnest. Well, it's not going to happen!'

'This is absurd.'

'You're damned right it's absurd! That's why I'm taking damned good care it doesn't get started!'

'What is it you're afraid of?' she asked, in apparent wonderment.

'I'm not afraid of anything.'

'Yes, you are. You're scared to death of something. You won't write a good book—you just turn out a trick musical. You back away from real things, real problems like South Africa, and choose to be a TV personality instead. Johnny, it's not good enough for someone like you. You're becoming a coward—a talented coward.'

'Well, hooray!' I said angrily. 'I've found my niche at last.'

'You've found a niche, and so do rabbits and mice. . . . Niche is a very good word,' she went on, with a calmness more than usually infuriating. 'Perhaps you do need one, perhaps you need that kind of hide-away. But not all by yourself. . . . If you won't come out of it, why not let me in?'

'It's a small niche,' I said, 'and you're a big girl now. But you're not going to get any bigger.'

'Can I have a drink?' she asked suddenly.

'Like me?'

'Just like you.'

'O.K.'

I poured out her customary modest martini, and passed it over to her. Our hands touched; it was the closest we had been to each other, all that day. But it still wasn't going to be any good; we were now both fully armed, and not for one second was I going to let down my guard.

Sipping her drink, wearing her most reasonable air, she said:

'Johnny, you're a clever man. Tell me what happened to us.'

'We evaporated,' I said, as curtly as I could.

'How could *we* evaporate? We had too much, just for it to disappear.'

'Maybe the sun was too hot.'

'What sun?'

'Oh, God, what does it matter?' I asked irritably. 'That was a silly metaphor, anyway.'

'All right,' she said, equable to an alarming degree. 'Something evaporated, and it isn't there any more. But everything else hasn't disappeared with it. That couldn't be possible. Not with us.' She was looking at me with serious, solemn eyes; it was a moment for extreme caution. 'We both have our faults,' she said. 'We're still human, thank God. You are perpetually afraid of something—of testing yourself

282

against some really great measurement, maybe. And you are vain—you have to be loved, one hundred per cent, all the time. You react to criticism like you react to violence—you think it's simply illegal. And you drink too much. But then there's me. I know the worst of my faults, and I give it to you on any kind of silver platter you choose. I am proud.'

I waited, but that seemed to be the end of this not too extensive catalogue. 'Well, that's just wonderful,' I said. 'I have three big faults, you have one little one. Three to one. That's quite a proportion. It makes a lousy martini, but as long as it makes you happy——'

'Pride is *the* fault,' she interrupted. 'It's at the very top of those seven deadly sins. Terrible things spring from it. Look it up, if you want to, if you need to. It's the worst sin there is, and I have it, and I'm sorry, and if it's contributed anything to the sort of mess we're in, I'm sorry ten times over.'

'That's wonderful,' I said again. My dialogue was not growing any more deft, but I could not help that particular shortfall, either. 'A becoming humility is just what we need, at this moment.'

'It's on the list of things we need,' she answered. She was in much better shape than I was, and the contrast was beginning to show. 'And because I love you—really love you, and want you—I don't mind listing it. But that's not really what we're talking about.' She gathered herself for a summation, for a flourish of feminine skills; and it was interesting, especially for a writer, and daunting, especially for me, to watch her doing it. 'Please come back home with me. Back to Marais-gezicht. We can work this all out there. But I *have* to go, Johnny. My people need me.'

'For Christ's sake, shut up about your people! You sound like Catherine of Russia.'

'That's not how I feel. . . . Pride again, perhaps. . . . But they do need me, and I need you.' It was the first time she had ever said it, since the wild old days when she had needed me in a different way; more than ever, I mistrusted it. 'You taught me such a lot, at the beginning,' she went on, 'when you were—well, when you were a good man. It wasn't on purpose, I don't think; it came just from listening to you, watching you, *living* with you. . . . I would never have asked Father Shillingford here, if it hadn't been for you. I used to think that kind of man was just a bloody nuisance. Now I don't. I know he is a saint. I owe you that, too. . . . Please stay with me now.'

'Or what?' I asked after a moment.

'Or?'

'There's always an "or" to these things. Take a look at the hand-book. . . . I *won't* go back with you, and get submerged and rehabilitated and generally castrated.' I had difficulty with the last word, which had never been one of my favourites, and I took another giant swallow to smooth things out. 'So what's the alternative?'

She said: 'We say goodbye.'

There was always a point in every nightmare when one felt: *This is all wrong; things don't happen like this;* and it came as a vile shock that I seemed to have reached it now. I reacted very quickly, on crude impulse. It *was* all wrong, but I couldn't cure it, and it seemed that Kate did not want to. I downed the last of my drink at a gulp, angry with her, angry with myself for feeling a perceptible twinge of fear. Fear was exclusively for other people. . . . Then I said:

'If that's the way it is, we'd better start practising. Goodbye!'

Then I gave her a wave, and walked out.

She called after me: 'Where are you going?' but I would not have answered, even if I had known. In fact, I did not know. I didn't even know exactly where I was. I seemed to be nowhere special, or—as in a nightmare—lost in a forest which might have been hell, and running furiously in order to keep up with the trees.

Kate was getting me down at last, and the sooner I was really drunk, the better.

Actually, I spent the night with Susan, and it was a flop, from beginning to end. Worst of all, it was a sexual flop.

When finally I shambled my way up to her apartment, in search of some sort of refuge, I found that I did not particularly like anything I found there. The place was in a detestable mess—untidy, dusty, totally uncared for; the bathroom was festooned with washing, almost impossible to negotiate, the kitchen piled with grimy plates and encrusted saucepans. I did not even like the look of Susan herself.

She had gone back to allowing people to fool around with her hair, and the result of what was probably a recent, three-hour session with some mincing young professor of the *coiffe* was a positive bird's-nest of loops, twists, streaks, and kiss-curls, framing her face as if with a lunatic halo. She looked like a film company starlet who wanted to

284

look like Brigitte Bardot; her aim, whether laudable or not, could scarcely have been wilder.

I complained instantly, and the move was far from popular.

'I have to do things with it,' she answered, in a not too friendly tone. 'Everyone does.'

'That's a damned good reason for leaving it as it is.'

'I *can't*. I'm on the *stage*!'

'That sort of hair-do won't make you a better actress.' I sat down with a thump on the cluttered sofa; a sharp cracking sound indicated that I had landed squarely on a concealed gramophone record. 'Well done, Steele,' I said. 'You've broken another record.'

'Oh Johnny,' she wailed, 'it's my Yves Montand.'

'More good news.' I looked about me, with a wobbling gaze. 'Why do you live in such a terrible mess?'

'It isn't a mess. It's comfortable.'

'It's an absolute pig-sty,' I said, 'and don't argue. . . . Well, come on, what do we do now? Entertain me.'

She was staring at me doubtfully. 'Would you like a drink?'

'I would like *another* drink. You can cut out the diplomacy.'

She poured out something which I hoped was Scotch and soda, and I drank some of it, though cautiously. I knew that I was raggedly drunk already, and that drink was doing nothing for me; probably it was taking something away—my nerves seemed to be yelping for a respite which they could not find. Susan started up the record player, with an insipid tune, a man playing the piano as if he had been scared by it when young, and then she began to talk, in a bright voice, about something terrible which had happened back-stage that morning, while I stared ahead, not hearing what she said.

The moment seemed to mark a very low ebb indeed—my wife out of love, my mistress out of wits; an old-fashioned domestic dilemma indeed, not to be solved in any way that I could see.

Presently Susan finished a long, involved sentence with the words 'awful', 'fantastic', and 'hilarious' in it, and then asked: 'Honestly, what do you think?'

'Christ!' I said, 'I don't know. I wasn't listening.'

'But I was *telling* you!'

'I never listen to theatrical chatter.'

'But it's *important*!'

'It's not. It's the dullest topic in the world. It's like—' I searched for a parallel, '—it's like local politics, and the awful thing the Mayor said to Councillor O'Toole about the sewage disposal plant. It's like the eight different ways of making a mint julep. It's like TV in the morning! Who cares?'

Susan picked out a simple, wounding word. 'Does that mean I'm dull?'

I considered, since it seemed to deserve a sensible answer. 'Yes, you're pretty dull.'

She switched off the music abruptly, and turned, and asked: 'Johnny, what's happened to us?'

The familiar ring of the question was not the most comforting sound in the world. 'You're stealing dialogue,' I told her, after a moment.

'I don't understand,' she said unhappily. 'I never understand you nowadays.'

'Nothing's happened to us. We're as good as new.'

'We're not.' She was standing over me now, looking down at me, considering—to the best of her ability—the problem of a drunken man who did not seem to love her any more. 'It's not the same now. It hasn't been the same, for a long time. And we *must* do something about it, before it's all spoiled.'

I squinted up at her. 'Tell me more,' I said. 'What do we do, to revive this magic memory?'

She was more determined, more prepared, than I had expected. 'We don't revive it,' she said.

'Farewell for ever? Well, well. . . . Strong stuff, Susan, old girl. I must remember that, for my next work of art.'

But the parallel with another recent interview was growing oddly close; a young man need never have left home. Sooner or later—whichever way I could manage it—I would have to start taking all this goodbye stuff seriously.

Her next words pointed up the fact.

'Be nice to me,' she said, 'and please listen. Don't let's pretend any more, Johnny. Things aren't the same, and we both know it. It was a lot of fun in Barbados, and fun for a little while here, specially when you were helping me so much. But it hasn't been fun for a long time, has it?'

'Some of it has been highly enjoyable.'

'Oh, *that* part's all right, when it happens. But I mean, the serious things, the being friends. . . . We don't seem to have anything left.'

'What serious things did we have before?'

She was still staring down at me, her face wearing a rare look of unhappiness and confusion. 'You know what we had,' she said after a moment. 'At least, you know what you *said*. . . . So it's silly to go on meeting, when there's nothing left any more except going to bed now and then.'

I sipped my drink. 'The practice is still well spoken of.'

'But if it's only that. . . . It's such a silly reason for——'

'For what?'

She said: 'I don't want to break up your marriage.'

I stared back at her, genuinely surprised. 'You couldn't,' I told her. Then I felt that I might soften this. 'I mean, it's not that kind of——'

'I know what you meant,' she said, interrupting me for perhaps the very first time since I met her. 'But even if I couldn't break it up, this sort of situation could. And it's not worth it. I *know*. That kind of thing never is.'

'Not worth what?' It seemed a good moment to be obtuse, and the effort involved was negligible.

'Not worth breaking up a marriage like yours.'

'Do tell me more.'

'I wish you'd help me,' she said, 'instead of joking and pretending.'

I had to resist this impertinence. 'I'm not doing either,' I said roughly. 'Not that you could tell the difference. . . . What do you mean, a marriage like mine?'

'I mean,' said Susan, serious and intent, 'that you still love her very much. There's not such a lot of that around. You should never throw it away.'

I had to think about that for a bit, before deciding how to answer it. For some reason, it seemed first and foremost a blatant intrusion; Susan simply was not licensed to operate in this area; her expertise was confined to smaller matters altogether. It would be better, I thought presently, to work her back towards her own ground; I wasn't equipped, neither on this evening nor on any average evening during my present lousy half-life of pressure and counter-pressure, to deal with inquisitive fingers from the nursering-wing of affairs.

But before I shoved her back into bed, a smart slap on her shapely ego would not do either of us any harm. . . . I lay back, and looked at her over the rim of my glass, and asked:

'How did you arrive at that acute analysis?'

She met my glance, rather hopelessly, and said: 'I knew this wasn't any good.'

'You're god-damned right it's not any good! I've never heard such a load of crap in all my life.' It was not a moment for delicacy. 'Love has nothing to do with anything we're talking about. There isn't any love in the whole world. There's sex, and there's habit, and there's phoney emotion, and there's greed, and these are the ties that bind. . . .' I pointed my finger at her, not too badly aimed. 'Now you want us to stop, because of—' I had almost forgotten, '—because of what?'

'Because you're still in love with your wife.' She had never said 'Kate', nor, come to think of it, had I. 'It's too good to be spoilt.'

'Just how did you work that out?'

She was being rather brave—the most annoying trait in any woman. 'It's obvious, in everything you do these days.'

'It won't be obvious, in the next thing I do.' I set my glass down, with no more than a minor crash, and levered myself off the sofa. 'Come on—let's go to bed.'

'Go to bed?' She sounded more surprised than I had ever heard her.

'*Go to bed*,' I mimicked. 'It's the thing people do when they want to insert object A into object B, in the interests of cementing their sacred union.' I had brought this intricate sentence out at a stumbling rush, afraid of pausing. Now I said, more relaxed: 'Come on, Susan. I'm tired. Let's get laid.'

She shook her head. 'No, Johnny. Not tonight. It's wrong.'

'What do you mean, wrong?' I was near to her now, for what I hoped would be a brief stop on the smooth, well-worn pathway to the semi-conjugal mattress. Except for the overcooked hair, she still looked beautiful. I was sure that I could manage it.

'It's wrong when people are quarrelling.'

'We're not quarrelling. We're reviewing current topics.'

'It would be wrong, all the same.'

I started to argue, then to wrestle, which was ineffective, then to argue again. Sometimes, in the past, it had been her availability which had vaguely annoyed me. ('Just pour hot water on that girl,' I had thought once, in Barbados, when she was briefly under the shower before our fourth bout of the day, 'and you get Instant Screw.') Now it was her refusal, perverse, unaccountable, against all accepted regulations. By God, one might have supposed that she had a mind of her own. . . . And what had happened to gratitude?

The wrestling match, verbal and physical, took some time and covered all sorts of territory, from the sofa in the sitting-room to the very front doorstep of love; but in the end she said yes, and stripped and bathed, as I did, and lay down upon our long-established work-bench, dutifully composed, undeniably good to look at.

It seemed that I had won my argument—which, in these hard times, was quite a change. But it turned out that I might as well have saved my breath.

Long ago, Eumor, an older man, used to use the words: 'It won't travel,' or some such phrase, to indicate a sad decline of his potency, in any pause between impetuous wooing and actual achievement. 'Sometimes I fear even to get out of the car,' he had once said, posing a serious problem in logistics. 'And if she keeps me waiting in the bathroom . . .' I had sympathised, though feeling superior; but now, for the first time, it was happening to me, and I was not superior any longer. I was livid.

I did my best, as a man must, but there seemed to be too many things against me. Drink had taken its toll; I had spent too much time and energy arguing; I had had a period of disliking her, and the sudden switch to amorous intent failed to pull the rest of the equipment with it. My body sagged, even as I tried to whip it into some kind of shape.

Susan did her best for me, and she was as beautiful and alive as ever. But something beyond lively beauty was betraying me. For all the talk, I did not want her enough to be able to take her.

Sweating, impotent—the gross and wounding word had to be used —I lay back in the tumbled bed, and thought of ways and means. There were none. Something really had gone wrong. Perhaps it was the bed itself, which seemed grubby and stale, the sour graveyard of a battle never joined, recalling too clearly the rank disorder of our lives. Perhaps it was something I deserved.

Perhaps this was, as she had said, the end of the line.

I did not like that thought at all, and I tried once more, with a desperate bruising intensity which made no gain of any sort. The times were out of joint, and a lot else besides. *Have you prayed tonight, Desdemona?* I thought, as I sought entrance to that ravishing body; and did you pray for this—and where is this, for God's sake?

Gone to graveyards everywhere.

'Why not just go to sleep?' Susan said presently. 'You're tired.'

'I'm not tired,' I mumbled, face buried in the pillow. 'I'm just no good tonight, that's all. I must have trod on a bad oyster.'

'It doesn't matter.'

'It should.'

Perhaps there was a term to adultery, as there was a term to marriage, and it was shorter, and I had found it. Our affair had been fun, as she had said; but now it had become nothing—it was the garbage of love, which had started to smell before it started to evaporate.

Between drowsing and thinking, between feeling sad and feeling a damned fool, between wanting another drink and wanting to throw up, I felt her stirring beside me. I wondered how it had been for her, pestered and sought after one minute, left vacant the next. If I were cast down, she was presumably still up in the air. There wasn't a thing I could do about that, either.

Of course, I might joke it up a little.

'The Sultan had nine wives,' I said, in the same anonymous mumble, 'and eight of them had it pretty soft.'

'All right, Johnny,' she said, in a small, cool voice. 'Let's say good-night. I have to work in the morning.'

'I'll say goodnight,' I said, 'and I'll sing the lullaby too. Let me tell you some more bad jokes,' I said. 'I've been wanting to use them for a long time, but I don't get many chances, so I store them up on the the last page of my manuscript book. . . . They're a writer's end-product, and you know what that is. . . . Do you know who was the most elastic man in the Bible? Ananias—he tied his ass to a tree, and walked into Jerusalem. . . . I heard that one at school,' I said, 'and it was terribly daring even then. . . . And did you know how they found out about Oscar Wilde? It was at a party, and someone asked where he was, and the butler said: "He's upstairs, feeling a little queer." And did you hear about the blind prostitute? You've got to hand it to her.'

'Time to go to sleep, Johnny,' said Susan.

'*Sleep that knits up the ravelled sleeve of care,*' I said. '*Sleep, twin brother of death.* . . . There's another rather funny story about Oscar Wilde. It happened at his trial. He produced a character witness, an officer in some regiment or other. And the officer, who wasn't too bright, said, absolutely straight-faced: "I am convinced that Mr. Wilde is a man of honour and integrity. Why, I would trust him with my own sister!" '

'So?' said Susan.

'So nothing! It's just a story. And don't think I'm anti-Wilde. I don't mind what he did. He could poke a canary to make it sing, as far as I'm concerned. He was a man of enormous talent, and that pays for everything. Like Maria Callas.'

'Maria Callas?'

'Maria Callas. The other kind of canary. She had a tremendous row with Rudolf Bing, and was sacked from the Met. Don't you remember? Well, I don't mind what she said to Rudolf Bing. She could stab Rudolf Bing with a poisoned tuning-fork, if she felt like it. Just as long as she sang like an angel. Which she did, unfailingly. . . . You've got to make allowances for people who have it.'

'Have what?'

'The spark. . . . Sometimes I wish. . . . I'm starting a new book tomorrow,' I told her, in all drunken seriousness. 'Something for the kiddies. It's called *A Child's Garden of Thalidomide*. Or else I'm going to start a new magazine. It's aimed at where all the heavy money is, so it's got to be called *Modern Widow*. . . . Sometimes you can make up good names for new firms. There ought to be an ambulance business called the Sick Transit Company. And then there's my new marina, to bring in the LP set. Let's see if I can pronounce it properly. It's called the Ludwig Vann Boat Haven. Very difficult, very classical. . . .'

'I don't know what you're talking about,' said Susan.

'Forgive us,' I said. 'We are of humble origin.'

'What's that supposed to mean?'

'Christ, don't you know anything?' I was sick of people who didn't know anything; they were worse than the ones who knew everything. 'It's in *The Brothers Karamazov*, or maybe *Crime and Punishment*. Those are books. . . . There was this captain—Captain Popoff, or Captain Pullizpantzoff, or something. He was a ranker, and he married a peasant woman who was always dropping social clangers, or spilling the samovar, or making idiotic remarks at parties. So whenever she did something particularly stupid, the captain would say: "Forgive us, we are of humble origin." Thus putting everyone at their ease.'

'Goodnight, Johnny,' said Susan.

'Lucky you,' I said. 'Nothing on your mind. . . . I was a dropout for the F.B.I. . . . Actually, when I was your age, I had a wonderful job. Stud groom at an elephant farm. The pay was lousy, but the tips were terrific.'

'Johnny, I've *got* to sleep.'

'People miss the point all the time. Like Oscar Wilde's character witness. Do you remember Lee Bum Suk?'

'Johnny,' said Susan. 'For heaven's sake!'

'Oh, he was a real man. Foreign Minister of North Korea, or something like that. But you've got to agree that it's an odd name. And we —that's the good guys—felt we had to point the fact out. Lee Bum Suk, we said. Ha, ha, ha! Not so! said the Chinese newspapers. This is a foul capitalist slander, a typical revisionist lie. As all the civilised world knows, his name is actually Bum Suk Lee.'

'Sleep, Johnny,' she said. 'Sleep, sleep. Please!'

I also was sleepy now, drowning out on a muddy, fouled-up stream-of-consciousness routine which, as they used to say on the music halls when the tuba blew out a rude note, was better out than in. But I still had a few left, with a little dredging. I might be no good to her, but, like the man in the hardware store, I could still talk a good screw, any day of the night.

'The motto of the Gordon Highlanders in France,' I said, 'was "Up kilts and at 'em!" And let me take you to the land of the nursery rhyme.' I gave it the light tenor treatment:

> 'Oh, have you met my daughter, sir?
> She can't control her water, sir;
> And every time she laughs, she pees—
> Don't make her laugh, sir, please sir, please!
> Oh damn you, there it goes again,
> A-trickling down her knees.'

'Johnny,' said Susan, 'just give it a rest.'

'Shall I sing you an old German raping song?'

'No.'

'Or my latest twelve-tone composition—Ecstatic Variations on a Theme by Me?'

'No. Go to sleep. Or go away.'

'Spoken like a true virgin. Oh yes, virginity. Virginity is the only realm where a girl will boast of her ignorance. Well, that *used* to be true. Now they seem to have taken the bit between their legs. . . . Drives women mad—smells like money—that's my after-shave lotion. . . . And I've just remembered a story about a public lavatory in England. The chaps had been behaving very badly there—boring holes

292

in the partitions, doing all sorts of naughty things to each other, committing sodomy every time they pulled the chain. So the authorities raided the place, and the policeman giving evidence said to the magistrate: "There were some absolutely filthy things going on, sir. In fact, when someone came in for a good honest crap, it was like a breath of fresh air." That's a true story.'

Susan didn't like true stories, presumably, because I didn't get any answer to this last contribution. My head had started to ache, and my mouth felt dry, which was a funny thing for it to feel after so much had been poured down it. There seemed to be a lot of traffic down on 54th Street; car doors slamming, and once someone running, like me. The rumpled bed felt like a corrugated sweat-box. I was going to have a hard time getting to sleep.

'Captain Snegiryov,' I said, after a long, long silence; and then louder: 'Of course! Captain Snegiryov!'

'Who?' asked Susan sleepily. 'What?'

'Captain Snegiryov. The man who said "Forgive us, we are of humble origin!" '

'God damn you!' said Susan. 'I'm not interested.'

At the very same moment, I wasn't interested either. Not in her, not in anything in the world.

'Then I surrender, dear,' I said. 'I'm a talented coward. It's the only kind to be.'

Not speaking any more, a talented coward to the last, I turned away from her, and thought secretly, scarily: This had better be the last time.

I walked back, on a damned cold December morning, nursing an imperial hangover, trying not to dwell on the phoney symbolism involved in my long zig-zag retreat up town, from West 54th Street to East 78th. I suppose I must have looked a bit wild, judging by the stares of passers-by; but God bless us every one! had these early-shopping matrons never seen a returning reveller with a creased suit, yesterday's stubble of beard, and two well-earned circles under his eyes? Just how insulated could you get?

Of course I was pale and wan, and a little rocky when it came to walking a straight line. What did they expect me to be? It was ten o'clock in the morning—a gentleman's dawn, having no connection with the sunrise. I had my rights, the same as any other card-carrying wino.

High as a kite, low as a flat heel, blinking like a lighthouse, feeling like hell, I plodded my way north-eastwards, towards home and beauty. Policemen gave me cold looks and a measured swing of the night-stick. Women averted their well-bred gaze. Dogs relieved themselves pointedly—especially poodles. Home was the sailor, home from the sea, and the hunter home from the hill he never climbed.

Kate—up early, like any percipient wife—said not a word when I got back. Obviously she was not fighting; if she were going to win at all, it was by not fighting. Though this was a change, it was not the most welcome change in the world. The least you could say to a returning dog was 'Bad dog!' and to a man, 'For God's sake wipe your feet.' All I got was silence, and a face of purest marble, and music, music, music. The guitar had started again, and its sad and searching loveliness plucked at the air, and at all defenceless things, and at me.

Pursued by several kinds of taunting ghost, head aching, feet as sore as sandpaper, I went upstairs.

I went upstairs, to be taken, in solitude, by a drenching despair which would not leave me, nor yield to the half-bottle of champagne I had to have, nor relent in any way. This really was all wrong, and I was beginning to know it. . . . If it needed a sickening hangover to tell me that I had been wandering a sordid by-path, then a hangover might well be part of every man's first-aid kit. . . . Susan was a dear girl, and a lovely one, but I must not go to that tainted well again.

Suddenly I began to need Kate, with all the old hunger; I began to feel the conviction, deeply disquieting, almost terrorising, that in spite of the rough edges and the smooth invigilation, I would never be happy with any other person. It was a totally confusing thought, and crossed up by a drinking man's morning miseries, and a fornicating man's remembered impotence, and the back-lash of a glass of champagne which was not doing its appointed work; but in essence I could see that it came down to marital politics, which were the same as any other brand—the art of the possible.

If what we had got was not perfect, if the terms were tough and the prospects wounding, then, the thing might be re-negotiated. But it must not be abandoned, while life was still in it.

In love and war, it seemed, you did best—or at least you were not disgraced—if you took all the ground you could get, but gave all you had to give in payment. And if panic were persuading me to this, then panic could have the credit. I wasn't using any credit-cards that morning.

I was on the point of going downstairs to give Kate a very cautious slice of this, as a matter of concealed urgency, in the most guarded terms available to a man feeling his way from one pitch-dark vault to another lit by a single candle, when the phone rang in my dressing-room. It was Erwin Orwin.

'What happened to you, Johnny?' he asked immediately.

'I'm sorry, Erwin,' I told him. 'I'll be along soon.'

'You got held up?'

'No. I had a hangover.'

'That's what I like about the British,' said Erwin. But whether he meant their hangovers or their transparent honesty, I did not know, and there was no time to inquire. 'Now listen,' he said forcefully. 'Are you happy with *Safari*?'

It was a startling word, one I had not thought to hear that morning. 'Happy?' I said. 'Yes, I think so. Why?'

'Here's why,' he said. 'Things have been happening to a couple of other shows. You don't need the details, but one of them wants longer on the road, and *Josephine* is starting to sag, here in town. What I aim to do is cancel the out-of-town tour of *Safari*, and open it cold in New York.'

'When?'

'About five weeks.'

'I don't see why not,' I said, though with an alarming sense of misgiving which was not related to the show. 'We've done our best with it. I think it's about ready to go, whether you put it on in Boston or here.'

'That's what I thought,' said Erwin. 'Otherwise I wouldn't be taking this sort of chance. But it won't be easy. We'll have to work like crazy.'

'O.K.'

'No more hangovers.'

'Oh, come on, Erwin—this was the first one.'

'It's the first one that got into the record books. I'll want you all the time, Johnny. How soon can you get down?'

'Half an hour.'

'I'll be looking for you.'

I put the phone back, with a feeling that something beyond price—

some healthy limb, some conviction of piety—had been ripped from me while I was off-guard. God, how did a man ward these things off, and still get a little sleep. . . . For now I had my urgent assignment, and it wasn't going to be Kate after all. Erwin's call had seen to that.

Now I was foul-hooked elsewhere, and I had no choice save to follow the wrenching drag of the line. For a thousand reasons, *The Pink Safari* had to have all the priority; I was doomed to give Kate second place again, and in our present wasteland the demotion might be fatal. This was the one priority she would never recognise.

But there could be nothing else on the list, till the show was mounted. And if, after that, there were no list left to turn to, I might be foul-hooked for ever.

CHAPTER EIGHT

ERWIN ORWIN'S after-the-first-night-parties were never geared for failure, and the party he put on for the première of *The Pink Safari* was no exception. It was, as always, held on stage, as soon as possible after the fall of the curtain; he kept the set as it was, except for taking out the back-drop, and filled the vast available space with tables, bars, an enormous buffet, and a throng of people to match.

It was part of Erwin's touch-of-Napoleon technique that he never followed theatrical fashion, neither in this particular area, nor in most others. He did things his own way—and thus, after a first night, he did not go to Sardi's. Sardi's, with bulging hampers, a fleet of heated trolleys, and crate after crate of the right stuff, came to him.

The curtain had rung down, reasonably near to schedule, at eleven-thirty; by twelve o'clock, the stage was jumping again. It was a merry charade, because we thought we had cause to be merry—the show had romped through without a hitch, the audience had seemed to love it, and everyone was saying, between drinks: 'They *can't* pan this one. . . .' These were famous last words, of course, and Broadway was littered with expensively embalmed theatrical corpses to prove it; but this time, this time it seemed they really *couldn't*. . . . So we celebrated, with a good heart, steady nerves—until the time for the reviews drew nearer —and most of the stops out.

An orchestra played for us, and in between times Teller's mother's cousin took over at the piano, pounding out the *Safari* tunes which people were already beginning to hum. The guests danced—there were loads of pretty girls available, all with hair like Susan's—and ate a lot, and drank more, and gathered into knots and wandered around the set, arguing, or melted into the shadows for a brisk clinch.

There was probably some kind of esoteric message in the fact that this celebration party, held on stage, put some people into the full glare, and others wandering in and out of the wings, and others nowhere to be seen. Life, my boy, life. . . . Myself, I had the glare, and it was beginning to blur a little at the edges.

It was a theatrical crowd, the famous and the infamous jumbled together like differing grades of egg; the only grade not represented were the critics on the dailies, absent with leave, crouched even now, with the knives or unguents of their trade, over the prostrate body of my brain-child. There were moments, many moments, when I did not care what they did with it; moments when this whole evening seemed to slop over into absolute falsity—a falsity presented in specific terms by our own *Safari* cast who, ruthlessly coy, delayed their various entrances until the moment seemed propitious, and then swept back upon the stage, ready, they hoped, to take the best curtain call of the evening.

Actors. . . . But I could not deny that they deserved it. They had all been wonderful, and they knew it, and we knew it, and thus they were entitled to this little extra slice of nonsense. Dave Jenkin, attended by his raucous girl friend, was especially prominent, prancing around the stage like a compatriot boxer at the moment of victory; but he had risen to the very top of his form that evening—agile, cheeky, sometimes very funny, and always timing to perfection—and he now had, as far as I was concerned, a free hand to put on any kind of an act he chose. He had proved himself a star. Let the star gyrate a bit.

I was gyrating myself, though in smaller and smaller circles.

People congratulated me. I congratulated people. Erwin Orwin held court behind a massive corner table, piled with food. Teller's mother's cousin gave of his best. On my side—it was a night for remembering that there were two sides to everything—I had Jack Taggart, looking

297

all-competent, and Hobart Mackay, looking out of place, and beautiful Susan Crompton, looking just fine.

Beautiful Susan was excited, but full of the pangs of remorse, for something really important. She had fluffed one of her only two lines, though with an air of such ravishing incompetence that the audience had roared with laughter. (I could imagine Erwin saying, out of the corner of his mouth: 'We'll keep that one in.') But Susan, at the moment, was not to be consoled. It was obvious that she would talk about this set-back for many months to come.

'I thought I'd die, right there on the stage!' she declaimed, as soon as we had met, and I had told her how wonderful she was. 'And I'd rehearsed it so many times!'

'It didn't matter,' I assured her. 'Really it didn't.'

'It did, it did!' she wailed. 'It was awful! And what will people think? What will *she* think?'

'She?'

'Your wife!'

I felt able to promise that Kate would not, for this particular reason, think any the worse of her. I had no doubt that this was true. I couldn't check it with Kate, because I couldn't see Kate, at that moment. I was not in good shape, for all sorts of reasons. It had been a long evening, a raw evening. I had spent a lot of it with Kate, but now, in the midst of the crowds and congratulations and the merry merry fun, I was finishing it alone.

It had been very exciting; one could not be blasé about an evening which had gone with such a triumphant swing, the glittering culmination of nearly a year's hard work. Like Dave Jenkin, I felt entitled to my own little prance of victory. . . . I had sat in a box beside Kate, with an unauthorised row of drinks close to hand, and watched the thing unfold, so well and so smoothly that presently I stopped sweating, and drank only to success, and for pleasure.

Safari had been funny, as I hoped it would—wildly funny, bitterly funny, cruelly funny on a cruel strand of the world's multiple troubles. I enjoyed it, and nodded when bits of it went especially well, and glowed a little when people laughed, and glowed even more at the final applause. But all the time, I could guess what Kate must be thinking. Indeed, I knew. Was racial strife ever funny? Were there jokes to be made out of side-by-side squalor and affluence? What had happened to *Ex Afrika*? What—that famous old conundrum, the despair of the leading *savants* of two continents—what had happened to me?

Her main reaction to the play itself had been silence; in fact, we had only spoken to each other twice during the entire evening. When Susan came on, Kate said:

'So that's your Miss Thing.'

'She was,' I said, with a slight extra emphasis.

'Well done.'

It was rather too elliptical for me.

Later she had seemed to have a moment of tears, though for what and for why I did not know. Was it when the Negro child died, and a single sad guitar theme picked its way out of the jungle of the native-location music? Or was it for other things? For me, for herself, for us? I could not tell, I did not know how to ask.

At the second interval, she put a curious question: 'Do you remember "God is black"?'

I did remember, though I could not see why she had recalled it tonight. It had been something long ago, in Johannesburg, when I had told her: 'If you want to know what it feels like to be a native in South Africa, go along to the steps of the Town Hall, and take a look at the pillar at the far end.'

I would not tell her why, so she had gone to look, and found what I had found earlier that day—the words 'God is black' scrawled in chalk on one of the civic pillars. When she came back, she had asked:

'But what does it mean?'

'Despair and hope, in three words.'

It was a hot day, and she was rather cross. 'You might just as well have told me what it was. I never walk as far as that.'

Now, in the theatre, it was my turn to ask: 'What made you think of that?'

'I was remembering,' she answered, and that was all she would allow me. Though we sat together, sculptured, like royalty, with fixed dynastic smiles, we were utterly divided still. It was part of the rawness of that evening, and it came at the end of five weeks of the same forlorn, contemptuous, bitter disengagement.

When next I thought about the time, it was one a.m.; the party was thinning out, though not very much—no party with a theatrical basis ever broke up before the food and drink were finished, and there were still those reviews to come. . . . I sighted Kate once, talking to Jack Taggart; across the stage, they noticed me looking at them, and they smiled back, but it did not seem that they smiled very much. Hate Steele Month was still on.

A rather pretty girl, with bare feet and her dress torn, came walking hurriedly out of the wings; then she turned, and called to some unseen adversary: 'You don't have to rape me!' 'I would say that was true,' said the cynical fellow standing next to me at the huge central bar, and I laughed with him. But suppose it had been my sister. . . . Dave Jenkin was doing a wild tap-dance routine in the middle of the stage, putting most of it out of bounds for other dancers. Erwin was at his post, still eating, talking very gravely indeed to one of his backers, who talked very gravely back.

I overheard Susan say: 'You know, I think you're absolutely right! I was *over* rehearsed!'

It was my newly adopted world, and I didn't like it at all.

Then the man on the other side of me suddenly turned out to be my publisher.

'It's past your bedtime, Hobart,' I told him.

'It's past *our* bedtime,' he said precisely.

'I hope no one misconstrues that.'

He wrinkled his nose. 'That would not surprise me at all. What very peculiar people you have in the theatre.' Then he turned to look at me more closely. 'Aren't you rather pale?' he asked.

'I've been working. *Si monumentum requiris*—can't pronounce the rest of it. And worrying. And of course drinking. All people like me are pale. . . . Tell me that you liked the show.'

'I liked the show.'

'More!'

'It should do very well.'

He was something less than effusive, and I couldn't quite let it go. 'Don't have a complete mental break-down over this.'

'No, I really did like it, Jonathan. I thought it was very good.' He added, with a certain amount of care: 'You know—of its kind.'

'Like a beautifully designed sewer?'

He laughed, while I drank. 'Like a beautifully designed musical. But don't forget, I published *Ex Afrika*.'

'There's plenty of *Ex Afrika* in this.'

300

Now he was looking worried, as if he did not know whether to answer me seriously or not; he seemed more than ever like a professor—a professor with an unruly class which might start acting out the Blackboard Jungle while his back was turned. At length he said:

'Well, it's half the story, isn't it? The funny half—no, that's not it exactly. The *top* half, sad and funny both, but basically the part that doesn't matter.' He looked at me carefully. 'You see I'm trying to be quite honest about this. . . . All the part under the surface, the core of *Ex Afrika*, is still in the book. And only in the book.'

I drank again. What was it Kate said about criticism? I *must* learn to be brave about it. . . . 'Then we're both satisfied. I have a show, you have a book.'

His brow cleared. 'I'd be completely satisfied if you'd write me another one.'

'I will, Hobart, I will. Don't crowd me.'

I passed my glass across the bar for a refill, and the barman, a refined youth not quite at home in these raffish surroundings, asked: 'Something similar?'

'Too right!' I said, in my Australian accent.

He sniffed as he passed the champagne glass back to me. I had made another enemy—and a barman at that.

'I'm not crowding you,' said Hobart.

'What?'

'You said, "Don't crowd me", and I'm not.'

'Oh.' He had sounded rather irritated. 'That's good to know.'

I had the impression that he was not going to talk to me very much longer.

'How are things at home?' he asked presently.

'Terrific,' I said. 'One long honeymoon.'

'Kate was looking very well.'

'What's "was"? She *is*!'

'I meant, when I talked to her.' He glanced at his watch. 'I don't think I'll wait for those reviews after all. I'm sure they'll be wonderful.'

'You wish to leave me?'

'It's time to go.' For a small man, he could be firm enough when he wanted to be. 'Good night, Jonathan. Let's have lunch, one of these days.'

'With a new book by Steele?'

301

'With or without a new book by Steele. But in a perfect world———'
he gestured, and smiled, and was gone.

I turned to the barman, and said: 'Something similar.' But he was
now a different barman, an oldish, disgruntled, rushed-off-his-feet man
who did not speak the language of leisure. He snatched my glass, and
asked curtly: 'What'll it be?'

'Good God!' I said. 'Don't you know a champagne glass when you
see one?'

He glared at me, and stuck out a bristly chin. 'Yeah. That's why I
asked. Champagne's finished.'

'Who says so?'

He pointed to an empty bottle. 'Look for yourself, Mac.'

'Good God! Don't you know who I am?'

'No.'

'Good God!'

Very weak dialogue, Steele, I thought, as I turned away; we won't
keep it in. But I knew where the champagne would be, if there was
any left in the theatre. Like Lord Muddley, it was the kind of thing
I heard about.

Erwin—enormous, overflowing, massive old theatrical tzar Erwin
Orwin—made room for me at his table as I sat down beside him.

'Hallo, Johnny,' he said. 'Have some more champagne. You know
my associate, Mr. Ehrlich?'

'No.' I shook hands with Mr. Ehrlich, a tall, thin, precise Jew with
very formal manners and, I should have guessed, lots of money. 'But
I do now. And yes, Erwin, I'd like some champagne. I feel bound to
tell you that in certain parts of this building, the champagne has run out.'

'Mine hasn't,' said Erwin. 'There's got to be a limit for actors,
that's all.' He snapped his fingers, and a man jumped forward, with
a magnum of Louis Roederer at the ready; he snapped them again,
and a cigar was brought, and a third man lit it almost before I knew it
was in my mouth. 'Well, Johnny, how does it feel to have a hit?'

'We have a hit?'

'What else? This is going to be the toughest ticket in town.'

'Five stars,' said Mr. Ehrlich. 'Not a star less.'

'Ehrlich is the German for honourable.'

'Even so,' said Mr. Ehrlich.

'Your girl was terrific,' said Erwin.

'All right, Erwin. But thanks for giving her a try, anyway.'

'Have you another work in mind?' asked Mr. Ehrlich.

'A novel.'

'May it make another great musical enterprise!'

We talked about that, and this and that, and the theatre, and how good Dave Jenkin had been, and how *The Pink Safari* would make a fabulous film (side-glances exchanged between Mr. Ehrlich and Mr. Orwin), until two o'clock, when there was a sudden outbreak of ooh-and-ah on the other side of the stage, and people came running in with the morning papers, and we had our reviews.

Suddenly everyone was kissing and laughing and shaking hands and slapping each other on the back. The party took a wild upward swing. Dave Jenkin was uttering loud yells of delight, hugging his girl friend, turning cartwheels all round the stage. The orchestra, which had been flagging, began to roar and thump out our songs, with many an extra clash of cymbals. More champagne appeared, released from some prudent reserve, and with it came fresh smiles and whoops and people joining hands and dancing. Erwin, delighted, put his arm round my shoulder; even Mr. Ehrlich gave my hand a small informal squeeze.

People crowded up to our table, waving newspapers, pointing to headlines, upsetting glasses, clapping me on the back, kissing the nape of my neck. 'They mentioned *me*!' Susan cried, and collapsed into the nearest chair, overcome by the sheer grandeur of fame. Someone yelled: 'Three cheers for *The Pink Safari*!' and the cheers came up like high-pitched thunder.

We had a hit.

They were fantastic reviews—the dictionaries must have been combed for adjectives, and we had enough quotable comments to crowd a full-page ad. '*Safari* a Smash!' 'Rip Roaring Success', 'Five Star Hit!' 'My fair *Safari*!' 'Dazzling Display of Talent', 'Resounding Triumph', 'You MUST take This Safari!'—there it was in black and white, quotable, memorable, unarguable. Erwin Orwin's press agents couldn't have done better. I couldn't have done better myself.

In all the swamping praise, there was only one example of the still small voice. It seemed to be speaking to me, in direct and cautionary terms. It was important. It was, inevitably, the *Times*.

Those readers (said the man, after calling the show 'an undoubted success') *who enjoyed that fine novel* Ex Afrika *may find themselves putting their hands over their ears—or even holding their noses—at* The Pink Safari. *But (as no one knows better than author-playwright Jonathan Steele) there are thousands of people in and out of New York who don't give a finger-snap what happens to novels, good or bad, but who do like plush musicals; and these devotees should keep the SRO notices nailed up at the Orwin Theatre for many a long month—or year.*

I thought: If we trim that down to 'Should keep the SRO notices nailed up at the Orwin Theatre', we couldn't ask for a better quote. And from the *Times*. . . .

It was the last snide thought of the evening.

Erwin was leaving, attended by a pallid, puffy-eyed, yet jubilant phalanx of his aides. 'Good boy, Johnny,' he said, as he shook hands, and then: 'Give me a call tomorrow. I've got some ideas.'

I was still sitting down—bad manners, but a matter of necessity. 'Did you read the *Times*?' I asked him.

'Sure,' he said. 'Wonderful review.'

'Not so wonderful about the book.'

'The book's great.'

'No, I mean the novel.'

'Oh, that. Well, of course they had to say something. Don't let it get you down.'

'But it's true.'

He was looking down at me with expert appraisal. 'Forget it,' he said. 'Go home. Get some sleep. You'll think differently tomorrow.'

'It *is* true.' I waved my hand round the *Safari* stage, brilliantly contrived for my last-act, lovable, loyal losers. 'This is all wrong. All wrong!'

Now he had a different look, or rather a very strange progression of them: near-anger melting into a gleam of anxiety, and then to one of his widest grins. 'Confidentially, I agree with you,' he said, and shook my hand again. 'But don't you tell a soul.'

I wasn't going to tell a soul, till I had sorted it all out. But someone, I found, was going to tell me.

The someone was my hot-shot agent and non-critical friend, Jack Taggart. He took the chair vacated by Erwin Orwin, and smiled at me, and said:

'Well, you did it.'

'Yeah.' But I was dispirited, and it wasn't going to change tonight.
'What did I do, Jack?'

'Made *The Pink Safari* a riot.' He had a glass of his usual whisky
and water in his hand, and he raised it, toasting me. 'Cheers. This
thing can't miss. Erwin was talking to me about a film deal.'

'Am I in on that?'

He sighed gustily; the theatrical atmosphere was catching, even for
him. 'Don't you ever read your contracts? You get a big cut anyway.
And if you adapt this thing as a screenplay, you just about double
everything. If you want to. Do you want to?'

'Hell, I don't know.'

He looked at me very soberly. 'You really don't, do you?'

'No.'

'Well, if you want my advice——'

'I want your advice.'

'I'll give it you in two words.' His corn-crake voice was suddenly
forceful. 'Forget it.'

This was confusing, and though confusion was nothing new, it still
deserved translation. 'Translation,' I said.

'What do you really want to do next?'

'Not another of these bloody things, anyway.'

'That's what I meant. You've done it once. Don't do it again.
Don't even think of it. Finish the book instead, or write a new one.'

When a neutral man, suddenly and at last, took a position, it was
always surprising, and I was surprised now. This was the first time
that Jack had ever offered a suggestion that wasn't strictly professional,
such as the choice between two differing rates of royalty. It was like
an unloaded gun firing, a man serving a writ, a talking horse. . . . But
there was much more to come.

'And while you're at it,' he went on, 'leave New York. For a while,
anyway. It's been nice having you, Johnny, but this town is not for
you.'

'How in hell do you figure that out?'

'It's getting in the way of your work.'

'You've been talking to Kate.'

'Sure I've been talking to Kate. The first time ever, about this sort
of thing. It turned out that we had exactly the same ideas.' He was
looking very thoughtful, staring at the table-top, fiddling with his glass.
'A lot of it is none of my business. But you as a writer—that is. There's

a whole range of new work for you to do, on race relations. It's the crucial thing now, I believe, and you know a great deal about it. You mustn't go to waste. . . . There are plenty of experts taking care of that damned east-west axis, hardly any working on the north-south one, the really important one. . . . North and south in this country, north and south in the world. We live on the rich top of it; down there they're boiling with anger and frustration, they're sick of the misery. . . . Do something about that, Johnny. Show it, explain it, do a little bit to cure it. It's your job. Panel shows, and this—' he waved his hand round the stage, '—and novels about the sex life of the rich white trash, *just—are—not!*'

This was too odd, too astonishing, for me to cope with, at that moment; I filed it away under 'Some Other Time', and went back to something else.

'Where is Kate, anyway?'

'She left,' he answered, rather shortly.

'Didn't like the reviews?'

'Not that, either. She left hours ago.'

'To go where?'

'Home.' He was standing up suddenly.

'That's all right, then.'

'I don't think home is 77th Street.' I saw that he had become very angry with me, for some reasons I couldn't work out. Ah well, he had only joined the majority. . . . 'I told you that already. The rest is none of my business, like I said. But I'll say this, damn it, and then goodbye.' He was looking at me in an extraordinary way, like a sentencing judge, like the sternest father in the world; it was a thousand miles away from all he had ever been. 'You need a fresh start, more than anyone I've ever met. And you need Kate. She has guts and integrity. She's the only one who can help you.'

'I don't need help.'

He said: 'My friend, you are dead without her,' and smiled a very bleak smile by way of goodbye, and was gone.

I called after him: 'Thanks, Jack!' It was meant to be sarcastic, but at that bad moment it only sounded true. Someone called out: 'Wonderful, Johnny!' and someone else—it was Sally Coates, who had played the lead and done such miracles with it—leant over and gave me a smacking kiss, and said: 'That's for being the perfect author!'

Suddenly I didn't appreciate it at all. It was all right for other people

306

to be ecstatic; but now something had reversed all the rules. Now I only wanted to know what Kate thought, I only wanted to please her. . . . On that instant, caught in the crowds and the cheers and the kissing on stage, I was lonely; irrationally, hopelessly lonely.

None of this was any fun if I couldn't show it off to Kate; and no fun either if she didn't laugh at me for doing so. She had become, once again, the only one I had to satisfy; the only begetter, and the whetstone to keep sharp on. I had to go back—go back all the way, as she had once said. I had to have her with me again.

It could not happen soon, nor easily; but it had to happen.

I stood up, on too swift an impulse, and inevitably, typically, I knocked over my chair, with a resounding crash. As people stared or laughed, and a waiter sprang forward to straighten things up, I decided that this had better be the last time I did *that*, too.

Susan was one of the people I passed on the way out. She might have been watching me for some time; her face was oddly concerned, even compassionate; she wasn't thinking about her career—she was worrying about me, perhaps wondering if I would make it, whatever 'it' was. She touched my arm as I drew near, and I came to a rocking halt.

'Going, Johnny?'

'Yes. Home. I can't stand this any longer.'

'Oh.' Her beautiful eyes—her very beautiful eyes—were looking directly into mine. 'Goodbye, Johnny, in that case.'

'I'll be in touch,' I said awkwardly, squeezing her shoulder.

She had never made me feel bad, bless her, and she did not do so now. She just smiled her lovely smile, and said: 'You do that. But goodbye, anyway.'

CHAPTER NINE

AFTER some extraordinarily bad shots with the key—which made me think of that final sign-off night with Susan, and did not seem very funny on that account—I managed to let myself into the flat, and stood in the hall, listening. The place was utterly silent, as it had a right to be, past four o'clock in the morning; but it was still not a night-time kind of silence—it was a strange and lonely void, empty and echoing, as if I had entered the shell of a house, long abandoned, not lived in by myself or anyone else.

There was something else very strange, too, but I could not pinpoint what it was till I had wandered in and out of several rooms, and surprised myself in distant mirrors. Every single door in the apartment was open. After that, it took very little time to discover that the place was empty.

Kate's bed had not been slept in, nor Julia's. Foolishly, I checked my own. The master had not sought his couch, either. . . . She was gone, it seemed, and without a word. But after a while I came upon the traditional note, propped up in the traditional place against the mantelpiece clock.

I am sorry, Jonathan (she had written). *I stayed for your Safari, but now I have to go back. People will come in to pack the rest of my things. Julia has gone direct, I shall be wandering a little. My love as ever. Kate.*

Standing there with the note in my hand, I remembered Jack Taggart saying: 'Home is not 77th Street.' I had missed the point, at the time he said it; but he had meant it literally. He must have known about this already.

Now there came flooding in, like the final swirl of a muddy tide, all the poisonous residue of the last five weeks, when I had wanted to talk to her and could not, when she would not talk to me in any case, when the twin pressures of overwork and loneliness had made these the worst few weeks of my life. I had learned more about marriage in that divorced time than ever before. . . . But now the bill had arrived, and I had not a cent of spirit left to pay it with.

I poured myself a drink—a very familiar reaction, a habit impossible at this moment to change—and wondered how to climb out of this hole. Presently I made for the telephone. It was nearly five a.m., an unreasonable hour for research, but I had to take a chance, I had to establish some basic bearings. I did not even know where Kate was.

My useful friend at Kennedy Airport was at his post, and—for a man working out the last hour of his night duty—remarkably lively.

'Hallo, Mr. Steele!' he said. 'How did the show go?'

'Very well indeed,' I told him. 'It should run a year. Would you like tickets for it?'

'Gee!' he said—and there was no reason why he should not be surprised—'would you really fix that for me?'

'It's as good as done,' I answered. 'Just give me a call when you've worked out a date with your wife.'

'Gee!' he said again. 'Well, thanks a million, Mr. Steele.'

'Tell me,' I said, 'did my wife get off all right? I couldn't make it to the airport myself.'

'Oh sure, we looked after her,' he said, switching to the executive stance. 'Course, she wouldn't have made it if the flight hadn't been delayed. But BOAC fixed her up, and we gave her a couple of drinks in the lounge.'

'BOAC?' I asked, carefully.

'Sure. That was the only available London flight. Pan-Am was gone, Trans-World only had this day-flight today, Air France———'

He rattled off a few of his ready statistics, while I thought: London. Why London? Then I remembered that she had written: *I shall be wandering a little.* I had my first clue, anyway.

He was still talking. 'Her maid went Pan-Am as far as Accra,' he said, important as ever, as if he had engineered the whole thing himself, revved up the plane, launched it into the air. 'She'll pick up the South African flight from there. And gee!' he said again, 'all that excess baggage. I thought the boys would pop their eyeballs. Two-hundred-thirty dollars—how about that?'

How about it, indeed. . . . 'Well, thanks,' I said, 'I just wanted to check.'

'You'll be following pretty soon, I guess.'

'I hope so,' I answered. 'I'm not sure I can make it just now.'

'Oh. . . . She said you might be, that's all.' His voice had grown a small edge of professional caution; he knew all about husbands and wives, and the way they travelled at short notice, and the way they sometimes didn't travel after all, and the virtues of absolute neutrality for airline personnel. 'Well, any time, Mr. Steele. Just give me a call.'

'I'll do that. And don't forget about those tickets.'

'You bet!'

He hung up promptly—the executive type always knew how and when to round off a phone call—and I was alone. Drink in hand, spirit in desperation, wife in mid flight, I was alone again, with a whirl of

309

thoughts and only a hungry despair to feed them on. But some of the thoughts were sharp and clear as icicles, and as piercing to the bared skin as any dagger.

A notably wise and perceptive writer (see under 'Steele' in the Yellow Pages) once laid down the axiom that there was a term to marriage, however good, however strong, and that when it was reached, only a fool would claim that it could be extended, and only a fool would try. The fellow was wrong, and he was feeling wrong now, and almost vomiting on the knowledge of it.

I had ship-wrecked myself on this same cocksure shoal of self-regard. I knew now, in solitude, that the very core of marriage was this permanence, with its good days and its bad, its highs and lows; and that only a fool—this fool—would wantonly throw it away. Isolation had not been the answer, withdrawal had not been the answer, Susan had not been the answer. There wasn't any answer, in the toadstool circle where I had been looking for it.

In the process, I had done to our marriage (everything now seemed fatally consigned to the past) what I had done to *Ex Afrika*—insulted it, cheapened it, diluted it into slops, turned honest laughter, bitter tears, into a giggle and a gulp. Once it had been precious; now it was the toughest ticket in town.

In fact, we *had* been building something real all the time, only I hadn't recognised it; or perhaps I had lived with our love for so long and in such security that it had merged with nature, like an animal in the forest. The animal lived and moved and watched and brooded, but a casual glance, or a preoccupied one, discovered only the vines and the dappled leaves of an accustomed scenery.

So with Kate and myself. In our forest, our love and need had always been alive, but they had grown vague, obscured against a shoddy backdrop of my own painting. I still did not realise this fully, but I knew that I was going to.

Indeed, I had to do so; otherwise the animal, long overlooked, long neglected, would spring and devour, taking the revenge of all discounted things. The revenge of *this* animal would be bitter loneliness.

Once I had told Kate that we had 'evaporated'. That wasn't true, either; it was part of the same dreary self-delusion. What we had done —and it was my sole fault—was to lose all sight and sound of each other; while she took her gentle ease in the cool shade, I was in another part of the forest, climbing trees, robbing nests.

I should have stayed by her side, drowsy if need be, asleep sometimes, but never out of touching distance. The only important thing now was to find out if I could still make my way back.

Light-headed with the long night, scared to death by the harsh abrasion of the world, I went into forlorn action. First I put down my drink; then I wandered into the study, and started opening drawers, looking for airline schedules. We always had a lot of them; they had never seemed really significant until now. But, rummaging in one of the bureau drawers, I came up with something else instead; a dusty, yellowing, still current piece of paper, and on it a scrawl of my own handwriting:

I Jonathan Steele promise not to behave like a bastard this evening. Signed: Jonathan Steele. Witness: Kate Steele, née Marais. X X X.

I had long forgotten what it was about. It wasn't dated, and it didn't have to be.

I missed her in London, and again in Rome. For some reason she was returning south, very slowly, by the way we had come on our honeymoon nearly seven years before, when she had said: 'Let's not just fly *over* Africa; it's such a waste,' and we had wandered and side-tracked at will, baffling several travel agents in the process. Now I hoped that it was because she wanted me to catch up, but the time for such self-assuring thoughts was long past.

Once I overshot her progress altogether, after a bad guess or a lapse of memory—who goes to Khartoum, and why, unless you do not mind where you go? In those days, we could not have minded. . . . Finally I caught up with her grounded plane at Kano, in Nigeria, where the huge gorging vultures stood hideous sentinel at every back door, waiting for garbage, waiting for people.

They frighted both of us, perhaps helpfully; and there in the desert, our desert, almost in the shadow of an ancient walled city which might have stood for the defiant, healing virtue of time itself, we began to talk again, after surviving half a day of terrible, disjointed, fencing mistrust.

Then we set to work to retrace our steps southwards—gingerly, fearfully, but together.